King

Angus Donald is the author of the bestselling Outlaw Chronicles, a series of ten novels set in the 12th/13th centuries and featuring a gangster-ish Robin Hood. Angus has also published the Holcroft Blood trilogy about a mildly autistic 17th-century English artillery officer, son of notorious Crown Jewels thief Colonel Thomas Blood. Before becoming an author, Angus worked as a fruit-picker in Greece, a waiter in New York City and as an anthropologist studying magic and witchcraft in Indonesia. For fifteen years he was a journalist working in Hong Kong, India, Afghanistan and London. He now writes full time from a medieval farmhouse in Kent.

www.angusdonaldbooks.com

Also by Angus Donald

Fire Born

KING OF THE NORTH

ANGUS DONALD

CANELO

First published in the United Kingdom in 2023 by

Canelo
Unit 9, 5th Floor
Cargo Works, 1–2 Hatfields
London SE1 9PG
United Kingdom

A CIP catalogue record for this book is available from the British Library.

Print ISBN 978 1 80436 233 4
Ebook ISBN 978 1 80436 232 7

Map by John Brodie Donald

Cover design by kid-ethic

Cover images © Shutterstock, istockphoto

Look for more great books at www.canelo.co

Printed and bound in Great Britain by Clays Ltd, Elcograf S.p.A.

I

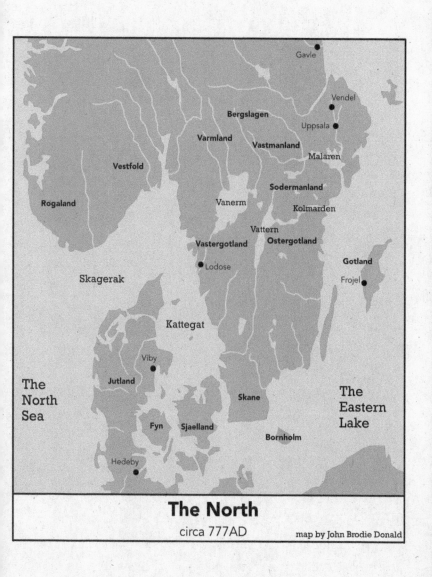

The North

circa 777AD

map by John Brodie Donald

Prologue

A life-long oath

It did not look comfortable, the age-darkened throne that Tor was staring at. High-backed, narrow, with broad, square arm-rests and fashioned from dense oak. It looked constraining, imprisoning. Like half of a wooden cage, and Tor knew something about those. She wondered what it would be like to occupy. Not just to rest on its smooth, unyielding surface; she wondered what it must be like to be a jarl, or even a king or some such high personage.

This was the throne of a jarl, her own Jarl Starki, lord of Norrland, a region in the furthest north of Svealand, but it could equally be the high seat of some petty king or local warlord. In a few moments, Jarl Starki would come out from behind the heavy, woollen curtain that shrouded his private quarters at the end of his great hall in the town of Gavle, and seat himself in it. And the ancient ritual would begin.

Tor was about to make a serious and solemn commitment. A life-long commitment. She was about to swear an oath of fealty to the man who would sit in that uncomfortable-looking oak throne. She would swear to serve and protect him, and to be his *Stallar*, the captain of his *hird* – as the commander of his household warriors was known. All two hundred and three warriors of the Starki *hird* would be under her authority. She could order them to kill – and to die – at her whim. For this honour, Tor would swear to keep to this mighty oath until either death or her lord dissolved it. It was, in its way, of greater import and moment than any marriage vow.

And she would do so. She would make the oath and keep it. There were few folk more despised than an oath-breaker. Any warrior whose word could not be trusted was worthless as a comrade. One such warrior might change sides at the height of the battle and stab you in the back. Or betray all your secrets to the enemy. An oath-breaking servant might steal his lord's silver and gold, or seduce his prettiest daughter. Or, worse still, ride off with his most valuable horse.

An oath-breaker was worse than a coward – a *nithing*, shunned by all decent folk.

Which was why Tor had wrestled with this difficult decision for a long, long time before she had finally agreed to it. Her brother Bjarki, whose comforting bulk was now slumped beside her on the bench at the side of the hall, while they waited for the jarl to emerge, had counselled against it. He felt that oaths were best avoided.

'Why bind yourself to another?' Bjarki had said to her. 'Why reduce yourself to a thrall, a mere puppet who moves to every jerk of the master's string? You have land, Tor, a fine home at Bearstead, silver in your coffers. What advantage does this binding oath bring?'

Oaths bound a servant to his master, a warrior to his jarl, a jarl to the king. Oaths were the mortar that held a people together, from the meanest thrall to the mightiest monarch. Without oaths, the Middle-Realm was a place of unpredictable violence, of betrayal and deceit, of fear and lawlessness. Of chaos. No one could prosper in this maelstrom.

Tor had not answered Bjarki's question. Yet she knew in her own heart why she was willing to make this commitment. For honour. For advancement. For power. And perhaps for the excitement, too. Jarl Starki's offer was the chance for her to be something greater than just a mud-spattered farmer, eking out a meagre living in the thin soils of the back of beyond. She truly loved Bearstead, her home in the remote northern woods, a full morning's walk north of the jarl's hall in Gavle, but she was a young woman who had seen only twenty-three winters. She was not ready to moulder away in the endless dank forest of the rest of her days.

Even so, this was a very significant step – to bind herself to this man, this jarl, for her whole life. She did not even know the man well, having only had a small amount of personal commerce with him over this past year. He was young and ambitious, she knew that, and she suspected that he harboured a deep love of money. But he was also a fair man who fought to uphold justice in the name of the king. She had liked and trusted his father, Viggo the White, and this young jarl, after a fraught period in which she and Bjarki had been outlawed by him, had eventually realised his error and done right by them. He was a good man, she thought, kind and decent. One whom it would not be too irksome to serve.

Tor looked up and saw the jarl was taking his seat at last in the uncomfortable-looking throne. His light brown hair fell to his shoulders, his beard was well trimmed; his nose was a little thin but he had an honest face, a face that was pleasing but not too pretty.

He settled in his throne and waved away a horn of ale proffered by one of his servants. He looked directly at Tor, and offered her a half-smile. His hall steward, the elderly man who ran the ceremonies and who was responsible for the provision of food and drink in his home, cleared his throat and said: 'Jarl Starki Viggossen, lord of Norrland, will now graciously accept the traditional oath of fidelity from his land-holder and shield-maiden Torfinna Hildarsdottir of Bearstead! Long live Jarl Starki!'

The few warriors and servants in the hall dutifully responded with: 'Starki!'

The steward drew a plain but well-polished iron sword from a tooled leather sheath and handed it to the jarl. Bjarki whispered, hot and breathy in her ear, 'There is still time to say no to him, sis. You *can* refuse the jarl, even now. But know too that I am with you, whatever you decide.'

Tor said nothing. The young jarl sat up straighter in his throne, and made a small beckoning motion to Tor, who stood up from the bench and walked a few steps towards him. She knelt stiffly in front of her lord, her mouth dry, her heart for some reason beating like a forge hammer. She looked up into her jarl's handsome face.

'Do you, Torfinna Hildarsdottir, swear to be my faithful warrior from this time forwards and for ever,' said Jarl Starki, 'with no deceit in your heart, nor with any trick or subterfuge, but do you instead freely make this solemn oath, by all gods, and in the name of your ancestors, that you will be true and loyal to me, Starki Viggossen, and to my descendants, as long as you shall live?'

'I so swear,' said Tor.

'Do you swear by all you hold sacred that you shall obey me in all things and never betray me to my enemies, nor stand with any who stands against me? Furthermore, that should you break the oath made this day, you beg the Norns who weave all life webs in the Middle-Realm to cut your life thread, and ensure you are dispatched at once to Hel's frozen realm where your spirit shall languish until the end of time and breaking of the world.'

Tor dry-swallowed. It was indeed a mighty oath. 'I so swear,' she said.

'And do you accept, from this day onwards, the position of *Stallar*, or captain of *hird*, and vow by all gods to behave in a manner fitting to that high office and to carry out your duties to me and those whom you are set above to the best of your abilities?'

'I so swear.'

'Then, Torfinna Hildarsdottir, you are mine – as I am yours,' said Jarl Starki, smiling. And he held out the burnished iron blade of his sword towards her face.

The metal was cold to her lips. She lightly kissed the point. And it was done.

4

Chapter One

The age-old sacrifice
Three months later

The doomed man looked directly into Bjarki's eyes. He was of middle years, bearded, with long, lank, sweat-dark hair, and Bjarki Bloodhand could see he was terrified, yet fighting with all his might not to show the world his shameful fear. There was a grim tightness around his mouth, and a glow coming from his staring blue eyes, seemingly caused by something more powerful than the red reflected firelight in the vast temple.

The man knew he was about to die; that there was no escape from this end; that there could be no reprieve. He fixed his eyes on Bjarki's, unblinking, unmoving; his pale gaze seemed to bore right through Bjarki's skull. Yet the man was trying to hold his courage high, even in the teeth of death, and for this reason Bjarki could not look away; he could not refuse to witness the valour displayed in the man's final moments.

Bjarki had seen eight others die in the same manner that this warrior faced, one each over the past eight nights of the great equinoctial *Disablot*, which was being held in this ancient temple at the centre of the royal compound of Uppsala. And while some of the victims had revealed their quality, others had screamed or wept, whimpered or soiled themselves; some had begged uselessly for mercy. Some were tellingly loose-necked, heads flopping like ripe barley heads, and had clearly been drugged with the juice of henbane or thorn apple, or numbed by quantities of mead. But this fellow's mind was clear, his jaw stiff and proudly lifted. So

Bjarki stared right back into the doomed warrior's eyes, trying not to blink, trying not to judge or taunt, their gazes joined together as if by an unbreakable filament of light between them.

'You are the One,' the man said. His voice was deep, low, and quavered only a little. 'You are the Reborn One they speak of in Fröjel, you are...'

Bjarki flinched. The man was a Goth, or a Geat, as they were also called; his mention of Fröjel, a town on the west coast of the island of Gotland, confirmed this.

He was also a complete stranger: how could he know anything about Bjarki?

A muscular young spearman, one of King Harald Fox-Beard's *hird* warriors, stepped forwards and cuffed the prisoner hard round the side of his bearded jaw, a thumping blow with his fist that snapped the bound man's head back and round.

'Be quiet, thrall,' the soldier hissed. 'Do not profane the *Disablot* ceremony.'

Their locked gaze broken, Bjarki felt a hot, shameful wash of relief. As if *he* had been reprieved from his own doom. He looked down and rubbed his suddenly watering, smoke-stung eyes. This bound prisoner deserved to die, of course, even if he now displayed remarkable courage. The man was known as Einar the Cruel, and that by-name was, apparently, richly deserved. He had been a sea-raider, using his sleek black ship and crew of vikings to ravage the lands along the coast of Svealand, burning farms, slaughtering husbandmen, raping their wives and daughters, then sailing away with his vessel loaded with silver, goods and slaves. That had been his trade for many and many a year, and the King of the Svear, Harald Fox-Beard, lord of Uppsala, the great man on whose land this huge, venerable temple stood, had finally lost patience and ordered the ambush and capture of Einar.

Jarl Starki had been given the task, and Bjarki's sister, Tor, who commanded the young jarl's *hird*, had quietly followed Einar the Cruel's black ship all along the coast on horseback. Then she and her *hird* warriors had attacked their land-camp in the dead of night, defeated Einar and killed or captured most of his crew.

So, yes, Einar the Cruel certainly deserved to die. And his death would be useful to the Svear people, too, in other more indirect ways. His blood would nourish the invisible spirits honoured at the annual *Disablot* festival, the *Disir*, the female entities of stone, water and wood that lived in and around the royal compound of Uppsala, and all over the North, too. Yet Einar's high courage demanded a suitable response from Bjarki. He felt he must look into the man's eyes as his end was enacted. It was simply the respect one warrior owed to another.

Bjarki could feel the meaty throb of the ceremonial drums vibrating deep in his bones, in his chest, too, and clearly hear the eldritch voices of the women – only the women – that drifted like smoke up into the high roof spaces of the great temple of Uppsala. The high-pitched singing made his skin crawl, and filled him with a kind of mad joy at the same time. A high priestess of Odin, a *Mikelgothi*, was speaking, her ancient language slow and pure. Bjarki knew the words by heart after attending eight such ceremonies during the eight previous nights of the *Disablot*. The *Mikelgothi* was calling on Odin, Thor and Freyr – the only three male gods worshipped this night – to witness this *blot*, to take part in the sacred feast alongside the female *Disir* sprits.

There were three tall wooden pillars running down the centre of the enormous Uppsala temple, with long fire troughs set in the packed-earth floor in between them. The god-pillars were intricately carved so that the ancient wood resembled the faces and figures of huge men. The centre one, the pillar by which Bjarki now stood in his ceremonial finery, depicted a solemn old man, wise-looking with a full beard and one eye-socket sewn shut.

It was the pillar of Odin – the All-Father. The Spear-Shaker. The Wanderer.

Bjarki glanced left and saw that the *Mikelgothi* was slowly approaching from the far end of the temple, from the west. She was clad in a fine white linen gown, clasped with precious gold at the throat and wrists, and with a gold chain tight around her ribs, just under her breasts. A line of eight white-clad female *gothi* followed her, and beyond them the crowd of ordinary celebrants pressed closer, filling the temple with their eager, fire-lit faces.

The *Mikelgothi* held up an almond-shaped stone knife in both her hands, as big and broad as a chestnut leaf, its dark ridges seeming to ripple in the reddish light coming from the central fire-trough. The finely chipped flint edges, Bjarki knew, were as keen as Frankish steel. But this was a magical blade, a true wonder, fashioned by the light elves in days of old and left behind here, abandoned in the Middle-Realm when all the Fair Ones returned to *Alfheimr*.

There were only perhaps three or four elf blades of this quality in all the world, and the sight of that knife made his flesh tense, and all the fine hairs on his body rise.

The high priestess passed by the first pillar, a carved image of the god Thor, and began to approach the Odin pillar in the centre of the temple and her tightly bound victim. The crowd surged forwards behind her, a murmuring mass of faces, but always keeping at a respectful distance.

Bjarki watched her advance. He knew this priestess well, this *Mikelgothi*. She was named Edith – a Saxon princess, far from her southern home. She was clever and strong, full of cunning and steeped in the tarry midnight arts of *seithr*, or so folk whispered. Bjarki had fought beside her brother, the Saxon war leader Widukind, in his homeland two years ago, and he had known this *Mikelgothi* then as a carefree girl – cheerful, flirtatious.

He had held a great affection for her then. And perhaps even something more. But many deed-filled months had passed since, and his life-thread had drawn him along other paths. He had not seen her since she bade him a fond farewell in a field near the river Weser, on the eve of a great battle against the hated Christian Franks.

This god-ridden night, as Edith approached along the centre of the hall with the ancient elf knife held up before her, she cut a very

8

different figure to the pretty maiden he had known for a time in Saxony. Her thin linen dress, which clung tightly to her slim form, was now lightly spotted with red from the many sacrifices she had performed over these past eight nights. Her oval face, fixed and stern, was painted unnaturally white with some paste, perhaps crushed chalk. Her lips were coloured a dark purplish, bruise-like shade, and her eyes were rimmed with lines of the same hue, as well as black and crimson. Her long golden hair, arranged into tight plaits, oiled, stiffened with glue and dyed white, red and purple, looked like a nest of snakes waving as she moved along the hall. She looked solemn, frightening – yet beautiful.

She was still singing, Bjarki saw, as he watched her approach, chanting the same fell dirge as the women who followed in her train.

Bjarki looked back at the doomed prisoner. He was tied to the thick oak pillar in front of him, Odin's pillar, and beside the base of the dark-stained wood was placed a small altar, a block of stone, knee high, a foot wide, and the length of a grown man. The prisoner was trembling a little. Bjarki could see that in the bunched muscles of his jaw. The man fixed his eyes on Bjarki's and they stared at each other, joined in an instant before eternity.

The *Mikelgothi* was beside them both. The wild, eldritch singing was reaching a violent crescendo, the low drumming harder than a running man's pulse – very loud.

'Do the right thing by me, highness,' whispered the doomed man, his blue eyes digging into Bjarki's face. 'I beg you, highness. When it is done, put a blade in...'

Again the king's guard intervened. He shoved the doomed man roughly on the shoulder. Bjarki reached for the horn handle of his seax, the foot-long, single-bladed fighting knife that always hung horizontally across his loins, and smoothly pulled the shining steel from its sheath. He felt the stir of the half dozen men around him, his own fighting men, warriors all sworn to him. He rolled his huge shoulders inside the heavy, discoloured and much-tattered bearskin cloak he wore. Then he looked beyond the prisoner tied to the Odin pillar, and lifted his eyes for an instant to see his sister's face on the far side of the temple, only three paces away. Tor was frowning at him.

She gave a tiny shake of her red head. Beside her stood a tall, thin-nosed young man, haughty, a thin gold circlet holding back his long brown hair, a fine, silver-stitched purple wool cloak falling from his shoulders, her lord, Jarl Starki; and beside this young lord of Norrland, in a wooden chair, sat Harald Fox-Beard, the king, an old man, his famous red beard now sparse and white, his once mighty frame hunched and skeletal, his skin mottled and sagging. Beyond the king stood a broad, brutal-looking man of middle years, Sigurd Hring, lord of Sodermanland, the king's cousin and his most powerful jarl. And peeping between Sigurd Hring and his elderly king was a face as weird and white-painted as the *Mikelgothi*'s. Abbio the Crow, another acquaintance from the Saxon war, drawn to Uppsala by the *Disablot*. This odd fellow was also a *gothi*, and some said a sorcerer, too. He was Widukind's counsellor.

All five were looking at the seax in Bjarki's hand. Tor shook her head again.

Bjarki looked quickly away from his younger half-sister. His eyes instinctively went back to the prisoner's and their gazes slotted into each other's once more.

The singing stopped. The drumming ceased. The sudden silence in the temple was a vast and terrible void. Then there was movement. The king's *hird*-men moved forwards and swiftly untied the ropes that held the doomed man to the pillar. Then they threw him, with unnecessary force, Bjarki thought, on his back onto the stone altar. One guard caught hold of his long, flailing hair and pulled his head back, right over the altar's edge, exposing the man's neck. The prisoner made no sound at all.

Bjarki saw the king lift his trembling, stick-like hand and make the traditional signal. Edith the *Mikelgothi* called out loudly: 'Odin! Hear us! All-Father, draw near and accept our blood sacrifice. *Disir*, gather; come spirits, take your rightful places at the high table of the gods! Here is your meat and drink, *Disir*

– sisters, spirits of wood and stone, of field and river: here is your lawful portion of the feast!'

She stepped forwards purposefully and sliced down once, a hard and smooth strike, across the prone man's exposed neck. The stone knife cut into the prisoner's flesh and a jet of bright blood immediately fountained into the air, splashing against the ancient wood of the Odin pillar. Edith herself had stepped back smartly out of the spray after making her cut, but another *gothi* stepped forwards with an iron bowl, and as the flow slowly subsided, she gathered the rich, bubbling blood in the vessel.

The prisoner jerked and twitched silently for a time, his bound feet kicking madly against the bonds. Then he lay still, his limp body slumped in its finality.

There was a huge collective sigh from the crowd of a hundred or so celebrants in the ancient temple. A relaxation of tensed muscles. An exhalation of pent-up breath.

Bjarki came forwards then; he bent down and, fumbling slightly, he found the corpse's right hand, where it was pinioned behind his back, and placed the horn handle of his seax in the dead man's curled fingers, then closed them tight round it.

'May the Bear guard you on your final journey, my sword-brother,' he said.

–

'You are a sentimental fool!' said Tor. 'That was a fine, expensive blade, crafted by none other than Harva of Finnstorp, by far the greatest smith in the North, whose grandfather learned the dark secrets of ironwork from Wayland himself! Do you think your seax will remain with the corpse of that murderous rapist? Someone will steal it long before they hang up old Einar the Cruel's worthless carcass in the sacred grove. You have simply thrown away a very fine blade.'

'He was a brave man,' said Bjarki, grimacing at his sister's fury and taking a sip from his brimming horn. 'He deserved to face the Old One with a blade in his hand.'

11

'You think a maggot like Einar will find a place on the benches in the Hall of the Slain? I very much doubt it! And if I find him when I get there, I'll kill the bastard all over again – and easily, since he won't have that Harva blade anywhere near him.'

'Stop harping on about this, sis. It is done. I'll replace the seax. We can afford to pay Harva the Smith to make me another one; perhaps an even better one, if we ask.'

That was true. They were wealthy after a perilous journey the year before to the Khaganate of the Avars, on the great plain of central Europe, during which they had discovered an ancient Goth king's hoard. It had been a gruelling expedition, they had lost many brave comrades and Bjarki had been so badly wounded that, only now, a good nine months later, was he recovered and back to his full, considerable strength.

The final *blot* ceremony was over and Bjarki and Tor were sitting together, a little apart from the rest of their party, in their camping place inside the fenced royal compound at Uppsala. The remote spot they had chosen to erect their half a dozen waxed linen tents and make their cooking fires was slightly to the west of three huge circular mounds. The Royal Mounds, these three grassy hillocks were called, and the Uppsala *gothi* claimed that they held the ancient bones of three famous heroes of old – mighty kings of the Svear, and human grandsons of the gods Thor, Freyr and Odin.

A quarter of a mile north of them, just outside the fence that encircled the royal compound, was the small sacred wood of ash and elm called the Grove of Skelfir, where all the bodies of the sacrificial victims of the *Disablot* – both human and animal – were taken by the *gothi* after sacrifice to be hung up dripping on the trees like gruesome Yule-tide hall decorations. From time to time, when the chilly wind blew in from the north, Bjarki caught the oily taint of rotting flesh on the air, and each time he smelled it, he pondered moving their little camp to a sweeter-scented spot, perhaps on the far side of the royal compound, near the king's hall and its outbuildings, more than a mile to the east. But the *Disablot* festival was nearly over, and when the wind veered again, it always seemed too much of a bother. There would be only one more day of celebrations, and then they would go home to Bearstead in Norrland, a five-day walk or two-day ride north of their little camp here in Uppsala.

A bustling market had sprung up in the southern part of the royal compound for the nine days of the *Disablot*, which Bjarki and Tor and their party meant to enjoy to the full the next day, now that all the sacrifices, the prayers and religious ceremonies were done. The *Disablot* market set up in the low-lying area to the south-east of their camping spot sold almost everything a Svear man or woman might reasonably desire – from delicate silver cloak pins to massive smoked elk carcasses, from huge barrels of powerful mead to beautifully painted lime-wood war shields, marked with birds and animals and swirling colours. Anything could be bought here from fancy necklaces made from bright burnished silver and blood-red carnelian beads, to sturdy male slaves stolen away from their homes across the seas, and absolutely indispensable to the hardy Svear farmers. It was the greatest market in all the North.

There would be trials of martial skill to watch as well, as part and parcel of the *Disablot* celebrations, various tests of a warrior's courage, strength and speed – sword duels, wrestling matches, spear-throwing and archery competitions. And the king himself, old Harald Fox-Beard, would make the traditional ship-captain's speech to mark the end of the festival, in the evening of the last day, at the Thing of All Svear, the assembly of all free-born males capable of bearing arms in his realm.

King Harald would be speaking from the Thing-Mound, a smaller, raised, flat-topped earthwork, at the bottom of the chain of three Royal Mounds. A platform on which all might see him. The speech would be made after any outstanding legal disputes had been settled, and all other business concluded, and Harald would name all the steersmen, or captains, of the ships' crews in his fleet for the coming year, and reward his jarls and *hersirs* with gifts of gold rings, and additional lands and honours.

Then the wild feasting would begin, which would last until dawn the next day.

Yet, in spite of all this excitement to come, Bjarki had had enough of these raucous celebrations to mark the turning of the Norse year. He simply wanted to go home to Bearstead. Einar the Cruel's death-gaze haunted him, and the nine bloody human sacrifices had increasingly sickened him. When he was younger he might have enjoyed taking part in the wrestling competitions or quarterstaff bouts, but he had no taste for it these days. Having survived to the ripe old age of five and twenty winters, he had seen too many real battles to find their peacetime approximations appealing. Besides, no warrior in his right mind would challenge him. He had a truly fearsome reputation. He was Fire Born, a *berserkr*, a Rekkr – and there were few people gathered in Uppsala for the *Disablot* who did not respect that high status.

'The prisoner, Einar, he *knew* me,' Bjarki said. 'He said something odd to me.'

His sister cocked her head at him, and said, 'He recognised the Bear in you?'

'I don't think that was it. He said this to me: "You are the Reborn One they speak of in Fröjel." What do you think he meant by that?'

'He recognised you as Fire Born. It is not as if it is some great secret. There you were, the big, bad warrior, with your scars and your scowl, a bearskin cloak marking your honour. He recognised you as Bjarki Bloodhand, the Rekkr of Bearstead, that's all. He hoped you would give him a sweet Harva blade to keep before he went off to the otherworld. There's no mystery here.'

'He was a Geat – a Goth from the island of Gotland. And he spoke of me as one who was *reborn*, not Fire Born.'

'Fire Born are reborn in the flames. You know that, oaf, just as well as I do.'

'Maybe you are right. But he called me "highness" before he died. Twice.' Bjarki waved an arm across the fire to summon one of his men with the ale skin. 'He was talking about the Angantyr business, Tor. About me… about my lineage.'

A grey-clad figure, an elderly warrior but squat and very strong, with a steel at his waist and iron in his hair, stepped forwards out of the gloom carrying a leather ale sack. He bent down in front of Bjarki and poured a stream into his out-thrust horn.

'Tell me, Kynwulf,' said Bjarki, when the man had finished refilling the vessel. 'Do folk here in Uppsala ever speak of me as... uh, as Angantyr? As the King of the Goths, as we understood it in your homeland. Or did we leave all that stuff behind?'

'You'll always be *my* king,' said Kynwulf. Then he indicated the five figures lounging around the far side of the fire, *Felaki* warriors who had followed Bjarki north after their lands were destroyed by the Franks. 'Their king, too. Your blood commands our obedience, because you are the heir of Angantyr, and it always shall.'

'He wants to know if he can strut about, nose in the air, calling himself king *here*,' said Tor. 'In Svealand. Or only in the back of beyond where you hail from.'

'My sister is teasing you, Kynwulf. Forgive her. But that prisoner tonight, the one we sacrificed to the *Disir* – the brave one – he said he'd heard, in Gotland, that I was *the One*. The Reborn One. Have you been speaking of my lineage to the Svear?'

Kynwulf looked uncomfortable. 'We speak with Svear people daily,' he said. 'We are not ashamed of how we come to serve you. So, naturally, we have spoken often of your bloodline and of the royal Goth ancestor whose lineage you claim.'

Kynwulf had helped a badly wounded Bjarki escape the vengeful Franks in the Avar Khaganate the year before, but then the old warrior had asked to return to his homeland to seek out any survivors of the terrible Frankish massacre of his village. Once there, Kynwulf had gathered up a dozen leaderless men and women from his burnt-out *Felaki* settlement and they had decided to abandon their ancestral lands and seek their fortunes – as their ancestors had before them – in the North. Six tough *Felaki* warriors now followed Bjarki, descendants of the original

Companions of the King. They believed Bjarki to be Angantyr, the legendary King of the Goths returned to life. Yet neither Tor nor Bjarki was entirely certain that this was true.

Bjarki looked up at his oath-man, weighing his words. The War Chief and his *Felaki* comrades had probably been spreading the story of their ancient king reborn all the way along their journey from Avar Plain to the Wendish port of Rerik – and across the whale-roads in the North. It was a fine tale and no doubt told with relish.

'It is no great matter,' he said, dismissing old Kynwulf with a friendly wave.

Tor leaned forwards to him then and spoke in a low voice. 'Have a care, brother, about bandying your royal title. We may have been able to persuade the *Felaki*, but if you go about flaunting your royal heritage – *our* royal heritage – then you may find your head swiftly removed from your body. There is already a king in Uppsala – Harald Fox-Beard – and he would not take kindly to anyone who tried to usurp him.'

'I'm not looking to usurp anyone. And I'm not making a claim to be the king of Svealand or anywhere else,' Bjarki replied to his sister in the same low tone. 'But I *would* like to know what people – particularly Goth folk, since Angantyr was their ancient king – are saying about me. That dead viking Einar the Cruel seemed to be suggesting that my name was often in people's mouths in Fröjet and, if that's true, where else do they speak it?'

'Have a care, oaf, that's all I say,' said his sister. 'And try not to...'

Her words were interrupted by a commotion of some kind, a man wailing in distress, calling out piteously, somewhere in the darkness, shouting Bjarki's name.

They both looked in that direction and saw a warrior, one of the *Felaki*, on his feet and speaking to a wildly dishevelled man, a weird-looking, dark and ragged creature, his hair plaited into ropes with his face painted as oddly white as the *Mikelgothi*'s for the *Disablot*, but with a recent cut over his right eye and splashes of fresh blood on his chalk-white cheek.

It was Abbio the Crow, counsellor of Duke Widukind of Saxony. The *Felaki* man escorted him into the firelight and Abbio slumped down in front of Bjarki.

'They, they took Edith,' he blurted, his eyes wild. 'They ssstole the poor *Mikelgothi* clean away.'

Chapter Two

A beardless nithing bastard

It took most of the night to get the story from Abbio. Tor was surprised how shaken he was by these events; she had known him a little in Saxony and he had always seemed to be a towering figure of power and mystery. He always carried a magic iron staff, the handle cunningly wrought in loops and twists, and dressed himself in stinking black rags and feathers, with tiny bones knotted into his beard. Two of his front teeth were missing, which gave his speech an unnerving sibilance.

He practiced *seithr*, she had been told, and he used these dark arts of magic, as well as more prosaic methods, to gather all the world's knowledge to him. He had been the cunning man who informed his lord Widukind during the war in the south about the movements of the Frankish enemy across the forests of Saxony, and his web of hundreds of informants reached right across the North and beyond.

Now he seemed almost girlishly hysterical, terrified by his experience.

'They came out of the night, while we were sssinging. The lasst traditional prayer to the All-Father after we had completed the ritual – the lasst ceremony of the *Disablot*. There were at least a dozzzen of them, warriorsss, brutal, cruel men...' He tailed off. Tor passed him a full horn of ale. She sensed the others in their party gathering around the speaker, listening, as Abbio drank. A pretty blonde called Inge, Tor's protégé, came and crouched at her knee, and Tor saw out of the corner of her eye Inge's servant and bodyguard Sambor, standing like a boulder behind her. The girl had been away visiting a friend for most of the evening – Tor knew not where – but Sambor had been with her so Tor had known that she would come to no harm.

'We tried to fight them but we are jussst *gothi* – only god-chosen folk were permitted to attend the Ccceremony of Conclussion… I cassst a sssspell but…'

'You were in the Grove of Skelfir when these men attacked you?' said Bjarki.

'What is the Ceremony of Conclusion?' asked Tor. 'I've never heard of it.'

'Horrible men, beasts, they cared nothing for the godsss – not even for Odin. They feared nothing, not even the power of the Dark Rites…' Abbio was mumbling. He had finished the ale in the horn and dropped it on the grass. Tor realised that the knock on the head had addled the poor man's wits.

'Tell us,' said Tor, 'who were these people?'

'Troll-kin, wer-monstersss… They had no resspect for anything sssacred…'

By dawn, they had a rough idea what had happened. A group of perhaps twelve warriors – not Svear, Abbio said he was sure of that, but Norse-speakers of some kind – had concealed themselves all day in the sacred grove and, when the Uppsala *gothi* had been occupied in a last *Disablot* ritual to wrap up the festivities, these unknown warriors had emerged from their hiding place and attacked.

They had trampled straight over the magical defences set up by the *gothi*, lines of thrice-cursed salt and urine, and four *nithing* poles, one in each cardinal direction, treating these spiritual deterrents as if they were nothing more than painted spears with gory horses' heads stuck on the top – which to an irreligious person or an ignorant foreigner was what they would appear to be. Two unarmed priests had been instantly killed by the attackers, several more were injured; but the most important priest of all, the *Mikelgothi* – Edith of Saxony – had been captured and carried away into the darkness over the shoulder of one of their attackers.

'And they cut down Einar the Cruel,' said Abbio. 'They got him down from his asssh tree and bore him away – gently, asss if he were a wounded man, not a corpssse.'

With the first grey streak of the day, Bjarki and his six *Felaki*, all armed and alert for danger, went to examine the sacred groves and see if there was any sign of the attackers. They left Abbio the Crow in the care of Inge and Sambor, while Tor went to rouse the fighting men of the Starki *hird*, and to report the matter to the king.

There had been much discussion about whether they should go and investigate the holy groves during the dark of night. But it had seemed not only extremely reckless to go charging blindly into the last place an armed enemy host had been seen, but also likely to be fruitless. If the attackers were gone, as seemed probable, what would they achieve trampling around in the dark except ruining the spoor?

Tor suspected that there was a further, deeper reason why Bjarki and his *Felaki* were so unwilling to search the Grove of Skelfir after midnight – the generations after generations of men and women who had been sacrificed to the gods and hung up there in the trees as offerings. The spirits of the dead, the *draugir*, as they were known, were said to be more plentiful in that small holy wood than fleas on an old hound.

Tor found her bivouacked troops – two hundred or so men of Jarl Starki's *hird* – in their own encampment in a sheep field on the far side of the king's hall. Evidently some garbled word of the night-attack on the grove had already reached their ears.

'What should be do, *Stallar*?' asked Gudrik, her *Merkismathr*, or second-in command, who had the honour of holding the jarl's Silver Fish banner in battle. 'We're prepared for pursuit, if that's your order. Is it true the Lady Edith was killed?'

'They took her. Alive. But we don't know who they were, or where they went. My brother is scouting the grove. For now, pick twenty swift runners and stand by.'

Inside the king's hall, the mood was more sluggish. Harald Fox-Beard had not emerged from his sleeping chamber and no one seemed inclined to rouse the old man.

Jarl Starki and Sigurd Hring, an older man, his scarred muscular arms adorned with many gold rings, and some other veteran warriors were sitting at the end of one of the long pine tables. Jugs of ale had been set out, along with bowls of hot porridge, and platters of bread, radishes and cheese, but no one was eating very much.

Tor received the distinct impression they were all suffering from a surfeit of ale or mead taken at the feast the night before.

'Lord, there has been an attack during the night on some of the *gothi*,' began Tor, looking at Jarl Starki. 'Two *gothi* were killed in the Grove of Skelfir, and some others injured. The assailants made off with...'

'Report to me, woman,' interrupted Sigurd Hring. 'And be brief, too.'

Tor ignored his rudeness. She continued speaking to her own jarl. 'The Lady Edith, sister of Duke Widukind of Saxony, and our honoured guest here in Upp—'

'I am the king's cousin, his *Armathr* and senior jarl here – you report to *me*!'

Tor allowed Sigurd Hring a brief glance. Then looked back at Starki, a single eyebrow raised. 'You had better make your report to Sigurd Hring, Tor,' said Jarl Starki with a disarming smile. 'As the king's *Armathr*, he stands in place of the king in his hall, when Harald Fox-Beard is indisposed.'

'The king is ill?' said Tor.

Jarl Starki gave a tiny shrug by way of an answer.

'Our beloved King Harald will no doubt be restored to his full strength after a little rest,' said the young lord of Norrland.

'If you don't tell me, woman, *this instant*, why you have disturbed our breakfast, I shall have your shrivelled buttocks whipped to bloody rags,' said Sigurd Hring.

Tor bristled and glared at him, her right hand hovering near the handle of her seax. Two of Sigurd Hring's nearest men growled in their throats like wolfhounds.

'Oh, don't do that, my dear Sigurd, don't *threaten* Torfinna Hildarsdottir,' said Jarl Starki, 'it always makes things *so* much more unpleasant. Her brother is Bjarki Bloodhand, don't you know?'

'I care not who her brother is, nor her uncle – nor her great-great grandmother. This woman will report to me *now* or I shall have her punished for her insolence.'

'Please, Tor, do not make my headache any worse,' said Jarl Starki, with a sigh. 'Just tell the *Armathr* what you know, and let us get back to our breakfast.'

So, obedient to her own jarl's orders, Tor made her report.

—

'That bastard Sigurd Hring said my buttocks were shrivelled!' said Tor, peering over her right shoulder and groping her behind. 'Do you think I'm flat-arsed, oaf?'

Bjarki was not accounted a man of very deep thought but even he was wise enough not to answer his sister's question on this delicate matter. He simply carried on packing a leather bag with his belongings, a good mail coat, a small cooking pot, a bag of dried meat, a warm woollen blanket and, of course, his tattered old bearskin.

The bearskin had been a gift from Tor, and cut from the She-Bear who had given Bjarki his *gandr*. The cloak had once been a rich, glossy black, but Bjarki had worn it in a dozen bloody fights, and the cuts and slashes of his foes had taken their toll. As had the blood spilled on the thick fur. Inge, a kind-hearted girl, had tried to clean the bearskin using a powerful lye-based soap. She had washed it thoroughly and rubbed soap into the blood and other stains. The result was that the once-jet-black cloak, though now clean, was a light brownish colour, even streaking to yellow in the parts Inge had washed most energetically. Bjarki did not care. He loved the garment.

'Look what I found in the grove, sis,' he said, holding up a long shiny object.

Tor could see it was the seax made by Harva of Finnstorp. She made a snorting noise, which might have been taken by some as an admission she had been wrong.

'So what else did you find?'

'A lot of tracks, the marks of a fight. It seems Abbio was right – about twelve men attacked the *gothi*. They had been hiding in the grove for some hours, waiting – we found their trampled hiding place. And we followed the tracks out of the grove and east towards the river. They had a ship moored there, a small one. They were overheard by one of the local fishermen from his bothy. A crowd of men, elated, raucous, getting into their ship and heading downstream towards the lakes in the middle of the night. The fisherman claimed to have heard a woman scream for help.'

'That's it, then. They're gone. They have a clear run down to Lake Malaren and the port of Birka, and by now they could even be out in the open sea – and sailing who knows where. Frisia? Francia? Hibernia? We've lost them, oaf. You will never see your pretty friend Edith again!'

'I know exsssactly where they are going,' said a sibilant voice from behind her.

Tor turned round to see the raggedy crow-like figure of Abbio standing there with his face now as dark as his filthy garb.

'How could you possibly know where they are going?' said Tor.

'From sssome of hisss foul crew – sssome of the men you yourself captured, Torfinna Hildarsdottir,' said Abbio. He ran a grey hand distractedly through his plaited hair, and Tor saw that there was fresh blood showing on his filthy fingers.

'We did not sssacrifice all of Einar the Cruel's crew. One or two of the younger ones were to be spared the knife and sssold as thralls. I questioned them this morn.'

'What did you learn?'

'They will go to Rogaland.'

'Where?' asked Tor.

'Rogaland,' her brother answered, on behalf of the Crow-man. 'It is far to the west, even beyond the Little Kingdoms, on the jagged coast that looks out towards the Western Sea. It seems that Einar the Cruel was ejected from Fröjet by the townsfolk – Abbio discovered all this today. The people of Fröjet hated him. They rely on the regular shipping trade that passes through their port – the very ships that Einar and his crew were despoiling. With Einar's vikings attacking their ships, many traders were steering clear of south Gotland. So no trade for the Fröjet folk. They threatened to hang Einar if he ever set foot on the island of Gotland again.'

'So he went off to this Rog-place?'

'Rogaland. He built himself a steading there, a fortress, really, overlooking the sea, with a snug little harbour, Abbio says, and he made it his winter lair. Einar could still venture out in spring and ravage the shipping in the Kattegat and the Eastern Lake, and along our eastern Svealand coast, but when the raiding season ended he could return to his hiding place in remote Rogaland in the autumn and feast and drink and boast of his deeds and count his stolen silver in safety all winter long. Einar's walled steading is at a place in Rogaland called Ymirsfjord, the Crow-man says.'

'Abbio discovered all that?' said Tor. 'I'm impressed. That is some fine work, *gothi*. Are any of the poor bastards you tortured this morning still able to speak?'

Abbio shrugged. He made all the dirty rags and feathers of his costume rustle.

'And you truly think that's where they are taking Edith, Crow-man?' said Tor. 'Wait, a more important question is: *why* would they take her there?'

'Where else *can* they go?' Bjarki answered for the scowling *gothi*. 'King Harald will surely be seeking them all over the Eastern Lake soon – a handsome reward offered for their capture. And the

24

waters around the Dane-Mark will be dangerous for them too; Widukind is closely allied to King Siegfried and so the Danes will also be searching for the sister of their king's good friend. They have the prefect hiding place at the very edge of the world. Somewhere few people ever venture to. They believe themselves safe there. Who would travel so far to rescue one woman?'

'I'm guessing that you would, oaf – judging by your hasty packing,' said Tor. 'But why steal Edith in the first place? Why do they risk so much for just one person?'

'Revenge,' said Abbio. 'And sssilver. Einar'sss great friend, his most loyal sssupporter, has been ssseen at the *Disablot*, one of the captivesss I questioned sssaid he had ssseen him here. He wanted to ressscue hisss beloved captain before the sssacrifice but found he could not. Instead, he and hisss crew chose to take their revenge on the onesss who killed him. And their revenge may not yet be complete.'

'You said "silver". Is this pirate, this "great friend", looking to ransom Edith?'

'Ssshe is a Sssaxon princesss. Would not her brother pay handsssomely for her?'

'He would,' said Bjarki. 'And if he does not pay up, Edith will surely die. But there is another peril, too. A reason why I must get to her fast. Abbio, tell my sister the name of Einar's friend, the one who took Edith, who is taking her to Rogaland.'

'Hisss name is Hjorleif Hjorsssson.'

'Now kindly tell my sister his by-name.'

'He isss more commonly known as Hjorleif Illugi – Hjorleif Evil Mind.'

'He delights in rape, Tor; he even boasts of it. Even among scum such as these Rogaland vikings, he is renowned for it. He likes to rape every woman he captures.'

–

Tor saw her brother off at the jetty by the river, the same place the night before that Hjorleif Illugi and his crew had so noisily departed with Edith. With him went Abbio and his six *Felaki* warriors; they set off in a small, light but swift-sailing fishing smack, the kind of boat that Bjarki had grown up sailing almost every day on the tiny Danish island of Bago where he was raised – and the same little boat that had brought them all down to Uppsala from Gavle.

Tor, Inge and Sambor would be walking home after the Thing of All Svear. She had been surprised when Abbio the Crow insisted that he must accompany her brother on this rescue mission into the wild and unknown west. She did not see him as the bold, adventuring type. But the strange, filthy little man has demanded to go: 'My lord Widukind made me promissse to take care of his sssister while ssshe wasss in Uppsssala. I have failed him. The leassst I can do is attempt to bring the Lady Edith back home sssafely,' he said.

While Tor felt a good deal of apprehension at Bjarki embarking on this risky journey to the west, she knew that, given the kind of man that he was, he was honour-bound to follow after Edith. He would have tried to rescue the Saxon princess even if he had no idea where she had been taken. And now that Abbio had so cunningly divined her abductors' destination, Tor was almost sure that Bjarki could find these pirates, defeat them with the help of his *Felaki* warriors, and then return home safely. It gave her a sense of comfort to know that, if she ever found herself in a similar predicament, her brother would hunt down her attackers, even if it meant going to the most distant stormy lands in all the Middle-Realm.

Back at their campsite, having bid her brother farewell, she found that Inge had prepared a cooked breakfast for her – bacon fried in a skillet with eggs, and toasted bread. Tor ate hungrily. After the long, sleepless night, she was weary and, asking Inge to wake her at noon, she rolled up in her blankets and fell into a dreamless sleep.

It was Sambor who woke her, with the news that her lord Jarl Starki urgently desired her company. Inge's Slav bodyguard and general factotum had only a few words of Norse and seemed reluctant to learn any more, and he communicated to the company mostly by grunting and pointing. But this morning he managed the simple phrase: 'Lord. Want. You. Now.' Tor had initially been suspicious of this foreigner, a short, immensely powerful, almost spherical warrior who had been tasked with protecting Inge by her grandfather, a Polans nobleman. The fellow had been foisted on them, and she did not know his true intentions. But after an encounter in Gavle, in which Inge had been accosted by a drunk in the market, she had changed her mind.

While Inge was at the cockle stall, examining the small clay pots of shellfish preserved in vinegar, a local blacksmith, a very powerfully built middle-aged man, reeking of ale, had moved in close behind Inge in the crowd and had attempted to fondle her buttocks through the gown she wore, as she haggled with the stall holder. Sambor had half-killed the fellow, lifting the blacksmith and hurling him to the ground, then pounding his face into pulp long after he had lost consciousness. Inge had had to summon some of Jarl Starki's *hird* – two of Tor's strongest warriors – to pull Sambor off his limp victim or red murder would have been done that morning.

So Tor now knew that Sambor's commitment to Inge was beyond question. And when the girl went off on her little errands, or to visit friends she had made during the nine days of the *Disablot*, Sambor went with her and Tor did not worry so much.

Tor found Jarl Starki with Gudrik, her *hird* lieutenant, at the Thing-Mound at the bottom of the line of three Royal Mounds. There were many people already there, ahead of the king's speech that evening, folk gathering in noisy knots around their regional leaders. Each territory in Harald Fox-Beard's realm, each village or district would be expected to build or buy – and then supply a crew for – a ship of war for the king. And they had all sent their representatives to the Thing of All Svear.

She found Jarl Starki with a dozen or so of his *hird*-members under a flapping standard – a silver fish on a field of sea-blue – near the westernmost Royal Mound, a few hundred yards north of the Thing-Mound. They were drinking wine, Tor could tell by the purple-stained lips of her young lord and his men. Wine-drinking was an affectation Tor despised, not only for the expense of the rare drink itself, which had to be transported hundreds of miles north from the distant Frankish lands, but also because she thought it an unmanly, Christian practice.

As she approached her lord, she saw, half a hundred yards beyond him, Sigurd Hring, the Jarl of Sodermanland, seated in a carved throne of sorts under a scarlet canopy, involved in some kind of grand ritual or ceremony. He appeared to be taking an oath of fealty from a very large bald man, a warrior, who was kneeling before him. When the fellow, after kissing the tip of the jarl's sword, stood up to his full height Tor saw he was, in truth, enormous, a genuine giant, taller even than Bjarki, but built in the same vast proportions as Sambor.

'Who is *that*?' she whispered to Gudrik, when she arrived at Jarl Starki's side, nodding in the direction of the giant. But it was her lord who answered for him, with a gust of sweet, wine-scented breath: 'That, my tardy *Stallar*, is the legendary hero Egil Skull-Cleaver, who has come to take service with my good *friend* Sigurd Hring.'

Tor noticed that there was an odd, angry tone in Jarl Starki's voice that gave the lie to the word 'friend'. She wondered if he were already drunk on the strong wine.

'Beyond him, you will notice another warrior of high renown, Krok of Frisia.' Tor watched as the giant withdrew from the throne, and a second massive warrior took his place. Krok knelt down before the throne and grasped the proffered sword.

'Sigurd Hring is acting as if he were the king,' said Tor. 'He is behaving as if *he* holds the power. I doubt Harald Fox-Beard will be pleased when he learns of this.'

'You have hit the nail directly on its broad head, my dear Tor,' said Jarl Starki, with a nasty little laugh. 'Sigurd Hring is demonstrating his strength for all Svear at the Thing to witness. He has been summoning heroes, the most famous warriors from across the North, gathering up renowned fighters to his banner for months, but *today* – the day of the Thing of All Svear – is the day that he has decided to take their oaths. And the jarl even brought along his *throne* to make it look all the more impressive!'

'What does Harald have to say about this? Is he not angry?'

'I could not tell you. The king has yet to emerge from his chamber. His servants say he has a bad cold in the head and needs to rest his aching bones a little longer.'

Tor bit back a curse. 'It is past noon. Surely, Harald must rise very soon from his bed, if only to dress himself and prepare for his *Disablot* speech for this evening.'

'You might very well think so. But, if the king cannot rise, if he truly is sick, I've no doubt that Sigurd Hring, the king's *Armathr*, will gladly step into his shoes.'

'Look, Tor, over there,' said Gudrik. 'See that beardless young fellow making his oath to Sigurd? He was the *hird*'s *Stallar* before you. You must remember *him*!'

Tor looked, and did remember. The clean-shaven young warrior now kneeling before the throne was Rorik Hafnarsson. Tor had killed his father, who had tried to cheat her, and when Rorik killed an old friend of hers in retaliation, she challenged him to a duel, from which he had fled, absconding with some of Starki's property.

'Ah, yes. I should have mentioned this, Tor,' said her lord. 'Sigurd Hring has asked me to forgive Rorik for his crimes against me, as a favour to him – and I have done so. Rorik will make his oath to the jarl. He'll be Sigurd Hring's man for life.'

'So, not for very long then,' said Tor.

'What do you mean?' said Jarl Starki.

'I mean I'm going to go over there now to gut that beardless *nithing* bastard!'

29

Chapter Three

A different world

Bjarki stood at the prow of the fishing smack, drenched to the bone, and peered through the lashing rain at the high black cliffs ahead. He turned and yelled an urgent command to Kynwulf, who was manning the steering oar, gesturing furiously to the *Felaki* War Chief to turn the craft away from the land. Even under the merest scrap of sail, the small boat was being buffeted alarmingly by the winds and the swell. The dark, angry-looking waves towered higher than the mast, hurling the fragile craft up and down like a child's toy in a wash tub. One such ugly wave, taken the wrong way, and the ship would be swept in and crushed against the granite cliffs and they would all be dragged down screaming to Queen Rán's watery domain.

This vertical coast was like nothing Bjarki had ever seen before. Raised on Bago, a flat, mud-and-sand island less than a mile wide, and now living in the low, undulating lake and forestlands of Harald's realm, Bjarki was unused to such a dramatic meeting of sea and land – these sheer forbidding mountainsides and narrow fjords a couple of bowshots across were alien to him. It was like a different world.

He made his way with difficulty back through the middle of the boat, passing the huddled *Felaki*, crouched in misery on their chests, and the black-rags of Abbio, his head over the side again, coughing up a string of yellow bile into the heaving water.

The weather had appeared calm this morning, when they had set out from a little sandy beach where they had spent the night, with only a distant shading of slate grey to the west to give any warning of this coming tempest. Abbio had promised that his prayers and the sacrifice of a few drops of his own blood, which he had made at dawn to Rán, the sea goddess, and her nine daughters of the waves, would secure them a smooth passage on the final leg of their journey. He had been mistaken.

As Bjarki passed by the miserably vomiting *gothi*, he had to restrain an urge to toss the irritating fellow over the side. At least the pelting rain and the sea spray would wash some of the stink off him. He smelled like a polecat – a long-dead polecat. He never seemed to wash his body, he could not navigate a sea-craft, he refused to row, saying it was beneath his dignity as a *gothi*. He did no chores around the camp they made each night on shore, and when he was not fiddling around with some disgusting bit of *seithr*, skinning a dead sea bird, or collecting up a handful of putrid fish guts, he was complaining constantly about the quality of the company's food, the inadequate size of their open vessel, the malevolence of the weather and the waves, about almost everything. It seemed his sorcery did not work either.

Bjarki bitterly regretted bringing the smelly *gothi* along on this mission.

'Take her a little further out,' yelled Bjarki in Kynwulf's ear. 'Two bowshots ought to keep us clear of those rocks. Aim for that tall sea-stack there – that's the one they call the Old Man, I think – but don't get too close to that either. I don't like the look of those big rollers coming in!' Bjarki pointed through the veil of rain at a teetering pile of rocks half a mile out which looked a little like a hunchbacked old man. Kynwulf, his beard and clothes soaked with sea-spray, grunted his agreement.

This was the seventh day since they had left Uppsala. The first night after a long haul south, they had made landfall at Fröjet, on the island of Gotland. This place was, as the name suggested, populated by Goths, a people originally from deep in eastern Europe who now occupied a wide swathe of land across the peninsula to the south of Svealand. The Goths spoke a very similar language to Svear and Danes, and shared the same gods and the same ways of living, but they were divided into three nations: the people of the island Gotland and, on the mainland, their far more numerous cousins the Ostergotlanders and the Vastergotlanders – the East and West Goths, who were divided by a long thin body of water called Lake Vattern. The Ostergotlanders lived to the east of the long lake, the Vastergotlanders to the west – and their western territory extended to the busy water lanes of the Kattegat, the seas to the north-east of the Danish Jutland peninsula.

Enquiries at one of the harbour ale-houses in Fröjet had confirmed what Bjarki and Abbio already knew: that Einar the Cruel had been cast out from the island some months earlier and had retreated to a remote fortified steading in Rogaland, which he had built at a place called Ymirsfjord. No one had seen Hjorleif Illugi for some months either but, after Bjarki produced a few silver coins from his pouch, one greybeard called Malfinn – whom Bjarki suspected had been a-viking with Einar the Cruel more than once – readily provided Bjarki with a detailed description of the route and the location of Ymirsfjord, including several important local sea-marks.

The second day's travel, on a heading more or less south-west, had taken them deep into Danish waters and, on the third day, they had been ordered to heave to by a large warship, a *busse*, filled with more than thirty mail-clad warriors, which was flying the famous Green Dragon standard of Siegfried, King of the Dane-Mark.

Bjarki was known by his reputation to the captain, who told him that a fast *karve* had been sighted the day before, and the helmsman thought he had seen a dozen crew and a woman in a white gown. However, when the Danish *busse* had approached, and ordered the *karve* to come under her lee, the unknown smaller ship had defied the order, hoisted sail and immediately sped away into a thick bank of fog, where it had soon been lost to sight. But the *karve* had been headed into the Kattegat, the captain said, through the narrow channel between the Danish island of Sjaelland, and the most southerly part of the main peninsula under Danish control known as Skane.

For the next three days, Bjarki and his crew-mates had sailed north-west up the Kattegat, with Jutland on their left and Vaster-gotland on their right, then turned west into the Skagerrak towards the Little Kingdoms, more than a dozen small patches of territory, some not much bigger than a valley, which had been carved out by a handful of refugees, outcasts and adventurers from the more prosperous and settled Svear, Goth and Danish lands to the east.

They had spent the sixth night at a damp, foul-smelling hall at a place called Oddernes, a short way inland from the wide, sandy beach they landed their ship on.

After some initial suspicion, the 'king' of Oddernes, a tough-looking old warrior called Ole Karlsson — whose subjects amounted only to four grown-up sons, one daughter, three daughters-in-law and five filth-covered grandchildren, as well as half a dozen iron-collared thralls — welcomed them to his realm. He fed them a rancid leek and oat pottage containing a few ancient bits of mutton gristle, stale rye bread and sour ale, and then determinedly set about trying to persuade Bjarki and his men to join him in building his sandy kingdom. He offered Bjarki his youngest daughter in marriage, suggesting they might spend that night together, to discover if they found each other agreeable, and if they did so, they could be betrothed the next day.

Bjarki politely demurred.

'I could use a good strong son-in-law,' said Ole. 'And my daughter Molfrid is fertile and pleasantly vigorous in bed.'

How King Ole knew that, Bjarki did not like to ask. He did however gain some valuable information about the exact where-abouts of the fortress of Ymirsfjord.

'There, highness, do you see it?' said Kynwulf. 'The inlet. That's the one King Ole was talking about. I think we could just about make it in there, if we tack out to sea and come around at it from the south-west.' Kynwulf was pointing through the veil of rain to a narrow opening in the black cliff face, a stone's throw wide, the wild sea surging and boiling between its walls most alarmingly. The inlet went inland less than a hundred yards, then widened. And Bjarki thought he glimpsed a patch of grey shingle at the far end.

'Give me the steering oar, Kynwulf, and get up amidships by the mast, and get two men on each side with the oars to fend us off.'

The War Chief relinquished his position, cupped hands round his mouth and shouted over the gale: 'Haugen, Rask, one oar each. Fend off on the larboard side. Bodvar, Harknut, fend off from steerboard side. Oddvin, up to the prow, quick lad – keep your eyes peeled for submerged rocks. Sing out if you see any nasty lurkers – and don't be shy about it.'

The five *Felaki* immediately moved to follow their War Chief's orders. Oddvin, the youngest, a mere stripling of only seventeen summers, clambering to the very front of the ship to watch their passage. Abbio couched, dripping, in the centre of the ship under the mast, looking balefully at Bjarki, as if his woes were all the Rekkr's fault. Bjarki ignored the *gothi*, settling down on the stern bench with the steering oar tucked snugly under his powerful right arm. He called out: 'Ready about! Watch your heads, you plough-pushers!' And swept the steering oar round so the ship's head came into the wind; then, with the square sail fluttering madly, she continued to swing onwards under her own momentum, the prow describing a smooth arc until the vessel found her new heading – south-west.

The ship surged forwards. Bjarki looked over his left shoulder. He could just make out the narrow inlet through the driving rain – just as described by King Ole and the greybeard viking in Fröjet, too – like a small black mouth in the forbidding, sea-washed wall of the cliff. The opening looked impossibly tiny at this distance. This manoeuvre, he recognised, would be as hard as a very drunken man trying to thread a needle – in utter darkness. With death as the price of his failure.

Bjarki counted thirty heartbeats and shouted, 'Ready about – and call on your favourite gods for aid!' He pushed the steering oar over and once again the boat swung around alarmingly, the prow now pointing due east directly at the black mouth of the inlet. The fury of the wind on his left side was intense, with little freezing packets of spray soaking his already drenched thin linen tunic, the small square sail was now bellied and taut as a drum; and the fragile little boat was speeding, hurtling, as fast as a galloping horse, straight towards the lethal cliffs.

Bjarki knew that if he got this wrong, if he made the slightest mistake, the frail craft would be dashed against the rocks, the timbers smashed, and they would all be hurled into the churning sea. They were a hundred paces away now, half a bowshot, and closing fast. Bjarki was a strong swimmer himself but he wondered how skilled the rest of his crew were. He guessed that Abbio the Crow would not be able to swim even a single stroke.

Heed me, Odin, he prayed silently. *Aid me in this sea battle with your rival Rán.*

He felt the swell lift the boat and push it sideways, an irresistible force, as if the sea goddess had heard him and wished to make her displeasure felt. He corrected the position of the oar slightly, angling the vessel to allow for the inexorable push of the sea. Another huge swell swept him further south; he was now way off target. The sail was pushing the craft at a dizzying speed straight into the side of the black, slippery cliff, which was now fifty paces from them – and rushing at them terrifyingly swiftly.

'Kynwulf, get ready to loose the boom!' he shouted. Then: 'You, Crow-man, if you have any sway at all with Rán of the Nine Waves, now is the time to wield it.'

He felt a sour fear rising from his belly, up into his tight throat, almost into his mouth. They were not going to clear the narrow entrance of the inlet, they were a dozen yards out. Another swell lifted and pushed the vessel even further off course. The boat seemed to shiver under him, as if she knew she was heading to her doom.

'Now, Kynwulf! The sail. *Now.* Watch your heads the rest of you!'

The War Chief tugged at a rope and the boom that was holding the square, rain-drenched sail aloft fell like a hanged man. The woollen sail suddenly collapsed in a sodden heap around the mast, and Bjarki pushed the steering oar out, far out, as far to the right as his long, muscular arm could reach. The resistance of the sea to the movement of the oar was enormous, and Bjarki summoned all of his strength to make the oar move through the water.

Immediately, the speed of the vessel slowed, and the prow of the boat swung round, and the ship squeaked through the mouth of the gap. There was a horrible bump and scrape, and Harknut shouted, 'Get away, you troll-turd,' wielding his oar to push the boat off a large shiny black rock at the entrance to the inlet. Something scraped noisily along the keel of the vessel. There was a judder that shook the whole hull, a scream and a splash, and Kynwulf bellowed: 'Oddvin!' When Bjarki looked right forwards there was no sign at all of the youngster at his watch-post on the boat's prow.

But they were now well inside the narrow jaws of the inlet.

Bjarki shouted: 'Take the oar, Kynwulf!' and while the older man hurried towards him, he stood and looked into the churning froth for some sign of the lad.

'There!' he yelled, thrusting the long oar into Kynwulf's hand and pointing with his own at a sleek head that had popped up from the waves five paces from the boat's side, before immediately sinking again.

'Take her right in to the beach, man. Don't wait for us,' Bjarki shouted to an astonished Kynwulf. Then the Rekkr dived over the side of the boat as lithe as a seal.

The cold water was a shock to Bjarki's whole body. He opened his eyes and could see nothing but a cloudy darkness. There was no sign of Oddvin. He turned this way and that. He began to feel a panic rising in his gorge, and growing pressure from holding his breath. He swam downwards, his blond head still questing from side to side. The pressure in his lungs expanding, almost intolerable now. He longed to gasp.

'You need my help,' said a dark, ursine voice in his heart. 'I can feel your fear.'

No, I do not need you. I only seek my prows-man Oddvin, replied Bjarki, silently.

'That boy is headed for Hel's realm – and you will follow him down, if you do not soon breathe good air,' said the voice. 'Go up, man-child, go up to the daylight.'

I must find him. He is in my charge. I shall not fail him.

Bjarki could see the shingle bottom now, and drifting fronds of thick green weed. It was calmer down here, away from the toil and roil of the storm on the surface. It felt almost peaceful. The vision now was fading at the sides of his eyes. Then he saw the boy – Oddvin – shockingly close. His mouth moving silently, opening and closing as if he was speaking – or screaming in terror. The boy's huge eyes staring at Bjarki.

Bjarki thrust out his right hand and gripped Oddvin's tunic by the loose material at the chest. His feet touched the bottom of the inlet. He felt his chest would explode; his hold on the world loosening. A subtle weakness was trickling through his body; his leaden eyelids were beginning to close. The whole world was slowly darkening.

Now, I need you, Mochta, he said inside his heart. *Grant me your great strength!*

Still firmly gripping Oddvin's tunic, he shoved off hard from the stony bottom. His body rose, aided by his flailing left arm and the wild kick of his feet, hauling the *Felaki* warrior up, up, with him. He felt his *gandr*'s great strength flow into his body like liquid fire; he felt the power infuse his kicking legs. He felt strong as a mountain.

'Swim, foolish man-child,' said the deep voice. 'Swim swiftly up to the light.'

His head broke the surface of the water, and he sucked in a breath and, feeling light and powerful, he hauled Oddvin's terrified face above the slapping waves.

The youngster gasped, spluttered and immediately began to struggle. Bjarki kept his grip on the folds of his tunic, and pulled him in close, their faces inches apart.

'Do not fight me! I will bring you to the beach,' he yelled. The storm was still in full fury, and a wave smashed into them, swamping Oddvin's head. The *Felaki*'s arm flailed out and he grasped Bjarki's hair, shoving his saviour under, seemingly trying to clamber on top of his huge body, as if Bjarki were some kind of human raft.

Bjarki let himself sink. He disengaged from the youngster. Then bobbed up, close by, and swung a short hard punch at Oddvin's jaw. The brutal blow landed on the point of his chin, and Oddvin was knocked back, his eyes wildly fluttering, and immediately began to sink again. Bjarki grabbed him, and flipping the boy, and turning on his own back, he cradled the unconscious young man's neck and chest against his own. Keeping Oddvin's chin above the water with his left hand, he began to swim, with short powerful strokes, towards the shingle beach now only fifty paces away.

Kynwulf helped him haul the boy's limp body from the waves. The War Chief bent to see that Oddvin was breathing, looked up at Bjarki, and gave him a brisk nod.

Together, they carried the insensible prows-man past the now beached ship and across the crunching stones to a place with a large overhang of rock that provided some shelter from the storm. They laid him down and his comrades wrapped him in a blanket and tried to make him comfortable. Bjarki slumped down on the shingle – suddenly exhausted and filled with a familiar melancholy that summoning the power of his *gandr* always left him with. He muttered, 'My thanks to you, Mochta,' under his breath, and thought he heard an ursine grunt from deep inside him in response.

After a while he lifted his head. 'How is the boy?' he asked Kynwulf.

'He's awake, highness. With a sore jaw. But awake and still alive, praise Rán.'

Bjarki peered out at the dismal, stony beach. The rain seemed to be lessening. Someone passed him a half-full sack of ale, and he drank deeply. A slice of bread and hunk of cheese were passed next. The rain was definitely slowing. Slowing. It stopped.

It was only just past noon but Bjarki felt as if he had been marching over bad terrain all day. He felt, in truth, almost as if he had just fought a hard, bloody battle.

'We rest here tonight,' he said. And there were general expressions of relief from the exhausted *Felaki* sitting all around him on the pebbles under the overhang.

His eye fell on Abbio. The Crow had spread out a small patch of old doeskin on the shingle, about the size of two cupped hands, and he seemed to be muttering some kind of prayer over it. As Bjarki watched, he took out a little leather pouch, loosened the drawstring, and holding it up to the air he said some magical words then emptied the contents of the sack onto the doeskin. A dozen small flat pebbles fell out onto the skin, and Bjarki could see that some of them had runes scratched on the different coloured stones' upturned surfaces, and some were face down and the rune could not be seen. He had seen Abbio perform this simple divination technique often before, indeed, almost every night on the voyage here. But it always made him feel a little uncomfortable; any kind of *seithr* did. Abbio gathered the stones with runes showing and laid them out in a line on the edge of the doeskin. He seemed to be reading them.

He turned and looked directly at Bjarki, his tiny blackbird eyes glittering.

'Edith isss still alive,' he said. 'But ssshe is in very grave danger at thisss hour.'

Chapter Four

A visit from the Honeyman

Tor glared at Jarl Starki. 'Say that to me again,' she grated. 'I surely misheard you.'

'You must forgive him, Tor. You must forgive Rorik Hafnarsson for his crimes against you – and for refusing to fight you in the *holmgang* – you must forgive him, just as I have done, for the sake of peace with his lord Sigurd Hring. We *must* try to remain on good terms with Jarl Sigurd – he is a rising power in Svealand. Perhaps our next king. I will not make an enemy of him just to quench your lust for revenge.'

'Fuck all that. I'm going to kill Rorik. I'm going to go over there and call him a coward to his face – then slaughter him. And nothing you can say, lord, will stop me.'

'This is an order, Tor Hildarsdottir. You will do nothing. Rorik is not important. You will remain by my side and far from that man. As your lord, I *command* you.'

Tor made a scrapping noise in her throat. 'That *nithing* killed my friend Ulli, the old steward of my steading. Rorik hanged him from a tree. I *shall* have my revenge.'

'Do you have any proof that Rorik Hafnarsson killed your steward? A witness?'

Tor said nothing; her eyes were now smarting as a result of her contained fury.

'You will obey me, *Stallar*, or you will become *my* enemy. Do not test me, Tor! I will destroy you. Destroy everything you have – Bearstead, your folk, your brother.'

Tor looked hard at her jarl. She could see that Starki meant every word he said.

'But lord...'

'You will return home to Bearstead, Tor, this is my command. You made an oath to serve me, did you not? Do you now wish to break it? Gudrik can take charge of the *hird* for a few days. Go home and reflect on your oath, Torfinna. Return in a week or so to my side, when you're reconciled to obeying my orders – or do not return at all.'

Tor dropped her eyes. A fierce battle raged inside her – all her instincts told her to ignore the jarl, draw a weapon and take revenge on Rorik. Fuck the consequences.

Another part of her saw Bearstead in flames. The jarl's men slaughtering Inge and the rest of her folk, her brother at bay, surrounded by Starki's warriors, and then them cutting him down. Almost as bad, to her mind, was the knowledge that she would be branded an oath-breaker. No one would trust her word again. She turned from Jarl Starki and, without saying a single word, she stalked away. She found that her treacherous eyes were filling with hot tears – and cursed her stupid weakness.

–

The familiar rhythms of Bearstead soon soothed her rage. And, five days later, after a long march home with Inge and Sambor, she allowed herself to realise that she had, for once, made the correct decision. She would surely take a fine revenge on Rorik in due course, but there was no particular hurry. Now that she knew where the *nithing* was, and whom he served, she could take her time, and do her duty to her friend Ulli secretly, without risking everything she loved. There was no need for Jarl Starki to know; there was no need for his relations with Sigurd Hring to be jeopardised. She would bide her time and, one dark night, she would slit Rorik's *nithing* throat – and tell Ulli to listen from the afterlife to the music of his death rattle.

Bearstead was a bustling place these days. After the arrival the previous autumn of the six *Felaki* warriors, and their four wives and five children, they had had to swiftly construct another timber and thatch longhouse to accommodate all the new members of the household. Indeed, Bearstead was swiftly coming to resemble a small village, or at least a hamlet, rather than just a steading, with a total population, now, when all of her people were present, of nineteen folk. Or nineteen hungry mouths. And while Tor and Bjarki were indeed wealthy after all their bloody adventures in the southern Slav lands, nineteen people needed a great deal of feeding.

They had cleared a larger area of forest – a hard, painstaking task, which had involved much digging up of stubborn roots, and clearing boulders from the thin northern soil. But they had managed to get a rye crop in before they went off to the festivities at Uppsala. And the extended kitchen garden behind the hall, dug by so many willing hands, provided them a steady stream of beans, leeks and cabbages.

Tor had invested in a herd of twenty black pigs, four goats and two dozen white ducks, whose rich eggs she enjoyed lightly boiled each morning. They bought oats, barley and dried peas by the sackful from the monthly market at Gavle – although Tor hated spending precious silver on food, and she promised herself that the next year, when her crops came in, she would sell her surplus in Gavle to recoup the money spent.

There was one luxury she *was* prepared to spend coin on – unless she could persuade the seller to accept duck eggs or sides of cured bacon – and that was honey. The Honey Hunter came once a month with his little donkey cart piled high with small barrels and pots of delicious, dark wild honey, jars and skins of fine mead, and stacks of roughly cast blocks of creamy beeswax, which could be made into candles.

No one knew his true name – he was always simply called the Honey Hunter, or sometimes the Honeyman – nor exactly where he lived, but it was clear he lived alone and somewhere in the vast forests north of Bearstead. He was heavily bearded, with long dirty brown hair, and his torn clothes were little better than a beggar's rags, but Tor knew for certain he was woman-less and child-less because he stared at the *Felaki* girls and their laughing children with an undisguised longing. However, when she asked if he would like to meet one of the *Felaki* newcomers, a handsome woman, still quite young, who had been widowed by the Franks the year before, he blushed and turned away and muttered that no, no, he was not fit for fancy female company.

Two days after her arrival at Bearstead, after the long tiring trek from Uppsala, the Honey Hunter drove his donkey cart into the stamped-earth courtyard, and reined the grey-muzzled beast in. His cart was immediately surrounded by all the various children of the steading, shrilly demanding that they be allowed to sample his wares, as well as Inge, who, while not exactly a child at the almost-womanly age of fifteen winters, still loved sweet honey more than any other food. And she was not alone: at least one of the *Felaki* women joined her in looking for a sweet treat.

The Honey Hunter generously obliged them all, honouring them with his shy, crooked little smile, opening up a large wax-sealed pot and giving each supplicant a large horn spoonful of the delicious brown liquid.

'May you be healthy and happy this day, lady,' he murmured, when Tor was finally able to get through the crush of folk, and inspect the contents of his cart.

'You too, Honeyman, healthy and happy,' Tor said, eyeing the stacked wares. She had several purchases in mind and hoped they would not cost her too much.

When the children, realising that they would get no more free honey, wandered away to play, Tor engaged the man in a little chit-chat and a few pleasantries. The Honey Hunter travelled to several farmsteads in the vicinity as well as visiting Borte, a village a few miles away, and Gavle for the monthly market. He had all the gossip.

A woman Tor knew in Borte had a fever and was likely to die. There had been a brawl in Gavle a week ago, in which some of Jarl Starki's *hird* had been involved, although no one had been killed, and Starki's steward had punished those to blame.

Eventually, when the talking was done, Tor purchased one large pot of best honey from the Honeyman, one small one, too, six fist-sized cubes of sweet-smelling beeswax, and a long leather skin of his strongest mead, which she thought Bjarki would enjoy when he returned from his rescue mission in Rogaland. She exchanged these items for a whole fresh goats' milk cheese, a side of smoked bacon, and half a sack of green beans, and she threw in a basket containing a dozen creamy duck eggs for good measure, since she was very pleased that she did not have to part with any of her precious store of silver coin. The Honeyman was happy too.

Before he left, he mentioned one more thing to her: 'Maybe this is nothing, lady,' he said, 'but in Bjorke they said strangers had been staying with Hrolf Gundarsson, for some days, maybe a week. Three foreigners from the south. Asking about you and Bearstead.'

'Foreigners?' said Tor. 'Goths? Danes? Not Saxons, surely.'

'Nay, they were Svear. But not from these parts. Strangers from Sodermanland.'

Sodermanland. The far southern territory of Rorik's master Sigurd Hring.

'A young fellow? Beardless? Handsome? One all the girls might giggle over?'

'No, older men, I was told. Seasoned warriors. But they have gone back south.'

—

Before Tor set out into the forest, she spoke to Inge and the girl's bodyguard Sambor.

'There have been strangers in the neighbourhood asking about me, and about Bearstead. It might be nothing. It might also be Rorik's friends looking to come here and attack us. Will you ask everyone to be careful when they're outside the walls of the steading? And we need to keep a watch, at all times, and especially in the night.'

Inge had to translate some of this to Sambor. But when the massive Polans warrior understood the situation, he growled assent and agreed to take precautions.

Tor took a thick blanket, a water flask, a little food and the small pot of honey, her seax and her favourite bow and a quiver packed with arrows, and set out early the next morning into the endless forest, heading north, but allowing her feet to wander.

She saw no sign of any other people – except once when she crossed days-old wheel tracks of the Honey Hunter's donkey cart – but plenty of animal spoor, and in the evening of the first day, she shot a young roe deer and made camp in a clearing.

She hung the deer up in a tree and gralloched it, cutting its belly open and spilling its purple insides all over the leaf-litter floor. The guts-smell was strong but that was what she wanted. She cut herself a sizeable chunk off the haunch and grilled it over her fire. As the dusk began to gather and the forest closed in around her, she wrapped the blanket around her body and waited. She keenly remembered, then, an earlier time in her life, when she had been all alone in a dark forest. That had been far to the south, in Saxony, and she had been undergoing an ordeal known as Voyaging in an attempt to become Fire Born, a Rekkr like Bjarki. The attempt had, of course, failed, and she had been utterly heartbroken, but as the years had passed, her regret had faded; and now, with Bearstead as her own steading, her coffers brim-full of Goth silver, a position of high honour with the Norrland jarl, and daily surrounded by the cheerful sound of voices, and the playing of children, she was not far from contentment. There was the problem of Rorik, and her delayed revenge, but it did not press on her.

She allowed her mind to wander as she drifted off to sleep. How was Bjarki? Where was he? Had he managed to find Edith, and extract her from the viking lair of Hjorleif Illugi? She knew that Bjarki desired Edith – he had mooned over her embarrassingly in Saxony, and he had no special woman, at present, no lovers at all, so far as she knew. It would be a good match – Edith of Saxony, a *gothi* beloved of Odin, and Bjarki Bloodhand, equally blessed, victor of so many battles – although she knew it would take her brother away from her side, and from Bearstead, too.

Edith was not made for a life in the backwoods. Even if she did decide to choose Bjarki – and she might not – she would surely not want to spend her life as a dutiful steading wife, milking the goats, making butter, weeding the leeks. She was born for great halls, bred to entrance men of power; made for silk clothes, servants and jewels. Tor did not begrudge her this soft life, indeed she admired Edith: the woman had grit.

Yet that kind of life could never be Tor's. She liked things plain, rough and dirty, joyous and wild. Soft silks and elegant manners would never suit her character. But could her brother Bjarki live in a fine palace? In many ways, he was softer than she was – despite his truly terrifying ferocity in the heat of battle. There was a subtle gentleness about Bjarki, a deep kindness to his spirit – the other side of the coin to the ravening beast, the blood-soaked maniac he became in the grip of his Bear *gandr*.

She heard a sharp noise. A breaking stick. And sat up swiftly, with her right hand falling naturally on the bone handle of the seax at her waist. She listened, and thought she heard the brush of fur against bark. She got up, shrugging off the blanket, and stepped to the wood pile. She threw a handful of loose kindling in the embers of the fire. All her senses were engaged. The fire flared, and she thought she saw a shape move out by the tree line. She put two logs on the fire, and sat with her back to the growing blaze staring out into the dark.

A pair of eyes, yellow as two tiny suns, stared back at her from the dark forest. She shuffled over to her bow, still seated, and strung the short weapon with a smoothness born of long practice. She selected an arrow, and pulled the full quiver over towards her thigh.

There was another set of eyes now, a little past the first one. And as she looked around she saw others too. A pack. Perhaps half a dozen. And they were not afraid of her. The past winter had been hard, and the pack was clearly hungry. And a fresh deer carcass was hanging from a tree only a few yards from her back, still dripping. The wolves smelled it. They wanted it; they would kill her, if necessary, to feast upon it.

A stray thought came into Tor's mind. All those years ago, when she was alone, naked and Voyaging in the First Forest in Saxony, she would have given her right hand, indeed she would have cut it off herself, to have been visited by a pack of wild wolves in the night. Now it was an inconvenience. She was not frightened. She had her bow. She knew the wolves were wary, struggling between instinct and hunger.

She said sternly: 'Be gone, grey sisters, and do not seek to steal from me. This meat is not for you – not this night. When I am done with it, you may feast to your hearts' content. Not till then. Go, or I will be forced to slay you. And I do not wish to.'

The wolves were spreading out, encircling Tor. She stood up, nocking the arrow to the cord. 'Go back into the darkness, my sisters. Lest I shoot you. Go. *Yaaaaaah!*'

She screamed the last word, and saw the skittering of the nearest wolf, a young female, at the human noise – but the others were not so easily impressed. There were low, grey shapes slinking in and out of the shadows all around the clearing. Tor put her back to a tree, and waited. They would rush her, all at once, she thought. And then she must begin to kill them. Could she get them all? No. One or two. Maybe three.

She could see at least seven out there. It seemed there would be blood spilled.

A little chill ran down her spine. Was this some silly joke of the gods? Odin possessed a dark notion of what was amusing, or so the wise ones said. That a woman who had long craved a meeting with Wolf *gandir* should die by the teeth and claws of their ordinary cousins. If this was her end, so be it. At least she would perish in battle.

No point in self-pity. She had made a mistake. It was time to kill. Time to die.

Tor drew back the cord of her bow and tracked the nearest low, slinking shape.

She heard a roar, a huge deafening sound, deep, dark and somehow meaty. And every wolf in that clearing checked and stood still at the loudness of the warning. There was a great crashing, the noise of breaking branches and muffled heavy thuds. The wolves whisked around like cats and vanished into the darkness between the trees, and a massive black bear came lumbering into the clearing, a monstrous creature with yellow eyes and long teeth. And the bear charged straight towards Tor.

Tor hurled bow and arrow away and ran straight towards the huge bear.

The two beings collided, Tor throwing her arms around the animal's bulk, her voice, muffled by his thick fur, cried: 'Garm, my lovely boy! How I've missed you!'

The two of them were rolling around on the leaf-litter of the forest, over and over, lit by the blazing fire, a furry growling ball of limbs and legs and happiness.

–

Tor walked slowly back to Bearstead with a haunch of venison over her shoulder, and a smile on her face that could have melted a glacier. She had spent the rest of the night and the next day eating honey and half-cooked venison and playing with Garm, a bear cub she had adopted in Thuringia six years ago, and a creature she had loved fiercely ever since.

The bear, now fully grown and distinctly dangerous, had once lived with Tor and Bjarki and had travelled with them, but that had become impractical, and they had faced a choice between caging Garm or setting him loose to make his own way in the forest. Once they had built their hall at Bearstead, things had become much easier.

The humans lived at Bearstead, and the wild animal marked his territory in the forests surrounding their hall, announcing his claim with renewed urine deposits and scat, and never straying, as far as Tor could tell, more than two or three days' walk away from his human friends. But Tor saw very little of her beloved Garm in the cold months of the year, since the bear ignored the lovely, warm hut she had built for him inside the steading palisade, and preferred to make his own bed for the winter sleep in some unknown den deep in the endless Svealand woods.

Now with the thaw of spring, they were reunited. Although the way that Tor was unerringly able to find this creature in the open wilderness was still something of a wonderful mystery to her. She suspected that Garm could smell her scent from a considerable distance away – as much as a full day's march, perhaps – but she had no way of knowing this for sure. When she had spoken of this remarkable skill to Bjarki, he had given her a different reason: 'Garm is no ordinary bear, sis. His mother Mochta once told me that Garm also is a *gandr*. You should not be too worried about losing him in the woods – *gandir* are always drawn to us humans, which is why Garm is always drawn to you. No, what you should be more worried about, Tor, is Garm finding his way into your heart, and becoming your *gandr*, not just your playmate.'

'Garm is *already* in my heart – and my lovely boy always will be,' retorted Tor.

'You know what I mean,' her brother had replied, smiling at her. 'All I'm saying is, be careful, sis: I think one battle-drunk Rekkr in this family is more than enough.'

When Tor returned to the steading, in the middle of the afternoon, she found the courtyard a hive of activity. Inge came out to greet her, her face white, her blue eyes alive with excitement. Inge took both Tor's hands and looked into her friend's face.

'A messenger arrived today from Jarl Starki in Uppsala. The poor fellow ran all the way here from Uppland without stopping. He's in the hall, sleeping like a stone.'

'What is it?' Tor was puzzled by Inge's obviously high emotional state.

'The jarl has ordered you to return to his side in Uppsala, as quickly as possible.'

'Starki's had a change of heart. What does he want with me?'

'It's Harald Fox-Beard. The King of the Svear is dead.'

Chapter Five

'Kill all the men'

'What do you mean *grave* danger?' said Bjarki. 'How can the danger be any graver now for the Lady Edith than it has been during these past seven days?'

Abbio shrugged. 'I know only what Odin tellsss me through the rune-ssstones.'

Bjarki cursed and tiredly got to his feet. 'Right, Oddvin stays here to watch the boat. The rest of you get all your kit together – we will head out immediately.'

'Highness…' said Kynwulf. 'Would it not be wiser to rest? The men…'

'Don't question my orders, old man. Get your people up and moving. Now!'

Bjarki knew he was being harsh but he had no choice. If Edith died, or was badly hurt as a result of a delay to rest his men, Bjarki would never forgive himself.

He heard her captor's by-name ringing in his head: Hjorleif Illugi – Hjorleif Evil Mind. And his reputation, too.

Bjarki looked up at the slate-grey sky. The rain had ceased and he thought he saw a few faint patches of blue over to the east. He believed it was about five miles as the eagle flies – say, an hour's march – to the steading at the end of the fjord where Einar the Cruel had built his hall. That was, if the information given by King Ole was correct. He wanted to get there in daylight, to look on the place from the cliffs above.

Ymirsfjord had been built at the base of a long, narrow inlet of the sea, he had been told, at least three miles long, with sheer cliffs on either side. It looked, Malfinn of Fröjet had said, like a furrow that had been scooped out of the land by a giant's spoon in the days when the Middle-Realm was still young and curd-soft. It was considered impossible to approach Ymirsfjord by sea, the old former viking had said, without the inhabitants being aware of the approach for several hours before the ship could be beached on the strand. They could not be taken unawares *by sea*, Malfinn has insisted. But *by land*, if you were hardy enough, and knew the proper route, you could reach the cliffs above the steading, descend quickly and take them by surprise.

Bjarki had rewarded the greybeard handsomely for this information with a bag of silver, while despising him for his treachery to his former comrades. Malfinn had taken his money but also sensed Bjarki's unspoken disapproval. He said: 'You think me dishonourable? There was no honour among Einar's filthy crew. Hjorleif, Einar's second, raped my wife – my *wife*! The only woman I ever loved. He forced her. And when I complained, he laughed and said she liked him far better than me. Then he and his cronies beat me senseless and left me for dead on a beach in Skane. Penniless and broken, no weapons, no friends. And, as far as I know, my wife is with him still. I believe you mean to harm him and his crew; maybe even kill Hjorleif Illugi. I say to that: may Odin All-Father aid you in your task, and take my blessings with you too!'

They left Abbio with Oddvin to watch their vessel and, carrying only weapons, armour and climbing ropes, they clambered up the rain-wet cliffs at the head of the inlet to the top. Abbio had said he would remain with the boat and work his magic to cast a spell of enchantment to hide the warriors while they approached Ymirsfjord.

'I am not made for battle,' he told Bjarki. 'I ssshall fight them my own way.'

They left a knotted rope, tied to a stake hammered deep into the turf at the summit, dangling thirty feet down the cliff, so that a rapid escape, should one be necessary, would be easier. In late afternoon, with the weather mercifully remaining dry, they set off in single file. Bjarki led the way and Kynwulf took up the rear.

Bjarki had little faith in the Crow's promised spell of invisibility, but he was relieved to be rid of the filthy little man. He kept his body low and advanced slowly north-eastwards, cautiously climbing a steepish grassy slope with the five *Felaki* warriors strung out in a line behind him. After less than an hour's uphill walk, Bjarki came to the edge of another sea-cliff, this one higher and far more vertiginous than the one they had scaled a little earlier. He crouched down near the lip and looked north at the dark, white-capped waves in the long fjord below.

It was a spectacular view. The fjord ran roughly east–west in a straight line for several miles – and the sea channel did indeed look as if it had been scooped from the soft rocks of the earth by some vast being with a spoon. The sheer cliff sides both north and south were covered with scrubby vegetation and the dark, shining sea was at least five hundred feet down from where he now sat.

He glanced behind him and saw all the *Felaki*, all except Kynwulf, who was fully alert, were lying prone. Some even seemed to be asleep. Dusk was not far away.

At the very eastern end of the fjord, perhaps a mile distant, Bjarki could make out the buildings of a walled settlement – presumably Ymirsfjord. A long hall from which a trickle of smoke seeped, creating a small haze above its shingled roof. Several outbuildings, hay barn, pig pens, stables perhaps, and a forge were arranged around a muddy courtyard. It looked, Bjarki thought, not all that much different to Bearstead, if his home could have been observed from above by some flying creature. Except that, outside the palisade of sharpened poles that protected the compound, a fat river curled towards the beach on the southern side. And there was a ship pulled up on the strand, too, the lean craft canted over on its side, and Bjarki thought he could make out two or three figures working on the weed-covered timbers of its hull. The ship was a *karve* like the one the Danes had tried to stop before it ran from them.

He crawled back to Kynwulf, taking care to make no visible outline above the cliff. 'It's not going to be easy, War Chief,' he said. 'We can work our way to get above Ymirsfjord before nightfall – but getting down the cliff is going to be hard.'

'What are your orders, highness?' said Kynwulf, a little sulkily. 'Whatsoever you command, we shall obey.' He was still smarting, clearly, from Bjarki's earlier rebuke.

Bjarki took a long breath. 'I want to hit them just before dawn. So we have a choice. We can get down there to the fjord tonight, and hide until first light, then make our attack. Or we can wait on top of the cliff, go down in the darkness just before dawn, and attack before they are awake. What is your counsel, old friend?'

'The men are all very tired...'

'I know that, curse you, but I still desire you to give me your wisdom.'

Kynwulf frowned at him reproachfully. 'I was going to say, highness, that the men are exhausted now but they are used to scaling mountains. We can climb down these cliffs, even in the pre-dawn dark, if need be. We have enough ropes. And it would be better if we rested on the top beforehand. I say we stay up here tonight. They'll climb better tomorrow; fight better, too.'

'So be it,' said Bjarki.

They crept a mile closer and slept above the settlement, wrapped in their cloaks, a little back from the edge of the cliff, under a pair of wind-stunted gorse trees.

Bjarki, although he was also near the limits of his own strength, found it difficult to drift off. Some of the *Felaki* were snoring, but that was not the problem. He was worried about the descent they must undertake before dawn the next morning which, despite Kynwulf's confidence, was a truly perilous one. He was also worried about Edith. Grave danger, Abbio the Crow had said. Grave. Visions filled his mind of poor Edith being ravaged by the entire crew of the *karve*, with Hjorleif standing over her, his erect member in his fist, saying: 'She likes me better than you, Bloodhand!'

54

'Highness!' It was Harknut, who had the watch, shaking his shoulder.

Bjarki sat up and looked at the iron, cloudless night sky. The moon was far to the west, near the horizon. It was a little less than full dark. Near dawn. Cold, too.

The descent went far better than Bjarki had hoped. The *Felaki* were indeed skilled in cliff-work. They fixed their ropes and clambered down as nimble as goats.

Bjarki himself found it more troublesome. He kept catching his trews and tunic sleeves on the wiry roots of the shrubs that grew horizontally out of the mountainside and in the greyish half-dark he found it hard to locate decent hand and foot holds. However, there was only one truly heart-stopping moment, when Bjarki, moving heavily because of the thigh-length, iron-link mail coat he wore under his ragged, discoloured bearskin cloak, misplaced his right foot, dislodged a rock, and caused a cascade of pebbles to tumble and rattle, shockingly loud, down the mountainside.

All six men froze on the cliff face, listening hard. But there was no sound from the sleeping Ymirsfjord steading. They were about fifty feet from the bottom when the wooden gate in the palisade creaked open and a man came out, stretching and yawning. It was now much lighter in the east, and beyond the mountains behind the settlement, there was even a faint pink tinge to the sky. Bjarki fretted that they had left the attack too late. A slow sea mist was rising, edging ever closer from the west. However, Bjarki had no time to wait for its cover.

'Hurry,' he hissed, as softly as he could, to the five half-seen *Felaki* behind him.

The early rising Ymirsfjord viking shut the palisade gate behind him, just casually pushed it closed with one hand. Then sauntered down towards the beach. He was bare-chested, shoeless, clad only in a pair of linen trews that came to his knees.

In the growing light, Bjarki could see the gate in the palisade was only half-shut. There was a half-foot gap. *Careless*, he thought. *Good*. The enemy were unprepared. He felt a flare of savage joy in his belly. He had contemplated an old manoeuvre in which they would boost a man or possibly two as quietly as possible over the palisade; men who would, once inside and with the good will of Odin, be able to open the palisade gates to their waiting comrades. Failing that, he was prepared to cut through the gate himself, with the big Dane axe that was strapped to his back – which would be noisier, and would limit the time they had before the warriors of Ymirsfjord were alert. Neither of these risky plans would be necessary now.

The gate was open. The path inside was clear. Odin was truly smiling on them.

The half-naked viking walked obliviously down to the shore and waded straight into the water, wincing a little at its spring chill, but soon his dark head could be seen swimming out further into the empty fjord, leaving lines and ripples in the dark mirror of the water like an otter. Soon, he disappeared completely into the thick mist.

'Hurry!' Bjarki said again, a little louder this time, as he stumbled down the last few feet of the cliff face, staggering and stamping, loosing yet more stones. He pulled the Dane axe off his back, loosened the seax in its loin-sheath and slapped an old iron helm, which had been tied to his belt, onto his head. The *Felaki* were gathering around him. He could smell their excitement, the fear and sweat of his comrades. He said silently inside his own heart: *Are you there, Mochta? You awake, gandr? The hour of bloody battle is at hand*. He felt a distinct stirring in the darkness inside his chest, a hard kind of breathlessness.

'Kill all the men,' he said. 'Leave any women and children alive, if you can. Most importantly, find Edith and guard her with your lives. Is everyone ready?'

–

The sensation was deeply familiar, he felt the thudding as his heart increased its speed; he could almost see the blood running round his veins like lines of liquid fire. He suddenly felt as strong as a

56

mountain, faster than a hunting hawk. He enjoyed the scarlet, blooming expansion of all his senses as he ran, swiftly, so swiftly, with all the *Felaki* around him like a pack of hounds on the hunt, towards the half-open gate of the steading of Ymirsfjord.

He found he was now humming to himself, a simple four-note tune, repetitive, rhythmical, ancient, and he could hear his warriors keening their war songs with him.

'It has been too long, man-child,' said a deep voice inside of him, the voice of his *gandr*, the She-Bear spirit that had inhabited his heart since he became a Rekkr.

'It is time for the blood harvest, man-child! Kill for me! Kill them all for me!'

Theirs had not always been an easy relationship: the Bear *gandr* desired blood, indeed, she needed it to sustain her shadowy life and seemed not to care if the warrior to whom she granted her power perished in the spilling of her nourishing gore.

At one point in their acquaintance, Bjarki had believed that the Bear *gandr* would drive him completely insane, would turn him into a blood-drunk monster, who would kill and kill until someone stopped him. But things were different now. Bjarki and Mochta had forged an alliance based on mutual help, and perhaps even respect.

Yet he revelled in the sensation of power as the *berserkr* fury rose up in him like a pot of water boiling over on the campfire. He kicked the half-open gate wide with his boot, a tremendous blow that swung it back. He and his warriors charged inside.

There was no one in the courtyard, just a pair of chickens pecking placidly at the dust. Bjarki looked left and right, and saw no other living thing. He let out a roar of rage. Directly ahead of him was the longhouse, twenty paces in length, with lime-washed wattle-and-daub walls, tiled with wooden shingles. In the centre of the wall facing him was a wide door under a carved lintel in the shape of a ship, two dragon heads at prow and stern. The door opened and a man came out, shirtless and hairy, scratching at his groin. He saw the intruders, six warriors brandishing their weapons, and opened his mouth to yell a warning. As he shouted, he turned and projected his voice inside the hall. And, as he turned back to look at the fast-approaching enemy, a small hand axe, thrown by a skilled *Felaki* warrior, chunked into the very centre of his naked chest and knocked him sprawling back inside the dark hall.

Bjarki was almost on top of him by now, charging and howling and slavering like a mad beast, he leapt over the dying man, and plunged into the dim interior of the hall. Which, to his utter astonishment, was packed with dozens of sleeping men.

He had expected a mere handful of enemies. Perhaps twelve. The same number that had attacked the *gothi* in the grove and kidnapped Edith. But in this hall, in various states of consciousness and undress, were three times that number. Bjarki checked, but only for an instant. There was no going back.

'All the more meat-bags for us to feast upon,' crowed his *gandr*. 'Kill them!'

And Bjarki began his grim labour.

He swung his long axe and crushed the ribs of the nearest man, a big fellow who was just rising from the bench on which he had been sleeping. Bjarki pulled his glistening axe-blade free of the man's chest, and split the skull of another foeman, a fellow lying just behind the first.

The *Felaki* were now bundling into the hall behind him.

'Kill them all,' Bjarki roared. 'The more of the bastards we slaughter now, the fewer there will be alive to fight us!'

He charged forwards, swinging his axe in wide loops, shedding droplets of blood with each wild swing; he cut down one man by the legs, the axe blade crunching easily through thigh bone and living flesh; another man lost his head with a single swipe, a third fellow had his chest hacked wide open, and behind Bjarki the *Felaki*, seasoned warriors all, howled their cries and followed their Rekkr lord's example.

They slashed and hewed at the half-asleep pirates – who were rapidly coming to their senses – accounting for half a dozen before the first enemy raised so much as a dagger in his own defence. Then the easy part was over. This nest of desperate men erupted like a prodded hive. The enemy found their weapons, rose and fought like lions for their lives.

Bjarki strode down the centre of the hall, killing as he went, slicing and striking, his axe blade trickling red all down to his two fists. The enemy came at him, singly and in groups, and he soaked up their blows with his mail, killing them each in return.

Two of the *Felaki* had bows and arrows and warded his back as best they could, shooting down his assailants with a swift and deadly accuracy. But there were too many of the enemy – after this first frenzy of killing, there were still more men coming forwards from the depths of the hall to assail the five *Felaki* and their king.

One tall Ymirsfjord champion strode forwards towards the *berserkr*, and shouted his challenge, before striking at Bjarki's head with a sword. The Rekkr met the long blade with his own axe head, and stopped it with a clang, but another foe swung hard at Bjarki, missed and cracked his sword instead onto the sticky shaft of the axe, snapping it, and tumbling the head and haft to the reed-strewn floor. The champion gave a cry of joy, seeing Bjarki with empty hands and an astonished expression on his blood-spattered face. The viking hero drew back his sword for the killing blow…

Bjarki leapt at him, like some huge cat, his teeth snapping at the man's nose.

They fell to the floor, struggling madly, the sword spilling from the champion's hands. Bjarki got a thick fold of face-skin between his biting teeth, jerked his head back, ripping, and the big man screamed like a woman in childbirth.

Bjarki got a hand on his Harva seax hilt, pulled the blade and buried it in the big viking's belly. Once, twice, a third for luck, he stabbed him. The steel sinking in deep. An instant later, Bjarki was on his feet once more, snarling, growling, slicing with the Harva, his mail-clad body slathered in gore, lips covered with creamy spittle.

Bjarki's end of the long hall was now depleted of enemies.

In the centre, Kynwulf had the *Felaki* gathered in a tight knot, fending off a ring of attackers, with sword and dagger, bow and arrows. Bjarki reached out a long arm and snatched up a last shrinking viking at his end, dragging him close and skewering him on his seax. He let the stricken, weeping man drop like a sack of wet sand, turned and looked up the hall at the ring of foes furiously hammering at the *Felaki*.

His friends. His people. He tilted his head towards the rafters and let out a hideous, scalding scream of rage.

Then Bjarki, armed only with a bloody seax, charged straight into the writhing scrum of a dozen enemies around the beleaguered *Felaki*, and began their execution.

He ripped and stabbed, cut and sliced, his bloody teeth snapping at anything they could reach. He severed limbs and punctured soft bellies; he carved a red ruin on their frail bodies, gibbering and giggling, scarlet matter flying everywhere in horrible, solid gobbets as his seax flew and cut and sliced. The *Felaki* surged out of their tight defensive ring, invigorated by the madness of their gore-drenched king. Bringing all their exceptional war skills to the shrinking, slumping, dying men of Ymirsfjord.

The terrified vikings had soon had enough. They were running, sprinting to the hall door, and out of it. The barley straw on the floor was now sodden red and carpeted with dead and dying men. The *Felaki*, panting and bloodied, looked about themselves in wonder. Bodvar was down, eyes staring, quite still. Haugen had two fingers missing, and Rask was tying his left hand-wound tight with a strip of grubby linen. The others had lesser hurts. Bjarki had a bloody gouge down his left forearm. He could feel the red mist of battle slowly clearing from his eyes.

He said: 'No prisoners. Send all these wretches onwards – do it swiftly!' Bjarki waved a hand at the piles of wounded enemies scattered across the floor of the hall.

He turned to Kynwulf, and merely nodded slowly, approvingly, at the old man.

'You're with me, War Chief; ward me while we seek out Edith – if she lives.'

Chapter Six

The king is dead! Long live the king!

Tor could not understand Inge's eagerness to return to Uppsala after leaving the royal compound only ten days before. Surely the girl must realise that the *Disablot* market with its myriad delights would all be long gone by the time they arrived?

Perhaps Inge was bored living in Bearstead. Tor considered this. It was possible. Inge had returned to the remote northern part of Svealand after their bloody adventures the year before in eastern Europe, leaving her grandfather, her only living relative, a Slav nobleman known as the Duke of the Polans, and saying she wished to see some more of the world. But during the past nine months she had seen little outside of Bearstead and the surrounding forests, except for a few trips to the monthly market at Gavle. The *Disablot* had been exciting for her. Not just the drama of the religious ceremonies – although she had confessed to Tor that she'd hidden her face in her hands when it came to the *blot* sacrifices – but the gathering of thousands of Svear from all over Harald Fox-Beard's kingdom to mark the turn of the year, to meet old friends and catch a glimpse of the king and his jarls in all their finery.

Inge had bought trinkets at the great market, sampled wares from a dozen steadings, and watched the ferocious combat competitions with a special interest; she had particularly enjoyed the one-to-one fighting with blunted swords. And, Tor noted, that she had cheered the overall victor of these mock-duels, a sandy-haired, sullen-looking warrior from south Svealand called Joralf, with an almost hectic enthusiasm.

The mock-fights were over; the king was dead and Uppsala would be a far more dreary place with all the lively country people gone back to their homes. Tor hoped the girl, who had insisted on accompanying her, would not be too badly disappointed.

They were approaching the northern gate of the royal compound at Uppsala along the rutted main road that came south for seventy miles all the way down from Gavle. Tor and Inge were both mounted, but Sambor was striding along beside Inge's dun pony on his own two feet, as silent and glowering as a cave troll. The temple in the centre of the royal compound was just coming into view directly ahead of them, about half a mile away. With its triple deck of wood-shingled roofs, which were guarded by six fierce dragon heads jutting from the gable ends, and its ornately carved oak pillars along the outside of the blood-red painted walls to support its extraordinary height, it did indeed look like a palace imposing enough for the gods.

Away to the right, in the western part of the compound, illuminated by shafts of late afternoon sunshine piercing the clouds, the humps of three Royal Mounds rose up in a slanting line, like a pod of grassy whales swimming in an earth-locked sea.

On the eastern side of the compound, beyond the great temple, was the king's hall, where, presumably, poor Harald was now lying on his royal bier, being tended to by his women. The funeral would be tonight – at moonrise on the Thing-Mound, the exhausted messenger had said.

'So who do you think will be the new King of the Svear?' asked Inge.

They were now about two hundred paces from the north gate, and Tor could see a pair of alert sentries already eyeing them warily.

'That will be for the king's council to decide,' said Tor. 'A gathering of twenty of the most powerful jarls, thanes and *hersirs* in all Svealand will discuss the matter tomorrow after Harald's body has been sent on its fiery way to the Hall of the Slain.'

'Surely it will be Sigurd Hring; he has the most warriors – the best ones, too.'

Tor thought about the many famous champions that Sigurd Hring had been gathering to his banner from far and wide. Even up in Bearstead, they had heard some of the names: Egil Skull-Cleaver and Krok of Frisia, whom Tor had seen make their oaths on the last day of the *Disablot*. These two men were renowned across the North as warriors of extraordinary strength and skill. But Sigurd Hring had summoned other famous fighters, too. There was Connor the Black, a mad pirate from Hibernia, who was rumoured to have made a death pact with one of his Irish gods; there was Hagnor the Fatbellied, a huge Danish outlaw, who was as famous for his ferocity in battle as for his enthusiasm for feasting and ale-drinking; Erland the Snake, from the island of Bornholm, was said to be the greatest swordsman in all the Middle-Realm. Also Gummi and Gudfast, two brothers from Estonia, who always fought in battle side by side. All these heroes and more had answered Sigurd Hring's call to arms.

The Jarl of Sodermanland had been planning for this for some time, that was quite clear to Tor. What could he have said to these heroes to induce them to flock to him? Only that he would surely be crowned the next King of the Svear, and he would then be able to reward them richly. But there was something else at work here, too, Tor felt, some element that she was missing.

'The king's council may well name Sigurd Hring as their choice,' she said, 'but his title can only be confirmed by his overlord – Siegfried, King of the Danes.'

'What have the distant Danes to do with folk in Svealand?' asked Inge.

'As I understand it, the royal line of Svealand is an offshoot of the royal Danish line. I am foggy on this, I admit. You must ask Valtyr Far-Traveller this sort of thing. But he once told me that, in name at least, the King of the Svear owed allegiance to the King of the Dane-Mark, and must do homage to him for his kingdom. In our grandfather's grandfather's time, according to Valtyr, a Danish sea-lord called Hakki conquered the warring Svear tribes and set himself up as their king, here in Uppsala.

'He was supported in his fight to unify Svealand by King Solve of the Dane-Mark, his uncle, who agreed to lend him warships and fighting men in return for homage and the recognition that he, Solve, was Hakki's overlord, and overlord of all Hakki's descendants and heirs in Uppsala for ever, or until the breaking of the world.

'King Solve claimed the old title of the King of the North – the supreme ruler of all the northern lands from Frisia to the Finnmark – because of his family's direct descent from Odin Spear-Shaker. Even some of the northern Saxon tribes used to pay tribute to the King of the North, in the old days, or so Valtyr Far-Traveller claims.'

'Who's King of the North now?' asked Inge. 'Is it Siegfried of the Danes?'

'No ruler has called himself that for generations. But, by tradition, the King of the Svear must go to the Danish king's court and kiss his sword before he is installed as king in his own country. You'll see. If Sigurd Hring is acclaimed king by the council, he'll go to Viby, or wherever King Siegfried is, and kneel down before him.'

They were at the north gate now, and one of the two sentries, an unkempt young spearman, took a few steps into the middle of the open gate and blocked their way.

Tor spurred forwards the last few yards.

'I am Torfinna Hildarsdottir, *Stallar* to Jarl Starki, lord of Norrland. I demand immediate entrance to the…'

'I was told to look out for you,' said the guard. 'You are Tor the Shield-Maiden. Sigurd Hring summons you to the king's hall, where he stands vigil over his cousin, Harald Fox-Beard. You're late, woman. I was told to expect you early this morning.'

Tor bared her teeth. 'I'm here at the summons of my own jarl – Starki, lord of Norrland. I own no allegiance to Sigurd Hring, nor will I come scampering like a hound whenever he whistles. Now, stand aside, before I lose my temper with you.'

'We will, all of us, be bowing down before Sigurd Hring in a day or two,' said the spearman sulkily. 'You would be wise not to anger the powerful lord of Sodermanland either before or after he ascends to the throne of the Svear. But it makes not a jot of difference now. Go to him. You will find you lord Starki by Sigurd Hring's side in the king's hall, both standing vigil beside the late king's body.'

If, by standing vigil, the insolent gate-guard had meant that Sigurd Hring was lounging at a long table with a horn of mead and a plate of ham and cheese, and playing a raucous game of *tafl* with Hagnor the Fatbellied, then he had been accurate. As Tor pushed her way under the leather door covering and entered the smoky hall, she saw the king in a crimson robe, a gold coronet on his snowy brows, lying on a raised platform at the end of the hall, on the dais where the high table usually stood. Sigurd Hring was sitting with a few of his men, throwing dice on the board across from a grossly fat warrior, who was laughing uproariously at something the jarl had just said. Jarl Starki, her own lord, was sitting with Gudrik and a handful of his *hird*-men at the far end of the hall, drinking ale. There were other high dignitaries, jarls and thanes, and here and there a famous hero that she thought she recognised. Servants scurried to and fro bearing heavy trays containing food and drink. Tor did not hesitate, she went straight over to Jarl Starki and made her usual bow.

'My lord, you called for me,' she said when Starki acknowledged her presence.

'Good, Torfinna, I'm glad you are finally here.' Her jarl looked tired, nervous.

'How may I serve you, lord?' said Tor.

'Sit and have a cup of ale, Tor. Then you can offer me your counsel.'

Tor did as she was bid. She took a sip and caught Gudrik's eye, the banner bearer was standing behind Starki, out of his sightline. Gudrik shrugged at her as if to say that he too was in the dark about the reason for the summoning. Yes, the king was dead. But she was not needed to help choose the next one. She was no powerful jarl, not even a *hersir*.

'I know, my dear Tor, that your temper is as fiery as your hair,' Jarl Starki began, keeping his voice low, and casting one telling glance across the hall at Sigurd Hring, who was just hurling his dice across the *tafl* board, to raucous encouragement. 'But this night I need you cool as a mountain stream. Can you do that for me, Tor?'

'Tell me what is in your mind, lord.'

'Naturally, it is the succession. The question of who is to be the next King of the Svear. Now, look around this hall – there by the water butt is Jarl Ottar of Vastmanland.' Tor looked over at a middle-aged man, a little overweight, a little plump, you might even say, but not soft-looking. A golden chain hung around his bull neck. His sword belt was made of pieces of expensive blue enamel, inset with garnets and sapphires. He wore a plush hat made of pine-marten fur on his overlarge head.

'And those two men sitting next to him are the jarls of Ostfold and Varmland.'

Tor noted two slightly nervous-looking younger noblemen sitting with Jarl Ottar.

'Camped outside this hall around this royal compound, or else housed in the king's various guest halls, are the thanes of Bergslagen, Vendel, Dalsland, Birka and Tivden, and more than a dozen important *hersirs*. And tomorrow they will all meet in here to decide who shall be the new king. It will be almost certainly one of the great men who is even now in the king's hall tonight.'

'And?' said Tor.

'The king must be of royal blood. A descendant of Odin All-Father of the Yngling line of ancient kings. And the most likely man to wear the Svear crown next, almost everyone agrees, is Sigurd Hring, Jarl of Sodermanland. Him, that noisy fellow, over there!' Starki jerked his chin towards the group round the *tafl* board.

'You are not telling me anything, lord, that I do not already know.'

'Ottar of Vastmanland is the son of Harald Fox-Beard's brother. He is very rich and has six hundred spearmen at his command and a better blood-claim to the throne than the lord of Sodermanland. Sigurd Hring has fewer than seven hundred warriors, including his new-bought heroes and their men, and only thirty warships.'

Jarl Starki leaned right in to her, so close Tor could smell the ale on his breath.

'Ottar and Sigurd are neighbours, their lands border each other, and they are bitter rivals – the enmity between them has lasted for more than twenty years. Three days ago, in secret, Jarl Ottar asked me to support his claim to the throne. And I am tempted. Between us, Ottar and I have more strength than Sigurd Hring. If we can persuade some of the lesser jarls and thanes to join us, we can muster a host far greater Sigurd Hring's. He would then have to accept Ottar as king and return to his hall in Sodermanland, his tail between his legs.'

'What has Jarl Ottar promised you?'

'The Thane of Bergslagen has already made his oath of allegiance to Sigurd. If Ottar were to be king, he would oust the thane and give me Bergslagen to add to my own lands in the north. Also he has promised that I will be his *Armathr*, his battle commander, whose word is as an order from the king himself. He also says he will betroth me to his only daughter, to be married in the fullness of time. Linhildr is her name. She is six winters old.'

'And what did you say to Jarl Ottar, lord?'

'I said I would tell him my decision before the council meets tomorrow.'

Tor sat back on her stool, and took a pull on her ale. She casually looked over at Ottar, who was now hectoring the two less powerful jarls of Varmland and Ostfold, wagging a finger at them, no doubt trying to persuade them to his cause. Then she looked at the table where Sigurd Hring and a dozen of his heroes were drinking and laughing merrily together. One of them, a tall, slim fellow – Erland the Snake, she thought – was dancing about trying to balance a full horn of ale on his nose. The horn tipped, the ale spilled, drenching him, and all the men at the table roared with mirth. At the far end of the hall, the king lay still in his cold splendour, ignored by almost everyone. Two serving women sat beside his body. One had clearly been crying.

'Tor? Look at me. What do you think? What is your counsel?'

Tor turned back and looked into Starki's eyes. 'I think Sigurd Hring is not a man who would go meekly back to Sodermanland with his tail between his legs. He yearns to be king. And his new men, these so-called heroes, all desire it too. They won't disperse. They came here for honours and riches; they will not all go on their way empty-handed.'

'He is an arrogant old cockerel – you know this as well as I do. Maybe he needs to have his comb trimmed by Ottar and me, and whomsoever we can find to help us.'

'I have no love for Sigurd Hring. But if you declare your support for Jarl Ottar tonight, there will surely be war in Svealand. Ottar and Sigurd are nearly matched and it will be a long and bloody fight for the throne. Hundreds will die. The whole Svear nation will be weakened. I do not fear war, but are you willing to risk all to be a king's lackey? Would you plunge our folk into a cauldron of blood to marry a child?'

'You think I must support Sigurd Hring? That overbearing prick?' asked Starki.

'If you declare for Sigurd Hring, Ottar will have no choice but to back down. Without you, he does not have the strength to stand alone. There will be no war.'

Starki put a hand on Tor's shoulder. 'Thank you, *Stallar*, for your wisdom. You are the best and most loyal of my followers. I must think on this matter some more.'

–

The Thing-Mound was surrounded by a ring of burning pine-torches, and at its flat summit the king lay on a platform of planks and branches well doused in whale oil.

Around the mound all the people of Uppsala were gathered, hundreds of them. The jarls stood in their finest cloaks, held closed with jewelled pins, golden torcs at their throats, bright gold rings on their bare muscular arms, silver-hilted swords at their waists. The *hersirs* in polished helms leaned on their long spears, sporting freshly painted lime-wood shields. The score or so of *gothi* were in their usual filthy robes, faces garishly painted, singing the old hymns, calling on the gods, and scattering red droplets hewn from the magnificent white stallion that had been sacrificed a few moments earlier in Harald Fox-Beard's name, a mount to bear him in a kingly fashion in the otherworld.

On the pyre, around Harald's corpse, had been placed his finest sword and seax, a magnificent shield beautifully decorated with his sigil of the fox, and a bow and a sheaf of arrows and various pots of mead and ale, fruits, cheese, fresh and dried meat and loaves of bread. His favourite boar hound, its throat slit, lay limply at his feet.

The *Mikelgothi*, a wizened old goat with a white-painted face and purple knotted locks, climbed slowly up the mound, leaning on his magical iron staff to make the ascent. At the summit, twenty feet above the crowd, he paused, panting slightly to stand beside the bier and the body of the king. A droning prayer filled their air like a swarm of bees. Then the *gothi* gave a cry and held up both shaking hands in the air.

At his word, four younger *gothi* moved forwards, scrambling the slope of the Thing-Mound with lit torches, which they thrust into the four corners of the king's pyre. The oil-soaked wood caught almost immediately and red flames became to lick up the side of the platform. The old *Mikelgothi* began uttering a series of prayers, calling all the gods to witness this passing of the king from the world of men, and urging them to welcome him to the otherworld, and for Odin to make ready for him a place of honour on the benches in his eternal feasting hall. The flames and smoke billowed around the old man, casting weird shapes around his already bizarre form.

Tor, standing with Gudrik and some of the men of Jarl Starki's *hird*, could barely hear the priest's words above the roar and crackle of the fire. Eventually, the old man fell silent and, with the pyre in full bloom, he began to walk gingerly down the slippery slope, every step carefully measured. As she watched him, Tor wondered again where her own jarl was. He had left her to watch the king-burning a while ago and, taking only one attendant, had wandered into the crowds around the mound.

She looked left and right, perfectly unconcerned for his safety – it would have been the grossest sacrilege to offer violence, even to a mortal enemy, at the funeral of a king – but curious as to what he was doing. The flames on the summit of the mound were now almost obscuring the whole platform. She thought she saw the king's body move, and her heart thumped hard, and then she realised that it was only the cold dead flesh's reaction to the fiery kiss of the flames. Looking left she saw some kind of commotion in the crowd, a stirring, and a broad man in a scarlet cloak coming towards her, with another more slender one following in his wake.

It was Sigurd Hring, and he seemed to be heading straight towards her.

The Jarl of Sodermanland stopped in front of her and looked her up and down in a most insulting manner, as if she were a side of bacon hanging at a butcher's stall.

'You are Jarl Starki's *Stallar*,' he said. 'The insolent woman who reported the grove affair to me at the *Disablot*,' he said. Then he surprised her by saying: 'You must be a very competent warrior indeed to have been chosen for that high honour.'

Tor could think of nothing to say. She was looking past Sigurd Hring at his companion. It was Rorik Hafnarsson – the man she fully intended to slaughter.

Rorik offered her a small, queasy smile. He looked terrified.

'They say you are sister to Bjarki Bloodhand,' Sigurd Hring continued. 'A Rekkr, I'm told, a real one, a Fire Born – not some mushroom-chewing mountebank.'

Tor said nothing.

'Answer me, woman!'

Tor wrenched her eyes off Rorik, and stared directly at Sigurd Hring. 'Did you come here to waste my time, jarl, or ask a question? Because I have yet to hear one.'

The jarl snorted with annoyance. 'They said you were a feisty one. Very well, she-*Stallar*, is Bjarki Bloodhand your brother? And is he indeed a genuine Rekkr?'

'Yes and yes,' said Tor, pretending to stifle a yawn. 'Was there anything else?'

'Tell your brother from me that if he is looking for a place of high honour in a king's court, among the greatest warriors in the Middle-Realm, he should make himself known to me. If he kneels before me, he shall be richly rewarded. Tell him.'

And with that, Sigurd Hring turned his back and stalked away. Rorik, however, twitchily stood his ground. Tor stared at him coldly, waiting.

'I need to say something to you, Tor. Since we are now likely to be thrown into each other's company.'

Tor said nothing. Her green eyes were as cold as the sea in winter. She was in truth struggling with the urge to draw her seax and gut this silly *nithing* right now like a landed trout. But the strict laws of behaviour at a funeral forbade her from doing violence. Even to this worm. And she knew Jarl Starki would be very, very angry with her. She would do it another time. No hurry. Quietly, privately... properly.

'We have had our differences, I know,' Rorik was still talking, but Tor's eye was distracted by a man climbing up the slope on which the king's pyre was merrily burning. It was Jarl Starki, standing tall, resplendent in his best silver-trimmed cloak.

'But I am prepared to forgive you for the death of my father, and I hope you will forget any quarrel that you believe you have with me. Our two lords will be in each other's company a good deal from this day on, and since I am to have the position of Royal Huntsman, assuming Sigurd Hring becomes king, I think it behooves us...'

'Be silent, coward,' said Tor, turning away. Halfway up the slope Jarl Starki was raising his hands for quiet. The crowd had noticed and was flowing towards him.

The Jarl of Norrland began to speak: 'Friends, comrades, honest Svear folk – as we gather here in sorrow this night to mark

72

the passing from the Middle-Realm of our beloved king, Harald Fox-Beard, I hope you will allow me to interrupt your grieving for just a few short moments to make a small announcement of my own.'

There were a lot of hushing noises from the assembly of Svear before the slope.

'I wish to tell you all this, good people. This very hour, I have knelt before Sigurd Hring, kissed his sword and sworn an oath of allegiance to him as my lord. I must also tell you that I shall also be recommending, at the king's council tomorrow, that Sigurd Hring be named King of the Svear. Hail Sigurd... hail our new king!'

'You see?' said Rorik. 'Your lord will serve mine as his *Armathr* and so, naturally, Tor, you and I shall see much of each other. Can we not bury our quarrel?'

'Bury our quarrel?' said Tor. 'No, I don't think so, *nithing*. I mean to bury *you*.'

Chapter Seven

Hero of the hour

Bjarki wiped his bloody seax clean on a dead man's tunic, sheathed it, and picked up a discarded Dane axe, a weapon that had once belonged to one of the Ymirsfjord vikings. He examined the curved iron blade at the end of the shaft closely, grunted his approval, then strode out of the longhouse, axe in hand, with Kynwulf at his heels.

The courtyard outside the hall was empty, and the gate still wide open. Bjarki knew that some of the men in the hall had fled the fight and with half his mind he wondered if they might be hiding in the vicinity ready to leap out and take revenge.

He could feel the familiar effects of the Fire Born rage subsiding in his blood – he felt cold, sick and embarrassingly tearful, as he always did after the Bear *gandr* had taken possession of his body. But the feeling was not as bad as it had sometimes been in the dozen or so times he had been possessed by the *berserkr* frenzy. And he had no regrets about the men he had slaughtered. They lived by the sword, and died by it. And while he had led Bodvar to his death, the *Felaki* warrior had died fighting bravely, sword in hand. There were worse ends.

He offered up a quick prayer to Odin, asking the god to claim the man as his own. 'I shall see you again, Bodvar, my friend – we shall feast together in Valhalla,' he said aloud.

'That was a fine slaughter, man-child,' said a soft ursine voice deep inside his heart. 'A worthy blood-shedding. I am now replete from the feast and I shall sleep for a long time.'

74

Bjarki and Kynwulf searched the big barn first and found nothing but a huge pile of damp hay and a mound of mouldering ropes. The animal feed shed was empty, except for a few scattered rye grains, mixed in with rat droppings. They looked into the forge, which was cold, the fire long unlit, with abandoned iron-working tools and half-finished farm implements scattered about. The various-sized hammers were thrown in a jumble in the corner, which irritated Bjarki more than it should. The people who had lived here did not cherish their tools, which meant they were careless folk. But he already knew that from the left-open gate. He unsheathed his seax and dipped it in the plunge trough, then cleaned it more carefully than before, scrubbing with a piece of rag, wiping all gore out of the grooves and patterns in the blade. His action a reproach to all forms of disorder. He dried the seax carefully and sheathed it.

Then he heard a scream. A woman's voice crying out in pain.

He and Kynwulf sprinted towards the sound, which was coming from a small log-built building near the main gate. Bjarki hit the door with his massive shoulder and it burst open immediately, causing him to tumble inside, totally off balance. He saw in an instant that the cabin was a temple to Odin. A crude carving of a huge one-eyed, bearded man stared at him from the far wall. In the centre of the room was a thick wooden pillar, crusted black with the dried blood of a hundred sacrifices. There was an upright wooden cage of sorts in the far corner, three paces from the door, with thick vertical wooden bars, a place to hold a sacrificial victim until his time of doom.

Inside the cage was a woman.

It was Edith, in a filthy white dress. A patch of bright red stained its side. She saw him, recognised him, and shouted: 'Bjarki, beware – look out!' and gestured to the side of the shed, a dark corner, where a large man was emerging in war helm and mail, a spear in his hand, the shaft above his shoulder, drawn back, ready to cast.

The man hurled the spear at Bjarki from five paces away, the sharp iron point driven by the heavy ash shaft powering towards him faster than the eye could see.

Bjarki, exhausted from the hall fight, drained of power after the departure of his *gandr*, found he could not move. He was frozen. Yet the spear flickered towards him.

And a blur to his left. Kynwulf, leaping forwards with the shield in his left hand pushed out in front of him. Just in time. The spear thumped into the extended shield, ripping it from Kynwulf's grasp, the spear-blade embedded deep in the lime-wood, and the transfixed shield smashing painfully into Bjarki's mailed left shoulder.

Bjarki gave a roar of anger, hurled the shield and its attached spear away from his body, took two steps forwards and swung hard with the Dane axe. The axe blade caught the man just above the left shoulder, clipping his mail and sliding onwards into the side of his head. The heavy, fast-moving axe blade crunched through the helmet's side piece, through skin and bone, and sank into the man's brain. He dropped like a wet sail when the boom halyards are cut. Dead before he even hit the ground.

Edith breathed out, long and loudly. 'Bjarki!' she said. 'I knew you'd come!'

—

They buried Bodvar, and dragged all the other corpses out of the hall, out of the fortified compound, all the way beyond the scrubby, ill-tended fields behind the settlement to feed the foxes and ravens. They found no more vikings hiding in the settlement seeking revenge. Some had fled, but the others were now all lying in a jumbled, reeking pile further up the fjord valley.

The spearman in hiding, Edith said, the one Bjarki had killed, had pinked her with his spear-tip only moments earlier to make her call out in pain and so draw his foes into the Odin temple, where he meant to lie in ambush and take at least one with him when he fell. He said their deaths and his would be a sacrifice to the All-Father.

He would have been successful, had it not been for Kynwulf's shield skill.

Bjarki thanked Kynwulf for saving his life. Then he dispatched Rask – a small, stocky man with a cheerful disposition, and the best sailor and woodsman among the *Felaki* – to return up the cliffs and across the land the way they had come, all the way back to the shingle inlet. Rask was ordered to gather up Oddvin and Abbio, launch their smack, and meet the rest of the company out at sea, by the weird stone stack known as the Old Man, at noon the next day.

With a morning fog rising all around the courtyard they tended to their wounds, drank and ate a little, and then the *Felaki* began searching the place for anything of value.

Bjarki found Edith on the beach, the dress torn open at the side, tending to the shallow spear cut on her ribs with a bloody rag and a pot of herbs and goose fat. She flinched when she saw the warrior coming and hurriedly pulled the filthy garment together to cover her modesty.

'I found these in a chest in the hall,' Bjarki said. 'They seem reasonably clean.'

Bjarki passed her a fine quality blue woman's gown, and a warm blue cloak.

Edith choked back a sob.

Bjarki, embarrassed, studied his blood-spattered boots.

'We will stay here the night, rest, and depart in the morning,' he said. 'On that.' He pointed at the beached ship, the *karve* that had brought Edith here from Uppsala.

'I'll just go see if she's seaworthy,' he mumbled. 'You try on your clothes.'

As Bjarki was about to walk away, he was astonished to find Edith's arm tight around his neck and her dark-golden head pressed into his chest. She was weeping, sobbing, her body convulsing with every breath. He held her clumsily, his heavy right arm curled around her narrow back, his bandaged left uncomfortably pinned to his side by her tight embrace. And waited for the storm of tears to subside.

Eventually, she pushed away from him, and wiped her nose with the back of her hand. 'You are a good man, Bjarki Blood-hand,' she said, her teary, blotched face smiling up at him. 'Don't ever let anyone tell you otherwise. Now go away and look at your ship while I make myself decent.'

Bjarki crunched over the shingle beach to the vessel, which was canted over on its steerboard side. Someone had given the hull a fresh coat of pine tar recently, but there was still a little worm damage visible beneath the sticky black surface. Only a little. He was relieved to see that the craft looked sound. It was seaworthy, at least.

While he poked and peered at the hull of the ship, his mind was also filled with the scalding memory of the sensation of Edith's body pressed up hard against his. The embrace had been brief and clumsy. But he could feel it still, burning into his bones.

He had harboured a certain tenderness for Edith in his time in Saxony, and had even dreamed then of perhaps one day making her his lover, or even his wife. He had believed that sentimental dream was long gone – nothing had ever happened between them physically – yet her embrace on the beach had brought those feelings to the forefront of his mind once more. Now he found he could think of nothing else. Even the viking ship could not hold his attention. He yearned for Edith. He wanted to rush and scoop her in his arms. To kiss her, to take her down to a cloak on the beach...

With a great deal of effort he wrenched his mind back to the task at hand. He knocked at a worm-eaten side-plank in the ship's hull with his knuckles. This was no time for love. This was a time for making travelling plans. The ship was sound, and he believed it would bear them safely to the Dane-Mark, where Edith could be happily reunited with her brother Widukind. The Saxon duke, he had recently heard, was in almost permanent residence at the royal court of Siegfried in Viby.

He tested a strake with a hard poke of his finger, and grunted in satisfaction. Then he reached up and, favouring his right, unwounded arm, he heaved, rocked and pulled the craft over back right-side up on its hull. There was space for a dozen rowers inside and that would be ample for them. There was no sign of the mast, the sail and the rowing oars, but he assumed they could be found back in the steading somewhere. They would need to stow some food and fresh water, too... Suddenly a wave of black tiredness hit him and he felt his vision blur and knees sag. It was just the effects of the *gandr* possession, he knew, but for a moment he felt weak as a kitten.

He plodded back up the beach to where Edith was now waiting for him. She was transformed by the new clothes, and had washed her face in the sea and neatened and tied back her long, beautiful dark-gold hair. Despite her ordeal, she looked radiant.

And she was smiling at him.

'I never said thank you,' she said. 'So, thank you, Bjarki. I owe my life to you.'

'I don't think they meant to kill you. I believe their intent was always ransom. Silver. Did they hurt you much? Apart from that spear jab in the temple, I mean.'

Edith did not answer the last part of the question. 'Many a ransom victim is killed after the coin is paid. It's more convenient – safer, too, from the abductor's point of view. It would be a mistake to have faith in the promise of a viking outlaw.'

Bjarki did not know what to say to that.

'We killed most of them,' he said eventually. 'A few got away. No one seems to know which one of them was Hjorleif Illu...' He stopped abruptly, embarrassed.

'Hjorleif was the man with the spear in the temple, the one whose skull you smashed in with your axe. So we need not think about that evil bastard ever again.'

'That's good,' said Bjarki, nodding sagely. 'Well, I had better get back to...'

'I know that you want to ask me, so just ask me. I owe you that at least.'

79

'What?'

'You want to know if Hjorleif Illugi raped me, but you are too kind to ask. Men don't like to face up to these things. But ask it and I will answer you truthfully!'

Bjarki looked into her lovely, heather-purple eyes. 'Did he?' he said softly.

'He taunted me, when I was in that cage. He pulled out his member and showed it to me. He played with himself in front of me. I think he thought I'd be aroused.'

Bjarki looked away. The fjord was now filled with a thick mist. He could barely see the water.

'He did not touch me,' said Edith. 'The only prick I received from Hjorleif, after being knocked about in the Grove of Skelfir, was the little spear cut he made in the temple to attract your attention. I did *not* lie with him, willingly – or otherwise.'

'You are safe now,' mumbled Bjarki. 'That's the most important thing.'

'No, it's not. Listen, Bjarki,' she said. 'You must ask another question. Why?'

'Why?'

'That evil bastard's by-name was "Illugi" – he was renowned for raping women and girls across the North. Why, then, would he not try to rape a helpless captive of his spear? I've seen five and twenty winters but I am not yet ugly. There is a reason he did not touch me. He had *orders* not to harm me. Orders from someone he feared. For only considerable fear would stop that dog from taking his disgusting pleasures.'

'How do you know this?'

'He told me. While he was parading around ridiculously with his trews round his ankles. He said: "I may not fuck you. My instructions are clear. But there is no reason you should not enjoy the pleasure of my body through the bars of your cage."'

The image of this scene in Bjarki's mind was making him feel a little queasy.

'So somebody very powerful ordered you to be abducted,' he said eventually.

'Yes,' she replied. 'And when I discover who that person is, I shall take my revenge on him in full measure, you may be certain of that.'

'Not if I discover him first,' said Bjarki. He grinned at her then – a tiny joke.

She smiled back, put her hand on his bearded cheek, and set his heart on fire.

–

They met up with Rask, Oddvin and Abbio by the strange sea formation called the Old Man, just before noon the next day. Bjarki was pleased with how his new vessel handled – they had named her the *Sea Elk* because she had a steady, almost stately quality, like one of those huge mountain deer. But he was even more pleased that they had discovered three chests of the vikings' stolen hacksilver before they left Ymirsfjord – some of which he had distributed to his joyful *Felaki* as the spoils of war – as well as several sacks of precious items, gold rings, silver buckles, a few gold and silver torcs, too, and assorted shiny trinkets which he claimed as the king's share. They had also stripped Ymirsfjord of all its food and several casks of mead.

The voyage back into the Kattegat was quick and uneventful, and Bjarki had the pleasure of Edith's company for the whole two days, since he insisted she travel in the *Sea Elk* with him, Harknut and Haugen Halfhand – as the *Felaki* was now called.

Abbio had protested at being in the smaller ship – with Kynwulf, Oddvin and Rask – but was mollified when Bjarki handed him a generous share of the loot.

Three days later, late in the golden afternoon, the two vessels sailed in consort, *Sea Elk* leading the way, into the crescent-shaped harbour at Viby, on the north-eastern coast of the long Jutland peninsula. Bjarki shaded his eyes under a hand and looked up at the king's great hall, which was stood high on a promontory overlooking the harbour from the south. Somewhere up there was King Siegfried, lord of the Dane-Mark, the most powerful man in the North. With him would be Widukind, Duke of Saxony, whose sister he had just rescued from dire peril. He would return Edith to her brother, but Bjarki also began to ponder what reward he might receive for his labours.

The two ships curled round the headland with the huge island of Sjaelland just visible, a low dark mass off away to their left, and a brisk easterly breeze wafted them swiftly into the wide bay of Viby. Only an hour later, they were stamping their boots on the slimy wooden jetty, getting a feel of the land again, and securing their two craft under the critical eye of the royal harbourmaster. While the five *Felaki* were making everything aboard secure, and Bjarki was arguing with the harbourmaster over the outrageous fees he was demanding, Abbio the Crow set off immediately for the great hall up on the southern promontory, shouting something over his shoulder to Bjarki about readying the welcome for this band of heroes, who had achieved such great things. 'The duke must know as sssoon as posssible that hisss sssister isss sssafe!'

Bjarki let him go. And reluctantly paid the outrageous mooring fee from his chest of captured hacksilver, but only after persuading the harbourmaster to provide Edith and himself with a basin of hot fresh water, some soap and a clean towel, and to allow them to wash their faces and brush off their salt-crusted clothes before their meeting with the king. Tor had commented often on his scruffiness and lack of good hygiene, and he did not want to disgrace himself in Siegfried's court in front of Edith.

Kynwulf and the *Felaki* found themselves cheap lodgings in a harbourfront inn, right next to the harbourmaster's very grand house, and by the time Edith and Bjarki, washed, brushed and more or less presentable, were finally setting off on foot up the narrow, curling road that led to the royal compound on the summit of the southern headland, most of the Companions were already drunk.

Let them each drink their fill, Bjarki thought. *They have more than earned it.*

He was also feeling oddly contented to be back in his home-land after such a long time. He had been raised on a fly-speck of an island called Bago, in the Danish archipelago, not fifty miles to the south of Viby, and every time he heard the Dane-Mark accent spoken by the people he passed – a softer speech than the harsh dialect he heard daily in Svealand – he enjoyed a little rush of pleasure at the familiar sound.

'The king will wish to reward you, Bjarki,' said Edith as they walked up the road to the hall, 'as will my brother Widukind. Have you given any thought to what you might like to receive from their hands? I suspect they would deny you nothing.'

Bjarki had, in fact, already decided what he wanted for his reward. He wanted Edith. He wanted to marry her and live with her the rest of his years. Yet he could not speak of it. Not to her. He loved her. But he did not know how she felt about him. He would not force an unwilling woman into his bed – as a reward. As if she were a pot of gold, or a prize sheep won in some fairground competition. He was no Hjorleif.

'I'll think about any rewards when – or if – they are offered,' Bjarki lied. 'But not before. It's bad luck. Gods don't like it when you assume you'll gain something.'

When they reached the gates of the royal precinct, they were swiftly admitted, and ushered across the courtyard to the great hall. The double doors were flung wide and Edith, her long white neck held high, entered the king's residence, with Bjarki walking beside her, smiling modestly. Up on the dais at the far end of the hall, raised a few feet above the common hall space, sat King Siegfried, whom Bjarki had met several times before, and beside him was Widukind of Westphalia, Duke of Saxony, Edith's brother. Also seated up there beside the king and duke was Abbio the Crow.

The filthy *gothi* was seated in a place of honour at the right hand of the king. He was drinking wine from a silver-chased horn, and the king himself was pouring out another measure for him with his own hands. Edith was spirited forwards by a pair of burly Saxon guards, and, after a warm brotherly hug, she too was seated at the long table on the dais next to Widukind. But when

Bjarki also tried to move forwards and join them, an aggressive young spearman blocked his path.

The warrior gestured brusquely with his spear tip to the benches where the fifty of the king's warriors were noisily feasting and drinking and jostling each other.

Bjarki indulged in a brief flash of anger, but swallowed it down and meekly took his place with the rest of the boisterous *hird*-men. He could see Widukind and the king fussing round Edith, pouring her wine, calling for the servants to bring food.

Bjarki shoved a couple of small spearmen aside to take his seat on the benches, and helped himself to a large mug of ale from the common jug. Then he watched as Widukind rose to his feet to address the whole hall. The duke looked older and less full of bounce and pride than the last time Bjarki had set eyes on him; his blond hair was a little thinner now, his waist a little thicker, his fine clothes just a little shabbier – but his enthusiasm for speech-making was clearly undimmed.

'My friends, my fellow warriors, my bold comrades, I give you a toast to my beautiful sister, the Lady Edith, who has been snatched from the jaws of the dragon, delivered safely from a nest of the filthiest depravity, freed from the clutches of the vikings of Rogaland who have plagued our good folk for so long. The Lady Edith!'

There were roars of approval from all corners of the hall and men shouting out praise. Bjarki found himself smiling and raising his mug, too, before drinking deeply.

Yet Widukind had not finished. He was still on his feet, with his silver chased goblet still held high in the air. 'And I ask you also, good people of the Dane-Mark, to drink one further toast with me this day, to my sister's fearless rescuer, to the great man whose deep cunning is matched only by his dauntless courage; to a mighty sorcerer, a wise *gothi*, a powerful man who wove a spell of invisibility – a magic mist – that allowed him and his handful of loyal followers to liberate my sister from a peril greater than death itself. Show your appreciation, good Sword Danes, for the hero of the hour, for my constant supporter, my brave comrade, my wise counsellor. My friends, I ask you to drink to the health, wealth and happiness of *Abbio the Crow*!'

Chapter Eight

The true King of the North

Tor peered over her shield rim at her opponent, a dark-haired warrior with a square hedge of a beard and a ferocious scowl. He too was armed with sword and shield and was creeping towards her, growling low, with a murderous expression on his face.

'Come on then, sonny,' she called out mockingly. 'I haven't got all day here.'

Her attacker gave an ear-splitting roar and charged at her, and in three quick steps his shield crunched massively into hers and his long sword chopped down viciously at her head. But, instead of meeting the man's attack head on, Tor pivoted to the left on her back foot, allowing her body to be pushed round by his momentum. She did not try to block his shield, but accepted its pressure, then shoved forwards and towards the left. At the same time as she turned, she ducked her helmed head in behind the shield's rim. The downward sword blow, now pushed from its original line, clanged against the iron rim of her helmet, but it was only a glancing blow since the black-bearded man was off balance. His powerful charge had been guided off to the left by the movement of her body and her protecting shield and the big man was now blundering past her. She struck fast with her sword, still pivoting round, her blade sweeping over and slapping his rump hard with the flat as he passed her by.

He yelled out in mild pain and surprise and there was a loud clatter of applause from the dozen or so watching *hird*-members.

'Did everybody see that?' said Tor. She looked at her audience. 'Watch me do it one more time!'

She demonstrated again but without the bearded man: the body pivot, the guiding movement with the shield and the counterblow to the attacker's passing rear.

'Back of the thigh, knee or calf,' she said, 'and you will drop any opponent. He's out of the battle for good. But, mark well, this move only works with a right-handed warrior attacking you. This is what you do with a leftie. Watch, closely.'

She then demonstrated a similar manoeuvre, the mirror of the last, but with the warrior passing her on the right. Instead of finishing with the roundhouse blow to the back of her invisible opponent's legs, she made a forward cut low and to the right.

'You'll snap his shinbone this way,' she said. 'Or, if you're lucky, take off a foot.'

The young man with the big black beard was watching her sourly from a few paces away, still rubbing his bruised behind.

'Now hear me,' said Tor. 'All we're going to do is shield-work today. How to block, how to parry, how to kill an opponent with your shield – which is useful if you lose your sword. Wiglaf, you're up again. Come at me, this time with a roundhouse.'

'Why is it always me who has to be your victim?' the bearded man grumbled, 'I'm black and blue just from this morning's work. Pick on someone else, *Stallar*.'

'It is because you're my favourite idiot,' said Tor. 'Because you were last to arrive at muster this morn. Stop whining like a child and come at me. Roundhouse.'

Tor was instructing the least experienced members of Jarl Starki's *hird* in a sheep pasture just outside the royal compound at Uppsala. She felt that she had been neglecting her lord's troops as a result of the momentous events of the past few weeks, and was determined to devote more of her time to them. Now that Jarl Starki was oath-bound to serve the new Svear king – Sigurd Hring – who had been acclaimed by the king's council three days before, Tor felt she needed to polish up the skills of the new *Armathr's* troops, and make their young jarl proud of them.

She was not the only commander who was training warriors in the grassy fields around Uppsala that sunny spring morning:

indeed, she could see at least three more groups training in various styles of warcraft without even turning her head. There were even a few horsemen thundering about poking at cabbages stuck on poles with their lances – and mostly missing. Uppsala had recently come to resemble a vast army encampment with fresh warriors trickling in every day, most of the new arrivals masterless adventurers from all across the North. Sigurd Hring was offering a bounty of a mark of hacksilver for every *bondi* – as free armed men were known – who volunteered to join one of his companies of men and who was prepared to serve him for one year and a day. It made Tor a little uncomfortable, if she was fully honest. Sigurd Hring was clearly preparing for a war. Or a major raid. But against whom?

She organised her people into pairs and, after demonstrating several aggressive uses of the shield, she allowed them to batter away at each other while she walked through the struggling knots of men, offering advice, scathing criticism and, very, very occasionally, high praise. Her attention was distracted from the shield lesson by the sight of Sambor, moving his bulk in an undignified shuffle, which was as close to a run as the big man could manage, coming across the fields towards her. Sambor never hurried. This must be something important. She went out to meet him and, when the big man had recovered his breath, she listened to his staccato tale.

'Little. Princess. Missing. Bed. Empty. All. Night.'

So Inge had stayed out all night. Tor's first thought was she must have injured herself; slipped and broken a leg perhaps, and was unable to come back to the small hut next to Jarl Starki's guest hall that she and Sambor had been allocated as their personal quarters. Sometimes being the granddaughter of a duke – even a distant Polans duke – could be very useful. Her second thought was that Rorik had got to her somehow. That he had injured her as a method of hurting Tor. But on reflection that seemed unlikely. Tor had made some discreet enquiries about Rorik only the day before. Where did he sleep? What were his duties? And had discovered to her disappointment that he had been sent away from Uppsala on a long-distance errand by Sigurd Hring immediately after his acclamation as their new king.

'Look. Everywhere. Hall. Stables. Everywhere. No princess,' said Sambor.

'We will ask at the sword square,' said Tor, pushing her panic down deep inside her. 'She likes to watch the individual bouts. Someone may have seen her there.'

The sword square was an area of packed earth, an equal-sided space, surrounded by ropes to keep the audience at a safe distance. It was situated a little to the east of the king's hall. Members of the royal *hird* and other warriors favoured by the new king used the ground as a practice place for swordplay, various types of one-on-one training, for mock duels and, occasionally, when tempers boiled over, real ones.

When they arrived there Tor immediately noticed Erland the Snake in the centre of the square mock-fighting two Svear warriors at the same time. She could see why they called him the Snake. The man was fast – unbelievably fast. And as sinuous as a reptile. He dealt out sword blows to both his opponents, blocking, attacking, slipping between them, turning this way and that, as swift as a striking viper and just as lethal.

Erland made the two men, both experienced Svear warriors by the look of them, seem like clumsy, incompetent fools, always striking where he was not. As Tor watched, he knocked one opponent down with his shield, and while the man was recovering from the blow, he attacked the other opponent, and just as he seemed to be winning that fight, Erland slipped and fell to one knee. Sensing an easy victory the Svear rushed forwards, his sword lofted high, to make the killing blow – and Erland lunged, driving up and forwards from his kneeling position to stab his blunted sword up into the leather-armoured belly of his foolishly charging, overexcited enemy.

The sword tip knocked the wind out of his astonished foe, and Erland stood smiling above him, helping the winded swordsman to his feet. It was all beautifully done, the false slip and fall, the recovery and lightning-quick lunge to the attacker's belly, and the astonished foeman so easily defeated. Tor was impressed, despite herself. The man was good. It occurred to her that this Erland was by-named Snake not only because of his sinuous technique but because of his serpent-like cunning too.

It was fascinating to watch the mock-duels in the square but Tor forced herself to look away. She scanned all along the ropes for a sign of her girl. And when she saw one little blonde figure her heart leapt, only to be dashed down a moment later.

It was not Inge – just some young Svear maiden eyeing up all the sweaty, muscular young men. On the far side of the square, Tor could see Gummi and Gudfast – the two near-silent brothers from a distant land called Estonia, one tall and dark, the other shorter and brown-haired – both famous heroes, apparently, and newly sworn to Sigurd's banner. They were sparring wordlessly with each other. Their sword blows were slow and deliberate, more like a dance than combat. Tor somehow knew, however, they could both move a great deal faster if they chose. The motions of the mock-duel were beautiful, to Tor's eye, and seemed to follow some long, complicated pattern of movement, that each had practised often and knew intimately.

Tor ran her eye along the ropes over on the far side, and saw no one who might be Inge. Sambor's ruddy face had gone unusually pale. She wondered what would happen if he returned to the territory of the Duke of Polans in the south and admitted he had lost his granddaughter in Svealand. Sambor looked pleadingly into her face.

'Ask. Speak. People. Where. Princess.'

Tor approached a warrior, a gigantic bald fellow who was standing at the ropes watching the bout between Erland and his two hapless opponents. Tor noisily cleared her throat, and the giant turned slowly and looked down at her. It was Egil Skull-Cleaver – another famous hero. Uppsala these days seemed to be filled with them.

'I am looking for my friend,' Tor said. 'She is nowhere to be found. A girl, about fifteen winters. Blonde hair. Blue eyes. Very pretty. Have you seen her?'

'No,' rumbled Egil. 'But she sounds like someone I would like to see.'

Tor glared at him. Egil held up both his big hands in mock surrender. He smiled, perhaps trying to be charming. Tor saw that several of his front teeth had been filed into points. 'And you, Red, are no great hardship to gaze on either,' the giant said.

Tor made a kind of low, growling noise in her throat and turned to walk away.

'Wait,' boomed Egil. 'There *was* a girl like that, I think...'

Tor turned back and looked up at the massive warrior, who had fallen silent.

'Spit it out, egg-head,' said Tor, her hands aggressively on her hips.

'She was talking and laughing with that young fellow from Sodermanland. The swordsman, the one who won the championship at the *Disablot*. I forget his name.'

'Joralf?'

'That's the fellow. I saw him over there by the ale butts a little while ago.'

Egil Skull-Cleaver pointed to the south-east corner of the square where a little canvas awning had been set up over a couple of huge, squat, open barrels of ale. A knot of warriors were standing around them, quenching their thirst after their fights.

'You're Joralf,' Tor said, a little later, addressing a lean warrior with sandy hair, shaved at the sides of his head, who was standing with a group, laughing at a joke.

'You are Torfinna Hildarsdottir,' said the youth, taking a swig of ale. Tor reckoned he could not be more than seventeen winters. But he had a commanding presence, a weight, even, as if he were years older and a warrior of high renown.

'I am looking for my young friend, a blonde girl...'

'You mean Inge?'

'Yes, you know her? Have you seen her today?'

'I saw her this morning,' said Joralf. For some reason his friends seemed to find this amusing. There were titters; one warrior even nudged his companion and winked.

'She was in good health? Not injured.'

'Very,' said Joralf. 'Glowing, you might say.' Again his friends all sniggered.

Tor could feel the tethers that restrained her temper fraying dangerously.

'Do you know where she is now?'

'She left here perhaps an hour ago. She said she was going back to her house.'

—

They found Inge in her hut, naked, crouched over a large bowl of steaming water, washing herself. Tor burst through the door and glared at her. Sambor took one look, let out a boiling stream of incomprehensible Slav, and quickly retreated from the hut.

'Where were you? I've been worried sick. Sambor has been beside himself.'

'I was with friends.'

'With Joralf?'

Inge looked surprised at that. 'Yes, with Joralf.'

'All night? Don't you *know* what men are like!'

'Do *you* know what men are like? When was the last time *you* had a man?'

Inge's words took Tor's breath away. She was stunned. Astonished by the girl's perceptive cruelty. It had been two years since Tor had enjoyed the attentions of a lover – and that relationship had not ended well. But she had never once spoken of her desperate loneliness, even to Inge. She felt a hard coldness close around her heart.

'Are you saying that Joralf is your lover? That he made love to you last night.'

Inge said nothing. But a small smile crept about her lips.

'I suppose you think you love him,' said Tor.

Inge stood up. She put her hands on her naked hips, and faced Tor directly.

'I do love him,' she said, her eyes sparkling. 'I love him with all my heart.'

'Then I think Sambor and I will have to go and have a little word with that boy.'

'No, Tor, *no*. You leave him alone. He is *my* lover and none of your business.'

'I shall just make it crystal clear to him the kind of behaviour I expect from...'

'No!' Inge shouted the word. 'You are not my mother. You are not my elder sister. You are no kin to me at all. You have no right to interfere in this matter. None.'

Tor was once again taken aback by the vehemence in Inge's voice.

'I only want what's best for you, Inge. I simply want to protect you from...'

'No! If you go and threaten my friend, if you even say a single word to him, I shall never speak to you again. I swear it. If you bother Joralf, I shall hate you for ever. Now go, get out. This is my house and I am trying to wash myself. Go away!'

And Tor found herself standing outside a slammed door.

In something of a daze – and since it was nearly noon and she was very hungry – Tor wandered over towards the king's hall in search of something to eat. She was still thinking about the boy-warrior Joralf and exactly what she would like to say to him. But she also knew in her heart that she would surely lose Inge if she made the Polans girl choose between her new man and her. What was she to Inge? A friend? She was more than that. Inge had been her thrall and Tor had freed her. But Inge had chosen to come back to Svealand with Bjarki and Tor, when she might have remained in the territory of her grandfather the Duke of Polans. She had said many times that Tor and Bjarki were her real family. Tor felt the same way. But what *was* she?

She realised then exactly what she was. Tor stood in the position of a *fóstra* to Inge. This was a common practice for families who had no children. They would accept into their homes a child of another family, perhaps a family that might have difficulty in feeding an extra mouth, and they would raise it as their own. In this way, the two families were linked in a foster-alliance, and would support each other in legal disputes and quarrels.

Tor was Inge's foster-mother and, as such, she *did* have certain rights over Inge. Yet Tor also knew she could not risk losing her love. So, she decided, she would *not* speak to Joralf. Not at the moment, anyway. Perhaps there was no need to. He knew who Tor was; and she was not without a certain reputation. Perhaps, if he proved worthy, Tor should start thinking about a betrothal between the two youngsters, even a wedding in time. She would need to seek out Joralf's family and discuss the bride price they must pay. It could not be too miserly for the granddaughter of a duke!

Cabbage soup and barley bread was being served out at the back of the king's hall, but up at the dais, another ceremony was being enacted. Tor was amused to see Ottar, Jarl of Vastmanland, and once a would-be king, kneeling before Sigurd Hring in his throne and kissing the blade the new monarch held out while making his oath.

She took her soup bowl over to the place on the benches where her own lord Jarl Starki was sitting with some of his oath-men, and plonked herself down beside him.

He threw her a keen glance. 'You were half-right, *Stallar*,' he said. 'Jarl Ottar has submitted to the king without a murmur. And a bloody war between the Svear jarls has now thankfully been averted. But Odin's battle ravens are gathering nonetheless.'

'I know,' mumbled Tor, her mouth full of bread. 'I guessed that Sigurd Hring had new bloodshed on his mind. Have you been out and about in the fields around Uppsala recently? He must have called at least two thousand warriors to his banner.'

'See that fellow,' Starki said to her, jerking his chin towards the dais. An ageing warrior, tall and clad in shaggy wolf furs and with rings of gold on both his muscular arms, was standing stiffly upright before the king. 'That scruffy old he-goat holds both of Sigurd Hring's balls in the palm of his hand – but he doesn't even know it.'

'What do you mean?'

'That is an East Goth. He is called Helgi the Wulfing – you will have heard of the Wulfings, the powerful clan that has ruled Ostergotland since our grandfathers' days. He is – I suppose you would call him a jarl. But they don't use the title – they haven't for generations. Goths have kings, so they claim. Every man with a dozen spearmen puffs himself up as a king down on the Ostergotland plain – over in Vastergotland, too, the Goths who live on the other side of Lake Vattern. But that big hairy fellow cannot call himself king before Sigurd. So he calls himself *the* Wulfing.'

'And?' said Tor, slurping another spoonful of soup.

'Sigurd Hring wants Helgi the Wulfing to swear the oath. To kiss his sword.'

'So?' Tor sometimes found Jarl Starki's roundabout methods of making a point tiresome. 'He's not a Svear. He's a Goth. Why should he swear an oath to *our* king?'

'He's *not* going to swear fealty to Sigurd Hring. He's already refused him twice. He is adamant. He's here merely as a courtesy, paying his respects to the new king and delivering a fine gift, in the cause of good amity between two neighbours. The Wulfing swears that Ostergotland will always remain independent of the much more powerful Svealand. He will not become involved in our wars. But what would happen if he changed his mind, eh? What if Sigurd Hring offered him whatever he wants to make him kneel? What would happen if Svealand and Ostergotland were firm allies?'

Tor did not reply to her jarl. She watched as Helgi the Wulfing sat on a stool beside the king and accepted a horn of mead with both hands. Her eye was caught by the two warriors standing behind the Wulfing lord, his two bodyguards or champions.

She knew them. She had fought with them. They were twins, almost identical to look at – Saxons from Westphalia, the homeland of Widukind. They were both short, strong men, with a thatch of grey-shot black hair. One was looking round the hall, his eyes roving and assessing. From the mole on his right cheek, she knew he was Fidor.

Their eyes met, and she inclined her head fractionally, to politely acknowledge him. She knew he deserved all due courtesy from her. For these two Saxons were warriors truly to be feared, unlike many of the so-called 'heroes' at Uppsala. They were Rekkr. Fire Born. The Wolf *gandr* lived in their hearts.

Fidor stared at her for a time, then gravely nodded in response.

Tor pushed away her half-eaten bowl of soup. The sight of the Fire Born twins had stolen her hunger. For the first time since he left, she wished Bjarki were here.

She became aware that Jarl Starki was speaking to her, very quietly. Something about the Danes and King Siegfried and doing homage for the crown of Svealand.

'What did you say, lord?'

'Shh. Keep your voice down. This is not yet known to all our folk. You will have to be discreet on your journey. Say you are visiting relatives or something, yes?'

'Forgive me, lord. What in Odin's name are you talking about – what journey?'

Jarl Starki leaned into her. 'Sigurd Hring has long had dreams of becoming the greatest monarch in the North. All of it – from Frisia to the Finnmark. He has told me, as well as a small group of his oath-men, that he has decided he will *not* swear fealty to King Siegfried for the crown of Svealand. This land is his by right, he says.'

'I don't follow you,' said Tor. 'What has this to do with my making a journey?'

'I have been asked by the king to send a trusted messenger to the Dane-Mark to deliver his decision to King Siegfried. I have chosen you to undertake this task.'

'You want me to go to the Danes? What about the *hird*? What about you, lord?'

'I'll be fine for a week or so. And Gudrik will command my *hird* while you're gone. He's done it before. It is a part of his role as *Merkismathr*. Hurry back to me.'

'And what am I supposed to tell King Siegfried, exactly?'

'Tell Siegfried that Sigurd Hring will *not* make the traditional oath for his own Svear kingdom. Tell the lord of the Dane-Mark that our king repudiates this outdated agreement. Tell Siegfried that Sigurd Hring now claims the title King of the North!'

Chapter Nine

An offer from the king

Bjarki opened his eyes. And the blinding world drove a spear deep into his forehead. He reached up a hand to clutch his aching brow and felt a bump the size of an egg on his brow. He looked at his right fist, at the scraped knuckles and the traces of dried blood. Then it all came back to him. Well, not all. But enough to make him wince.

He rolled off the bench on which he had been sleeping and dry-heaved on the straw-covered floor, producing only a few gobbets of thick and yellowish spittle. He sat up, his head spinning, waited till it stopped and looked cautiously around. He was in a tavern of some kind. Small and filthy. Rank smelling. He had no idea where. There were two tables and benches and a counter with a huge wooden barrel on it, and scattered clay mugs, some of them broken. A puddle of brown vomit lay by the door. There was no one around. Not even a thrall. Bjarki had an overwhelming urge to piss. Hardly daring to fully open his eyes, he stumbled towards a door, stepping carefully over the vomit, and lurched out into the appalling light of the morning.

He was on the harbourfront of Viby. And before him were a dozen moored ships of various sizes. A few people passed by, giving him scornful or amused glances. But he did not care. The sea was a dazzling blue, the sky equally azure and bright. The sun not yet at its height but well advanced in its day-journey. *Water!* He needed water. First a more urgent matter. He stumbled around the side of the tavern and unlaced his trews and relieved the pressure on his bladder in a steaming stream against the wall.

Last night. Fragments of his memory jostled for his attention. He had left the hall in the middle of Widukind's speech, furious, sickened by the falseness of it all.

The Saxon prince had waxed full about Abbio's virtues and, without knowing anything about the events at Ymirsfjord, had merrily fabricated what he assumed had happened. He spoke at length of Abbio summoning his powerful *seithr* to mask the cunning attack he had led on the fortress with a magic fog; the Crow-man heroically in command, wielding lethal thunderbolts with one hand and a shining sword with the other, bringing red slaughter to the cowering vikings, and later enjoying the tearful gratitude of his rescued sister, before wafting them all safely back to the Dane-Mark to enjoy the praise of all right-minded folk. Bjarki had not interrupted, nor made any protest. He had simply risen from the bench while Widukind was in full flood and walked out of the hall. Then he stormed down to the harbour where he slammed open the door of the first tavern he found, and demanded ale – and lots of it.

He had drunk his fill and then moved on to another place, and drunk some more. At some point he had met the *Felaki*, who were also impossibly drunk, and they had sung battle-songs together, and drunk some more together. Later they had gone away and left him alone – he thought at his own insistence. He had played at dice with some new folk; there was a pretty girl he tried to kiss, who laughed and danced away; then he had quarrelled with a group of hard men, warriors, Sjaellanders, he thought, Danes of some kind, anyway.

They had been disparaging about Bago. Or perhaps he had been disparaging about Sjaelland. There had been a fight, anyway. He knew that by the state of his knuckles, and the lump on his head. And one of his ears was sore and swollen too. He hoped he had not killed anyone. Or injured them too badly. With some trepidation, he looked into his heart but found no signs his *gandr* had been summoned to aid him.

Just a brawl then. But he still felt that horrible feeling he had when he knew he had misbehaved but could not quite remember how or why. A general feeling of guilt.

'Highness?'

Bjarki turned his aching head and saw young Oddvin standing beside him.

'Kynwulf sent me to ask if you would like some breakfast. He is grilling just-caught mackerel on the jetty down by our ships. He has plenty of fresh ale, too.'

He had not killed anyone, at least that was the verdict of the *Felaki* over breakfast, but he had badly battered a group of five Sjaellanders, warriors sworn to Jarl Harald Wartooth, the most powerful man in the Dane-Mark after King Siegfried. But no one had been killed or crippled, it seemed. The *Felaki* seemed to think that it had been a joyous night, well earned after their Rogaland adventure. Bjarki's guilt began to subside, and he forced himself to eat a few mouthfuls of the delicious hot mackerel and take a sip or two of ale.

He knew that he must go up to the great hall at some point and make his salute to the king. He was a visitor in the Dane-Mark, a guest, and it would be discourteous not to do so. But his heart balked at the thought of encountering Widukind again. He was not sure that he could listen to another extravagant paean of praise for Abbio the Hero, without punching at least some of the Saxon's teeth down his lying throat.

And he needed to keep the duke on his side; he needed Widukind's goodwill if he was to ask for the hand of his sister Edith. Perhaps he would let a few hours go by, let his headache ease a little, and walk up in the cool of the evening; Edith, he was quite sure, would tell her brother the full, true story of the rescue.

Bjarki was not given the time to recover. A royal messenger arrived at the jetty not long after he had finished his mackerel, a lad of about twelve, on the cusp of manhood, who seemed mightily impressed with the gravity of his mission: delivering the king's summons, his invitation to Bjarki Bloodhand to join him as soon as it was convenient. Which meant, of course, at once.

Bjarki had only a moment to wash his face in harbour-water and pull on a clean tunic. An instant later, or so it seemed, he was standing before Siegfried in his private quarters. The king's steward handed him a horn of ale and Bjarki drank it gratefully. The king looked him up and down and said: 'A few more years on you, a few more scars, too, but I am pleased to note that you, Bjarki Bloodhand, are the same good man who fought beside me at my Dane-Work and held back the Frankish hordes – oh, it must be a full five years ago. It is very good to see you, my friend!'

'Highness,' said Bjarki, cracking a smile. 'You seem in good health yourself.'

This was a black lie. Siegfried had become an old man since Bjarki had last seen him: his almost translucent facial skin was wrinkled, sagging and mottled with brown spots; he had large dark hollows under his pale, wet-looking eyes. His sparse white hair was wispy and stuck out everywhere at alarming angles.

'Well, I am not. But you're kind to say so. I've been hearing about your exploits recently, young Bjarki,' said the king, waving him towards a nearby three-legged stool and siting down himself in an oak chair. 'About the perilous voyage into the western wilds of Rogaland to rescue the Lady Edith, of course, with brave Abbio...'

Bjarki clamped his jaw at that, but said nothing.

'...but also of your journey to the far Kingdom of the Avars last year...'

Bjarki was aware, from a flicker of movement in the corner of his eye, that another man had entered the king's chamber. This figure was also an old man, tall and thin, dressed in a long grey robe and leaning on a wooden staff. Bjarki glanced at him, and flashed a smile. It was Valtyr Far-Traveller, an old and trusted friend.

He looked back at the king, who was still speaking. '...an eventful journey in the south, I hear. A lucrative one, too, very lucrative. They say you became rich...'

'You should not believe every bit of gossip you hear, sire,' muttered Bjarki.

The old king gave a short laugh, not much more than a wet cough. 'I'm not after your silver, Rekkr. I have enough treasure of my own. I'm very happy that you should be rich. Makes a man less susceptible to bribery, I find. A wealthy man needs a huge sum to make him turn his head. Beggars will do anything for a silver penny.'

'We did bring home a few trinkets to Bearstead, sire. That cannot be denied.'

'Good. I congratulate you. But you discovered something else, apart from great riches, on your long southern journey, did you not?'

Bjarki frowned. He looked at Valtyr, who offered only a bland smile in return.

'I refer, of course, to your kinship with Angantyr, legendary King of the Goths. You discovered that you were of his royal blood – your *gandr* told you, yes? And yes, it was Valtyr who told me, so you can stop scowling at him like that. Some folk, I have heard, say you are the King of the Goths reborn. Your men, your *Felaki*, the descendants of the King's Companions, follow you because they believe it so.'

'I do not claim to know the full truth of it,' began Bjarki, shifting uncomfortably on his stool. 'But my *Felaki* do seem to think...'

The king cut him off.

'Your royal blood does not intimidate me, Bjarki. I trace my line back to Odin. My family have been Kings of the North since Thor was shitting in his baby's napkin. No, I care not if you call yourself the heir of Angantyr and true King of the Goths – indeed I encourage you to do so, since it may help in the task I would set before you.'

Bjarki blinked. He looked suspiciously at Valtyr. Then turned back at the king.

'What task?'

'You tell him, Valtyr, my throat has become very dry,' said Siegfried, beckoning to a hovering servant with the wine jug. It was hot in the chamber, Bjarki realised. A large brazier was burning in the corner, even though it was near noon, its burning coals making the room uncomfortably warm. *He truly is an old man*, Bjarki thought.

'Jarl of Vastergotland,' said Valtyr.

'What about him? Whoever this mighty personage might be,' said Bjarki.

'It's you. Or rather it could be you, if you were to agree to the king's proposal.'

Bjarki thought about this extraordinary proposition for a while. Vastergotland – the land of the West Goths – was across the straits from the Jutland peninsula, on the other side of the Kattegat. Its fishing port, Goteborg, was on the west coast of the Vastergotland mainland about a hundred and twenty miles as the eagle flies north-east of this royal hall in Viby. Two days' sail with a fair wind. Maybe even less. Not far.

Vastergotland and Ostergotland, the twin inland territories of the Goths to the south of Svealand, were divided by Lake Vattern. Both were considered independent territories, in name, at least, but Vastergotland had long had deep ties to the Dane-Mark. Some might even say the area was under the sway of the Danish kings. For as long as Bjarki could remember, Vastergotland had been ruled by a Danish warlord called Raefli, but he had heard the man died recently of a leg wound, the injury taken during a hunting accident near his hall at Lodose.

He was invited to become the Jarl of Vastergotland. That was the king's offer.

'No,' Bjarki said.

'What do you mean – no?' said Valtyr, sounding offended.

'I mean – no, thank you, highness,' said Bjarki, remembering his manners.

'Why do you refuse me?' asked the king, his voice now cracked and feeble.

'There is no such thing as the Jarl of Vastergotland. Goths do not have jarls. They have war chiefs, they have law-speakers, and they have kings. They do *not* have jarls. It is a foreign title to them; and I would be seen as a foreign master imposed upon them.'

'You wish to call yourself King of Vastergotland?' said Siegfried. 'Very well, Bjarki. As long as you make your oath to me as your overlord, you can call yourself king over there. Call yourself a god, if you like. Call yourself the King of the Gods. Ha-ha!'

Bjarki saw Valtyr frowning at this levity. He took the gods very seriously.

'Why me?' Bjarki looked from Valtyr to Siegfried and back again.

'I know your quality, Bjarki Bloodhand,' said the king. 'I know you would be a wise ruler. I made you Master of Hellingar in the great battle against the Franks at the Dane-Work and saw then that you had the makings of a fine leader. My friend Widukind says you made an excellent Jarl of the Three Rivers and Warden of the First Forest. Furthermore, the rumours that you are the heir of Angantyr, King of the Goths – or the man himself reborn – will do you no harm in Vastergotland, I am sure. But, most of all, because you are the best man for the job. You are a Dane, in whose veins flows the royal blood of the Goths. You are a warrior of renown – the Bloodhand, the famous Rekkr – and you are a decent man – and, I discover, rich – so you will not be tempted to accept too many bribes. You're a perfect candidate. Will you not accept?'

'I would have to swear an oath to you?'

'Not this again,' said Valtyr. 'Every warrior has to make oaths, Bjarki.'

Bjarki ignored him. 'I must acknowledge you as my king?'

'Yes, acknowledge me as your sole overlord, your lawful king. You would be my oath-man. I cannot make you my general, my

Armathr – I expect I shall soon be obliged to give that position to Harald Wartooth of Sjaelland. His power is growing and I need to keep him sweet. But you would be obliged to obey me, to support me in all my causes – fight for me, or send me warriors and supplies, if I went off to fight a war somewhere, although that seems an unlikely prospect at my advanced age. You would be my man in Vastergotland, my representative, in residence at the jarl's hall – beg your pardon – in the royal hall at Lodose. You will also be obliged to employ my shipwrights to build me nine or ten new warships from the local timber; you would recruit suitable crews for these ships; you would have to keep order in your lands, collect taxes, dispense justice, protect the people from all evil…'

'I accept,' said Bjarki.

'Just like that?' Valtyr was surprised. 'I expected much more resistance.'

'You do not know me as well as you think. Besides, he is offering me a crown.'

'Under my authority,' said Siegfried.

'Under your authority, highness,' Bjarki agreed.

'Well, then. Let us waste no more time. Kneel before me, Bjarki Bloodhand, kneel, King of Vastergotland, and make the solemn oath of fealty to your overlord!'

–

Bjarki found Edith in the dairy, where she was talking with the Master of the Royal Herds, who was apparently an old friend of hers. The comforting smell of cows still filled the air of the empty, straw-strewn shed, an earthy, motherly scent, although the cows had long been milked dry and dispatched to their green pastures.

'I saw you leave the great hall last night, when my brother was so lavishly praising Abbio,' Edith said, when she had dismissed the herd-master. 'I know you are angry that you did not receive recognition for your bravery. But I want you to know that I know what you did for me. I owe you a debt of gratitude, Bjarki. One I fear I shall never be able to fully repay.'

'That is all in the past,' said Bjarki. 'I was angry then, but I no longer care that Abbio schemed to steal my glory. He is welcome to it. The gods know what I did and will punish him for claiming the renown that is due to me. I've already forgotten it.'

'I have *not* forgotten it. Nor shall I. Not only because you were cheated of your reward – but because I cannot rest until I know who ordered Hjorleif to abduct me.'

'I *have* been rewarded, in a way,' said Bjarki. 'But I would claim a richer prize, as well. But only if you, dear Edith, are willing. First I must tell you how I feel...'

'Bjarki, no. I beg you. Do not speak of it. Words will only make it all worse.'

'I must tell you. I must tell you while I have the courage to say the words.'

'Bjarki, please do not...'

'I want *you*, Edith. I need you with my whole aching heart. You are the only woman for me, and I pledge myself to you, here and now, for all our lives. Edith...'

'No! Bjarki, you do not understand...'

'Edith, please, just hear me out. I know that you are a princess of Saxony, that you are the sister of a duke, a fine lady born to wealth and luxury. And that I – I am just a simple Bago-born oaf, a plain, un-pretty warrior. But all that is about to change. King Siegfried has offered me my own kingdom to rule – under his authority. I am to be the King of Vastergotland. A king, Edith! A king! I shall reside in a palace with many servants and attendants. And I have money, too, enough to buy you whatever you desire: trinkets, jewels, maids to help you in your daily life – all of this you shall have, all this and more. If you will but accept my offer of marriage. Come with me to Vastergotland as my wife, come as my *queen*! Come with me and we shall be so happy together in my royal hall at Lodose. All you have to do is say you consent.'

'I cannot. I'm deeply honoured by your offer, truly I am. In other circumstances I would willingly consent to bind myself to you for all our lives. But, alas, I cannot.'

'Why not?' Bjarki realised that he had seized Edith hard by both shoulders. 'In Odin's name, why can you not accept me? Is it my lowly rank? Is it my scars, or my rough clothes? Do I not speak as elegantly as you are accustomed? What is it, Edith?'

'None of those things. They do not matter to me in the slightest. It is this: I am *already* betrothed. I was hand-fasted last night. I made a solemn vow before the king, and before my brother, and to the man I am to marry. I made the betrothal oath in the great hall at Viby before the whole Danish court. It is lawful and binding, Bjarki; it is just as binding as the marriage vow itself. To break my vow would cause a world of hurt – for my brother, whom I love, and for the old king, too. I would be ashamed, too. I would be a worthless woman, a faithless one who broke her sacred oath.'

'Who is the man to whom you are betrothed?' asked Bjarki, staring hard at her, although deep in his heart he already knew what the terrible answer must be.

'I am to be the wife of Abbio the Crow. He asked for my hand as his reward for rescuing me from Rogaland. My brother begged me to accept him and... and I did.'

Bjarki let his hands fall to his sides. Abbio. The man who had stolen his glory, the creature who claimed credit for the rescue at Ymirsfjord, had also stolen his bride.

Chapter Ten

Bearer of bad news

The king's steward, although a small, thin, nervous-looking man of advancing years, had a fine, rich speaking voice, and he used it to its full effect that afternoon.

'Torfinna Hildarsdottir, *Stallar* to Jarl Starki of Norrland; envoy of Jarl Sigurd Hring of Sodermanland, craves an audience with King Siegfried of the Dane-Mark!'

Tor stepped forwards out of the throng in the great hall in Viby, and stood before the royal dais. She looked up at the set of older men sitting at the long table staring down at her from the long table, waiting for her to speak.

She was known as a shield-maiden of high courage, her bravery proven many times in battle, but even she was not indifferent to her own death. She was the bearer of bad news, indeed the bearer of what might be conceived as a gross insult to the King of the Danes and his powerful jarls, and the furious recipients of such tidings were not unknown to take out their anger immediately on the luckless messenger.

Accordingly, she had dressed in her finest clothes and armour, as if for a battle, and held herself ready to fight for her life, if necessary. She wore stout boots, and a set of dark leather hunting trews and tunic, over which she had donned a good-quality byrnie of mail links that covered her upper arms and fell to her thighs. A fine sword was belted at her waist, and a seax sheathed across her loins. Her bright red hair was washed and braided neatly into two pigtails; and she had drawn a thin line of black kohl under each of her two large green eyes. She wore no helm, but held a plain steel cap with a nasal guard in the crook of her arm. And, slung over her narrow back, was a freshly painted lime-wood shield, decorated with a figure of a ferocious bear, red tongue extended, standing upright, clawing at a green-and-brown tree shape – a device of her own making meant to depict her home Bearstead in the Svealand forest.

She scanned the line of eight men seated at the dais before her – some of which she knew, some she did not – and immediately felt her apprehension lift a little, for there, seated two along from the elderly King Siegfried, was Bjarki, her older brother. How he came to be here, she did not know. But her heart soared at the sight of him. However badly her message from Sigurd Hring was received by these grim lords of the Dane-Mark, she knew that Bjarki would never allow her to be hurt, let alone killed out of hand. She loudly cleared her throat.

'Lord king,' she began, 'I come to you with a message from my lord's lord, formerly Jarl Sigurd Hring, who is now the new King of the Svear. He says that...'

Siegfried held up a hand of command; Tor found herself immediately falling silent.

'Shield-maiden, Sigurd Hring is *not* the new King of the Svear. He has been chosen by the king's council, and acclaimed by the people – those tidings have already reached us, and we congratulate him. But he is not truly the King of the Svear until he has done fealty for his crown to me, his overlord. The proper term for Sigurd Hring is "king presumptive" – he presumes he will be the King of the Svear but is not, in fact, such. Not yet, at least.'

'Um, this is indeed the meat of the message I am to convey to you, highness.'

A hush fell on the hall. The air around Tor's ears seemed suddenly much cooler.

'Deliver your message,' said the king. Tor could see Bjarki was frowning hard.

'Sigurd Hring asserts his right as a free-born warrior of Svea-land, and as a high-born descendant of Odin All-Father, and one of the ancient blood of the Yngling kings, to name himself king of his own people in line with their wishes and those of his king's council.'

Tor could still hear her master Jarl Starki slowly repeating these words for her to learn. 'And make sure you mention his descent from Odin, this is very important,' Starki had said. 'Kings have to have some connection to the gods, however distant or even false, otherwise they aren't considered special. Any man with a dozen followers can call himself a king – look at the Little Kingdoms and all those viking-lords out west – but Sigurd Hring has to seem like a true ruler. The great-grandson of a god.'

'Furthermore,' Tor continued, forging onwards into the increasingly frosty silence in the great hall, trying to keep her voice level and resisting the urge to hunch her shoulders, 'King Sigurd Hring hereby repudiates *your* claim to overlordship, King Siegfried, and any suggestion that the Kingdom of Svealand is in any way or fashion subordinate to the Kingdom of the Dane-Mark. The overlordship is now moribund, set aside for ever, King Sigurd proclaims. Moreover, he claims, by right of the true Aesir blood that flows in his veins, by the strength of his arm, and by the acclamation of his jarls and all the Svear people, the honour of styling himself by that most ancient of titles in these lands – King of the North.'

Tor paused for a breath. But before she could continue, Siegfried spoke again. 'Have I got this right, woman? You have the impudence to come to my own hall in Viby to tell me that, not only am I no longer Sigurd Hring's overlord, but that – I can scarce believe it – Sigurd Hring claims he is now *my* overlord as King of the North?'

'My lord's lord foresaw that you might take issue with this new…'

'Take issue? Take *issue*? I should have you slain on the spot for your…'

'My king,' said Bjarki, 'if I might offer counsel. Torfinna Hildarsdottir is, in delivering this message, simply obeying the orders of her own lord, as her oath compels her to do. We should listen to her words in full, then deliberate carefully on what is to be done.'

Siegfried turned and stared down the table at Bjarki for a long, long moment. Tor saw her brother look directly back at his king, calm, steady, totally unflinching.

'This impudent she-wolf is your half-sister, if I recall. She is the one who set the rotting head of the traitor Snorri Hare-Lip before me. Dumped it on my dinner table.'

'She did,' said Bjarki. 'And I believe it vital we hear what she has to say.'

Then the king turned back to look at her and made an abrupt motion with his hand that might have meant, 'Continue, then, if you must.'

'Sigurd Hring foresaw that you might take issue with this new order of affairs and he offers to satisfy your bruised honour in the traditional way of the North.' Tor took a deep breath. 'He will settle this matter with you in combat upon the field of honour. Sigurd Hring, King of the Svear, invites you to meet him, with all your champions, oath-men and armed followers, at a place to be named by you, on the first day of the month of Heyannir, the mid-point of this summer. That is, lord king, in three months from this day. He will do battle with you and your men, in the sight of the gods and the ancestors and all of the Middle-Realm on that day, and the victor shall win the right to call himself King of the North henceforth and for ever.'

–

Tor was coldly dismissed to the back of the hall and King Siegfried retired to his quarters with Harald Wartooth, his most powerful jarl, Bjarki Bloodhand, Valtyr Far-Traveller, Widukind of Saxony, and the current Master of Hellingar, Lars Crookback, who, along with two other ageing Danish jarls, had command of the southern portion of the Jutland peninsula, and who was charged with defending the Dane-Work.

'What is your counsel?' said the king. 'What message shall I send to Sigurd the Upstart?'

'Simple!' said Jarl Harald Wartooth, a ferocious old warrior, strong as an ox, with drooping grey moustaches and a single tooth that protruded like a tiny tusk from his lower set of tangled yellow teeth, from which he received his unusual by-name.

Harald Wartooth had a reputation for loving war more than any other human activity and some wag had named the unruly fang his 'war-tooth', and accused him of growing it deliberately to be able to gore his enemies in battle. 'We fight them, highness,' Harald now said, 'we slaughter them, we crush them and we hang that traitorous goat-turd Sigurd Hring by his stinking entrails from the nearest oak tree!'

'But do you truly have to fight him?' said Valtyr. 'Whichever side wins, the slaughter of so many of our fine warriors would weaken the whole North. Why not just tell him you assent to his claim to be King of the North? It is not as if you were using that dusty old title. Let him have it. Be magnanimous. Sigurd Hring can rule over Svealand; you shall continue rule here as before in the Dane-Mark.'

'By Odin's eye,' said Harald Wartooth. 'You cannot refuse a challenge! Folk will think you're weak; they'll think you fear Sigurd Hring. You would be shamed.'

Lars Crookback said: 'You *must* fight him, highness. He has insulted you. You have no choice but to meet him in battle if you wish to remain King of the Danes.'

'I know *that*,' snarled Siegfried. 'When I was younger I would have torn the balls off any messenger who spoke the words I received today. I asked for your counsel, not a statement of the obvious. I must fight him. But where? How do I win?'

'I was in Uppsala for the *Disablot*,' began Bjarki. 'Even then Sigurd Hring was gathering men to his banner in vast numbers from all over the Middle-Realm. He...'

'We'll obliterate him,' said Harald Wartooth. 'Danish warriors are the finest in the North. My own Sjaellanders could crush any army from Svealand alone. We will confront this Svear upstart head on and slaughter him – his milk-sop hired men too!'

Bjarki said: 'Sigurd Hring has summoned the greatest heroes in the North to his side, warriors of renown such as Egil Skull-Cleaver, Erland the Snake, Hagnor...'

The Wartooth interrupted again: 'These are merely masterless men, outlaws and vagabonds. But if he had Thor himself fighting by his side, we would still beat them.'

'Yes, Jarl Harald, thank you for that most valuable contribution,' said Siegfried. 'Now, kindly be quiet and allow the King of Vastergotland to speak. Bjarki, continue.'

'I only wish to point out that Sigurd Hring has *already* gathered a mighty force in Uppsala,' said Bjarki. 'So we should treat his army with respect. He has been planning this war for a long while. His army may even be as strong as yours, sire.'

'Nonsense,' said Harald Wartooth. 'Svealand is much smaller than the Dane-Mark. Much of it is just empty forest. In our grandfathers' grandfathers' days there were only a few dozen goatherders up there, a handful of fur-trappers and runaway thralls. Even today I doubt Sigurd Hring can muster even a thousand spearmen...'

'Do we agree we *must* fight the battle?' asked Valtyr. 'Is there no other way?'

He was ignored.

'Sigurd Hring already has many more than a thousand spears,' said Bjarki flatly. 'I've seen his troops with my own eyes. I hear he's also brought three companies of Telemark archers over from the Little Kingdoms to fight for him. He may yet find more allies...'

'The Ostergotlanders will not fight with him,' said Lars Crookbank. 'I happen to know that Helgi the Wulfing visited Uppsala but refused to bend the knee to him.'

'No doubt we will discover how many warriors Sigurd Hring has gathered when we meet him on the field,' said the king drily. 'The question is, where should it be?'

Valtyr said: 'If we must fight, then choosing the site is crucial. And Sigurd Hring is willingly giving that advantage away to us.

Which means he is very sure of his victory. He is saying he can destroy you and your Danish force, sire, at any place we are pleased to name.'

'Then we must choose wisely,' said the king.

'Not in the Dane-Mark,' said Jarl Lars. 'The devastation of thousands of warriors passing through Sjaelland or Skane could ruin farmers' livelihoods for a generation. Not in Sigurd Hring's own lands, either, where every steading we pass might conceal an ambush.'

'Where then?' The king idly scratched his sparse white hair.

'There is a place on the southern border of Svealand,' said Valtyr. 'On the march between Sodermanland, Jarl Sigurd's own fief, and Ostergotland. If we seek permission from Helgi the Wulfing – perhaps sweeten him with a gift – we can enter his territory and fight on the plain below the Kolmarden, that high wooded ridge that separates the two nations. There is an area of flat land, perhaps five miles across, treeless, and with deep water on both sides to guard our flanks. There is a little village there called Norrkoping, if I recall rightly. Famous for its salt-cured salmon. Finest cured fish in the North, the Norrkopingers always like to boast. Though I've never tasted the stuff myself.'

The king was slowly nodding his white head in approval.

Valtyr continued: 'Best of all, it is situated on a deep inlet of the Eastern Lake called the Braviken. An easy place for our ships to reach. We can bring our troops right there. No long marches with folk getting lost or losing heart and deciding to go home. We could sail our warriors right up to the battlefield.'

'I know that place,' said Lars Crookback. 'It is overlooked by a high forested plateau. I would not care to attack up that slope if they were standing at the summit.'

'So we will fight them on the plain beneath,' said Harald Wartooth. He turned to face Widukind of Saxony who had so far played no part in these discussions.

'You, Saxon, our people have aided yours in the past. Will you stand with us?'

'Alas, Jarl Harald, I have few enough warriors as it is, a bare handful, and they are needed in Saxony. I fear I must husband them for the fight against the Franks.'

'He is right,' said Valtyr. 'If we were wise, we would *not* spend our strength warring against each other but all unite against the common foe – the Christians!'

Once again, Valtyr was ignored.

'You cannot spare even a hundred young Saxon spearmen? Or some Angrian cavalry?' said the king. 'I've been a good friend to you, Widukind, in the past when you begged for *my* help.'

'You have indeed, King Siegfried, and I shall be for ever grateful…'

'Grateful but not helpful,' said Bjarki. Widukind shot him a hard look. Bjarki looked pointedly at the sword now belted at the Saxon's waist. It was an antique blade, well made and with a blue jewel at the pommel. Bjarki knew that sword. It had once, they said, belonged to a god. And it had cost him a great deal of blood and pain.

'I *am* truly grateful, lord king,' continued Widukind. 'But sadly I cannot spare even a single man to fight at your side. However, I shall have my fearless sorcerer Abbio make up a powerful *nithing* pole for your men to take into battle. Such is the power of these *seithr* talismans that your victory is assured. I will also ask him to use his considerable powers to curse Sigurd Hring. Abbio will fill his belly with fire snakes or cover his skin with boils.'

'Boils?' said Bjarki. 'Are you promising to give our enemy pimples?'

–

'You've certainly set the dog upon the doves, Tor,' said Bjarki, an hour later. They were sitting together in a nook at the rear of the hall, sharing a jug of ale.

'You think I wanted this mission? My lord Starki commands and I must obey.'

'I simply don't understand all this madness,' said Bjarki. 'All Sigurd Hring had to do was come here and bend the knee, kiss the sword, have a friendly cup of ale and go home – and he could rule in Svealand however he sees fit. The overlordship is only an old courtesy title. King Siegfried does not seek to interfere in Svealand. For years the old arrangement has worked perfectly well for both Danes and Svear.'

'Two old men,' said Tor. 'Two old kings. That was the problem. Harald Fox-Beard and Siegfried had known each other and trusted each other for many decades. Then one dies and the new King of the Svear has a chance to finally realise all his grand ambitions. Sigurd Hring looks across the sea at Siegfried of the Dane-Mark and sees a feeble, slack-bellied old nanny-goat who can easily be pushed around. And Sigurd Hring wants to rule the whole of the North, Bjarki. He truly does. He believes that as King of the North he will preside over a great blossoming of all our peoples. A time of peace and plenty, he says. He may even be right. For too long we have fought among each other. Raiding, feuding, fighting wars. The last time we were united was against the Franks at the Dane-Work five years ago. Sigurd Hring thinks we could all be united once again. The whole North from Frisia to the Finnmark. One people. One nation. Under his wise and just rule. All under the all-powerful King of the North.'

'You think he's right?'

'I don't know. He made a fine speech about it just before I left. You should have heard the cheering. Sigurd Hring talked about one big slaughter to end all slaughter.'

'That's insane. Killing folk to stop killing other folk? It would never end.'

'So what will you do, oaf?'

'Me? I'm going to Vastergotland. To a place up the Gota River – I'm taking up residence at the hall at Lodose. Don't laugh, Tor, but Siegfried has named me king.'

'What?' Tor did not laugh but she let out a snort. 'You're a king – *again*?'

'You are drinking ale with the new King of Vastergotland, Bjarki the First!'

'I'll have to start calling you "highness" again, instead of plain old oaf.'

'I could make you Princess of Vastergotland and then we'd both be equally grand.'

'Oh yes,' said Tor. 'I think I'd make a fine princess. I have *all* the airs and graces.' They were both laughing now. 'Wait, I thought you'd be taking along Edith Swan Neck as your queen. I know that you like her. I believe she likes you, too.'

Bjarki stopped laughing.

'Edith has become betrothed to Abbio, Widukind's good friend and counsellor.'

'Thor's hairy balls!' Tor put a hand on Bjarki's forearm. She could see how wounded her brother was by this. 'She chose *him*? That suppurating pile of toe-rags, over you? After you rescued her from the grip of Hjorleif Illugi? The woman is mad!'

Bjarki said nothing. He finished off his mug of ale.

'Listen, before I go back to Svealand, oaf, do you want me to quietly feed Abbio to the Viby foxes? I need to practise my silent killing.' Tor was only half-joking. She had spent much of the sea-journey to Viby thinking how she might successfully achieve the discreet murder of Rorik.

'No. Of course not. If I cannot have Edith by fair means, I'll not have her at all.'

'Well, if you change your mind, I'm always... When are they to be married?'

'Sometime in high summer. After the great battle is won.' Bjarki sighed and looked at his sister. 'I think you had better pack up our things at Bearstead and bring our people down to Lodose as soon as possible, don't you, sis? You don't want to risk being trapped up in Norrland when this stupid war starts.'

'What are you talking about? I'm not leaving. And I'm not going to live with you in your fancy palace in Vastergotland. Bearstead is my home. Your home, too.'

'But Tor, you cannot fight for the upstart Sigurd Hring against King Siegfried.'

They stared at each other, a horrible realisation dawning for both of them.

'You *must* come back to Svealand, oaf,' said Tor. 'Sigurd Hring would have you fight for him. He asked me to tell you he would welcome you with honour to his court, alongside the other heroes. He'll reward you. He won't make you king but...'

'No,' said Bjarki. 'It's not about being a king. Siegfried is in the right in this quarrel. Sigurd is a traitor; he must bend the knee. I cannot fight against my king.'

'I made an oath to Jarl Starki to be loyal till death,' said Tor. 'I'll not break it.'

'I made the exact same oath to the King of the Dane-Mark,' said Bjarki.

'We cannot meet each other across the shields. I cannot try to kill you,' said Tor.

'I cannot fight you either, Tor. But what are we to do?' asked Bjarki.

Chapter Eleven

An unavoidable challenge

The hall at Lodose was in poor repair. The rye straw-thatched roof was green with mould and weeds were sprouting everywhere. One part of the wall on the south side had a large hole in it, and Bjarki found what must have been the birth-nest of a wild sow in one corner of the building. It was clear by the cobwebs and dust that no one had lived here for months and that, for years before that, it had been badly neglected.

'I've seen better kept shit-houses,' said Kynwulf, kicking at a wall beam that was rotten at the base, and dislodging a large chunk of fibrous timber. 'We'd be wiser to burn the place to the ground and build a whole new hall up from the warm ashes.'

'Nonsense,' said Bjarki. 'A few days' hard work – with the help of the local folk – and it will be almost as good as new. I might even extend it. Or build a guest hall.'

The locals, Bjarki's subjects, were a surly, suspicious bunch of mostly dirt-poor wretches who did their best to avoid any interaction with the heavily armed Danish newcomers. About five hundred Vastergotlander families lived around the triple-ramparted fortress of Lodose, which was perched on a disc of raised land on the east bank of the Gota River, a day's march – or half a day's sail – inland from the sea.

The Lodose people farmed barley, oats and rye on the flatlands hereabouts, kept pigs, goats, cows and sheep and hunted deer and boar in the thick surrounding forests. There were plenty of fish in the river, too, just for the taking – and in early winter the waters flashed bright with spawning salmon. The rest of the Vastergotland population, another thousand or so families, lived along the Gota River between Lodose and Gotaborg, a small port on the Kattegat; or they built their modest steadings further north and east on the shores of the great lakes Vanerm and Vattern. There were a few remote farmsteads in the forests, too. But the rest of the country was almost all dense, virgin woodland.

Fishermen in Gotaborg netted their huge catches of silvery herring in the waters of the Kattegat, and hunted crabs and lobsters all along the shore, but the town was in an exposed spot, close to well-used trade routes and vulnerable to any passing vikings who looked to enjoy a little rape and plunder at their expense. So, in times of trouble – or outright war – the people of Gotaborg, and all the folk living along the Gota River, tended to flock to the fortification at Lodose and seek the protection of the Danish nobleman and his warriors who ruled Vastergotland from inside its strong triple walls.

The most recent incumbent of Lodose had been a warlord called Raefli Hawk-nose, an uncle of King Siegfried's who had sat undisturbed in his remote riverside fortress for forty years and done little except hunt boar, chase the local Goth women and drink himself insensible every night on local mead. Bjarki reckoned the people of Vastergotland would enjoy having a young, energetic ruler, if only for the novelty.

It was not, however, a large kingdom. By custom, the ruler's writ stretched from the shores of the Kattegat east for four days' march through the thick forests as far as Vattern, the long thin lake that ran roughly north–south and formed the boundary between his western kingdom and Ostergotland. Northwards the kingdom extended along the river Gota two days' walk up to Lake Vanerm, beyond which was the Svear territory of Varmland. South of the realm was Skane, part of the Dane-Mark.

So while the actual hall at Lodose might have been in disrepair, its defences still made it a formidable fortress. On its raised circular patch of ground, the hall and its outbuildings was surrounded by three layers of earth ramparts and river-fed moats. A visitor could only gain entrance to the Lodose compound by a narrow wooden bridge on the south-east, landward side, one that could be swiftly dismantled in time of war.

Just to the north of the Lodose compound was a small harbour with three wooden jetties poking out into the river, as well as several warehouses, grain stores, dwelling places and fishermen's huts on a broad spit of stony land next to the water. The town of Lodose, if such a small settlement could be called that, lay east of the fortress between the arms of a stream that divided and flowed into the Gota here. There were about a hundred huts and hovels, a busy forge, a mill wheel by the river, three ale-houses and several cook shops. There was also a temple for sacrifices – the locals favoured Thor rather than Odin, a more uncomplicated if less powerful deity.

'We need to introduce ourselves properly to the fine people here,' said Bjarki to Kynwulf. 'I cannot hope to rule them if they do not know me – and trust me, too.'

'In six days, it is the Feast of Idun, the goddess these people here venerate as the embodiment of spring,' said Valtyr, who had wandered over to listen to their talk.

Valtyr had insisted on coming to Lodose with Bjarki, and King Siegfried had quickly agreed, giving the one-eyed traveller the title of King's Envoy. Valtyr was supposed to act as Siegfried's representative in Lodose but Bjarki suspected the Danish king wanted just to get rid of a meddlesome, often drunken, long-time guest by foisting him on Bjarki.

'The Feast of Idun is the celebration to mark winter's end,' Valtyr continued. 'They have sports and games and drink a good deal, and make offerings to Thor.'

'Sounds just what we need. Kynwulf, have your *Felaki* and the captain's men go out into the town and tell everyone that we shall be celebrating the sacred Feast of Idun in the sheep pastures by the river in six days' time. There will be competitions of strength, courage and skill – with prizes awarded to all the winners by me personally. Be sure to mention there will be plenty of free food and drink for all who attend.'

'They play *Knattleikr* here,' said Captain Mogils. 'It's their favourite pastime.'

'What is that?' Bjarki looked at the young Danish warrior.

Bjarki had come to Lodose with three ships, his own two vessels and another, larger one, gifted to him by Siegfried. As well as his five *Felaki* bodyguards, the Danish king had given him a *lith* – or company – of fifty trained spearmen under a captain called Mogils, and a shipwright called Rudolf and his team of carpenters.

'It is a game of two teams of ten men armed with clubs – and a ball,' said Mogils. 'I used to play *Knattleikr* as a boy on the island of Fyn. You try to hit the ball over the enemy goal line with a club. It's quick, exciting and hardly anyone gets killed these days…'

'Excellent,' said Bjarki, rubbing his hands together in satisfaction. 'The centrepiece of the Feast of Idun will be a game of – what did you call it? *Knattleikr*?'

Mogils nodded. 'My men could make up one team – I have some fine players.'

'Yes, good, Danes versus Vastergotlanders. The winning team will be given… a prize ox. Valtyr, that's your task, go out and buy me a fine-looking ox that I can present as a reward to the winners. Off you go. Go, spread the word in Lodose about the Feast of Idun.'

Kynwulf saluted and turned to go. 'And send Rudolf the shipwright to me, will you, War Chief. Let's see what he and his men can do about the state of this hall.'

–

The next six days were filled with activity for Bjarki – which was as well because his nights were filled with dreams of Edith, from which he would awake drenched in cold sweat and feeling a horrible sense of panic and despair. He wanted her. However much he told himself he could never have her, his sleeping mind clearly disagreed. Yet he felt foolish to be coveting a woman who was promised to another, even if that other was a 'suppurating pile of toe-rags', as Tor had called him. But, try as he might to banish her, Edith occupied many of his night hours, coming unbidden into his dreams, and looking more desirable each time she visited. For that reason, busy days filled with work were a balm for Bjarki, giving him no time for foolish longings.

The Danish shipwrights aided by some of Captain Mogil's men attacked the hall with gusto, pulling down rotten thatch with hooks on poles and cutting pine shingles to replace the entire roof. Then they set about digging out all the worm-eaten support beams and replacing them with new timber. Bjarki sent men into the forests to identify the right trees for the hall repair, and also for the beginnings of the programme of shipbuilding commanded by King Siegfried. He accompanied the warriors out to the woods on the first dawn, and worked beside them that day, marking out suitable trees with his axe. Then he came back with the ox-teams the next day, and they dragged the trunks down to the river, to be stripped down ready for the saw pits.

After the first two days, Bjarki was obliged to base himself each morning in the hall, and direct all his efforts from there. And when the noise and bustle in the half-dismembered hall became too distracting, he retreated in the afternoons to a large waxed linen tent in the fields, to hold councils with the shipwright and his crews, as well as with Captain Mogils – who he had entrusted with the task of recruiting keen young Goth warriors to fight under Bjarki's banner – and Oddvin, who had charge of the provision of all the food and drink necessary for the great feast.

Sitting at the tent's entrance on a late spring evening, bone-tired, and eating his supper pottage, Bjarki watched the apparently tireless Captain Mogils training his team of ten *Knattleikr* players in a nearby field. The players seemed to rush around the small patch of pasture like excited children, swiping at each other with their clubs and shouting out in outrage when they were hit. Occasionally the twig-and-wool ball would shoot out from the melee and there would be wild cries of enthusiasm.

Everyone seemed to be having a good time.

He had asked Valtyr to be in charge of the religious side of the Feast of Idun – a few basic animal sacrifices, some songs and prayers. Yet, despite the old man having suggested the idea on their first day in Lodose, he now seemed to have lost interest.

Valtyr spent most of his days in the ale-houses near the port, drinking and talking to the Vastergotlanders. By mid-afternoon, he was usually to be found slumped and snoring on one of the benches. On the fifth day, Bjarki had to take over another task he had asked the old man to undertake: the attempt to buy an ox from a farmer on the southern pastures of the settlement. The farmer who owned the huge red-brown animal seemed to think Bjarki was a wealthy idiot who would pay the animal's weight in silver. Eventually, he asked Haugen Halfhand, the canniest of his *Felaki*, to purchase a young black bull from a different farmer.

The strange attitude of the local people was puzzling to Bjarki. He and his followers were all working very hard to improve the dilapidated hall – which was as much a public building, used for many events involving the whole of Lodose, as it was his royal dwelling – and he was very open-handed, offering food and drink and cheerful conversation, even jokes, to any Vastergotlander who came near to him.

Furthermore, in the few days he had been in Lodose, he had had his carpenters repair the three wooden jetties that every fishing boat here used. He had also mended several gaping holes in the palisade that surrounded the town. No one could say he and his people had been idle. Neither had he injured or dispossessed anyone – and one of Captain Mogils's men, who had got drunk and broken into a house and stolen some fine linen, he had had publicly whipped as a warning to his comrades not to break Bjarki's strict rules of behaviour. But the Vastergotlanders turned away from his friendly greetings when he walked through the streets, and no one – not one single person – had willingly come forward when he called for volunteers to help organise the feast, or to assist in the repairs to the roof of the Lodose hall.

They clearly did not like him. It was as simple as that.

And this hurt him more than it should have. He was used to being liked. Some people thought he was stupid, but *he* knew he was not. Some people thought he was a blood-drunk maniac, but he was no longer the mindless *berserkr* of popular legend. Most recognised him for what he actually was: a kind, amiable man, principled and decent. A skilled and ferocious warrior in battle but very far from a wicked man.

'Why do they dislike me?' he asked Valtyr, in one of the old man's half-sober hours the day before the Idun feast. 'You talk to them: what did I do to anger them?'

'It's not what you have done. It's who you claim to be. Their king.'

'They don't like having a king? Why not? I have asked nothing from them.'

'They don't dislike the idea of a king. They treated old Raefli Hawk-nose as a king. Even called him "highness". He did nothing for them but seduce their daughters and drink all their mead. But you, popping up out of nowhere and going round telling people that you are the true heir of Angantyr, King of the Goths, rightful ruler of all Gotland, well, that has put their backs up just a bit. Hey, ale-wife, another jug here!'

'But I haven't told anyone that... Oh, the *Felaki*. Yes, I understand you now.' Bjarki thought for a moment. 'Is there anything I can do?'

'Aye, lad, get that lazy slattern to bring me another jug of her best ale!'

'I meant about the Vastergotlanders.'

'Oh them. Well, you could kill a few. You know, on the principle that if they don't love you, they might as well fear you.'

'I'm not going to slaughter my own people to terrify them into liking me.'

'Just an idea,' said the old man.

—

Bjarki did not need to slaughter any of his subjects. They seemed willing enough to kill each other in the name of sport. Bjarki sat under a striped awning that had once been a ship's sail, on his new throne, a plain chair swiftly crafted from a local oak tree by his busy carpenters, which had been placed on a dais and raised him a good five feet above the games fields. This allowed him to see everything in the pastures north of Lodose and, more importantly, to *be* seen by all those Vastergotlanders who were competing for prizes that sunny day.

There were sword matches, with blunted weapons, taking place in a roped-off square, off to the right. Some of the combatants were surprisingly competent, even highly skilled. And the fury with which they attacked each other was alarming given that this was merely play-war. Two wrists and one shinbone had already been broken by the midday suspension of activities for the meal. Bjarki watched everything and tried to remember the faces and names of the better swordsmen: he'd been sent here to recruit an army of warriors, after all.

Over in the wrestling square, a far smaller space than the sword-fighting arena, greased men, naked to the waist, grappled with each other until they could pin their slippery opponents to the earth – or until the loser admitted defeat by slapping his palm on the ground. One stubborn man had already been killed – a snapped spine – his corpse carried off in a cloak by four men to be tended to by his weeping widow.

However, not all the games were as lethal. Over to the far left were the roped-off spear-throwing lanes, where men, and a couple of women, too, vied to hurl a javelin the furthest. The missile had to stick into the ground, with the shaft above the close-cropped grass. If the ash-wood shaft touched the grass the throw was disqualified. Next to the spears was the stone-throwing alley. Big men cupped a small boulder under their chins and after taking a short run-up they flung the stone one-handed as far as they could. The best of them could throw a head-sized rock a good fifty feet.

Beyond the stone-throwers, at the furthest distance from Bjarki, so far that he could not make out the faces of the competitors, were the archery butts: a couple of dozen men and women shooting at straw targets two hundred paces away from them.

Much closer to Bjarki's dais were the food tables, groaning with sliced roast beef, haunches of roast venison and wild boars' heads, piles of boiled fowl with a spicy sorrel gravy, steamed fish from the river with sauces of herbs and yoghurt. There were also small round loaves of flatbread stacked in tottering piles, huge cauldrons of soup, big cheeses, sweet preserved fruit in pots, honey jars and broad bowls filled up with nuts.

Next to the food tables was the ale and mead, with Valtyr dispensing foaming jugs to the revellers from a line of oak barrels, and keeping his own horn topped up, too. The Vastergotlanders were in good appetite that day, and streams of people visited the refreshment tables and went away with loaded platters and brimfull cups.

Bjarki watched it all, sipping frugally from a horn of ale, and nibbling a hunk of bread covered with a thick slice of beef. He did not want to be accused of greed by these people, whom he suspected already despised him. From time to time, Kynwulf or Captain Mogils would bring forward a victor of one of the competitions and Bjarki would praise them lavishly and hand over a fine silver-chased drinking horn, or a golden cloak-brooch adorned with garnets, or a small purse of Frankish coins. Much of the treasure he gave away came from the viking hoard he had taken in Rogaland, so he did not begrudge it all that much. Moreover, a king had a solemn obligation to be a generous gift-giver to his people.

Occasionally he encountered a friendly face: his *Felaki* comrade Harknut won the light javelin-throwing competition, and came second in the heavy spears – and Bjarki gave him a golden arm ring; and one of his Danish men, Hjolfi, took the archery prize – shooting as well as any Telemark man at two hundred paces – and he received a fine, dog-head silver torc from his king.

Bjarki, very bored now, and struggling not to show it, watched the sun inch its way across the cloudless blue sky. The *Knattleikr* match would take place in the late afternoon, when all the other competitions had been concluded. He knew that ferocious betting was taking place on the outcome all across the fields. Valtyr had wagered a purse of silver with some important local personage called Glamir on a victory for Captain Mogils's team – and Bjarki was worried that the drunken old fool would not have the coin to pay off his debt when he lost.

Bjarki stifled a yawn. He had never imagined being a king would be so dull. He found, despite his efforts, that his eyelids were closing. He jerked his spine straighter.

Suddenly, Valtyr was at his elbow, breathing fumes like an open ale-house door.

'I told you about this fellow Glamir, did I not?' the old man whispered in his ear. 'The law-speaker, Glamir Raeflisson? Wake up, Bjarki. You must remember I mentioned him.'

Bjarki realised that he had momentarily fallen asleep in his throne. There was a balding middle-aged man standing below the dais, staring contemptuously up at him.

'Whumf?' said Bjarki, wiping a thread of drool from his slack open lips and hauling himself upright in the uncomfortable chair. 'So what is happening, Valtyr?'

Valtyr pointed at the man. Bjarki rubbed his eyes clear and looked down at him.

He was very pale. Skin like snow and his sparse hair a shade of blond that was almost pure white. He looked like one of those strange men who, by some magic, are born with fish-belly skin and pink eyes, but this fellow's eyes were a shade of blue.

Bjarki looked at the man, who stared right back at him – arrogantly, fearlessly.

'I am Glamir, son of Raefli, Law-speaker of Lodose.'

'Oh, yes, Glamir, yes, indeed,' said Bjarki. *The son of Raefli,* he thought. *One of the last ruler's by-blows, risen to prominence. A law-speaker, a man of consequence.*

'I am honoured to make your acquaintance, law-speaker,' Bjarki added. 'How may I be of service? A knotty matter of law that you wish to discuss with your king?'

'No, not law – but custom. The custom in Vastergotland is that once every year in spring the king must accept a challenge to combat with any man who issues one.'

Bjarki sat up even straighter. He was completely awake now.

'Do you now issue such a challenge?'

'I do. I, Glamir Raeflisson, challenge you, Bjarki Bloodhand, to combat in the wrestling square yonder before the whole of Lodose. The victor shall be the man who pins the other to the earth, or forces him to submit to the better fighter. You accept?'

Bjarki studied the man carefully. He was unremarkable to look at, medium height, stocky, well muscled but not the strongest-looking man Bjarki had ever seen.

'You want to fight me?'

'I do. I would wrestle with you, king. No weapons. Only the natural strength we were born with. I am trusting to your honour that you will not invoke the spirit of the Bear in our friendly bout. Fight me as a plain, ordinary man, not as a Fire Born one.'

Valtyr leaned in and whispered: 'His reputation is as a superb wrestler. He has triumphed in the square over every opponent. You must *not* fight him. You will lose.'

'Do you dare to accept my challenge, lord king?' said Glamir.

'I accept. But, first, there is another matter that I must address.' Bjarki reached into the sack beside his feet and pulled out a fine silver and amber cloak-brooch.

'Take this gift, Glamir Raeflisson, as a prize for your prowess, and to mark your many victories today. It may be that I am in no mood to reward you after our match.'

Chapter Twelve

The king's favour

Sigurd Hring received Tor in the king's hall in Uppsala. He was playing yet another game of *tafl* but this time with her own Jarl Starki. Both men watched her as she entered the hall, shook off her rain-soaked, leather-lined cloak, hung it on a peg and strode over to the table.

'The Danish king agrees,' she said, with no preamble. 'First of Heyannir. The field they nominate is on the Sodermanland and Ostergotland border, at Norrkoping.'

'I know it,' said Sigurd. 'They make the best salt-cured salmon there.'

'Did they give you any difficulties?' asked Jarl Starki.

'No. My brother was there to watch over me.'

'The Fire Born? He was with Siegfried? Did you tell him there was a place of greater honour for him with me, at *my* side?' asked Sigurd Hring.

'I told him. He said no. Siegfried has made him the King of Vastergotland. I doubt you can match that. He will fight with Siegfried.' Tor strove to keep calm.

'Then he will die,' said Sigurd Hring. He moved a piece on the *tafl* board. 'I have you now, Starki. You – much like that fool Bjarki Bloodhand – are a dead man.'

Tor wandered away towards the ale butts and drew herself a foaming mug. She glanced around the hall and saw the *nithing* Rorik Hafnarsson laughing with a group of the king's newly recruited heroes. She wondered if they knew what a coward he was. Perhaps she should tell them. No, another time. She was bone-tired from the three-day sea journey from Viby and wanted very much to sleep for a day and a night.

However, before she indulged that pleasure, she thought she would first go and see Inge and check that her girl was happy and healthy and had not done anything outstandingly foolish during her week-long absence. She was not worried, Sambor was there to protect her. But she just hoped Inge had not fallen pregnant. If she knew anything about the behaviour of young men, she knew that they were seldom cautious in matters of love. She doubted that Inge's handsome new swain was any different.

Inge was not pregnant, so far as Tor could tell. But she *was* in a bad condition.

The girl was pink-eyed from weeping and seemed to have lost weight even in the seven days Tor had been gone. She had taken to her bed in the stuffy little guest hut that she and Sambor shared and she had scarcely left it for several days in a row.

'Princess. Sick,' said Sambor, when Tor arrived that evening with some fresh baked bread and hot bean soup for them all to share. 'Bed. Three. Days.'

Tor sent Sambor out of the hut. Then got down beside the bed and gently washed Inge's face with a cloth and warm water, wiping away crusted snot and sleep-sand from her eyes, but that small act of tenderness made the girl burst out in a fresh gale of tears. Tor cradled the girl and fed her spoonfuls of hot soup, and sops of barley bread dunked in a cup of ale. Tor found she was humming a Svear lullaby that her own mother had sung to her. Eventually, after a little care, Inge composed herself.

'Do you want to tell me about it?' Tor asked.

Inge shook her head. 'No, no, I can't tell *you*…'

'What did he do?' Tor asked. 'Did he hurt you?'

Inge looked up at her with an almost panicked expression. 'No, not injured hurt.'

'Tell me what happened.'

'Promise me, Tor, that you will not harm him. Promise me!'

'I don't think I can do that, my girl.' Tor could feel a knot of anger in the pit of her belly. She would drown that bastard in his own blood for making poor Inge cry.

Inge started weeping again. 'You'll kill him. I know it. I don't want him dead.'

'Just tell me.'

'Promise you will not hurt him.'

With a sigh, Tor gave her oath. After a while, Inge stopped crying and blew her nose. 'He meant to be nice, I truly think he meant to be nice to me. But he said...'

A fresh squall of sobbing. Tor stroked Inge's fine blonde hair.

'He said... He said I was the best-looking girl he had had this year.'

For a long moment, Tor was confused, unsure how to react.

'And it's not even full summer yet. He told me that I was prettiest of them *all*.'

'All?'

'I asked around and folk said he has a new girl every week. Sometimes two in a week. And I thought I was special to him. I thought he loved me. Only me...'

Tor rocked the girl until she fell asleep. She would keep her word to Inge. She would not go after Joralf, although, as all gods knew, that lad needed a good hiding.

Was she going soft? First Rorik had escaped her vengeance, and now Joralf. Was she becoming old? No, she knew she was neither. She would leave Joralf in peace, for Inge's sake, for the time being – but she might do something about Rorik.

A tiny idea took root in her brain, and began to grow, reaching towards the light.

The next morning she helped Inge and Sambor pack up their things and, with an escort of six *hird* spearmen, she sent them north back to Bearstead. Inge could nurse her broken heart by her own hearth, surrounded by friends. She also told Inge to be sure to take a big pot of honey out to the woods and leave it somewhere for Garm to find.

Then she went to confer with Gudrik in the *hird*'s allotted barracks. The competent *Merkismathr* had smoothly taken over the training of her jarl's *hird*, and after talking with Gudrik for a good while, she spoke briefly with one of her *hird* spearmen, a fellow who originally hailed from Vendel, a village to the north of Uppsala. Then, finally, she went back to the king's hall to wait upon Jarl Starki.

'Where have you been today, *Stallar*?' said Starki, crossly. He was sitting in a nook at the side of the hall while a man-servant trimmed his blond beard with shears.

Tor debated telling him of Inge's love troubles and decided against.

'Busy,' she said.

Starki chewed his lip but said no more. The barber finished his work and bowed. 'Your hair, lord, is becoming overlong. Shall I trim it for you – just round the neck?'

'Not now. Go away, you idiot. I seek counsel from my long-absent *Stallar*.'

'What have I missed?' Tor asked. It was clear that Starki was in a foul mood.

Starki glared at her silently for a while. Tor waited, looking right back at him.

'Before I made my oath to Sigurd Hring, he promised me that I would be made his *Armathr*, yes. I was to speak with the king's voice. You remember, Tor, yes?'

'And he did make you his *Armathr*. Has he now removed you from your post?'

'Oh no, nothing so straightforward. If he removed me from that position of honour, I would be entitled to take my *hird* and go home to Gavle. My oath to him would then be void. He would have broken the agreement between us. No, *I wish* he had dismissed me. What he did was much, much worse. So much more humiliating.'

'Tell me.'

'He has appointed two other warriors as *Armathir* alongside me. There are now three of us jostling to be his right-hand men;

133

three of us who, apparently, all speak with the voice of the king in his absence. And who can say if he will stop there. Why not make every petty lord and minor *hersir* an *Armathr*; why not every shit-brained, sheep-fucking spearman?'

'Who are the other two?' said Tor.

Jarl Starki was still spitting with fury. 'What?'

'Who are the other two men Sigurd has appointed as his *Armathir*?'

'Jarl Ottar of Vastmanland and Hagnor the Fatbellied.'

Tor nodded. 'Makes sense. Ottar has six hundred spearmen. That makes him a powerful ally. He is a worthy *Armathr*. And Hagnor is emerging as the leader of all the sell-sword heroes. He is certainly the one among them with the finest reputation.'

'Hagnor was a hunted outlaw only two months ago. A reaver, a drunken pillager and child-slaughterer... You think that fat viking makes a better *Armathr* than me?'

Starki's voice had risen, and Tor looked around to see if anyone was in earshot.

'Get a hold of yourself. Sigurd Hring has made his choice. Whining won't help.'

'You serve *me*, you ungrateful bitch – you are supposed to be on my side!'

'I *am* on your side, lord. My counsel is that you curb your temper. Calm down.'

Starki stared at her. He took two deep breaths. 'And this counsel is coming from the famous hot-head Torfinna Hildarsdottir!'

She allowed him a chuckle at his joke.

'You are still *Armathr* – you are still in a position of high honour,' she said. 'And there is nothing you can do about this change. You cannot break your oath to the king and quit Uppsala; you must stay here, keep your mouth shut, work hard and try to gain the king's favour. We go into battle in just over two months – there is plenty of time for things to improve. Jarl Ottar is an arrogant fool. And Hagnor the Fatbellied is no more than a greedy little thief. Who will prove himself greatest *Armathr* of the three of you? You will, lord. And everyone will see that this is so.'

'I remember now why I took you into my service,' said Jarl Starki, smiling wryly.

'I've a suggestion, too, as to how you might win greater favour from the king.'

'Oh yes?'

'After all the feasting and drinking at the *Disablot*, and at the old king's funeral and the new king's coronation, most of our warriors are badly in need of some hard exercise. I suggest that you propose a royal hunt – with hundreds of men driving wild game towards the king. There will be some good sport, a great slaughter – and we can all feast mightily afterwards on the day's bag. I am told by one who knows that the old woods west of Vendel are thick with game just now.'

'A royal hunt, yes! We have been idle too long. Sitting around playing *tafl* and scheming and drinking all night. You are right, my excellent *Stallar*, this may win back the king's favour. He has spoken to me often about his love of the chase.'

—

The rain had ceased but the bed of pine needles under Tor's feet were spongy to her tread. She stopped walking and listened hard. She could hear the sound of barked orders, in a familiar, royal voice. She smiled grimly to herself, and stepped under the canopy of a spruce tree, leaning her heavy hunting spear against its trunk. She peered around the gnarled bark, looking through the dense trees, and caught a glimpse of a slim figure in a green huntsman's cloak, with a thatch of fair hair, flitting between the trees, moving right to left across her field of vision. He vanished into the dark forest.

Tor took the long, waxed linen package off her back and crouching in the pine-needle litter, she began to unroll it. Inside was a short bow, two strings and two arrows. Two should be enough, she thought; if she missed with the first shaft, she might have a shot with a second, but no more after that. Her quarry would be alerted and already running for its life. If she could not achieve her goal with two arrows, she would have failed. And, if she merely wounded the quarry with one of the arrows, she could not close and finish the task with her spear or seax. An accidentally lethal arrow out in the field could be explained away; an accidental throat-slitting could not.

The king's party were away somewhere to her left in a small clearing. Sigurd Hring and his three *Armathir*, including Jarl Starki, as well as some of the heroes, had picked the place. The servants had set up tables of food while the hunters chose their stands, and boasted about how many creatures would fall that day to their spears.

Several miles away to the west, in the dense pine-wood forest, three hundred warriors in a line half a mile long were thrashing the tangled undergrowth with their spear shafts moving the game inexorably towards the excited royal hunting party. They had been beating the forest since before dawn, and it was now nearly noon. In a little while, there would be a thunder of hooves and a wall of frightened, tumbling beasts would erupt out of the trees, surging towards the king and his favoured oath-men – fallow, red and roe deer, mainly, perhaps a stately elk the size of a horse, as well as a few wild boars, the most dangerous game of all, which could rip a man with his tusks from knee to neck in an instant, and which consequently was the beast of the hunt that would bring most honour to the man who managed to slay it.

There would be other creatures as well in the throng: wolves, foxes and hares trying to slip through; iridescent-breasted caper-caillie and black grouse hurtling low through the air in a clatter of feathers. These game birds were customarily taken with arrows, shot on the wing – a most impressive feat. It was that difficult practice that gave Tor a reason to carry her bow; as well as the dozens of other bow-carrying hunters out on the field this day who might conceivably have loosed a man-killing shaft.

Her bow strung, one arrow knocked to the string, the other stuck in her belt, Tor advanced cautiously through the trees towards the last spot in which she had seen Rorik Hafnarsson. As she stalked her quarry, she recalled the sight of her friend Ulli, the steward of Bearstead, as she had last encountered him. He had been several weeks dead, decomposing and dangling by his neck from a pine bough outside the Bearstead gate. This had been Rorik's handiwork. Or one of his men. It made no difference.

'Ulli,' she whispered as she took another step forwards. 'Vengeance is nigh, old friend. Prepare to greet your murderer in the afterlife. And give him my salutations.'

It had not been difficult to detach Rorik from the king's party. He was the Royal Huntsman and therefore responsible for providing the day's sport. Tor had merely mentioned to the new *Armathr*, Hagnor the Fatbellied, that the line of warrior-beaters were taking an inordinately long time to drive the prey onto their spears, and that their lavish midday feast would be long delayed as a result, to make the fat man act.

Hagnor had called out some teasing comment to the king, suggesting that his lazy men were all asleep in the forest rather than eagerly pursuing the game, and Sigurd Hring had dispatched Rorik Hafnarsson at once to see what was going on and to chivvy his line of troops to greater speed.

When Rorik had set out, Tor muttered something to Jarl Starki about women's troubles and had slunk away in the thick woods, circling around after she was out of sight of the party to follow Rorik's trail. The Royal Huntsman, despite his title, was not a man at home in the woods. Rorik stumbled and tripped over roots, bawling loudly to attract the attention of the line of warriors, then often heading in the wrong direction. Tor feared that his antics would scare all the game in several directions. By slaughtering the clod, Tor thought, she might well be ensuring the success of the hunt.

She had him in sight now. He was moving south-east, back towards the party, but still a few hundred paces out and, she was sure, invisible to the king and his hunters.

Now was the time to act. Rorik stood in a patch of sunshine, fifty feet away, looking this way and that like a lost lamb seeking its mother. He scratched his fair head. Tor drew back the string on her bow, all the way to the ear, she sighted on the centre of his chest – a heart shot – instantly lethal, but if she missed she would pierce his lungs, liver or his belly, and give him a wound that would be fatal in due course.

Tor took in a deep breath, half released it. Now was the time. And she...

'Wolf-sister?' said a voice behind her.

Tor whirled round, loosing the string as she did so. The shaft thwacked into a thick patch of brambles a dozen feet away. Tor looked into the bearded face of Fidor the Rekkr, and beyond him to Fodor his twin brother. Both men were dressed in the skins of wolves, as befitted their status as Fire Born men inhabited by a Wolf *gandr*.

Tor had completely forgotten about the party from Ostergotland, which had been invited north to join in the festivities. It was another doomed attempt by Sigurd Hring to persuade Helgi the Wulfing to stand with him in the great battle against the Danes.

'What quarry, Wolf-sister?' asked Fidor. He looked puzzled. Tor looked back at the now empty patch of sunlight where Rorik had been standing only a moment ago.

'I thought I saw a fallow deer,' she said. 'There by the alder bush.'

'Neither of us saw any creature but that man, the king's huntsman,' said Fodor.

The twins, Tor remembered, had some eerie spirit-link that allowed one to speak for both. Indeed, she knew this pair of warriors shared a single *gandr* between them.

'He must have frightened the deer away,' said Tor, knowing this made no sense. She quickly followed up with: 'Why call me Wolf-sister? I am no Fire Born.'

'You endured the Fyr Skola, and ran through the Fyr Pit,' said Fidor. 'You have undergone Voyaging – although the Wolf did not come. You share the blood of Bjarki Bloodhand, a fellow Fire Born. We have fought beside you. You have our respect.'

'You honour me,' Tor replied. These two warriors were unnerving, but they were fearsome in battle when the *gandr* came to them. Their respect was indeed an honour.

'Tell us, then, Wolf-sister,' said Fodor. 'Is it true that the Blood-hand will stand against Sigurd Hring on the great day of battle?'

Tor's shoulders sagged. She had been trying very hard not to think about this.

'My brother feels that his oath to King Siegfried supersedes all other claims on his loyalty. He will indeed fight shoulder to shoulder with the Danes at Norrkoping.'

'This is very sad,' said Fidor. 'We three are the only living Fire Born in the Middle-Realm. We know of no others. The Fyr Skola is in the hands of Christians and will never produce another Rekkr. Helgi the Wulfing will *not* support the Svear – but Sigurd Hring will win his fight nonetheless, we have seen it. Your brother will fall. And there will be one less Rekkr in the world when the ravens feast on the harvest.'

Tor shrugged as if unconcerned. But she could feel despair welling up inside her.

'Have you reasoned with him, Wolf-sister?' said Fodor.

'I've argued. I've pleaded. I've begged him not to fight. But he will not relent.'

'Then Bjarki Bloodhand shall meet his doom that day,' the Rekkr said.

Chapter Thirteen

A man's true quality

Bjarki stripped off his shirt, handed it to Valtyr, and then scooped up a handful of sun-warm pig's lard from the tub beside the wrestling area and began rubbing the grease into his much battered, dimpled, burnt and scarred naked flesh.

Word of the bout had spread fast and folk were flocking towards the square.

His opponent, Glamir Raeflisson, on the far side of the roped-off square, had similarly disrobed and was rubbing his own white torso with half-melted pork fat. The pale man was a good deal smaller than Bjarki and with a completely hairless body. But that body had clearly been formed by hard labour and harder knocks. Bjarki reminded himself that this man, this wrestler, had vanquished all his opponents in his matches that day. Yet he looked so calm and rested.

A Judge of Games in sombre black stepped over the rope that marked the side of the wrestling square and walked into the middle of the twelve foot by twelve foot space, holding up his ash wand of office. Bjarki had seen several of these figures marshalling the contests that day. This judge was an older man, a Vastergotlander of middle years, someone whose name Bjarki did not know but suspected he should.

'Today's final wrestling bout is one of consequence,' the Judge of Games said, loudly, so that all those gathered around the square might hear. 'Bjarki Bloodhand, who claims to be heir to great Angantyr, and the King of the Goths reborn, and therefore rightful King of Vastergotland, has consented to try his skill in combat, with empty hand and open heart, against our own Glamir Raeflisson, Law-speaker of Lodose.'

Bjarki hoped there might be cheers then. He heard nothing but a surly silence.

'This will be a battle without prize or penalty – save for the honour and renown of the two participants. The rules of the match are as follows: no weapons to be used *at all*, no hidden blades, no rocks, no dust gathered up from the dry earth. There is to be no gouging of eyes and no biting. This will be a contest of blows, holds and throws. Neither combatant may use witch-craft or any kind of *seithr* or spiritual help from any other realm *whatsoever*.'

The Judge of Games looked sternly at the Rekkr, who grinned at him in return.

The feast-day crowds were now thickening on all four sides of the roped-off enclosure. Many hundreds of people, contestants in previous competitions, warriors, townsfolk, were drifting forwards to watch. Bjarki spotted Captain Mogils and his *Knattleikr* team around him. Their match would take place after this bout.

Bjarki wondered if he would be in a fit state to watch it.

'There will be three rounds,' said the Judge of Games, 'each round to be ended only when one man is pinned to the ground by both his shoulders for my slow count of three; or if a man strikes the earth three times in surrender. Or if he dies, or is rendered unconscious. If one contestant wins two rounds in succession, he shall be declared victor of the match; if all three rounds are fought, the man with the most rounds won is the victor. Do you both fully understand and accept these rules?'

Glamir half-nodded, the very merest inclination of the head.

'No,' said Bjarki.

'You do not understand the rules, highness?' said the Judge of Games.

'Oh, I understand them. I do not *accept* them.'

'You wish to refuse the challenge?' This was from Glamir on the far side of the square, delivered with an edge of contempt in his tone. Jeers came from the crowd.

'No, my objection is to the lack of a prize. We fight for honour and renown, yes, that is true, but I have a great deal of honour and renown to lose today. Far more, I would say, than you, Glamir. I am a king, by my blood and by lawful decree of your overlord King Siegfried of the Dane-Mark. But I'm also Fire Born, a Rekkr beloved of Odin. Who are you?'

Bjarki could see two little spots of high colour appear in Glamir's pale cheeks.

'I am the Law-speaker of Lodose and the son of Raefli, lord of Lodose...'

'And your mother? Was she Lord Raefli's lady wife?'

Glamir glared at him. 'My mother was Hilda, a fisher-wife of Gotaborg.'

'I do not seek to shame you,' said Bjarki. 'Nor to disparage your lineage. But I risk a greater humiliation than you, should I lose this match. Moreover, I'm forbidden by your rules from using my *gandr*-given power as a Fire Born to defeat you. I am no wrestler, I make no claim to be one, I have fought in your open-hand manner, without weapons, perhaps twice before in my life. If I am to risk my honour in this bout, at the very least, I demand a suitable prize – if I am, by Odin's whim, granted victory.'

'I am a poor man,' said Glamir. 'I have no silver to offer you as a prize.'

'I do not seek wealth. I have silver. I seek something of greater value – loyalty.'

'What do you mean?'

'If I am the victor, you, Glamir Raeflisson, will kneel before my throne and kiss the sword. You will swear to be my man for the remainder of your life. You agree?'

'And if I am the victor?'

'You say you are a poor man. I shall change that. If you are victorious, I shall give you the weight of a man's head in good Frankish silver coins.'

Bjarki could see Glamir swallow hard at his words. There was a gleam in his pale blue eyes, too. 'I agree,' the Lodose wrestler said. Then loudly, 'Let us begin!'

There was a huge cheer from the crowds at his words and the black-clad judge held up his ash wand for silence. It took a good long time for the noise to die away.

'The first round begins… now!' the judge said, and swept the wand down.

Bjarki and Glamir circled each other inside the square, both men moving sideways like crabs and watching their opponents intently. Bjarki knew this fellow was a much better open-hand fighter than he, and he was genuinely curious to see how his attack would unfold.

When it came it was deceptively simple. Glamir came forwards in a sinuous glide and seized Bjarki's right arm with both of his hands, gripping his forearm and upper arm, pulling the bigger man forwards, off his balance. Bjarki swiped at him with his left hand, a wild slap that Glamir easily ducked, and instinctively pulled his body back, resisting the tug of the Vastergotland man. In a trice, Glamir stopped pulling, gave him a shove backwards instead, and Bjarki went down like a felled oak and landed flat on his back in the dust, with all the breath in his lungs coming out in one loud whoosh.

Glamir leapt on top of Bjarki, his left hand, right forearm and full weight pinning the Rekkr to the earth. Bjarki, gasping, heard the judge sing out, 'One… and Two…'

Now he knew he was in a proper fight. Bjarki heaved up, his whole body convulsing, and he lifted his right shoulder off the ground. Glamir's grip on his greased shoulder slipped and Bjarki was able to struggle to his knees. Only to receive a full-bodied punch in the face from Glamir's right fist that immediately slammed him back down in the dust.

Glamir tried once more to cover his body with his own; but Bjarki dealt him a tremendous slap to the right ear, knocking him off and away. Then the Rekkr moved away, scrabbling up to his knees, coming slowly upright. Bjarki was dazed, his nose dripping blood. He heard a dark voice inside his heart say: 'Get him, man-child, kill him – *use me, use my Bear strength to rip him limb from limb!*'

Bjarki ignored the voice. He was on his feet now, but swaying a little, and Glamir was coming in again, low and smooth, both his fists clenched. Bjarki let him come right in then palmed the man off, a mighty open-handed shove to the centre of his chest, and as the Vastergotlander staggered backwards, Bjarki followed him fast and went in low, grasping at his knees, ducking a wild punch from Glamir that hissed through his long hair.

He threw himself forwards again, keeping low, and slapped at his opponent's left ankle. Bjarki's long arms and lunging reach paid off – he hit his mark and Glamir's left leg flew up in the air and the law-speaker thudded down in the dust. Then Bjarki immediately sprawled on top of him, grabbing at his greased shoulders, trying to pin the man to the ground. But Glamir squirmed, wriggled, got two good grips on the bigger man and, to Bjarki's astonishment, flipped his massive body over onto his back. Glamir somehow now had his powerful right leg across Bjarki's upper chest and neck, and was pressing down hard.

Bjarki heaved once, pushing down the earth with both palms, but Glamir kicked out and got his second leg under Bjarki's rising head and, with both muscular legs now wrapped around Bjarki's neck, he began to squeeze. Bjarki could feel his neck constricting, crushed between the man's iron thighs. He elbowed the fellow's torso, felt the short vicious blow land well, and heard the breath expelled from Glamir's lungs. But his vision was flashing red and black and there was no let-up in the terrible squeezing pressure around his throat.

The darkness was growing at the edge of his sight. And Bjarki slapped his palm against the earth, once, twice, three times. Immediately, the killing pressure around his neck ceased. He hauled in one massive breath, another and began to cough madly.

'First round to Glamir Raeflisson!' The Judge of Games's words seemed to come to him from a very distant land.

Bjarki sat up, blinking. He saw Valtyr crouching in front of him with a wet rag, mopping at his bruised face. The old man looked very worried. 'This is not red war, Bjarki,' he said. 'Remember: this is merely a sporting contest. A game. He is clearly the better man; the better wrestler. You cannot beat him. Tell Judge Hakkon you concede the bout, pay the victor his coin with grace and let us stop all this nonsense.'

'I will not,' said Bjarki.

–

The temptation to summon Mochta from her lair deep in his heart was very strong. But he knew he would feel that he had cheated if he did so. As he circled Glamir for the second round, crab-walking again, he could feel his own natural anger simmering hot through his veins. This Lodose fellow was quick, ruthless and skilled indeed. But Bjarki knew that he was the far stronger man. How then could he use that superior strength to his best advantage?

Glamir came gliding in, crouched low, his big grappling hands reaching out. Bjarki pretended to move away to his right, then pivoted on his heel, closed and smashed his left fist into Glamir's belly. The pale man grunted, a great huff of air, and recoiled, neatly stepping back out of his reach. Bjarki rushed in, reaching out to grab his shoulder and waist. He jerked Glamir towards him, half-turned, stuck his hip into his opponent's belly and pulled.

The manoeuvre seemed to be working, Glamir's greased belly slid over his hip, Bjarki's opponent was unbalanced, leg flailing. Then suddenly it was *not* working.

Glamir grounded his leg, twisted round and Bjarki found himself lifted off his feet and crashing down to earth again. He bounced and rolled, just as Glamir launched himself at his prone body. Bjarki rolled clear, Glamir missed and hit the earth, landing on both his elbows, and Bjarki rolled back, smothering the smaller man with his greater bulk. He got both hands on Glamir's shoulders, forcing them down. And the Vastergotland man twitched his head sideways and butted Bjarki in the right eyebrow, splitting the skin. The Rekkr recoiled. And Glamir was on top of him again, forearm on one shoulder, his broad chest pressing the other down. Bjarki roared and heaved up and, this time, managed to dislodge the Vastergotlander. He reared up and smashed his forearm hard into Glamir's chin, rocking his head back.

Bjarki grabbed him but his opponent struggled free, slipping from his double grasp. So Bjarki hit him again with his forearm, an even more powerful blow. Glamir's eyes rolled back in his skull. Bjarki flipped the man onto his back, hauled himself over Glamir's chest, pressing down hard on both his opponent's shoulders, using his full weight, and heard to his relief the Judge of Games counting slowly out 'One... and two... and three!'

–

One victory each. One more bout to decide. Both men were exhausted, panting. Blood was still dripping down the side of Bjarki's face, despite Valtyr's ministrations with a damp rag and a dollop of pig's fat. They faced each other for the final round. Glamir grinned at him from ten feet away, showing his teeth, his own once-pale face now very red and swollen.

'You've only wrestled twice before, eh, king? I would never believe it.'

Bjarki was too tired to reply.

The crowd chanted: 'Gla... mir, Gla... mir, Gla... mir...'

A lone voice in the throng, Mogils's perhaps, shouted: 'Long live the king!'

The fighters circled briefly then threw themselves at each other. Each seized the other, their muscles straining, chests pressed together, arms wrapped. Bjarki could hear the man panting hot and calling on Thor in his left ear. He shifted his own grip, joined his own arms behind the other man's back and squeezed the champion as tightly as he could.

He heard a rib creak and the breath hiss from his opponent's gummy lips. The hug of a bear – but not with the impossible power of a *berserkr*. He was using his superior strength. Yes, this was the only way to victory. Bjarki squeezed again, even harder than before. He straightened his broad, muscular back, lifting Glamir's heavy frame clean off the ground. The man's legs were dangling uselessly, but he was now beating his skull sideways against Bjarki's, in increasingly weaker head butts. Bjarki was bearing the man's whole weight in his arms and crushing his chest in a lethal grip, inching it tighter. He relaxed a fraction, adjusting his grip. One more good heave and even this brave fellow must call out in surrender.

But as Bjarki strove for a new, tighter grip, Glamir's feet kissed the earth, just briefly, and he back-heeled at once, kicking out the rear of Bjarki's right knee.

The blow struck home and their combined weights collapsed Bjarki's knee. He sagged and almost fell. But just managed to recover. Glamir had his feet on firm earth now. He slipped a foot between Bjarki's boots, his deft hands grasping and hauling at Bjarki's limbs and – *whump!* – the bigger man was savagely hurled to the ground. Bjarki landed flat on his back; winded once more. Glamir immediately thumped down, landing with one bony knee on Bjarki's exposed belly. A bout-finishing blow as potent as any mule's kick.

Bjarki's body convulsed upwards. And his jaw met Glamir's swinging right fist, a crunching blow that knocked the king back, his skull thumping hard on the ground.

Even in his dazed state, Bjarki could feel a huge weight on his shoulders, and his mind recorded the judge saying 'One... and two...' before everything went dark.

–

Bjarki was unconscious all through the *Knattleikr* match that followed his wrestling bout. But Valtyr was jubilant at Captain Mogils's victory over the Vastergotlanders. He proudly showed the still-confused king the purse of silver he had won from the *Knattleikr* match and teasingly offered to lend it to Bjarki so that he might pay his debt to Glamir. Bjarki only came to himself fully that evening, when he found he was sitting in his throne at the end of the hall. He had a splitting headache, and much of his body ached and throbbed as if he'd been savagely beaten. Which, indeed, he had.

Bjarki looked round the hall. Above him, all the thatch had been replaced, which was just as well since he could hear the patter of rain on the new wooden tiles. The fire pit stretched out ahead of him and beyond it was a long table, where his closest men sat. To the rear of the hall were several tables and benches for the lesser folk.

Food was being served, a roasted wild boar as well as some other large platters, the contents of which Bjarki could not make out clearly in the gloom. When a full plate was brought up to him, he waved it away, and asked the servant to refill the ale in his horn. In truth, he wanted his bed, more than anything else. But he knew it was his duty to oversee the Feast of Idun as its munificent host, and Valtyr had also said that he should try not to go to sleep too soon – something to do with a very common danger that followed on from a man being rendered unconscious.

Valtyr reappeared at his side, with a mug containing some foul-smelling black liquor. 'Drink all this down, for the pain, highness!' And for once the old man did not sound as if he were mocking Bjarki's title. 'Oh, and Glamir wishes to speak to you.'

'He wants his prize money,' mumbled Bjarki. He beckoned Kynwulf, who was standing guard two paces away. 'Get one of the *Felaki* to fetch out about ten pounds of hacksilver from my coffers, will you?' The War Chief grunted and slipped away.

'Tell Glamir I will see him now, Valtyr. He has more than earned his prize.'

A few moments later, Glamir appeared at the end of the hall and began to approach the throne. His face was badly bruised, Bjarki could see, and his features swollen almost out of all recognition. But his eyes glittered and he had clearly bathed and changed into his best clothes. He approached the throne and made a low bow.

'Law-speaker,' said Bjarki. 'I congratulate you on your victory in the square today. It was an honour to meet a man of your strength and skill in combat – if a painful one. I acknowledge you bested me and am ready to reward you as promised.'

He turned and looked over his shoulder for Kynwulf.

'Highness,' said Glamir, 'I am here this night, not only to claim the fortune in silver that you promised, but for another reason, too. I may say that it has been an honour for me, as well, to try my strength against yours. And while I did indeed prove the victor, I salute you as a worthy opponent, and a man who deals honestly and fairly with his fellow men. You did not need to fight me. You might have refused. Yet you accepted, knowing my superior skills. And you might easily have used your Fire Born strength to destroy me – yet you chose not to. You showed me your true quality this day, highness. I am here this night to show you mine.'

To Bjarki's surprise, Glamir Raeflisson, moving very stiffly, knelt down in front of his throne and bowed his balding head.

'Draw your sword, my king,' he said. 'I would swear my loyal oath to you.'

As Bjarki rose to his feet – also stiffly – and drew his sword from his scabbard, he heard the warriors in the hall push back the benches and bellow their acclamation.

'Long live the king! Long live the king! Long live Bjarki Bloodhand, rightful King of Vastergotland!'

Chapter Fourteen

The jarl's whore

Tor searched the whole of Uppsala, from the Grove of Skelfir, still adorned with the dangling decomposing bodies of the *blot* sacrifice, to the several barracks of the royal army, to the store huts and sheds near the three Royal Mounds, even to the extensive latrines of the king's hall – and found no sign of Rorik Hafnarsson at all.

No one in the king's household seemed to know where the Royal Huntsman was; but one seemingly half-witted kitchen maid admitted that the day before she had made up a bundle of twice-baked bread, cheese and radishes for him, and a large sack of ale, as if he was preparing for a long journey on horseback. That was all the information Tor could garner. Rorik had vanished from the face of the Middle-Realm.

Tor's own duties soon overtook her and put an end to her futile search and her speculations. Rorik was beyond her reach. For now. As far as she knew, he had not seen her stalking him in the forest during the royal hunt, and he could have no idea how close he had come to death. She decided to let things settle for a while. There might be more opportunities to take her revenge on Rorik during the preliminaries to the battle at Norrkoping – or even during the battle itself. Plenty of arrows would fly, hundreds would die. Who then would mark the loss of one fallen *nithing* huntsman?

She took Jarl Starki's *hird* in hand, making them practise the basic manoeuvres of any army in the pastures outside the Uppsala compound again and again and again, until the two hundred Svear warriors moved like one vast being with a single mind. One of Tor's favourite exercises was to simulate an unexpected attack. The members of the *hird* might be widely scattered about the field engaged in spear drills, or sword duels, and then Tor – or sometimes her second-in-command Gudrik – would scream out '*Skjald-borg*!' at an inappropriate moment, and Tor would count slowly under her breath to see how long it took her scattered troops to coalesce into a tight, triple-ranked shield wall along an invisible line she indicated on the turf.

After three weeks of this, the *hird* could form a formidable, spear-bristling wall in less than ten heartbeats. Which was good enough, Tor reckoned. The last man to join the shield wall was always sent off with jeers on a five-mile run round Uppsala.

Tor would then walk along the front of the forty-yard-long *skjald-borg* and kick savagely at a few of the faces of the shields, to see that the formation was tightly knit.

At sundown, she would join Jarl Starki in the king's hall for a proper meal. But her lord was often rather poor company. Any favour the jarl had accrued from the success of the royal hunt had faded. On that day in the woods outside Vendel, while Tor had been stalking Rorik, the new *Armathr*, Hagnor the Fatbellied, had skewered a magnificent wild boar but, rather than kill it himself, he had invited the king to have the honour of dispatching the wounded creature. The king had been more than delighted to share in Hagnor's glory and the two men now were as close as brothers.

This left jarls Ottar and Starki, the two other *Armathir*, eyeing each other suspiciously, both relegated to the far ends of the king's table. Neither man trusted the other an inch after the manoeuvrings before Sigurd Hring's ascension to the throne.

Tor was not interested in the power wrangling of the Uppsala court; nor did she have any fresh wisdom to impart to Jarl Starki. She usually sat in stony silence with him and consumed her meat and drink, then as soon as it was polite, she went off to her bed in Inge's hut. Her lord had no taste either, it seemed, for the nightly carousing of the king and Hagnor and whichever of the heroes joined them in their raucous after-supper ale-drinking. One night, a month after the royal hunt, after Jarl Starki had departed for his own guest hall, Tor was about to rise, nod to the king and slip away, when Hagnor the Fatbellied called down the table: 'Hey, *Stallar*, they say you're a dauntless warrior, and a real fireball, so why do you never drink with the rest of us?'

Tor, half-risen from her stool, sat down again. 'What does drinking till you lose all reason accomplish, Hagnor? I like to keep a clear head for my duties to my lord.'

'Duties to your lord, eh?' leered a hero called Krok, from the Frank-conquered lands of Frisia. 'At this hour of the night, what duties might those be, eh, pretty one?'

Tor stood up. 'If you are calling me the jarl's whore, why not simply say so?'

Krok chuckled uncertainly. He looked around for support from the other heroes.

'*Is* that what you're saying, you limp-dicked, maggotty arse-boil?' said Tor.

Krok scowled at her. 'What did you call me?'

The king intervened. 'That is enough! I will have no quarrelling among my best warriors – you should all be saving your strength to fight the Danish enemy.'

But Krok was on his feet now, glaring at Tor down the table, grinding his teeth.

'Want to settle this, big man?' said Tor. 'Here, now, sword and seax – in front of your friends? *I'm* ready to go, you oily goat-fucker. Though I doubt *you're* man enough.'

'No!' Sigurd Hring's voice boomed out like thunder. 'You shall not fight. I forbid it. I will not have bloodshed. You – Krok. Sit down, now, or by all the gods I shall make you. And you, Torfinna Hildarsdottir – go to your quarters this instant!'

Tor shrugged and made to leave, and halfway across the hall, as she glanced back at the long table, she saw a furious Krok being poured more mead by the king. And Hagnor watching her as she walked away. He caught her eye – and lifted his pudgy hands to make a series of silent motions as if he were clapping them in praise.

–

Hagnor the Fatbellied came to seek Tor out the next day, when she was training the *hird* to make an attacking formation known as the Boar's Snout. Two warriors formed the flat face of the Snout – traditionally the best and bravest, but also those with the best armour and shields – three men came in behind them, four behind those three, and so on, and the rest of the company funnelled in behind them in a V-shape like the head of the fearsome wild pig. It was a time-honoured formation used for splitting open an enemy *skjald-borg*, like an iron wedge being forced into a log by a hammer-man.

'Tighter!' shouted Tor. 'You're not a crowd of giggling market-girls, you're the head of a fierce boar thrusting his way through a thorn hedge. Close up, milk-sops.'

She saw Hagnor watching the show and called a halt to the lesson.

'Drink and rest time,' she commanded. 'You, Hafsteinn, will heave your fat arse once round the Royal Mounds and back before I finish my horn of ale. Go on!'

'I see Jarl Starki's *hird* is becoming a truly formidable fighting force,' said Hagnor courteously. 'You seem to have them well in hand. My congratulations…'

'What do you want?' said Tor.

Hagnor laughed.

'That is what I like about you, woman. No give. You won't give a man an inch.'

Tor looked up at the fat man coldly. 'Is this what you came out here to tell me?'

'No. In truth, I came out of curiosity. I wanted to see more of you. You won't drink with me in the king's hall, so I thought I'd come to see you at your labours.'

'Well, now that you have seen me, what…'

'I also come with orders from the king,' said Hagnor hastily. 'And before you say anything, Starki has endorsed these orders, too. You're to do Sigurd's bidding.'

'What orders?'

'The king orders you – um, he invites you, politely – to go down to Norrkoping to scout out the site of the battle. He wants you to look for suitable places for his jarls to make their stands. Check the wooden defences he is constructing on the ridge. Look for where to place the famous Telemark archers, for instance. He wants a full report from you in two weeks. He said only someone of your experience would be able…'

'Does the king think I'm stupid? Do you think I'm a fool, too?'

'What?'

'I know, you know, and everyone else in Svealand knows that King Sigurd has been sending scouts and teams of woodsmen down to Norrkoping for the past month and more. I heard that Erland the Snake has been thoroughly surveying the ground for weeks, at the king's command. Why would he need me to go as well? He's sending me away. That's it, isn't it?'

'Ah…' said Hagnor. 'Well, the situation is… I mean, the king feels that…'

'Spit it out, man!'

'The king feels that you are a stone in his shoe at court. You like plain speaking, Tor? Well, here's some of the plainest. Rorik Hafnarsson claims he saw you stalking him last month up in the woods near Vendel. He says you meant to shoot him dead with an arrow during the hunt. He claims you have a feud with him over some trivial matter, something about his father and some money he was owed, and are determined to murder him. The king listened to his Royal Huntsman and sent him off on a distant errand to take him out of your murderous path. He decided not to confront you at the time. But last night, that matter with Krok of Frisia… in truth, I thought you handled him well… He insulted you, as good as called you a whore, and you made him eat his own shit. Me, I salute you. The king, well... Sigurd Hring thinks you are disrupting the good fellowship of his court. He does not want to lose you as a fighter – and he is grateful for your loyal service, and for the service of your lord Jarl Starki – but, frankly, he doesn't want you slaughtering his best warriors in pointless duels.'

'So I am being punished – sent off on a fool's errand – because that big idiot Krok insulted me? You admit he called me a whore. Why am *I* being made to suffer?'

'I did not say it was fair or just. I said the king commands it, and your jarl agrees. Besides, riding down to Norrkoping and having a look around for a few days is not much of a punishment, is it? If you wish, I will ride with you part way and...'

'No. I'll go alone. Tell the king that I shall obediently depart from Uppsala tomorrow before sunrise. But now I must get back to training my *hird*.'

'Very well,' said Hagnor. 'I'll just...' But Tor had already turned her back and was striding towards her lounging troopers, ordering them all brusquely to their feet.

–

Two days later, at a little after noon, Tor halted her horse at the top of a very long escarpment and looked left over the shining bay called the Braviken, which stretched miles eastwards until it disappeared into the grey sea beyond the Svealand coast.

Where the Braviken inlet met the land it branched into two forks: the nearer, the northern one, was seemingly right below her horse's hooves. The further southern one that curled round a marshy headland was the mooring place of a dozen fishing vessels.

The escarpment, which ran east to west for a good hour's ride, for perhaps five or six miles, was called the Kolmarden and it formed the boundary of an area of dark forest that stretched behind her, north, deep into Sodermanland, Sigurd Hring's realm.

South of her position was a steep slope that had once been heavily wooded but had now been roughly cleared of its covering of trees; evidence of the work of Sigurd Hring's woodsmen, under the direction of Erland the Snake. The bare slope was now dotted here and there with the sawn-off stumps of once-mighty pines and spruces, but not all the undergrowth, briars and brambles had been fully cleared away.

The cut-down timber had been stacked in heaps near the very top of the incline, and Tor assumed that between now and the battle the trunks would be notched and stacked and arranged into proper fortifications, some sort of chest-high barricade or rampart running all along the lip of the escarpment would be appropriate. But it would hardly be necessary, she thought. If Sigurd Hring took his stand at the top of the escarpment, the steep approach to his lines would daunt even the boldest attacker.

At the bottom of the slope, a very long bowshot away, was a flood plain several miles deep and a similar distance wide, which was dotted with square fields of green barley, oats and peas, as well as a few areas of pasture and several orchards.

A fertile little patch of country, then. And this placid, sleepy landscape stretched all the way south to the village of Norrkoping, about six miles south of her position.

The settlement, of about a hundred houses, workshops, smithies and fisheries, which she could only dimly make out under a light cloud of grey cooking smoke, was a traditional marketplace, she had been told, where hunters from the dense forests of Sodermanland and farmers from the open Ostergotland plains met to exchange their various goods. It was also a place that trading ships could easily reach by sea, via the long Braviken inlet. Indeed, the trading village and its fields were situated between two great bodies of water – the glittering Braviken to the east, and to the west, a wide blue expanse of fresh water called Lake Glan.

The Kolmarden was like a great wall to the north of the village farmlands. A natural barrier. Away to her right, a wide, well-made road snaked down the incline from the north directly towards

Norrkoping. And the road that her horse was on now ran south-west and joined that northern road just before the nearest patch of green barley below the slope. Tor could also just make out a rough, muddy, deeply sunken track, half-hidden from view, which led north-west from the fields of Norrkoping, up the slope to run parallel with the coast of Lake Glan and which disappeared into the forest half a dozen miles to the west.

So, three roads of varying quality converged on the battlefield here – from the north-west, north and north-east. Three routes led to this wide patch of fertile farmland, squeezed between the two bodies of water, beneath the forbidding Kolmarden wall.

It was a perfect site for a battle, Tor recognised. She could see why Sigurd Hring had readily agreed to fight here. He could march his troops to war on roads from the west, north or east, take up an easily defensible position on the summit or lip of the escarpment, and invite his foe to attack him up the steep slope. It was also obvious – to Tor, at least – where the king must plant his banner: in the very centre of the Kolmarden ridge, about four miles west of where she now was, high above the fields of Norrkoping. Their Danish enemy would have to come at them up a very steep hill, charging over difficult half-cleared ground that would tangle their boots and break up any large formations. The enemy warriors would then have to throw themselves – individually or in small groups – at the Svear lines, at hundreds of men packed tight in the shield walls, or behind tree-trunk barricades. The Danes would be slaughtered.

However, she could also see why the Danes might have chosen this place for a battle. It was right on the doorstep of Svealand. If Sigurd Hring lost the battle, the Danes would soon be rampaging through his ancestral lands, looting and slaughtering without hindrance. And the Braviken inlet allowed the Danish king to bring troops in vast numbers right up to the battlefield using his very large fleet of warships – he could also bring up any number of reinforcements, too, should he require them.

Yet, while a frontal attack up the Kolmarden would be very hard for the Danes, they had no other realistic options if they wished to bring the battle to their foes. The Svear eastern flank, where she was now sitting on her horse, was guarded by the deep Braviken fjord, which met the sheer cliff face of the Kolmarden at the water's edge. The Danes might try to land warriors there but Svear archers, slingers and javelin men placed high above could destroy them before they got clear of their ships. And they would *still* have to fight their way up the cliffs. The Svear left flank was secure.

The Svear right flank, to the west, was warded by the blue waters of Lake Glan. It might just be possible for the Danes to work their way around this body of water, circling it sunwise, but it would require several days' hard march through thick forest and treacherous marshes. They might get lost. The left flank, she thought, was also reasonably secure. That left the centre. The Danes *had* to come up the middle, they had no other option; they had to attack their enemy on the ridge north of Norrkoping.

Sigurd Hring would have good views over the whole field from that central position. And he could easily issue his flag signals to both his right and left flanks, should he wish them to advance or retreat. The centre position would be the beating heart of the Svear line. The heroes – Hagnor the Fatbellied, Krok of Frisia, Erland the Snake, Connor the Black, Gummi and Gudfast, Egil Skull-Cleaver and all the other stupid, drunken blowhards – would probably fight right there, near the king and his elite household troops, in the very middle of the Svear battle line.

Jarl Ottar of Vastmanland and his six hundred warriors would most likely be placed over on the left, in the position of greatest honour. He would demand it as the king's most powerful jarl and his *Armathr*. But Ottar would require a goodly number of archers, slingers, too, and javelins, as well, to guard the cliffs above the Braviken. And he would get them. Which mean that her lord Jarl Starki – the third *Armathr* – would have to be given the right flank to ward, to the west, between Sigurd Hring's banners and the shores of Lake Glan.

Tor looked west at the endless rolling forest in that direction and sighed. She knew she had better go and take a good look at the shores of that lake before she left this place; it was her duty to ensure her jarl's position was scouted before the battle.

She followed the track that ran along the top of the Kolmarden for an hour and then dipped down and joined the sunken road that led north-west away from the plain, spurring her horse up the slippery, muddy slope. As her horse climbed, the track led her deeper and deeper into the dense Svealand forest. To her left, as she sploshed along, she occasionally caught glimpses through the trees of the rocky beach and shimmering waters of Lake Glan. Then, after half an hour of hard and muddy riding, she lost sight of the lake altogether, as the wilderness closed in all around her.

As the afternoon faded, she pushed on, until she found the track itself dwindling under her horse's hooves. Soon it became no more than a faint double line through the dark, close-growing trees. A pair of ruts made by the infrequent passing of some heavily laden cart could just about be made out. Beyond the two faint lines, on both sides, she was completely enveloped by the forest.

Around dusk, she smelled woodsmoke, and reined in. Then, guessing its likely origin, she guided her horse off the faint set of cart tracks and, following her nose, she rode on to an even fainter path through the dense trees. And, a few hundred paces later, Tor found herself in a small woodland clearing with a huge mound at its centre. A trickle of pungent grey smoke was rising from the middle of this enormous brown earth-heap the size of a moderate village house.

Two very dirty men, hands and faces stained black, one older, one a mere stripling, gaped in astonishment at the sight of her – a pretty female warrior with her sword at her side, seax at her waist, and the big painted shield slung over her leather-clad back. But the two men recovered their wits and soon invited her to pass the night with them, and share their meagre supper of bread, bacon and mead.

They were charcoal-burners, Tor knew, folk who made their living in these dense woods by felling trees, chopping them, and slowly charring them inside the great earthen mounds – turning them after a few days of slow baking into lumps and sticks of valuable charcoal. Every blacksmith in Svealand needed a charcoal-burner's wares to work his iron. And would pay a high price for the best quality fuel.

Yet charcoal-burning was a lonely and sometimes dangerous trade. These men spent many weeks and months of the year alone in the deep forests creating their black lumps and sticks from green wood, and braving wolves, bears and outlaws while they worked. Then they had to transport the heavy sacks of their product to remote settlements and farmsteads to sell it. This work produced a strange breed of man (there were few women charcoal-burners) – tough, independent but sometimes more than a little odd. These two fellows seemed to Tor to be normal enough, and they were obviously delighted to find a new face to stare at.

After sharing what news she had of the outside world with the two men, and a pair of fat hares she had shot the day before, Tor was content to lie back and listen to their tales of backwoods life. The younger one, excited by the company, claimed he had seen a family of trolls the week before, marching across a clearing.

The oldster told him he was a liar. 'They was orcs, you ninny. You only see trolls in the mountains, not in these lower parts.'

'So what is the nearest town around here?' Tor asked them after their supper. 'Where do you take your hard-won charcoal when you have finished cooking it.'

'When the firing is done, we fill up the cart with our sacks, and hitch up old Frigg,' he jerked a thumb at a mossy old mare that was placidly cropping the grass a stone's throw away by the edge of the clearing, 'and we take the new burn over to Finnstorp. That's the nearest. The forges of Finnstorp would run cold without what we bring 'em every month.'

Tor had heard of Finnstorp. They made fine swords there. Seaxes, too. Harva of Finnstorp had made the seax that Bjarki had given to the dead man Einar at the *Disablot*.

'Where is Finnstorp? It's in Varmland, isn't it? It must take an age to get there.'

'Nay, lass. Finnstorp is on the east coast of Lake Vattern. Near the top. Those forges need plenty o' water, as much as they need our 'coal. Our Frigg can amble up yonder in three or four days, pulling a full load of new burn. The boy here could run up in two days, though he'd likely get lost. Nothing but trees 'tween hither and yon.'

Later, wrapped in her old, warm cloak, looking up at the indifferent sparkle of the endless stars, and listening to the old man's gentle, almost musical snoring, Tor thought about poor, heartbroken Inge, and her beloved Garm, and her honourable but stubborn brother Bjarki – and, most of all, about the great battle that would soon take place at Norrkoping in which she and Bjarki must face each other over the shields.

Chapter Fifteen

'Sail to save my sister's life'

The shipwrights laid the keels in oak, selecting trees for felling that already had some natural curvature, and building up the skeletons of the ships from this keel-line. Each vessel was constructed from overlapping planks of oak fixed to the frame of the ship. The big, half-built craft were set out in a line just back from the muddy shore of the Gota River, a few hundred paces to the south of Bjarki's royal hall at Lodose.

This meant that from sunup to sundown, Bjarki had the chunking sound of adze on wood, and the rasp of saws and the hammering of mallets in his ears, as well as the smell of freshly cut wood in his nostrils. He did not mind. He had always liked the sharp, sappy smell of a carpenter's workshop. And the ship building was going apace, proceeding faster than he had expected. He enjoyed the sight of the line of war vessels growing, even seemingly blooming like great wooden plants, along the shore.

He was up long before sunrise, anyway, and when he wasn't overseeing the construction of these ships, he was in the fields and pastures around the town exercising his troops. Or appointing captains and commanders to positions in his *hird*.

The oath that Glamir Raeflisson had made after the Feast of Idun had changed everything. Bjarki had had no idea of the influence Glamir truly wielded. But it was as if by making his vow publicly, the pale wrestler had opened a spigot of warriors, a gush of men eager to serve their new king. Bjarki now had hundreds of free-born Vastergotland recruits who sought the honour of fighting in his ranks. He could pick and choose. Fortunately, at least two-thirds of them were already partially trained in war – Vastergotland men were bred to war, apparently – and almost all possessed a weapon of some kind, an axe or spear, or a seax, or even just a pig-slaughtering knife.

He organised the warriors in *lith*, or companies of fifty, under a captain who was usually a Dane – one of Siegfried's oath-men who had come over with him from Viby – but occasionally he appointed a local champion, a man who had the confidence of the warriors under him. The captains were responsible for training their *lith*, making sure they were housed and fed, and for their troops' discipline. Bjarki was ruthless about demoting any captain who allowed his men to misbehave or cause trouble.

The *lith* competed with each other in various martial exercises, most overseen by Bjarki. It was, in truth, not very different to the activities of the Feast of Idun, although on a grander scale and with no prizes save for prestige among their peers.

One of Bjarki's favourite exercises was a race in which two or three *lith* had to run to a point perhaps ten miles away and return – but every warrior in the company had to return before the result was acknowledged. Any members of the *lith* who were injured, or too exhausted to run, must be carried back by all the others. All fifty men had to return to make their run complete, which forced them to work as a team. Other exercises were feats of strength and mock battles with sticks and shields – although Bjarki and Glamir were careful to make sure the pretend fighting did not get too out of hand. He wanted no man killed or maimed in training.

The law-speaker soon became invaluable to Bjarki. Glamir was respected by all in Lodose, Gotaborg and the remote surrounding steadings. He would accompany Bjarki when he was inspecting the troops lined up in the fields after an exercise and whisper small but telling pieces of information about the men Bjarki was greeting.

'...next man is Hedvig, a hunter from up in the Kullen hills, his wife makes excellent mead from wild honey. Eight children, three of them boys.' Glamir had a prodigious memory, something which all law-speakers relied upon, and he seemed to know everything about everybody.

'Ah, Hedvig,' Bjarki would say, stopping in front of a scrappy-looking runt of a man with no front teeth. 'Your *lith* did well today. They must be drinking your wife's mead! That's what gives them heart. When will I see your boys in the shield wall?'

Bjarki knew it was a kind of deception, which made him a little uneasy, but the toothless grin of pride on Hedvig's face made up for it. As well as the knowledge that this old warrior would go into battle alongside him, and die beside his king, if asked.

He soon made Glamir his *Merkismathr*, his banner-bearer, and included him in his inner circle of counsellors. These consisted of Kynwulf, Mogils and Valtyr – when the one-eyed old man was awake, present in the hall and still mostly sober.

It was a reasonably sober Valtyr who brought him the news, when he and Glamir were conferring with the shipwrights on the riverbank about the shortage of pine-tar. Bjarki noticed the old man out of the corner of his eye, waiting, tugging his beard, almost hovering, clearly with something important to say. He ended his conversation.

'I will send a boat to Viby for more pine-tar, Rudolf,' he told the master shipwright, 'but until that arrives, we'll have to spread what we have more thinly. If we run out before more comes, we'll work out how to brew our own from pine bark.'

He turned to the old wanderer: 'Yes, Valtyr?'

'There is a *karve*, a big one – twenty-six rowers – coming upriver at speed from Gotaborg, flying the Green Dragon of the Dane-Mark and the Red Boar of Sjaelland.'

'Harald Wartooth?' said Bjarki.

'Looks like him,' said Valtyr. 'One scout claimed he saw that bone-headed blow-hard in the prow, with his big tooth sticking out of his skull like a unicorn's.'

Bjarki welcomed the Jarl of Sjaelland into his hall with a feast, the best meat and drink he could provide. He could tell the Wartooth was pleased to be so honoured.

'I can see you've made yourself comfortable here, Bloodhand,' he said jovially.

'There are good, honest folk hereabouts. They tend their crops and livestock diligently, and there are plenty of fish in the river and the woods are stuffed with game.'

'That's just as well, because the king asks that you provide him with some of the rations for the army – dried meat, pickled fish, twice-baked bread, and so on – when we sail in five weeks. My steward Boldi has a list of what Siegfried requires of you.'

'I shall be honoured to provide the king with whatever we can spare.' Bjarki lifted his ale horn to the steward, a sour little man, crop-haired and hunched, sitting further along the table, who gave him a flicker of a grin and raised his horn in reply.

'Well, I'm not just here for this excellent food,' said Harald Wartooth, wiping his moustaches, belching loudly and pushing away his empty platter. 'The king wants a report from me on the ships you are building. I saw some on the shore when we docked. Will they all be ready to join the rest of the fleet by mid-Solmanuthur?'

Bjarki finished his mouthful of roast pork, dabbed his beard with a linen cloth, and said: 'Not all of them, I'm sorry to tell you. And not even by the end of that month. I aimed to build the king nine ships but we were lacking in materials: pine-tar for waterproofing the hulls, enough heavy cloth for all the sails, flax rope for the rigging. There is no time to make more. If I had another two months, maybe… But I *can* promise to put five seaworthy *busse* in the Kattegat by the third week of Solmanuthur, filled with eighty warriors each. I hope the king deems this sufficient.'

'He won't. Kings are rarely grateful. But my opinion counts much more. And I'm pleased you have four hundred Vastergotland spears to add to my Danish host.'

Bjarki looked at Harald Wartooth sideways. Why had he said *my* Danish host? Also, he seemed to be criticising the king, and claiming he was more important, perhaps even more powerful than the ruler of the Dane-Mark. *What did this mean?*

Bjarki said nothing. He reached for a piece of bread to mop his greasy platter.

Harald Wartooth let out a hearty guffaw. 'You think I've turned traitor, eh? Ha-ha! Is *that* what you think, Bloodhand? If I *had* turned, I'd be here with a thousand Sjaelland spears – and you'd be raven-food, for all your *berserkr* ferocity. I know your loyalty to Siegfried. He made you a king – how could you *not* be loyal? You would be the first to be removed from the *tafl* board, if I did decide to betray him!'

'I find your mirth in poor taste,' said Bjarki stiffly. He hated being laughed at.

'I see word has not yet reached you in this backwater,' said Harald, still red-faced with merriment. 'The King of the Danes has confirmed me his *Armathr* – he's given me command of his entire army and his fleet. He has also made me his Royal Champion. And he has entrusted me with the important task of kicking the backside of that contumelious little turd Sigurd Hring at Norrkoping. So that's why I say *my* Danish host – and that's why I'm glad you can supply *me* with ships, dry rations and an extra four hundred hopefully well-trained shield-men.'

'The king will not fight at Norrkoping?'

'Are you deaf? I have command. I'll guarantee him his victory when we meet the cowardly Svear in battle. The king is old. He can barely lift a sword, let alone wield one. I shall fight for him, and with *four thousand* Danish spears at my back!'

Harald took a swig of ale and, from his pouch, he took out a length of flax yarn, which he used to clean around the large tooth that jutted from his lower gum.

It made sense, Bjarki admitted to himself. But he found that he was disliking the bombastic Harald Wartooth more with every passing moment. However, this red-faced braggart was indeed the most powerful man in the Dane-Mark. His fief on the big island of Sjaelland was known for its rich soils and burgeoning population. Bjarki reckoned the Wartooth could muster two thousand warriors from his own lands easily. It made sense for him to be

Armathr. It was a sensible choice. Nevertheless, Bjarki felt uneasy that this stupid, ageing, walrus-moustached buffoon was to have command of the Danish army. That he'd have the fate of Bjarki's folk in his hands.

'What other news from the king's court in Viby?' Bjarki asked.

'Not much. The king leaned hard on Widukind of Westphalia, and the Saxon has grudgingly promised one *lith* of his spearmen to join the cause. And a few horsemen! As if cavalry will have any role to play on the battlefield. And your friend Abbio the Crow is getting married – maybe you knew that. To that Saxon chit he rescued.'

Bjarki found he was gritting his teeth.

'I rescued Edith – it was me and my *Felaki* warriors. One of them was killed in the fight. Abbio was sitting on a beach far away when we attacked and rescued her.'

'Is that so? That's not what the skalds are saying – there is a charming rhyme that, whatsisname, the king's court poet, has made up. How does it go? Dum di, dum di dum… when fearless Abbio raised his magic fog… dum di dum … and slew the foe at Rogaland, down to the meanest dog… Rather good, eh? Wait, I'll ask my steward: Boldi, how does that splendid poem go? The new one about Rogaland. The king's favourite. Sing it, man, sing it for our host, the new King of Vastergotland.'

'Perhaps I might have the pleasure of listening to this poem another time.'

'No, no, Boldi will sing it. It's a fine heroic lay. I only hope to have one as fine sung about me after my death.'

Bjarki looked at the older man. He was past his prime, of course – perhaps more than sixty winters old. Yet he seemed to be bursting with health.

'You speak of your own death. Are you stricken with some ailment, *Armathr*?'

'No, you fool, in the great battle. I'm getting old. I won't live for ever. My father died when he was half my age. So at Norrkoping, I hope to win a great victory, then die laughing at the last, when I've enough glory to make the skalds sing of me.'

'A fine ambition, Wartooth. For myself, I plan to survive the battle, if I can.'

'Well, you're a youngster. Still full of fire and piss. You have plenty of time to make a name for yourself. But we were talking of music. Boldi, sing the song about the rescue in Rogaland. "The Triumph of Abbio", that was its name. Go on, sing.'

'Alas, I shall not be able to hear that… at the present time,' grated Bjarki. 'In truth, I fear I must now retire to my chamber. I find suddenly that I have a headache.'

'Indeed?' said Wartooth. 'Probably not enough ale. Have another drink!'

'Thank you, but no. But tell me, before I go. Has a particular day been chosen for the marriage of that… of the *gothi* Abbio and the Lady Edith of Saxony?'

'Yes, I believe so. The king has chosen the fifteenth of Heyannir. Which should give us time to thrash the Svear, and the survivors time to return for the celebrations.'

'Don't take the gods' favour for granted, *Armathr*. They will curse us if we do!'

'I have four thousand of the best warriors in all the Middle-Realm. Four thousand trained Danish shield-men! And my spies say the traitor Sigurd Hring can field only two thousand at best – even with all his so-called heroes. Even Odin Spear-Shaker would struggle to give us a defeat with the odds tilted so much in our favour.'

As Bjarki walked away from the hall towards his own quarters, he felt a shiver of dread. This arrogant old mutton-head had the fate of the Dane-Mark in his hands.

—

In the clean light of morning, Bjarki felt a little better at their prospects in the great battle. They outnumbered the Svear two to one. *Two to one*. And Bjarki knew the Svear troops as well as he knew his own Vastergotland men who would face them.

There was not much difference in their fighting quality – a few of them were skilled men of war, but most were merely brave farmers with a spear and shield and a thirst for glory. And, since the fighting qualities of the warriors on opposing sides would be roughly similar – setting aside all the heroes, who presumably were competent – the numbers on each side counted for much more than they otherwise might.

Four thousand against two thousand – if Harald Wartooth's spies were correct. The gods might intervene, of course, the weather might turn, a calamitous mistake might be made by either side but, taken all together, it seemed likely that Siegfried, or rather his *Armathr*, would be victorious. And Sigurd Hring's army would be crushed.

When he was washed and dressed, he went to seek out Valtyr, and found him in a stupor in one of the tool sheds by the shipyard, his skinny arm curled round a jug.

He tried hard to rouse the old man but, failing to get any sense out of him – and because he did not have time to wait for the Far-Traveller to sober up – he simply picked Valtyr up bodily and carried him down to the river Gota and threw him in.

A few moments later, Valtyr emerged from the water cursing and spitting, his grey robe flapping wetly around his long white shanks.

'If I were a younger man, I'd gut you like a trout for that,' said Valtyr.

'Do you think, even in your prime, you could ever have bested *me* in a fight?'

Valtyr swept back his long grey hair, plastering it to his scalp. He adjusted his sodden eye patch. 'Maybe not. But I would have made such a valiant attempt that all the finest skalds in the North would sing of my efforts till Ragnarok.'

'Do not mention skalds to me this morning, old man.'

'So then, Bjarki,' said Valtyr, 'what is it? Why this brutal awakening?'

'I need you to do something for me.'

'This is how you ask for a favour? By trying to drown me?'

'Stop whining and listen.'

'Did you bring any ale? My mouth is very dry this morning.'

'The river is just there. I could put you back in again, if you like.'

Valtyr gave a snort of irritation. 'Tell me what you want, you great bully.'

'I think we shall win this great battle in Svealand, do you agree?'

'My cause is the North – not Dane or Svear. I think we will all *lose* the battle. The winners shall be the Christians who are the true enemy to all folk in these lands.'

'Tell that to Egil Skull-Cleaver when he comes howling at you with his double-bladed axe. But let us set that aside. Do you think the Danes will win at Norrkoping?'

'It seems likely. The Danes have the stronger force. And right is certainly on their side. Which means the gods will probably favour them over Sigurd Hring.'

'I think so too. But Tor is determined to fight for this arrogant Svear upstart and, given her temperament and renown as a warrior, she will probably be fighting in the front rank, and will almost certainly be slain. I will not allow it, Valtyr. I cannot bear it.'

'It would grieve me deeply as well,' said Valtyr.

'Then do this for me, old one, for our friendship and the love I know you bear for my sister. I want you to go to Bearstead – or Gavle or Uppsala, or wherever Tor may be – and bring her safely back here to Lodose before the battle is joined.'

'She will not come willingly.'

'She may not – but you must try to reason with her. Try to persuade her that throwing her life away for the cause of this ambitious fellow Sigurd Hring is futile. And if that does not answer, you must use guile and, as a last resort, force. I will give you Kynwulf and a good ship – the *Sea Elk*, the *karve* we captured in Rogaland – and you must use all of your deep knowledge.

I understand there are potions, concoctions of herbs, that can render a woman unconscious… You know this better than I…'

'I do know a little of such matters…' The old man seemed oddly uncertain.

'Do not fear Tor's wrath. If you have to knock her senseless and bind her to bring back here, I shall take the responsibility on my head. I'll not let her harm you.'

Valtyr stared at the mud of the bank for a long time. Then he looked up at Bjarki. 'You are going to owe me a very great favour, Rekkr. I shall do this for you, son, but you must swear to do my bidding – only one time but without question – when I call upon you to do a task for me. Agreed? Will you do my bidding, once, in the future?'

'I swear it,' said Bjarki. 'Now go, sail to Svealand, sail to save my sister's life!'

Chapter Sixteen

Unworthy blade

Tor found that she was very glad to be back at Uppsala and surrounded by the familiar faces of her *hird*. Yet there were a large number of unfamiliar faces too in the royal compound. The warrior population of Uppsala seemed to have swelled a good deal in her absence. There were unfamiliar-looking squat, shaggy men wandering around with oblong shields, painted in black geometric lines and shapes, lightning bolts, squares and diamonds. And, while she was not entirely sure, she thought she heard these warriors talking together in the Wendish tongue.

Gudrik put the *hird* through their paces for Tor to see and she realised that in her weeks away they had all improved considerably. Gudrik was clearly a better troop commander than she was, or perhaps he was more attentive to the training of his warriors. Yet the *hird* seemed pleased to see her, and when Gudrik shouted out 'Skjald-borg!', they formed up in a bristling line before her in, at her own count, only eight beats of her heart.

Their bearded faces grinned at her triumphantly over the shields, and although she tried to look stern, and kicked hard at parts of the wall, she couldn't help but grin back at them. They were truly impressive: skilled and disciplined. They knew it, she knew it. She invited Jarl Starki to come and inspect his accomplished *hird* the next day.

After making her report to Sigurd Hring about the battlefield site on her first day back in Uppsala, and making her suggestions about the correct placement of the various Svear contingents, the king had not troubled to hide his extreme boredom. Sigurd Hring knew all of this already, and Tor soon ended her description of the terrain, bowed as humbly as she could, and silently withdrew from the king's hall.

She had stayed away from the royal court ever since. She knew if she returned there she would encounter Krok of Frisia – and it would be likely to end badly.

Jarl Starki was in a foul temper when she collected him from the stables to bring him up to inspect the *hird*. The gallop he had enjoyed on the heathland north of the compound had not lifted his mood, which was caused by being slighted by the king.

'The right wing, the *right* fucking wing. All the way over by Lake Glan – that's what he's given us! Some fool suggested this as a good place for us to stand. And he has agreed. The Danes will never attack us up on the right. They will come straight up the middle or try to land troops from the waters of the Braviken on the left flank.

'Jarl Ottar has the left, of course – the position of honour,' he said. 'Where all the fighting will be. We'll stand there on the right all day and watch the battle from the beach on Lake Glan. Perhaps we can have a refreshing dip if things get too dull.'

'I'm certain we will have a chance to show our mettle, lord,' said Tor. 'Their host is numerous, I'm told. The king will surely call on us when he needs reserves.'

'Haven't you heard? Sigurd Hring has a whole new army that will form his battle reserve – an army of dirty foreigners. Wends. Slavs. From the lands around the port of Rerik. A thousand Wendish warriors from the Obodrites tribe under a smart fellow called Prince Witzlaus, a seasoned warrior, everyone says. They arrived last week. Sigurd Hring has promised them lands in the south of Jutland if he wins and is declared King of the North. He'll be their overlord, but the Wends will control all from Flens to the Dane-Work. He has even promised them Nordalbia – Saxon lands.'

Tor said: 'Duke Widukind has allied himself with the Danes. Therefore the Saxons are now our enemy, too.' Nevertheless she felt a cold hollow open under her ribs at Jarl Starki's shocking tidings. When she had fought with the Saxon army, some years ago, Prince Witzlaus of the Obodrites had made a surprise attack on the unguarded eastern Saxon lands, which had drawn the East-phalians, whose land it was, out of the fight against the invading Franks, with calamitous consequences for Widukind's remaining Saxon troops.

How the wheel turns, she thought. *My friends are now my enemies; an old enemy will fight beside me when I face in battle the folk who used to be my friends...*

'I believe there will be more than enough blood to go around, lord,' Tor said.

The *hird* performed magnificently, marching and running, staging mock attacks and making their various formations impeccably. Tor was intensely proud of them.

When the display was finished, Jarl Starki drew his own sword and rode down the line of his excited, red-faced troops, the blade held high, to accept their cheers.

Then Tor, Starki and Gudrik sat down at a trestle table, set up by the *hird*-men, to eat a bite of bread, some radishes and pickled herring. As the ale was poured out, Tor said casually: 'May I trouble you for your sword, lord? I would take a look at it.'

Jarl Starki, whose mood had been much improved by the exhibition of prowess by his troops, readily agreed, hauling out the old blade and handing it over to Tor.

As the men ate, Tor looked down the polished length of plain, sharpened iron, and examined the bone and oak hilt, and the twist of gold wire around the pommel.

'Hmm,' she said, dismissively handing the blade back to Starki.

'What exactly do you mean, *Stallar*, by "Hmm"? You don't like my sword?'

'It was your father's sword? Yes, I remember Viggo the White drawing it.'

'It was indeed Viggo's blade. He fought many a famous battle with this sword.'

'Hmm,' said Tor. Gudrik frowned at her from the far side of the trestle table.

'Speak your mind, *Stallar* – do not hum at me like a bumble bee.'

'It is a fairly decent blade,' said Tor. 'No doubt serviceable in battle. But...'

'What? But... what?'

'It's not worthy of you,' said Tor. 'You are *Armathr* to a king. You need a fine sword to demonstrate your status. No wonder Sigurd Hring has little respect for you.'

As she spoke these words she felt a rush of hot shame in her belly, and her mouth felt greasy for having uttered them. Bjarki, she knew, would have disapproved.

Jarl Starki simply glared at her, all the colour leaving his face.

'Forgive me, lord, for speaking too plainly,' said Tor. 'But what I say is true. And I have a remedy. If you will hear me. Have you heard of Harva of Finnstorp?'

'I know of him,' said Starki. 'They say he is the greatest living smith in the North, whose grandfather learned the secrets of the trade from Wayland. He has his lakeside forge in Sodermanland. Very choosy about his customers, or so I've heard.'

'I've spoken to him. My brother has a seax made by Harva, the sweetest blade.'

'And?'

'The battle will take place twenty-four days from tomorrow. I believe I can persuade Harva to make you a fine sword, a truly superior weapon – perhaps the best blade in all the North – before that time is up. If I went to him now, and stood over him at his forge, I could bring you a magnificent sword for you to wield in the fray. The battle of Norrkoping will be remembered by folk for a hundred years, and the warriors who fought in it too shall be remembered. Perhaps years from now folk will speak of bold Starki, who slew so many at Norrkoping with his sword Leg-biter...'

'Not Leg-biter!' Starki's face was now alight with enthusiasm. 'I want a steel sword, in the Frankish manner, and it shall be known for ever as... *Dane-slayer*!'

'So it shall be, lord,' said Tor. 'I shall ride in the morning to Finnstorp...'

'Wait, wait just a moment, Tor. How much is this fine sword going to cost me?'

'I shall bear the cost, lord. My gift to you for the favour you have shown me.'

'Truly? Then ride, *Stallar*, ride to Finnstorp and bring Dane-slayer to my hand!'

Self-disgust was rising so fast in Tor's gorge she had to choke down a whole cup of ale to wash it away. Yet it had to be done. She knew this was the only way.

—

As she was packing up her belongings in the hut that had once been Inge's abode, and thinking about her coming journey, she was surprised to hear a knock at the ill-fitting door and when she opened it, even more surprised to see young Joralf standing there, twisting his hands around each other, an anguished expression on his handsome face.

'Where is she?' he said.

Tor gave him a long hard look. The young warrior seemed genuinely distressed.

'You speak of Inge?'

'Yes, Inge; of course, Inge. Where is she? I must talk to her.'

'Not here.'

'I can see that.' The hut was one small room, all of which was visible from the doorway. 'Where is she?'

'Why do you wish to speak with her? The last thing you said to her wounded her very deeply. I shall not permit you to hurt her again.'

'Tell me where she is!' Joralf's tone had changed; he grabbed a bunch of Tor's tunic cloth in the front and raised his left hand, open palm, as if he meant to slap her.

Tor seized his right hand with hers, twisted his against the wrist joint and immediately brought the younger, stronger man to his knees, hissing in pain. Tor carried on twisting, forcing the swordsman's body lower and lower towards the earth to save his arm from breaking. Eventually, Joralf's face was flat on the ground, and Tor put one boot on his neck, and pressed his half-shaved head into the soft wet earth.

'Shall I snap your wrist now, you spoilt little baby?' she said.

Joralf gave a groan of pain. 'Let me go, you bitch!'

Tor loosed her seax from its sheath at her belly with her left hand, and showed it to Joralf. He was immobilised but his eyes widened at the sight of the foot-long steel blade.

'It's not a Harva,' she said. 'But it will castrate you neatly enough, I think.'

'Gods curse you – kill me, if you will. I don't want to live without her anyway.'

Tor gave his arm a last little tweak, which elicited a scream from her victim. Then she released him and stepped back. But she kept the seax blade low in her hand.

Joralf slowly got to his feet, rubbing his twisted arm and glaring at her.

'Do you love her?' asked Tor.

Joralf nodded. 'With all my heart.'

'You made her cry. Talking of all the other girls you had been with.'

'I was stupid. I wanted to impress her. To make her jealous...' The young warrior was weeping now. Tears running down his cheeks. 'I didn't... I did not realise that I loved her till she had gone. A week ago or more. I must see her. I have to tell her I made a mistake. Where is Inge... please... tell me. You must tell me.'

'If you hurt her again, I *will* cut your balls off – you need to understand this. It is not an idle threat. Hurt her, you lose your balls; hurt her badly, I take your life, too.'

Joralf nodded. He wiped the back of his hand across his teary, snotty face.

'Inge is at my steading – Bearstead. Go to Gavle in Norrland, and walk north for half a day. The nearest village is Bjorke, you can ask for directions from there.'

'I thank you. And know that I will never hurt her again. I swear this by Freyr.'

'Don't make oaths. Just imagine how it will feel when I cut off your little balls.'

Tor walked her horse down the gentle slope towards the waters of Lake Vattern. Some of the lands had been cleared hereabouts for pasture and crops but these oases of civilisation were fringed with dense dark spruce and pine forests, of the kind she had travelled through for the past three days. The village of Finnstorp, off to her right, was a dirty smear of muddy houses and workshops along the rocky coast, with a large grey cloud of smoke sitting above it. It did not seem a picturesque place, despite the magnificence of the sunny lake beyond – which was narrow enough at this north end for Tor to glimpse its distant tree-fringed shore.

While Tor had not come here to enjoy a pretty view, she did note that that distant shore was Vastergotland, the very edge of her brother's realm, and her mind briefly winged away to him, wondering what he was doing this sunny day, and whether he had been accepted by the Vastergotlanders as their king. However, she soon dismissed him from her thoughts: she had a far more urgent matter on her mind.

She found Harva's forge without difficulty, and dismounted and tied her horse to the wooden rail before knocking on the doorframe beams to attract the master smith's attention. She could clearly see two men at work inside the forge under a low tiled roof. The forge was open on all sides, save for a waist-high wall, to allow the thick smoke from the huge bed of red charcoal in the centre to dissipate more easily.

The older of the two, Harva, she assumed, was a short, powerful fellow, naked apart from trews, shoes and a thick leather apron, who was rhythmically pounding a small strip of red-hot metal with a large hammer. The second man, who was holding the hot strip of iron in a pair of tongs, occasionally turned it so that the older hammer-man could pound a different side. The air by the forge, despite the lake breeze, was filled with the pungent smell of burning sparks and charcoal smoke, and Tor was reminded of the peaceful evening she had spent in the forest with the two friendly burners by their mound near Lake Glan. That charcoal-burners' camp, she reckoned, was two or three days' walk through the forest east and a little south of Finnstorp.

She knocked again on the doorframe, more loudly. But, once again, she was ignored. She had to wait until the smith had finished his pounding and instructed the younger man, his apprentice, presumably, to replace the cooling iron bar back in the furnace-fire, before he would even acknowledge her presence.

Harva the Smith came over to the doorway and peered out at her curiously. He was a mole-like man, with tiny eyes in a narrow balding head, and very strong paw-like hands speckled with tiny burns – but his chest and arm muscles were enormous.

She greeted him courteously, and told him want she wanted from him.

'I cannot do it, woman. I simply do not have the time or the spare forge-hands.'

'But you have more than two weeks – perhaps even twenty days – to make the jarl's new sword. He needs to have it for the first day of the month of Heyannir.'

Harva gave her a twisted smile. 'I know, I know, the great battle. Folk speak of little else. But I cannot make your jarl a sword in time for the fight at Norrkoping. I could not make you one for next mid-summer either. Do you think you are the only warrior of the North to come to me looking for a Harva blade? I've had hundreds of visitors. I have had enough requests to keep me busy for the rest of my days, and my son's days after me. It is out of the question. I cannot do it. My apologies – but no.'

Tor reached inside her jerkin and pulled out a heavy leather bag. She set it down, chinking, on the top of the waist-high wall that separated her from the smith.

'This is ten marks of Frankish silver *denier* coins. Will that change your mind?'

'You think I care about *money*? My work is an offering to my ancestor the great Wayland, who learned smith-craft from Brokkr and Eitri, the Dwarf-Masters of old.'

'I *must* have a sword.'

'I cannot make one for you.'

'What can you suggest?'

Harva scratched his bristly chin. 'I'm not the only smith in Finnstorp, you know.'

'Who would you recommend?'

'Nissa is not bad, although he overheats his iron on the second casting. And his caulking is a little shoddy. But Nissa might have the time to make you a new sword.'

'Master – the bar is the colour of sunset, it's ready for the flatter now.' This was the young apprentice, perhaps even the smith's son, calling Harva back to his anvil.

'I don't like the sound of shoddy,' said Tor.

'I must go. The heat is correct,' said Harva.

'If not Nissa – who else might I try?'

Harva flicked the bag of coin with one finger. 'If you have silver, you could just *buy* a sword. I mean simply purchase one that was originally crafted for another warrior. But that's bad luck. Least my father always said it was. A sword has a spirit – a *gandr* of iron – and should not be bought and sold like a ewe at market. I make my swords for a chosen warrior, only he and members of his bloodline should wield it.'

'Master, the colour of the iron, the colour is just right now...'

'I must go.'

'Where could I *buy* a sword then?' Tor hated the desperate note in her voice.

'Top of the street, by the tall birch, ask for Usko the Trader, he has swords, seaxes, buckles, cloak pins – all manner of shiny trinkets. And *he* loves silver!'

Tor bought the most expensive sword she could find from Usko the Trader's storerooms. It was a gaudy-looking object, a rich man's toy, with a fat ruby set in the silver pommel and two sapphires on each end of the silver cross-guard. The hilt was made from polished walrus ivory, inlaid with carnelians, and the broad blade had the rippling wave pattern of hard, good-quality Frankish steel, with a sinuous design like a curling vine in beaten gold running down the centre of the fuller, almost to the tip.

Tor hated the thing. But it *looked* like a fine sword, and that was what mattered.

She also bought two large leather buckets from the man, and a small leather cup.

That night, she camped out on the edge of the vast forest under a trio of mighty oaks and looked down as she ate her meal at the twinkling lights of Finnstorp below.

She had filled one of the leather buckets with lake water, and now set it between her knees, in front of the small campfire on which she had grilled half a leg of venison. She drank water from the bucket with the leather cup, with a strange and fixed determination. Cup after cup. Several gallons in all. Drinking long into the dark night. And when she found she needed to relieve herself, she went over to the second bucket a few paces away and did her business in there. In the dawn, after a final release, she was pleased to see more than a gallon of pale liquid sloshing at the bottom of the second bucket.

With the sun a hand's breadth above the horizon, she packed up her camp, mounted her horse and, very gingerly carrying the full leather bucket across her thighs, rode off very slowly into the dark, near-trackless Sodermanland forests.

Chapter Seventeen

If it seems too good to be true…

Bjarki supported Rask with both his arms, keeping the *Felaki*'s head above the water. It was late afternoon, and still warm. The warrior was lying flat across his forearms, while Bjarki tried to encourage him to move his arms in circular motions and kick with his feet. Rask kept saying, 'Yes, highness, yes!' but his whole body was rigid.

'We are in five feet of water,' said Bjarki, exasperatedly. 'If I let you go – which I swear I will not do – even your short legs would reach the river bed.'

'Yes, highness, yes!' said Rask. He was a compact, middle-aged man, and quite fearless in battle, a fine sailor and an expert tracker and woodsman but, at the river Gota's edge, he was strangely stricken helpless with terror.

He made tight, frantic little motions with his arms and, from time to time, his feet jerked. 'Try to be calm. Make the movements wider and slower. Remember: the water is your ally. The river will gently support your weight and carry you along.'

'Yes, highness, yes!'

Bjarki let him struggle on for a while, then said: 'Very good, Rask. I think you have grasped the rudiments. I'm going to release you now. Are you ready to swim?'

'Yes, highness, yes!'

Bjarki dropped his arms and Rask sank like an anvil under the rippled brown water. Bjarki wondered if the little fellow had heavier bones than ordinary men. Rask had disappeared. Then he surfaced like a small porpoise, further out into the river, with almost half his body shooting high out of the water. Rask gasped, flailed about, thrashing his arms and whipping the waters white before sinking down again.

When the little *Felaki* surfaced for a second time he was once again further from the shore. Out of his depth. And now he was being carried away by the strong current.

Bjarki cursed and plunged in after him. In a few short, powerful strokes, he had caught up with the little man and was soon dragging him swiftly back towards the riverbank. Back on land, Oddvin handed a miserable-looking Rask his wool cloak.

'So...' said Bjarki, looking at his men. 'Who else would like a lesson?'

Oddvin, Harknut and Haugen all looked at each other. Then Haugen Halfhand spoke: 'Some men are just not made for the waters, highness. We are not fishes.'

'But I could teach you! It is simplicity itself.'

The three dry *Felaki* looked at each other. No one said a word but they seemed to be conferring about something. Rask was sitting on the bank, wrapped in his warm cloak, looking like a half-drowned cat. He coughed hard and spat out a gout of water.

The silence stretched out until it became too long. Uncomfortably long.

'Perhaps we have all had enough swimming for one day,' said Bjarki. 'The hour grows late. It is time for food and rest – and ale. Come, let us return to the hall.'

'There is another matter we should like to speak to you about,' said Harknut, who was the leader of the *Felaki* in Kynwulf's absence. 'If you will permit it.'

'Speak!' said Bjarki.

'We wish to speak about us – about the honourable brotherhood of the *Felaki*. About the tribe of traditional warrior Companions to the King of the Goths.'

'You must know that I hold you all in the very highest esteem,' said Bjarki.

'We too are greatly honoured to serve you, highness,' said Harknut. 'And yet there is a thorny matter. And we four – and Kynwulf – are all concerned about this.'

'What problem?'

'We were six – six Companions. And then Bodvar was killed in Rogaland. And now Kynwulf has gone to Svealand to fetch your sister. Now only we four remain.'

'I prize your service very highly.' Bjarki had an icy feeling in his belly. He half-expected the *Felaki* to tell him they were going home; that they were leaving him; that they'd decided they must return to their village in the hills above the Avar Plain.

'We *Felaki* are too few,' said Harknut.

'Each one of you is worth five ordinary warriors, perhaps even ten!' said Bjarki, and he was pleased to see all four *Felaki* grinning at his clumsy compliment.

'Yet we feel we must enrol more warriors into our brotherhood,' Harknut continued. 'Five *Felaki* is too few. Angantyr the great king had thirty oath-sworn Companions to protect him. In his final stand at the Troll Stones, he had twelve men at his side to face the Hunnish foe. A big fight is coming and we five – while we would all give our lives for you, highness – cannot guarantee your safety in a battle.'

'I hear you,' said Bjarki. 'How would you enrol more warriors in the *Felaki*? How would you choose them? How many would you seek to be in your company?'

'Oh, we think we would need another five, at the least,' said Oddvin. 'Another ten would be useful. But I doubt we can find ten warriors of a high enough quality.'

'We have nearly five hundred warriors in and around Lodose – you may take your pick of them. Or would you prefer me to choose the men for you?'

'If you will choose thirty warriors whom you might find acceptable, highness,' said Harknut, 'we will pick out those whom *we* consider worthy to be *Felaki*.'

'Then I shall send you the thirty men tomorrow morning, Harknut,' Bjarki said, and he began to walk back up the beach towards the earth walls of Lodose.

Off to his left he could see Glamir Raeflisson deep in conversation with the king's shipwright Rudolf. And six large ships of war that were almost rigged and ready to put to sea. Harald Wartooth would be pleased when they met up with the Danish fleet at Viby in a dozen days' time. He had promised the old walrus five ships of war and now he was able to deliver six, each with a crew of eighty warriors. So the Wartooth would have nearly five hundred spears to swell his ranks at Norrkoping.

After Harald Wartooth had left Lodose, a week previously, Bjarki had abandoned work on three of the unfinished ships and concentrated all his wrights, timber, tar and other resources on the other six. In the next few days, they would be put to the test on the river and, after a live cockerel had been sacrificed on each, they would fill the benches, go down river to Gotaborg, and all six would put to sea.

The shadows were lengthening that afternoon, and Bjarki had only walked halfway round the walls of Lodose, still a hundred paces from the entry bridge, when he was intercepted by a running child, whom he recognised as a hall servant.

'Highness, highness,' squeaked the boy. 'The wolves have come to Lodose.'

The *Felaki* were immediately all around Bjarki, and bristling with aggression.

'What do you mean, Hunlaf?'

'Two wolves – in human form – are here. In the hall. They seek an audience with you, highness. We gave them meat and ale. Like men. But they are Wolf-men.'

–

Bjarki had not seen these two particular Wolf-men since they had all fought together in Saxony against the Franks. They had been strange creatures then, silent and watchful but proud, too, and easily offended. It appeared that they had not changed. They were Fire Born. Actual men – but Bjarki could see why the child had thought them wolves. They were twins, in early manhood, but with wiry grey and black streaked hair and pale inhuman eyes. They had long-nosed, pointed faces and were clad entirely in wolfskin, fur cloaks with wolfskin jerkins and shaggy wolf-trews. Their muscular, scarred arms were bare and browed by the sun, and each had one fat silver arm ring on the upper part of their left arm. A plain but well-kept sword hung at each of their waists and a throwing hatchet was tucked in their belts in front.

Fidor and Fodor were their names, and Bjarki knew these twins to be formidable warriors who were both inhabited in battle by a single Wolf *gandr* which they had summoned in the First Forest years ago. They were a fearsome pair, and while Bjarki was not at all afraid them, he knew them to be fully worthy of his respect.

'Lord king,' said Fidor, who could be distinguished from his brother by a small brown mark on his cheek, 'we offer you greetings, and thanks for your hospitality.'

'Fidor of Wolf Lodge! Rekkr, I welcome you and your brother to Lodose.'

There followed an awkward silence. All three men just stared at each other.

Bjarki, now in plain, dry clothes after the swimming lesson, sat in his throne and looked down at the shaggy pair who stood before him. They seemed older, and even wilder and more formidable than last time he had seen them. They had never been overly civilised but there was now something eerily feral about their demeanor.

They both gazed at him in silence.

'It has been some years since we last met,' said Bjarki, at last. 'Am I to take it that you no longer serve Duke Widukind of Saxony?'

'We stayed with Widukind in Nordalbia a month after you left us. With Jarl Ulf. But we are not men for feasting in great halls and sleeping in soft beds,' said Fidor.

'I can see that. What did you do next?'

'Widukind sent us back into the First Forest to make war on the Franks there.'

'They learned to fear us,' growled his brother Fodor. 'The Red Cloaks and the Green, and the Black, too. We killed many a Christian who strayed from the straight Frankish roads and wandered off into the forest. It was a time of death. A good time.'

'For a year or more, we killed the Franks. Just we two,' said Fidor. 'With no message from Widukind, nor his jarls or *hird*-men. Only forest sounds in our ears.'

'And the death screams of our enemies,' said Fodor.

'We were forgotten,' said Fidor. 'Abandoned by the duke in the wilderness.'

'So we returned to Nordalbia,' his brother said, 'and when we did, we found Widukind gone to the Dane-Mark. Jarl Ulf did not welcome our presence in his lands. The Franks possessed Saxony. Widukind was finished. The war was over, we found.'

'We went north. You'd say in the Fyr Skola, Bjarki: when in doubt, go north.'

'It is a fine principle to live by,' said Bjarki. 'Do you now seek a new lord, a king to serve? I could find a place in my *hird* for two mighty Rekkar such as you.'

Fidor laughed. It was a weird, grating sound, like iron being scraped over rock.

'We have a new lord, and a new homeland, with the Wulfings of Ostergotland. We are honoured there. It was Helgi the Wulfing who commanded us to visit you.'

At these words, there was a stiffening of spines from the *Felaki* who surrounded Bjarki on his throne. There was a vague tone of menace in the twins' odd words.

Bjarki sat perfectly still. He was unarmed but for his Harva seax. His sword and axe, shield and armour were in his chamber curtained off behind his throne. These two men were killers, raised in the same bloody tradition as he. *Did they mean him harm?*

'So you serve Helgi; he is a man of high renown. Why did he send you to me?'

187

The twins ignored Bjarki's question and turned to face the warriors of Lodose in the hall. There was a long, silent moment, in which death fluttered very close and anything might have happened. The twins stared at all the Vastergotlanders in the hall. Then Fodor turned back to the throne and said: 'We came to hail you, lord king!'

Bjarki grinned. He had tensed himself for violence. He had felt the stirring of Mochta in his heart at the sight of these two fearsome Wolf-men just a few feet away.

'You came to my hall, from the hall of Helgi the Wulfing in Ostergotland, yes? You walked through some two hundred miles of thick forest just to hail me king?'

'That is indeed the truth – we swear this by the Great Wolf,' said Fidor.

'But it is not the *only* reason we came to your hall, Fire Born king,' said Fodor.

'Oh, yes?' said Bjarki. He leaned back in his throne. He was, in truth, impressed by the courage of these two Rekkar. But he did not believe a word they said. They might easily have been sent here to murder him. Yet there were fifty Vastergotlander warriors in his hall. Not to mention Bjarki himself. Who, with half of his mind, was now wondering if he could beat both the twins in a fight. One, he was sure he could put down. Two of them...

'Yes,' said Fodor.

'Go on, then. What other reason did you have for honouring my hall with your presence?'

'As I said, we were sent here by Helgi the Wulfing. With an offer for you.'

'Perhaps you would prefer to discuss this in private,' said Fidor, gesturing at the growing crowd of muttering Lodose warriors who had pushed forwards to listen in.

'Perhaps, in your own quarters,' said Fidor. 'Just the three of us.'

'No, I don't think so,' said Bjarki. 'I'm more comfortable here. What offer?'

Bjarki adjusted his belt and fine tunic. He was careful not to touch his seax hilt.

Fidor shrugged. 'So be it. Helgi the Wulfing proposes an alliance of all Goths.'

Bjarki sat up a little straighter in his throne. 'What?'

Fodor said: 'The Vastergoths and Ostergoths are divided only by Lake Vattern – they are one people, united by blood, and separated only by a thin strip of water.'

Fidor said: 'The Wulfings were invited to ally themselves with Sigurd Hring. To fight beside him against the arrogant Danes. And against you, Bjarki, and all the men of Vastergotland. Helgi refused. To his mind, there was no sense in Goth killing Goth to decide which foreigner may call himself King of the North. Why should brothers from east and west spill each others' blood to make a Svear or a Dane their overlord?

'Helgi said to us: "The Goths now have their own king."' Fidor made a gesture at Bjarki with his hand. 'We now have a Fire Born warrior, beloved of the All-Father. The living heir of great Angantyr, King of the Goths, or so it is said, who resides here among us today. Why should not a true-blood Goth monarch rule justly over us all?'

'You mean *me*?' said Bjarki. And immediately regretted his stupid question.

'Do you know of another who fits this description?' said Fodor, frowning.

Bjarki swallowed. He turned to his steward: 'Bring ale for my guests!'

His brain was whirling furiously. *Could this offer be genuine?*

'Let us speak plainly: you want me to be king of *all* the Goths, yes? You – and more importantly Helgi the Wulfing and all his clan – want me to be the king of *both* Vastergotland and Ostergotland? Helgi will bend the knee to me and kiss my sword?'

'That is his offer,' said Fidor.

'And we – a united Goth homeland, under my rule – would throw off the yoke of the Dane-Mark, yet also have no alliance with Sigurd Hring of Svealand either?'

'This is what Helgi proposes,' said Fodor. 'And he offers you the hand of his eldest daughter Ynghildr to strengthen the alliance between East and West Goths. He says his grandchildren – the strong warriors you shall make with Ynghildr – will rule all Gotland when you and he are sipping hot wine with Odin in the Hall of the Slain.'

'She is tall, fair and smiling, a graceful woman – of just seventeen winters,' said Fidor. 'She is ripe. Her face as round and beautiful as the full moon. I have seen her.'

'What of the island of Gotland?' said Bjarki – just for something to say, some argument to make; his mind whirling, all his thoughts crashing into each other.

'What of it?' said Fidor. 'They know you there. Folk in Fröjol speak often of the heir of Angantyr. If they wished to join us, we would welcome them. If not, we could leave them be – or compel them to submit. It would be your decision alone as king.'

'And you two – you are also Fire Born – you would serve me willingly? You are Saxon, not Goth. But you two would also swear a mighty oath to me as your king?'

'We have served you before. We *know* you. We have seen the Bear inside you.'

At that moment, the steward appeared with a tray and a jug of ale. While the man was serving the cups out to the two Wolf warriors, Bjarki was thinking hard.

For the first time in an age, he wished Valtyr was near at hand. Sober or drunk, he would have valued his counsel.

'I will sleep on it,' he said. 'And give my answer in the morning. My steward will see that you are provided with food and a place to sleep. I'll consider the offer.'

–

Bjarki sat hunched on a three-legged stool in his private chamber. Alone but for a horn of mead and his thoughts. He did not feel tired at all. Indeed, his heart was beating very fast and his whole body was quivering slightly. *Could this offer actually be real?*

He did not know Helgi the Wulfing at all except by his grim reputation – as a ruthless and cunning warlord who had come to dominate all Ostergotland with his large family of ruthless warriors. The Wulfings were a Wolf-*gandr* worshipping clan, he knew, who claimed their descent from Loki, through the trickster god's animal-son Fenrir the Wolf, famed for biting off the hand of the gullible war god Tyr.

It was no surprise the twins had found themselves welcome in Wulfing territory.

If Bjarki became king of all Goth lands he would be as powerful as Sigurd Hring – his numbers a match for the strength of Svea-land. If he combined his forces with Sigurd Hring's, a new army of Goths and Svear would match the mighty Danish host.

A Goth nation united at last. With him as its king. It was a dizzying idea.

Could the offer be real? And could he truly trust Helgi the Wulfing?

The answer to the second question was obvious – even to Bjarki, who was not famed for his deep thinking. No, he could *not* trust the Wulfings. If he allowed himself to make a peace with the Ostergotlanders, and join forces with them, he might be setting himself up for a trap. They might murder him even as he ascended the throne.

What would Valtyr say? What would Tor's counsel be? He wished his sister was with him, too. Valtyr would be in favour of unity, Bjarki thought. Fewer factions fighting each other would make the whole of the North stronger. That would be Valtyr's view. The old man would surely urge him to accept Helgi's generous offer.

And Tor? Perhaps she, too, would urge him to join the Wulf-ings, and ally with Sigurd Hring and his Svear. And together they would all throw off the Danish yoke.

But something Tor had said to him long ago now surfaced in his mind.

'If something seems too good to be true, oaf, it most probably is,' she had said.

This offer seemed too good to be true. Helgi the Wulfing was surrendering his power to Bjarki. Why would he do that? Because he loved peace? Because he loved the idea of a Goth nation? Because he loved Bjarki? None of these seemed plausible.

And not only power: his beautiful young daughter was to be given to Bjarki.

The offer *was* too good to be true. And did he truly want to marry some moon-faced young girl anyway? No – his heart still belonged to Edith. Hers was the face that he saw, her lips that he kissed in his dreams. Yet Edith was promised to another, and soon she would be married to Abbio the Crow. In Viby. In King Siegfried's hall.

And what of the King of the Dane-Mark?

Siegfried had made him King of Vastergotland. And Bjarki had sworn a binding oath to Siegfried. A vow to be ever loyal to the Danish king and fight for his cause.

Bjarki was no oath-breaker. And he realised then that he had made his decision.

Chapter Eighteen

'You move very well'

Tor reined in before the south gate of the royal compound at Uppsala. She was tired, her horse was tired, and she wanted more than anything to find her people, eat something and climb into a very hot bath. It was noon and the bathhouse would be empty at this hour, which was good. But whether there was any hot water was another matter.

There were two spearmen at the gate she did not recognise. Beyond them a long, lean man was lounging against the side of a wagon piled with sacks of grain.

The two spearmen blocked her path with their crossed spears, and Erland the Snake pushed himself off the side of the wagon and sauntered towards her. He moved beautifully, Tor thought, a hip-driven liquid slide more than a walk. It seemed effortless, elegant. He stopped at her horse's nose, grasped the bridle, and smiled up at her.

'You are the shield-maiden,' he said, nodding slowly to show his recognition.

'I'm one of several,' she replied. 'I think there are about a dozen with the army.'

She was not in the mood to bicker or argue with him. She wanted to get in to the royal compound, have her bath, and go about her business without interference.

'But you are the only one who can fight,' said Erland. 'You have been *trained*. I saw you exercising some weeks ago with your jarl's *hird*. You move very well.'

'For a woman?'

'For any warrior. I'd back you with silver to win against nine tenths of the men in the king's army, in a proper fight. Where did you learn to use a blade so well?'

'My mother hired swordsmen to teach me, when I was but a child... Is this important? I would like to enter the compound and see my jarl. Kindly let me pass.'

'Of course.' Erland released the bridle and stepped back and to the side – another fluid, dance-like movement. He was still smiling at her in a familiar way she did not much care for. She had the feeling that he could see into her skull and knew her secret thoughts. That he already knew about the deceptions she meant to practise.

She walked her horse a few feet forwards and stopped beside him.

Before she could speak, Erland said: 'One day, when I am not on duty, we shall have a friendly bout with swords, you and I. It would be something to watch, I think. I'm better. But you would be a worthy opponent. We might even make a tiny wager.'

'Or a big one,' she replied. 'But when I am not so travel-raw. Until then, nimble-pins, stop grinning like a monkey and tell me where the king is. In his hall?'

'The king has gone hawking this day, with some of his favoured oath-men.'

'With the Royal Huntsman too?'

'Rorik Halfdan? Yes.'

'Why do you call him that?'

'His mother was Danish, or so I heard tell. I also heard a rumour that you have a blood feud running with that young fellow. I am surprised that he still breathes.'

'I, too, am astonished at my forbearance,' said Tor. 'I'll remedy it soon.' She nodded at Erland, kicked her horse into a canter and went thudding through the gate.

Despite what she had said to Erland the Snake, Tor had no immediate plan to slaughter Rorik. Indeed, she was glad the cowardly worm was out of her way that day. She had things to do. She rode directly to the king's hall, dismounted, tied her horse up outside, and taking a cloth-wrapped package from a saddlebag, she pushed inside the half-open door.

She found the king's steward in a side chamber off the main hall, in a flour-dusted space where the racks of barley bread were allowed to cool after baking. The man was just biting into a delicious-looking cheese pie but, with fine courtesy, he set aside his snack and listened most attentively while Tor explained why she was there.

'A costly gift, you say, and for the king?' the man said, wiping crumbs from his chin. 'Why do you not give it to him yourself? He will be back tonight for a feast – everyone will be here, all the great heroes and the jarls, all the noblest oath-men – why not give it to him then, and receive the gratitude of Sigurd Hring. He might even reward you.'

'I must be away before dusk,' said Tor, which was true. 'I have business to conduct for Jarl Starki.' That was a lie, but she tried not to let it show in her face.

The hot pie smelled delicious. And she had half a mind to ask him for a bite of it. But she restrained herself.

'You give my gift to the king, lord steward, and explain it is a special sword that comes from the village by Lake Vattern where Harva the Smith plies his trade.'

That was not *exactly* a lie.

'A Harva blade, eh?' said the steward, smiling. 'That is a fine gift indeed.'

Tor did not correct him – was that lying? No. It was simply a ruse of war.

'I shall ensure the king receives it. On his behalf, I thank you warmly.'

As Tor walked away, now properly hungry, she heard the old man muttering: 'A Harva blade, a Harva blade… A genuine Harva sword right here in my two hands!'

Tor arrived at Bearstead three days later, and was surprised to see Valtyr sitting on a stool outside the longhouse in the sunshine, with a jug of ale at his knee and a full, foaming horn in his right hand. On the short ride north from the town Gavle, where she had been speaking with some shipmasters, she had been pondering the problem of shipping a wild creature to the south, a journey of several days, and who should ward it on the voyage; now, it seemed, a solution had presented itself.

'I spy Torfinna Hildarsdottir, rightful Queen of Bearstead, who is returned to her forest realm at last,' the one-eyed old fellow said, rising unsteadily from his stool.

'Valtyr Far-Traveller, drunk again and spouting the usual nonsense,' she replied, smiling, then submitted herself to a brief, ale-perfumed embrace from the old man.

'Have you decided to sit out the great battle here, Tor? By my calculations it takes place in only nine days' time. It would be a wise decision, I think. Put your feet up in Bearstead, and let the rest of the North uselessly tear itself apart at Norrkoping.'

'You know me well, old fool. What do *you* think?' said Tor.

'I think you will choose, once again, to rush eagerly to your destruction,' said Valtyr. But before they could begin to argue, Tor saw Inge and Joralf coming round the side of the barn, holding hands, and she was pierced by a shaft of pure happiness.

'We all go to our destruction in our own way, old man,' she said, patting his arm. 'Have another jug of ale, why don't you. Have two, if you've a proper thirst!'

They feasted that night, and all was well. The *Felaki* women, at the urging of Kynwulf, cooked a vast meal of suckling pig, roast venison and buttered turnips with fresh baked bread, egg puddings, fruit pies and cheese. The leader of the Goth women – Harknut's wife Trudi – apologised for the lack of mead, saying the Honeyman had not been for weeks and there was not a drop of sweet stuff left in the steading.

Tor's suspicious were raised when she saw that Kynwulf was at the steading without Bjarki, and immediately guessed what her oaf of a brother had in his mind.

She called both Kynwulf and Valtyr to counsel with her when the meal was resting comfortably in their bellies. And they sat by the glowing hearth, the three of them, talking long into the night, drinking ale, discussing many options and shaping their plans. And when Tor finally went to bed long past midnight, she was content.

In the dawn, comforted by the agreement she had reached with both men, Tor set out into the forest, alone with her bow and a blanket, a coil of stout rope and an old leather collar. She was venturing forth once again in search of her beloved Garm.

–

The bear scented that something was wrong long before Tor did. The woman and the wild creature had found each other with the usual lack of difficulty about half a day's walk out of Bearstead to the north and west. They had wrestled and played together until dark, before eating and sleeping the night curled up together in a rowan bush.

Tor had not needed to use the collar and rope, after all, for Garm had followed her willingly, lolloping along beside her striding form all the way back to the gates of Bearstead. But once there, Garm had begun whining, growling and acting strangely.

Tor, too, felt a hum of imminent danger. She nocked an arrow to her bow and advanced carefully. One of the gates of the steading was open, which was unusual, and as she drew closer, Tor could hear the wailing of a woman in terrible distress.

Tor edged round the gate of the steading, bow at the ready, and looked into the courtyard. The first thing she saw was a little donkey cart loaded up with boxes and jars, but no donkey.

She saw Kynwulf, on his knees in the far corner of the court-yard, retching, a thin yellow drool pouring from his open mouth.

The woman's wailing was coming from inside the main long-house, and Tor advanced slowly, cautiously, her bow still held at the ready. There were other voices too, less loud but calling out in pain and sorrow from inside the house. She was aware that Garm had entered the courtyard and was sitting on his haunches, looking about him with bemused interest.

The bear moved towards the laden donkey cart.

'No,' said Kynwulf, his voice weak. 'Don't touch the honey. Don't eat it.' The old warrior lurched to his feet. 'Don't eat. Poison!' he managed to yell out.

'Get away from there, Garm!' Tor shouted, just as the bear shoved his snout into the jars and packages on the cart's bed. Tor flung away the bow and arrow and rushed headlong towards her enormous pet. The animal took one tiny, delicate sniff of the contents of the donkey cart, then reared his huge black head back in disgust.

'Get back, Garm!' Tor was beside him now, her arms around his massive neck, trying to haul him away. Their strengths were so absurdly mismatched that she made no impact on the animal at all. But Garm's extraordinary sense of smell had identified the acrid tang of poison better than any human's could, and after a final cautious confirmatory sniff, the bear ambled away from the honey cart of his own accord.

With a sense of horror and dread, Tor ventured into the house. Once through the door, she immediately saw the occupied straw pallet on the floor beside the hearth fire, with a small blonde head resting on a rolled-up blanket, eyes closed. She rushed forwards, fell to her knees beside the pallet, reaching out for the bone-white face with both her hands. Inge's cheeks were icy cold, and Tor leaned in, putting her ear to the girl's lips. No breath stirred. None. Tor fumbled at her throat for a pulse. Nothing.

Tor sat back on her haunches, and let out one long shuddering breath of sorrow.

She stared down at the white little face. So still. So calm. *Even in death*, Tor thought, *she's as beautiful as the frost. A frosty dawn that will never become full day*.

Joralf thumped down beside her by the pallet; his lean face, too, was pale and stained with tears. But not from poison. His body sagged, seemingly unstrung, almost as if he were drunk. He reached out and took Inge's small hand in both his big ones.

Tor half-expected the girl to open her blue eyes and smile happily up at him.

'She ate the honey cake,' Joralf said. 'She ate it before I could stop her. The others, too. The children were there first… at the cart… then Inge, she took one and… we were talking while she chewed. I *saw* her swallow… and I did nothing.'

It took a little while for the story to make any sense at all to Tor. It was Valtyr who explained it to her, patiently, even soberly, over the next few pain-dulled hours.

They had not seen the Honey Hunter arrive but, during the night, while Tor had been off in the forest with Garm, the Honeyman's cart, loaded with delicious goods, had been left abandoned just outside the steading's front gates. The donkey was long gone, perhaps ridden away by whoever had left the cart there.

The Bearstead folk had pulled the little vehicle inside the courtyard themselves that sunny morning and examined its bounty. It seemed like a gift from the gods. Or from the kindly Honeyman. There were the usual pots and barrels of sweet wild honey, skins of mead and blocks of wax, and a platter wrapped in cloth containing a dozen sticky honey cakes, containing berries and nuts and – so it seemed to Valtyr – serious quantities of a natural *eitr*, a powerful poison that grew wild in the woods.

'I think it was the juice of the plant that folk call the wolfsbane,' said the old man. 'It is naturally acrid, so the honey was necessary to conceal the bitter taste.'

'This can be no accident, then?' asked Tor.

'No. The cakes were deliberately poisoned. Whoever left the cart here meant to kill as many people as he or she possibly could.'

Inge was not the only one who had been killed – murdered – by the honey cakes. All but one of the five children had succumbed to the poison, and two of the *Felaki* women were also dead as well. Kynwulf had only had one small bite of his cake – he had set the rest down to enjoy later. And that had saved his life. The surviving wives of Harknut and Bodvar – Trudi and Elsa – were both numb with grief and exhausted from their crying. Valtyr had been spared because he had been sleeping off his ale in a pile of straw in one of the Bearstead barns until late that morning, and Sambor had been busy chopping wood for the pile when the women and children had flocked round the Honeyman's cart and eagerly helped themselves to the tainted sweets.

'Who. Does. This. Bad. Thing?' Sambor spat at Tor.

The Polans warrior was red-faced with anger. He had utterly failed in his task to protect the daughter of the Duke of Polans, who was in his charge. He was quivering with rage – and perhaps shame as well. 'Tell. Me. Killer. Name,' he begged Tor.

Tor herself was surprisingly calm. The truth of the carnage inflicted on the folk in her home was in the very front of her mind. But, at least for now, she *felt* nothing, just a black emptiness inside. Four Bearstead children were dead and cold. Two women of her household had perished in agony. Inge, whom she had loved like a daughter, was gone as well. Yet she had no tears to shed for any of them.

She left the compound, after locking Garm in his shed with the remains of the suckling pig – the shed that her boy never used – and went alone into the woods. She felt she had to get away from the horror and grief – from the cold, hard emptiness of so much death. Valtyr was busy organising the burials of the two *Felaki* women and their four children. Joralf was digging a deep grave for his lover Inge. The surviving *Felaki* women were clearing up the vomit and faeces – the seven deaths had been neither clean nor quick. Tor felt she must get away for an hour or so. She had to leave Bearstead. She wanted to be certain of the truth before she acted.

She found the Honey Hunter's corpse half an hour's walk west of her steading, the old man lying like a discarded pile of rags beside the main path to Bjorke.

Someone had cut his throat open, and a wide red smile yawned under his chin. His eyes were staring and Tor closed them. Then she knelt down beside him and touched the spilled blood on his neck with one shaking finger. She pulled open her leather jerkin with her left hand and with her bloodied finger she painted the rune associated with the god Vidarr between her small white breasts. Over her heart.

She felt the cold forest air caress her bare skin and closed her eyes tightly.

'Hear me, Vidarr, hear me, son of Odin, hear me, O Great One who hunts down the wicked and delivers them to their doom. Aid me in this necessary task. Aid me in my quest for justice. For I must have vengeance on the one who killed this old man. Hear me, Honeyman, the one who slew you shall pay the full price. I shall have my vengeance, too, on the one who killed my Inge, and the poor women and children of my steading, all those who looked to me for their safety. I hereby pledge my life to this revenge. May I rot for ever in Hel's chilly realm if I fail in this my sacred duty.'

She opened her eyes and looked at the corpse. He seemed to be laughing at her.

Tor threw back her head and roared out the name of her quarry to the heavens.

'Rorik Hafnarsson!' she bellowed. 'Roooorrrrriiiik! I'm coming for you. I shall hold your miserable life in the palm of my hand. Your death shall be neither swift nor easy. I shall relish it. You shall see your doom coming from afar and be powerless to stop its slow approach. This I swear on the shade of my beloved daughter, Inge!'

Then, at last, she allowed herself to release all the pent-up sorrow in her heart.

Chapter Nineteen

'Death to the king!'

Fidor and Fodor received Bjarki's decision to reject Helgi the Wulfing's offer in stony silence. The Wolf twins simply stared at him with their odd pale eyes for much longer than necessary after he had finished speaking. And Bjarki felt a strong urge to explain again that his first loyalty must be to the King of the Dane-Mark, who held his oath.

He managed to hold his tongue.

'I can offer you food and ale for your journey,' said Bjarki, eventually, 'and perhaps an escort, if you require one. But I must ask you to leave Vastergotland as soon as possible. If the gods are kind, we shall meet again in happier times.'

'We require nothing from you,' said Fidor. 'And I shall say only this before we depart: it is clear you do not trust Helgi – and perhaps you do not trust us either. But Helgi's desire for a unified Goth land will not alter. One day he will achieve a union of our people, of Vastergotland and Ostergotland, and Gotland Island, too, with your help or without it.'

'And we *shall* meet again,' said Fodor.

Bjarki could feel the four *Felaki* around his throne bristle at the implied threat. But he calmly said: 'You have my leave to depart Lodose. Go now and go quickly!'

When the two brothers had stalked out of the hall, Bjarki beckoned Rask to him.

The small warrior had fully recovered his swagger after his ordeal in the river, and looked up eagerly into Bjarki's face.

'Follow them on the journey back to Ostergotland,' Bjarki said. 'Go as far as the borderlands at the base of Lake Vattern. But go no further. I wish to be sure they are no longer in my domain. Do not let them see you. Do not engage them in a fight. If they attack you, run like the wind. But it is far better if they do not see you at all.'

'As you command, highness,' said Rask.

–

The thirty unarmed warriors were lined up in a row in the sheep pasture to the south of the Lodose hall. Each man's face was a mask of impassive concentration, his body stiffly upright, feet together. Bjarki knew some of them by name, others by their appearance. A few he did not know at all. They were all young – younger than most of the *Felaki* whose ranks they hoped to join – the eldest being a little less than thirty summers, by the look of him. They had all been chosen for him by Captain Mogils, and they were the best of his five hundred or so *hird* troops in Vastergotland, and the ones Mogils claimed were the most loyal to their king.

Bjarki walked along the line, trailed by a nervous Mogils, with the three *Felaki* hovering nearly, and looking down their noses at the rank of immobile Goth warriors.

'You have been chosen because you are the best in Vastergotland,' said Bjarki. 'And I have need of the best in the ranks of my Companions. But the choice will not be made by me but by Harknut Harknutsson, this man here, who commands the *Felaki* in the War Chief's absence and who will name those who are to be honoured.'

The thirty warriors said nothing.

'Are you all willing to be tested this day?' said Bjarki.

There were mutters of assent. Harknut stepped forwards. 'You will speak loudly and clearly when the king asks a question. He said: "Are you ready to be tested?"'

This time the response was a bellow of noise from thirty throats. 'Yes, sire!'

'Very well,' said Bjarki, 'Harknut, these good men are now in your hands.'

Bjarki stepped away from the line and found that Haugen Halfhand had brought along a three-legged stool for him to sit on. Reluctantly, he plumped down and watched as Harknut spent a little time talking to every single man in the line. He seemed to be asking about their families, their experience of war, everything relevant, even asking about their gods. The conversation was too low for Bjarki to hear clearly.

He looked up at the blue sky, and watched the clouds shift and form, swirling and changing their shapes like gigantic armies manoeuvring on a battlefield. He wondered if clouds ever fought amongst themselves as men did. Did they struggle and fight for power like humankind? Were clouds in truth alive? With feelings and personalities? Or were they just the visible breath of gods, as some *gothi* claimed?

It took a full hand-span of the sun before the first test of the candidates began, which was a simple demonstration of each candidate's fitness to fight a hard battle. Harknut indicated a green field of ripening rye, which was about a thousand paces away, to the east of the Lodose hall, the last cultivated field before the forest wall began, and ordered the men to run there and each bring back to him one unbroken stalk of rye. It was a straightforward test of speed. The thirty young men pelted off towards the rye field, and returned a little while later panting, and clutching their carefully preserved stalk.

The last few men to return, and those who had returned with carelessly broken stalks, were brusquely excluded from the competition. Bjarki rose from his stool to say something kind and encouraging to them but Haugen put a firm hand on his shoulder to silence him. So five hangdog young men duly left the testing field, some glancing enviously back over their shoulders at their more successful comrades.

For the next test, Harknut had them all jumping high into the air, and slapping their own calves with both palms. He walked along the line and encouraged them to jump higher, and slap their legs harder. They were all soon exhausted by this simple jumping exercise. Bjarki observed the grim determination in some of the men's faces and was impressed. When any man stopped jumping, Harknut told him he was out.

When five men had been dismissed, Harknut stopped the exercise and allowed the remaining twenty men to drink water or ale and rest for a little while on the ground, rubbing their blotched legs. The remaining candidates were all red-faced and breathless, some exhausted, but were aware they had achieved something worthwhile by their hard labours. And they were still in this testing game.

After a decent length of time, Harknut ordered them all to their feet, and the final twenty were put into ten pairs. Each pair was ordered, on Harknut's word of command, to wrestle the other fellow to the ground, and pin him there for a count of three. No biting or gouging was allowed. A few blows, grunts and meaty thuds later, and another ten men – the losers in their respective bouts – were sent despondently back to their barracks, some scowling, some of them limping and bleeding a little.

That left ten warriors in the competition, breathless, hot, beaming at each other.

There was now an air of relaxation and quiet triumph among the remaining candidates. Bjarki tried hard to appear similarly relaxed as well.

He sat on his little stool and smiled genially at the final ten Goth warriors.

'My friends,' he began, 'you have all shown yourselves to be the best...'

An ear-splitting scream ripped the air. Oddvin, youngest of the *Felaki*, had drawn his seax. He was standing ten paces behind Bjarki with no one between them.

Oddvin bellowed: 'Death to the king!' and hurled himself at Bjarki. He sprinted forwards, his seax held high in the air, the foot-long blade gleaming in the summer sunshine. It took him only three heartbeats to reach the king, the blade hammering down towards Bjarki's head. Yet his terrible killing blow never landed.

Three of the candidates reacted fast. One immediately threw himself at Oddvin and caught his swift-moving right arm, just as it was chopping down towards Bjarki's head. The second hit Oddvin's body, with his arms around the *Felaki*'s waist, which knocked him flying. And the third – a man called Black Ivar – jumped directly between Oddvin and Bjarki, and spread his arms wide, protecting the king with his own unarmed body. A fourth warrior leapt on top of the struggling mass of Oddvin and his assailants and pinned the would-be murderer's left arm. Then one more jumped forwards and pinned his kicking legs, receiving a painful knee in the face.

The rest of the group, five candidates, simply stared, gaping with astonishment.

Bjarki stood up. 'Stop. Release him. Let go of Oddvin now – this instant!'

Oddvin immediately stopped struggling. The unarmed men pinning him to the ground raised their five heads in surprise. 'Let him go,' said Bjarki, coming forwards.

The men released Oddvin, some frowning in puzzlement, and Bjarki reached down a massive hand and pulled his youngest *Felaki* warrior to his feet.

'There was never any danger,' he said. 'This was simply today's final test.'

Harknut stepped forwards. 'You five men,' he said, pointing at the ones who had not reacted swiftly enough to the apparent danger to the king, 'you can all go back to your homes now. The king thanks you for your efforts, but your competition is over.'

Five disappointed men began to trudge their way over the fields back towards Lodose. Harknut, Oddvin and Haugen surrounded the remaining five. Harknut said: 'There will be one more test for you men – after supper tonight. But perhaps it will not prove too irksome. After the feast, we shall see if you can hold your ale without puking. Some may fail. But, for now, you five may all consider yourselves *Felaki*.'

There was a good deal of cheering, grinning and slapping of backs, and Bjarki embraced each man to welcome him to his service, and there and then, Bjarki took their oaths. His new Companions, his five new *Felaki*, each in turn knelt before his three-legged stool, said the time-honoured words of the vow, and put the blade of his sword to their lips. And that night they all feasted together like the heroes of old.

–

Three days later, they launched the six ships into the river. Bjarki acted as the *gothi*, since the Vastergotlanders had always, time out of mind, combined the roles of ruler and priest in one man. Glamir was on hand to advise Bjarki in the rituals, having seen his father Raefli perform these rites on many occasions. And Bjarki, accordingly, shouted loudly to attract the gods' attentions – particularly Rán, goddess of the sea, and Njord, who controlled the winds – and at each ship he was handed a bound black and red cockerel. Bjarki sliced through the bird's neck with his seax, and directed the hot blood to spatter the prow of the ship, saying: 'May the hearts of the warriors aboard this fine vessel' – and he named the ship – 'be as brave as fighting cocks, and their passage across the sea be as calm as the crossing of a mill pond, and may this good ship always bring them safe back to harbour when the voyage is done!'

Then the nearly empty ship was shoved down the strand, over a series of smooth wooden rollers on the beach, and straight into the river with an almighty splash.

It took a considerable time to launch all six ships, most of the afternoon, in fact, and Bjarki was drenched with sticky chicken gore by the time he had finished. So, when the last vessel was bobbing in the middle of the stream, the captain hauling up her square sail with the new flax rigging, Bjarki, without removing any of his clothes, plunged in to wash the blood off.

He was rinsing his long hair in the river, squeezing it out, and scrubbing at his blood-crusted hands, when Black Ivar swam up to him, with a few brisk easy strokes.

'A ship has arrived, sire – another ship, not one of those we launched today,' he said. 'Harknut says you should come see. It has something very unusual on board.'

It was the *Sea Elk*. And the unusual thing was a huge black bear, squatting in the prow and regarding the town of Lodose and the mass of gathered people with interest.

-

The *Sea Elk* was returned but Tor was not with her. The crew consisted of Valtyr, Kynwulf, Sambor, Joralf and two *Felaki* women – one of whom was Harknut's wife Trudi – and one orphaned *Felaki* child, which they were taking turns to care for.

And, of course, Garm.

Rask, too, had returned from following the Wolf twins east to the border with Ostergotland but Bjarki could barely bring himself to listen to his report. His mind was whirling, skidding from this matter to that, careering between fury and grief.

'My thanks, Rask. You did well,' he said distractedly to the little warrior. 'Get some food and rest.' He summoned Valtyr and Kynwulf and asked them to repeat their report of events in Norrland, and explain why Tor had not returned with them.

Valtyr told him sombrely once more about the deaths of Inge and the *Felaki* women and children and the poisoned cakes. Bjarki looked at him with disbelief.

'This man Rorik left poisoned food outside Bearstead, meaning to kill as many of our folk as possible,' he said. 'Women, children... What kind of man *does* that?'

He found that tears were running freely down his blond, bearded cheeks.

The death of Inge was... incomprehensible to him. She had been so vital, so filled with potential. So alive. A happy, carefree girl, the living joy of Bearstead.

'So Tor is staying up in Svealand to take revenge on Rorik Hafnarsson? Good.'

'She burns for revenge, yes,' said Valtyr, 'but more than that, she's determined she will not break her oath to Starki. She says she would rather die than be forsworn but...' Then the one-eyed wanderer revealed to Bjarki what was in his sister's mind.

—

Bjarki gathered the full armed might of Vastergotland on the strand before the six moored and fully rigged ships. There were nearly six hundred fighting men and a handful of shield-maidens, all standing there looking at Bjarki who was wobbling on his little three-legged stool near the water's edge so that all there might see him.

Each warrior had a spear, shield and helm, at the very least, and most had seaxes, wood axes, or throwing axes as well – a lucky few even had swords. They had leather armour for the most part, cuirasses, double boiled to make the leather tough enough to turn a blade, and some of the veterans had iron mail-link byrnies.

There were a dozen or so archers, too, lightly armoured for swift movement on the battlefield, and some of the local lads, deemed too young to fight, were armed with leather slings and pouches filled with round river stones. Those who survived the battle expected to gain a rich booty from the enemy corpses – swords, precious jewellery, golden arm rings, pouches of hack-silver. More valuable than any prize of war, one who stood at Norrkoping and lived would be famed throughout the North.

Around Bjarki, tottering on his stool, stood his Companions.

Ten *Felaki* warriors, under their War Chief, Kynwulf – men judged the finest warriors in Lodose. Perhaps the best men in all the North, Bjarki believed. And they were more than eager for the coming fight. Each Companion had a new round lime-wood shield, decorated with broad alternating swirls of white and red, which grew like curved blades out of the central iron boss, with an image of a rearing black bear depicted on the top white swirl – Bjarki's personal sigil. And to one side of the *Felaki* stood Glamir Raeflisson, his *Merkismathr*, the banner bearer in full war gear and carrying an ash pole with another image of the black bear, flapping in the breeze.

'Brave warriors of Vastergotland,' boomed Bjarki, trying to make his voice reach to the furthest ranks. 'We are about to embark on the greatest adventure of all. Our friend and ally King Siegfried of the Dane-Mark has summoned us, as his loyal oath-men, to support him in the fight at Norrkoping. We shall oblige him – willingly. The folk of Vastergotland shall never be found wanting on the day of bloody battle.'

Loud cheers from the more eager warriors, some of whom had been drinking.

'We fight for our honour, our wives, our sweethearts, our children, and for the future of Vastergotland; and so that no man may say, when the trumpet called and the war drum beat out its summons, that King Bjarki's warriors held back from the fray.

'I know in my heart that each and every one of you will fight with courage, as your ancestors did before you, with valour and skill, for the glory of Vastergotland. I know, too, that the traitorous Svear, the lickspittle toadies of so-called King Sigurd Hring, will be sent reeling back, filled with the shame that is the lot of all cowards.

'Some of you may fall in the great battle that is to come, some of you may perish in the fray and the blood-frenzy... but your names shall live for ever, and be spoken of in reverent tones until the ending of the world. A seat awaits all who fall in battle at the table of Odin, Spear-Shaker, who loves a proud warrior, and who will greet you in the Hall of the Slain with a foaming cup, when the red day is ours.

'Remember: you fight for Vastergotland, you fight for your families. And you fight for me – for Bjarki Bloodhand, King of the Goths! And I shall remember and reward each and every man and woman who stands with me on this day of glory.'

The tumult rolled around the whole valley of the river Gota, the cheers echoing back from the edges of the forest. 'Bjarki... Bjarki... Bjarki... the... king!'

After a little while, Bjarki held up his hand to quiet the cheering horde.

'Your *lith* captains will tell you which ship to board. And that ship will take you to Viby, where you will meet up with the grand fleet of King Siegfried – and the mightiest array of vessels the Middle-Realm has ever seen. From there you will sail round the peninsula into the Eastern Sea, and up to the inlet of Braviken that cuts into the land at the old border between Ostergotland and Svealand. There, under the shadow of the long Kolmarden ridge, you and thousands of Danish warriors under the king's *Armathr*, Harald Wartooth, will fight – and triumph! – and gain lasting fame.

'And while I shall not be sailing with you this day, I shall meet you there, in the lee of the Kolmarden, to join you in the fray, by your side, as your brother-in-arms.'

There Bjarki paused to let the message sink in. There was a murmuring from the crowd, and one voice shouted out: 'So you're not going to sail there with us, Bjarki?'

'I shall join you in a few days. I swear this on my honour. Only my death can prevent it. But I cannot sail with you this day. Never fear. I leave you in safe hands. Captain Mogils, whom you all know by now, has accepted the role as my *Armathr*. Mogils shall be your commander, and Glamir Raeflisson, my *Merkismathr*, shall lead you into the field, holding up the Bear banner that is the honour of our people!'

The gathering of warriors seemed uncertain about this. There were a few cheers but the murmuring increased as many a man asked his neighbour what it all meant.

'Let me hear your voices,' bellowed Bjarki: 'For victory, and Vastergotland!'

Six hundred warriors dutifully bellowed back: 'For victory, and Vastergotland!'

The next morning Lodose town was a forlorn place. A few score of mostly elderly warriors remained to guard the hall and their homes and fields. But there was a quiet to the town that was eerie. The sound of women's voices could be heard everywhere, with no men present to bid them to be silent. Bjarki met his Companions in the hall. He was dressed for travel – loose clothing, stout boots, the Harva seax at his waist, and his ragged, horribly discoloured bearskin on his back. All his war gear was packed up in a bundle.

The thirteen warriors gathered in a circle: ten Companions, Joralf the Swordsman, Sambor the Polans – and Bjarki Bloodhand, King of the Goths.

To one side, at a long empty bench, sat Valtyr Far-Traveller, who already had an ale jug and a cup on the table beside him, and a befuddled grin on his wrinkled face. The King's Envoy had volunteered to remain in Lodose and act as ruler in Bjarki's stead until the fighting was done and the king returned to his hall. Outside the opened doors of the Lodose hall the dark, humped shape of Garm, tied securely to a massive door post, snoozed quietly in a warm pool of summer sunshine.

'Is everyone prepared?' asked Bjarki, looking round every face in the circle.

There were a series of nods and muttered assents.

'Then, my friends,' he said, 'let us go to war!'

Chapter Twenty

'Where have you been?'

The death of Inge had settled over Tor like a coating of ice, a brittle, translucent shell that allowed her to observe the world but did not allow the world to touch her.

When she had dispatched the living folk from Bearstead with Valtyr, and said the final words over the graves of all the dead, she nailed the door of her longhouse shut with a couple of planks, let the pigs and ducks loose to fend for themselves, barred the entrances to the various outhouses, stables and barns, then saddled her horse and rode south, through Gavle and on towards distant Uppsala to rejoin the men of her master Jarl Starki's *hird*.

Battle called to her.

'Where have you *been*?' said Gudrik, when she arrived at the jarl's guest hall inside the royal compound. 'The battle is in three days, Tor. Jarl Starki has been going mad wondering where you were. He wants his Harva sword. He thought you might have gone over to the enemy, joined your traitor brother in the Danish ranks. Where were you?'

'I regret that you have had to carry so much of my burden, Gudrik,' she said.

'I don't mind that. What I don't like is a nervous jarl barking questions at me all day. Questions I cannot answer. Tor, will you please go and explain yourself to him?'

Tor shrugged. 'Maybe later.' Then she told her hard-pressed *Merkismathr* everything about the honey-poisoning of Inge and deaths of her people at Bearstead.

Gudrik was shocked. 'You think this was the work of Rorik Hafnarsson?'

'He has been seen in the area recently. And some men from Sodermanland scouted my steading several weeks ago. Yes, it was Rorik. I am certain of it.'

'You must tell the jarl, or tell the king – have that wretch hanged for murder.'

'The king protects him. And I have other plans for Rorik. When do we march?'

'Tomorrow at dawn. Sigurd wants us in our positions on the Kolmarden a full day before the first of Heyannir – in case the Danes try an early surprise attack.'

Tor managed to avoid speaking to her furious jarl on the two-day march down to the border of Sodermanland, which was quite an impressive feat. They saw each other at a distance several times as the whole Svear army and its allies moved south along the crowded roads, but when Jarl Starki beckoned her she simply waved back cheerily and disappeared into the marching throng.

Starki did not pursue her, he was himself busy with supervising his household servants and his lengthy baggage train, while Tor and Gudrik equally had their hands full with keeping the two hundred and three warriors of the *hird* in line and cosseting the eighty-one untrained levies. These hapless levies were essentially no more than poorly armed Norrland peasants, some of whom had never travelled more than a day's walk away from their stead-ings before. Most were bewildered and frightened and acted like children – in contrast, some were oddly boastful considering that they had never fought a battle. Many of them would no doubt flee at the first sight of the enemy host, but a few dozen would find their courage on the day of battle – and a good handful might even make decent warriors in time. If they survived long enough.

Word had spread fast through the army about the poisonings at Bearstead, and many well-meaning folk tried to offer their condolences to Tor and share their sense of outrage. Inge had been well liked in Norrland and popular with many folk around

Uppsala, too. The name Rorik Hafnarsson was muttered with anger. But the murderer himself had disappeared once more. However, Tor responded indifferently to these kindly meant words of comfort. She refused to allow them to penetrate her shell.

However, she could not ignore her lord for ever. She was eventually summoned by him to a council of war, two days later at dusk – when the whole Svear army was arrayed along the ridge of Kolmarden – in the king's tent in the centre of the line.

As she rode along the ridge, she paused and looked down over the tops of the few remaining trees towards the flat lands directly north of the little settlement of Norrkoping. The village itself was now deserted, she could see only one thin plume of smoke and a single wink of red fire at one window in the town. The local people, knowing that the calamity of war was upon them, had gathered up all their children, their possessions and their animals and fled the area.

There appeared to be no sign of the Danish enemy, either, on the eve of the appointed day of battle; the long inlet called the Braviken was empty of ships, save for a couple of abandoned fishing vessels moored in the southern shore. But no, Tor realised that she was quite wrong. As the molten setting sun ignited the huge stretch of shimmering water in dazzling golds and bronzes, she reined in her horse on the edge of the escarpment and squinted to the east under a shading hand and observed what looked like a very dark shadow at the extreme end of the Braviken fjord.

It was ships, dozens of them. No, scores of vessels, all of different sizes. All turning in from the distant sea and gliding into the mouth of the bay. More and more appeared, one after the other, and began their haul down the Braviken towards her.

As the Danish fleet approached, Tor was taken aback by its sheer size. She had known that Siegfried was a powerful monarch, ruling over many lands, territories and islands, but even so, it was awe-inspiring to see so many powerful warships gathered in one place. She found it very difficult to estimate the enemy numbers accurately – the vessels were now so thick upon the water they were almost impossible to count, and the low sun was shining directly in her eyes – but she guessed there must be a hundred or so *karve*, plus at least fifty larger *busse* heading up the Braviken that golden evening under their full-bellied, stripped sails, each ship bearing at least a *lith* of trained warriors, along with countless smaller craft holding but a handful of troops.

Could the Danish king truly have raised four or five thousand warriors for his array? It seemed impossible. The Svear army, she was fairly sure, was only about two thousand strong, including her own jarl's two hundred and eighty shields, and Jarl Ottar's six hundred men, and all the vaunted so-called heroes and their followers. There were some Wends, she had heard, under Prince Witzlaus, the king's reserve force, but these foreigners had not marched with the army and she knew not where they were this evening.

Even with the Wends, however, Sigurd Hring was badly outnumbered.

She wondered if her brother's Vastergotland warriors were among those on the ships now running in a shapeless pack down the centre of the long inlet, their various battle standards streaming out in the breeze. Perhaps they were: the sides of each ship were adorned with the painted shields of the warriors it contained, a stirring sight, but she was too far to see if the Bear sigil of her brother was displayed.

Tor watched until the darkness grew too thick to see and then spurred her horse and hurried along the ridge track, heading towards the king's council tent.

–

Tor was not the only one who had witnessed the dramatic arrival of the Danish fleet. The large waxed linen tent was crowded with warriors animatedly discussing the matter, many nervous, many marvelling at the unexpected size of the enemy host.

'They say Siegfried summoned ten new *lith* from the Little Kingdoms – five hundred shields just from those fjords and mountains in the back of beyond,' one warrior was saying as Tor pushed through the throng to take her place beside Starki.

'Where have you been?' snapped her lord.

'Riding along the ridge, watching the enemy fleet arrive in the Braviken.'

'I don't mean today, I mean… Ah, it matters not, I suppose. But I hope you brought my new sword with you. Have you Daneslayer with you?'

'I secured a sword for you from Harva's village, but I had to give it away.'

'What?'

'Hush now, lord,' said Tor, 'I believe the king wishes to address us.'

It was true. Sigurd Hring was in the centre of the tent, a commanding figure in a scrubbed byrnie and gleaming helm, guards round him, holding up a hand for silence.

'My subjects, friends and comrades, we meet here on the eve of battle, and I am aware that I am meeting some of you, perhaps, for the very last time. Some of us may well fall tomorrow. But most will surely live to take a share in our glorious *victory*! Yes, *victory*, my friends. At this hour of peril, I have one word for you… *Victory*!'

There were a few murmurs around the tent but if the king had been expecting a huge roar of general approval at his words he was destined to be disappointed.

'Yes, my friends… *Victory*!' continued the king, looking expectantly around him. 'We shall surely have a fine *victory* over these cowardly Danish pig-dogs!'

An uneasy quiet in the tent. One man clapped – and stopped. A lonely sound. One muttered: 'There seem to be a very large number of these cowardly pig-dogs.'

Someone else whispered: 'What exactly *is* a pig-dog?'

'The foe are plentiful, this is true,' said the king, rubbing his hands together, almost gleefully. 'But that will only make our *victory* the sweeter. The more enemies there are, the more glory to be earned – every true warrior knows that. And a glorious *victory* it shall be,' he went on. 'For we have all the greatest heroes in the North fighting with us.'

Not all of them, Tor thought. *Bjarki Bloodhand yet stands against you.*

'See there,' said the king warming to his task, 'there is Egil Skull-Cleaver, who killed six men in a fight in Vestfold without taking so much as a scratch!'

He pointed at the warrior standing in the corner of the tent, looking embarrassed.

'Over yonder is Hagnor the Fatbellied!' The fat man gave an ironic bow. 'Hagnor once tore a Goth's head off his neck with his bare hands,' said Sigurd Hring.

'I did,' said Hagnor, beaming. 'Then I took a massive shit down his windpipe!'

'Behold Erland the Snake – the greatest swordsman in all the Middle-Realm!' Tor caught Erland's eye, and the sinewy warrior had the temerity to wink at her. She looked away. Sigurd Hring was pink in the face. A bead of sweat ran down his jowl. 'And we have many more famous and doughty warriors besides them, ah...'

He seemed to have run out of heroes to name. The king was not very good at this, Tor realised. She had been moved before by great battle orators – Widukind of Saxony was a master of this kind of speech – but Sigurd Hring was clearly not one of them. Even her oaf Bjarki was better at giving a good, spirit-lifting talk before a fight.

'We have the slope of the Kolmarden on our side, too. And the natural courage of all Svear, whose ability to lift their hearts and, er...' The king was floundering.

He recovered himself. 'And I have a new sword, a Harva blade no less, with which to massacre the Danish foemen and put more fear into their quaking bellies...' He drew the showy Finnstorp blade from its leather sheath and brandished it high in the air. All eyes in the tent were drawn to the bejewelled and gleaming steel.

'This blade was created by a master smith and given to me by one of my most loyal warriors here.' Sigurd looked directly at Tor and gave her a weird kind of leering grimace. 'With it, I shall make a great slaughter. It is a talisman, a shining beacon that tomorrow will lead us to *victory*! A victory that will be spoken of...'

As the king stumbled on with his clumsy speech, Tor looked again at the gaudy sword in his hand, which now seemed even more crudely ostentatious than ever.

She glanced sideways at Jarl Starki, and saw that his mouth was a grim line.

She saw him draw in a breath as if to speak, and seized his forearm in a strong grip. 'Lord,' she said, 'I will explain things to you after this council. But for now, I beg you, hold both your tongue and temper. Do you hear me, lord? Say not a word.'

Starki glared at her, but he said nothing and only gave a brisk jerk of his head.

—

Sigurd Hring's speech rambled on for some time but eventually he ran out of things to say and ended where he started, shouting, 'Victory... victory... *victory!*'

Hagnor the Fatbellied and Egil Skull-Cleaver led the muted cheers and weak applause. Then the king began to set out the individual dispositions for the next day.

The Jarl of Norrland was assigned the position on the extreme right, along with some of the lesser thanes and *hersirs* of Svealand. The king himself was to stand in the centre of the ridge where this tent had been pitched with his household troops and the heroes and their men. Jarl Ottar and his six hundred Vastmanlanders were, as expected, given the honour of holding the left flank above the Braviken.

Starki could barely contain his bubbling fury and, the instant the king declared the council concluded, he strode out of the tent without a single backward glance.

Tor hurried after him and caught up by the horse lines where both their mounts were tethered. As they rode west along the ridge line together in silence, Tor could already see the campfires of the Danish forces on the broad plain below and to her left. There were a great many sparks of firelight down there tonight. How many would be there the next night, she wondered. Then she forced her mind back to her angry lord. She thought about how she would make this next and most important move. And having reached her decision, she simply said: 'Lord, rein in here a moment, will you. I would speak with you now. It is a matter of great importance.'

Jarl Starki's expression was unreadable in the dark. But he did rein in and they both sat there in the saddle, side by side, while their horses cropped the grass.

'Will you now explain to me, woman, why you gave *my* sword to the king?'

'I will,' said Tor. 'But there are other important matters to discuss as well.'

'Is that so?'

'Yes. But first the sword. The king caught wind that I was bringing it to Uppsala – I don't know how – and he asked to see the blade the moment I arrived. He admired it and said that *he* should possess a sword of this quality, since he was king and you were merely a jarl. He invited me to make a generous gift of the fine Harva sword to him – and I could not refuse mighty Sigurd Hring, King of the Svear.'

'Why not? You refuse people all the time. You often refuse to do what *I* ask.'

Tor hesitated. She did not like lying to her lord. But there were greater issues at stake than this small deception. It was simply a ruse of war, she reminded herself.

'He threatened me with death, lord. And when that did not change my answer, he threatened to have you deposed and another jarl put in your place. He said Egil Skull-Cleaver was looking for a seat, and your hall in Gavle would suit very well.'

'And so you handed over my sword, to save my hall,' said Starki. He sighed.

Tor peered at him. In the faint starlight, she could not tell what he was thinking.

'And that is why you have been avoiding me these past few days. You felt shamed by being robbed of my prize in such a humiliating way. I see that now. Well, I suppose it was just a sword. I did not pay for it. I would rather keep my hall and possession of the jarldom of Norrland. You chose a wise course, *Stallar* – as always.'

Tor felt wretched manipulating a man she liked. A good man. A decent lord, if a little weak and stupid. Nevertheless, she struggled on with her self-appointed task.

'Lord,' she said, 'I do *not* think I have chosen wisely. Let me now tell you why.'

–

Tor made a last tour of the sentry lines, making sure the *hird* were bedded down in their correct positions for the night – after all, tomorrow was the first day of Heyannir and the Danes might attack at any time after first light – then she walked down to the shore of Lake Glan, sat under a tall spruce and stared out at the dark, calming waters.

She felt very uneasy about what she was about to do. It went against the grain of everything she believed in – loyalty, honesty, steadfastness in perilous situations. Even so, it must be done. She suddenly felt filthy, grimy beyond belief, and tried to remember the last time she had thoroughly washed. So she stripped off her mail, armour and worn old leathers and walked, fish-belly white and naked, into the lake.

A while later, feeling a little better, she emerged and dressed once again. But she was oddly reluctant to return to the *hird* up on the Kolmarden ridge, even though she knew she needed to sleep, and she sat again and allowed her mind to dwell on Rorik.

She had been only a little surprised that Rorik was not present at the king's council earlier that evening. No one had seen him for some days. Presumably he was wisely avoiding her out of fear of her vengeance. Everyone in the Svear army must know what he had done at Bearstead – word of his poisoning was on everyone's lips, she knew that, although that kind of talk always ceased when she came into earshot.

Murders were common in Svealand, even killings of women and children, but the indiscriminate, callous nature of the poisonings disgusted most honest folk. Rorik had made an error in attacking her in this cowardly manner. The sentiment was entirely against him. Several Svear warriors whom she did not know had approached her on the march and expressed their condolences. One fellow, a grizzled father with two daughters, had offered to help her hunt down and kill Rorik – an offer she'd refused.

Tor wanted to do this herself – slowly. When she caught up with him, she would bind him and take her time. An ordinary death would not do for Rorik Hafnarsson. Inge, Ulli and the *Felaki* women and children deserved something more significant.

When she caught up with Rorik she would decide the exact manner of his death. Whenever that might be. Yet in truth, with Rorik gone, there was one less thing for Tor to worry about on the eve of battle. If she survived this fight, she would find time to hunt the coward down. And Bjarki would surely help her, if he also survived.

Not that that would bring Inge back to life. Her Inge. Her daughter. So young and pretty, and so in love, so incandescently happy. Inge. A whole life seemingly stretching out before her with handsome young Joralf, perhaps a baby one day, and her own steading, maybe near Bearstead, so Tor might visit them often. Tor, alone, unseen, and now very cold after her chilly dip, felt a wrenching sensation deep in her heart, as if the great muscle had been torn in two parts. She squeezed her eyes shut but it did no good at all. All the scalding sorrow came flooding back out once more.

She indulged herself for a little while, then cuffed the tears away, wiped her face, and got to her feet. Inge and Rorik. Both of them must keep for another day.

She had a battle to fight. Men to lead into peril. And a betrayal to accomplish.

Chapter Twenty-one

The honour of a royal visit

'I have seen the lake, highness,' said Rask, emerging suddenly, blinking, from a thick patch of bracken like a mole popping its whiskery head out of a hole.

Bjarki, who had his mouth full of cheese and dry twice-baked bread at that moment, merely waggled one finger at Rask in acknowledgement. They had been marching hard, dawn to dusk, more or less due east, for the past three days, with Rask scouting out the near invisible tracks ahead through the forest. The little *Felaki* warrior was, in truth, only following in the footsteps of the Wolf twins, who had returned uneventfully to Ostergotland only a few days before. But without Rask's craft to guide them through the dense conifers from Lodose to the south shore of Vattern, they would probably have become hopelessly lost among the endless trees.

Bjarki swallowed his mouthful and got to his feet. 'How far, Rask?' he asked.

'A morning's march, highness, more if you mean to move stealthily. There are fishing huts down there on the beach. I saw a drift of blue smoke on the breeze, too.'

'Boats? A good-sized vessel that could take us all?'

Rask nodded.

Bjarki crossed the small clearing where they had decided to take their midday meal and march-break and approached the big, dark, mounded shape of Garm on its far side. The huge animal was lying with his head cradled in his wide paws beside Sambor, who had taken over the duties as his keeper, and who was now lounging against his warm furry side. Bjarki did not think that any other man of the expedition would have been allowed to take such a liberty with the young bear – nor that any other warrior would have dared attempt it. But Sambor and Garm seemed to have formed some kind of alliance since the terrible events at Bearstead. Bjarki was almost certain that the bear knew that Inge, his long-time friend and companion, was no more. Maybe he could even smell Inge's lingering scent on the Polans warrior who had been her servant and bodyguard. Maybe the bear just liked Sambor, the only man apart from Bjarki, who could come anywhere near matching the animal's strength.

The bear lifted his head at Bjarki's approach and stared at him impassively with his yellow eyes. Bjarki squatted down next to Garm and offered the creature a chunk of hard cheese, which the bear accepted and gulped down, hardly chewing at all.

'We have to go on a boat again, Garm,' said Bjarki, fondling the bear's furry ears. 'I'm sorry; it can't be helped. I would leave you behind in these woods to live on your own but I need you. Tor needs you. A short boat ride and you will see her.'

Bjarki did not know if the bear understood him but there *was* unquestionably some connection between the bear and the *berserkr*. Mochta, Bjarki's *gandr*, had been Garm's mother. Mochta had told Bjarki that Garm was not an ordinary bear but also a *gandr* – though, so far as Bjarki knew, the bear had never inhabited a human.

Garm made a grumbling noise and rubbed his muzzle against Bjarki's knee, which the warrior took as comprehension and acceptance of his lake-going ordeal.

He stood up and called over to Rask. 'No need for stealth. This is *my* kingdom. The folk fishing by the lake shall be granted the high honour of a royal visit this day.'

In the event, the folk of the fishing village were sadly denied the honour of a royal visit because, the moment they spied the huge forms of Bjarki, Sambor and the enormous black bear Garm shambling out of the trees, as well as lithe young Joralf gliding forwards with his sword drawn, and ten well-armed and warlike Companions, they immediately fled for their lives. Some of the fisherfolk ran away along the coast and dived into the gloom of forest further up the way, others jumped into their fragile skiffs and coracles and headed out to the safety of the lake.

A few of them attempted to launch the largest ship of all – a large *karve* with a sail and places for thirty rowers – but, at Bjarki's command, the Companions charged forwards to stop them and the terrified fishermen abandoned their effort to get the ship down the wooden rollers and into the lake and fled howling with fear along the shore.

It was a stroke of luck. Proof the gods favoured them. Bjarki had been hoping to come across one ship that could carry them all, but he would have accepted a few small ones. His only objective was to get all of his small company onto the water.

He closed his eyes and muttered a simple prayer of thanks to Odin All-Father.

Bjarki tempted Garm up the ship's gangplank with a bag of cheese rinds and got the animal settled on board with surprising ease – it was almost as if the young bear *had* understood their conversation in the forest – with Sambor coming up behind the animal on the wildly bouncing plank carrying his leather collar and tether rope. The rope and collar proved unnecessary, Sambor found, as Garm laid himself comfortably in the belly of the *karve* and began happily chewing through the mound of rinds.

The rest of Bjarki's company saw to the sailing of the ship, with Kynwulf taking the tiller and Joralf, who had been raised by the busy shipping-ways of Lake Malaren, tending to the single, square, forest-green sail. Bjarki himself delayed their departure by a few more moments when he suddenly remembered something, and jumped off the ship. He splashed then crunched his way back up the stony shore. He went into the largest fisherman's hut and laid a finger ring – a fine golden item – on the half-rotten wooden table in the centre of the shack's only room.

'They may not wish to meet me at this time,' he muttered, as he left the fish-guts smelling shed and crunched back down the shore to the *karve*, 'but I'll not have any of my subjects saying I'm a thief!'

Then they were away.

The sailing was easy, a brisk westerly wind filling the big green sail and driving the ship north at a spanking pace. Five hours later, they approached a wooded island in the middle of Lake Vattern, and tied the vessel up under a curtain of long willow branches. They made their camp for the night and Oddvin, who had been exploring, returned a little later with a small buck he had managed to shoot with his bow at the north of the isle, which meant hot, rich meat for their supper around the campfire.

After the meal, Kynwulf told a story about Hervor, the daughter of Angantyr, King of the Goths, who was a famous shield-maiden. She rejected the womanly ways of most of her kind and became a raider, a reaver, a warrior who took to the rowing benches with her fellow vikings and sailed the seas seeking plunder and adventure.

She dressed like a man, the War Chief said, in leather and iron helm and mail and fought as ferociously as one too. No mortal man could best her in a fair fight.

As Kynwulf began his long story, Bjarki's mind naturally flew straight to Tor. He knew his sister must be grieving Inge, and he guessed she must also be feeling very much alone. Her friends were with Bjarki – even Garm, who was snoozing at the edge of the firelight with a gnawed deer leg trapped under a paw – and all about Tor now were enemies. Hervor the Shield-Maiden would have been contemptuous of her plight – in fact, Kynwulf was even now getting to the good part, where Hervor challenged the champion of the King of the Danes to single combat and slew him in front of their whole army. Tor, too, could put on the mask of fearlessness, like Hervor. But his sister was just an ordinary woman

– not some dauntless hero from a campfire yarn. Bjarki often felt the strong urge to comfort and protect his younger sister. Not that she would ever allow him to do that. Not in front of others.

Then Bjarki wondered whether Tor had yet encountered Rorik Hafnarsson. And, if she had done so, what the consequences might have been. That murdering bastard would surely be dead now, there was no question of it, but he hoped Tor had been discreet in this rightful slaying. He doubted it. Anyway, it mattered little. Rorik was bound for Hel's icy realm sooner, if not later. If Tor did not get to him first, Bjarki would kill him, though Rorik would likely perish in the battle with so many others. Just as he and Tor might also meet their ends at Norrkoping. It seemed likely.

What if they did not die? What if, somehow, by Odin's whim, they survived?

What then for Tor? Back to Bearstead? No. With the sad little *draugr* of Inge ever hovering by the hearth? Bjarki could not imagine Tor finding any peace there ever again. She must come to live with him in Lodose. There was plenty of room in the royal hall. It would be a fine place to make their home. Perhaps there might even be a good and decent man in Vastergotland who would prove worthy of her. And an equally good woman for him? No, never, his heart belonged to Edith. It always would... *Edith*. He pictured her then at her wedding at Viby, a happy and smiling Edith, in a long, flowing blue dress, her bright, red-gold hair intricately bound up and adorned with a circlet of fresh summer flowers, taking Abbio's filthy hand in hers...

'No!' he bellowed, astonishing the circle of listeners to Kynwulf's fine story.

They all stared at him. Kynwulf's mouth was wide open, one hand raised high.

'Are you quite well, highness?' asked Haugen, the nearest *Felaki*. Bjarki saw he already had a drawn seax in his mutilated left hand. 'Is there some danger here?'

'No – but we must not stay up all night listening to tales. We all need to sleep. There is a hard march to be undertaken. A long, hard march. And a battle to fight!'

—

They left the island before dawn and set out in the *karve* in the half-light into the mists of the lake. The south-westerly breeze was fair and growing stronger, and with the green sail hoisted and filled, they made good time, skimming over the lake like a giant dragonfly. After several hours of uneventful, dull sailing, around mid-afternoon, Bjarki could see a settlement on the eastern bank, a long string of buildings along the water's edge, over which a dense and dark cloud of smoke permanently squatted.

'Does anyone recognise this place?' Bjarki asked his shipmates, most of whom looked back at him blankly. 'Have we come to the right town – what do you think?'

'The smoke seems right,' said Harknut. 'And I hear the music of the hammers.'

Bjarki listened. There was a faint, regular *tink-tinking* noise on the breeze.

Joralf raised his hand: 'My father brought me here once; I remember. When he wanted a sword made for him. I am sure this is the right place. This is Finnstorp.'

—

They landed a mile to the south of the town. Bjarki did not want a repeat of the panic they had caused when they approached the fishing village in the south. But this was enemy territory, too. The very western edge of Sodermanland, the domain of Sigurd Hring, so-called King of Svealand – the man who dearly wanted to be King of the North. Bjarki picked a spot at the edge of the forest, a hundred paces below the town, guided the *karve* in, disembarked, and told Kynwulf to set sentries and make camp.

Then he set off – alone – into the village of Finnstorp.

He walked up the only street, feeling a little vulnerable, and asked a young-ish man pushing a handcart full of iron scrap where he might find Harva the Smith.

The fellow told him – and seemed unsurprised to see a big stranger in his street.

A little while later, Bjarki was leaning on the half-wall and peering inside a dark square space lit by a huge, crackling fire, where two sweating men were hard at work. The balding older fellow, with a short, muscular, ape-like body, was bent over a glowing metal shard by the forge fire, holding the piece up with his tongs and peering a little suspiciously at it. The younger man, a slim but equally hairy fellow, half-naked and drenched in grease and grit, was drinking thirstily from a long leather jug.

The older said something to the younger, then shoved the metal bar back into the heap of glowing charcoal in the square hearth in the centre of the forge. The younger man began to work a huge pair of squeaking leather bellows with a long tar-black wooden pole, and the big fire in the hearth glowed cherry red and spat golden sparks in the air.

'If you have come to ask me to make a sword, warrior, you are much, much too late,' said the older man, without turning around. 'The great battle is in three days' time and even some of my best clients have been disappointed. If Erland the Snake came and begged me for a sword, if Egil Skull-Cleaver wanted a pair of new axe blades, I'd say no to both. Save your breath, man, and don't disturb me at my work.'

'I have not come for that,' said Bjarki. He stayed where he was, leaning on the half-wall. The older smith looked round at him, seeing him properly for the first time.

'Why then?'

'I want you to put an edge on this,' Bjarki said. He pulled the seax from the sheath at his waist. 'It is too keen a blade to give over to a common knife-grinder.'

The squat bald man came over and took the seax from Bjarki's hand.

'It's one of mine,' said Harva. 'And you sailed up from the south to bring the blade to me. Yes, I saw your ship. Hmm. Well, I thank you for that – for not allowing some ham-fisted nail-maker in Ostergotland to spoil my edge with his granite wheel.'

He turned the foot-long blade over and over in his powerful, fire-scarred hands.

'I did not make this for you, though,' he said. 'I made it for another man.' He looked up at Bjarki, questioningly. 'How do you come by it?'

'It was my father's blade. I took possession of it when he... when he died.'

Bjarki did not say that it was he and Tor who had killed their father Hildar, a blood-drunk Rekkr who was driven mad by his *gandr*. It had been a necessary killing.

'I made it for a madman, I recall. He frightened me. And you have his look.'

Bjarki said nothing. He just shrugged one shoulder.

'I'll put a razor edge on it for you, son, when I've finished tempering this spear-blade,' Harva said. 'Wait on that bench over there. I shall not keep you too long.'

'My sister came here to see you, maybe two weeks ago. She is named Torfinna Hildarsdottir. Red hair, a small but fierce girl...'

'I remember *her*. She tried to *buy* one of my blades.'

'Do you know where she camped during her stay here?'

'Down by the Three Oaks. I'll show you when we're done here,' said Harva.

In the morning, after a hearty breakfast of grilled mackerel, hard bread and cold venison, Bjarki attached the collar round Garm's neck and the stout rope to the collar.

'It's just so we don't lose you, boy,' he whispered in his ear, kneading his massive neck muscles to soothe the creature. The bear growled at him grumpily.

When they reached Three Oaks, Garm's manner changed abruptly. From sullen anger the animal suddenly seemed filled with eagerness. A playfulness that he had not displayed since he was a cub. Garm sniffed the damp earth greedily, nostrils flaring.

'Seek her out, boy, seek out Tor,' said Bjarki, stroking his furry right flank, but keeping one hand very tightly on his leather collar. 'That's her scent. Drink it all in.'

Garm jerked on the rope, lunging forwards, nearly pulling it from Bjarki's hand.

Bjarki hauled the eager bear back by his leash. It took all his great strength.

'Lead the way, boy, take up the spoor and we'll follow. Can't let you run ahead. Can't risk losing you in the forest. But think, Garm, in two days we'll see our girl!'

Chapter Twenty-two

'Svealand shall burn!'

The Danes came out with the dawn. Tor watched them spilling like dark wine onto the plain north of Norrkoping, where many of them had rested during the warm night.

The fighting men were unencumbered by baggage so presumably, Tor reckoned, they had left their belongings either in their ships or in the village, under guard to keep them safe from looters. But they all had spears, shields, helms and most had armour.

Hundreds more men were debouching from their ships, too, and were soon striding across the pastures to take up their loose positions on the field of battle. There seemed to be many more enemy vessels moored in the Braviken that morning than there had been the night before; reinforcements had arrived during the night.

Tor made no effort to calculate the numbers of the enemy. Five thousand; or six, even? Who could say? No point counting. Overwhelming numbers. That was enough.

The newly arrived ships were mostly moored with the others on the southern inlet, in the fork beyond the marshy headland by Norrkoping, and as far away as possible from the northern cliffs on which the six hundred Vastmanland men of Jarl Ottar stood ready, supported by some two hundred of the archers of Telemark.

The Danes had wisely kept their ships out of range of the bows of these famed backwoods killers – who had taken a fortune in silver from Sigurd Hring to come down from their mountain fastnesses to fight for the king. A Telemark archer, it was said, could shoot the eye out of a bird on the wing. And he might even ask which eye.

In the centre of the enemy line, a mile north of Norrkoping, Tor could make out a strong block of armoured men under a banner hanging vertically from a crossbar on a long pole – something red on a blue field – probably the Red Boar standard of Harald Wartooth, the *Armathr* of King Siegfried. The supreme commander of the Danish army would plant himself at the centre of their line, that was for sure. And now she could see contingents of spearmen filling in on both sides of the *Armathr*'s position. To the west, there were horsemen gathering in the flats near the shore of Lake Glan.

The Danes had picked their place to stand – a fair distance, perhaps two miles, from the bottom of the stump-covered slope of the Kolmarden. If Sigurd Hring wanted to attack them, he would have to come down from his heights and go south. But that would be madness. Why would the king give up his advantageous position?

Tor turned her horse and rode slowly back to the camp near the main road where Jarl Starki was at his breakfast. Eggs hard-boiled in the shells, cheese, bread and ale.

'They're making their lines,' she said as she stepped down from her dun and threw the reins to a dark, bearded *hird*-man called Wiglaf, who was on guard duty.

Jarl Starki was seated before a small table. He waved in a hospitable manner at the food spread out before him. And when Tor had helped herself to a cup of his ale and a hunk of wheat bread, she told her jarl what the situation was down on the plain.

'Their line is too far away for us to attack it,' she said. 'Unless we come down from this ridge. Which we will not do unless Sigurd Hring goes completely insane.'

'The king might *make* us go down to fight on the flat,' said Starki. 'He might.'

'No. He's not a fool. He's an arse but not a fool. He'll wait up here. The enemy have come here from Viby – they'll come a little further if they want to engage us.'

The Svear army was spread out all along the extended length of the Kolmarden ridge, each separate contingent of warriors occupying a section of the summit, but with large gaps between each of the solid blocks of Svear shield-men. When the Danes came up the slope against them — and Tor was sure they would — the units on either side of the point of attack could easily close up and concentrate to face the foe.

But with those huge numbers, Tor thought, the Danes could attack at several points and still outnumber the defenders. Would they do that? She did not know. In the centre of the ridge, a mile west of the north–south road, was the king's position, and where a mud-coloured pavilion had been set up to house him and his household.

Sigurd Hring's black Raven banner flew above the massive, circular brown tent, the bird of ill-omen painted in white on the strip of dark cloth. The king's sigil, this symbol of Odin Spear-Shaker, was meant to strike terror into the hearts of all his foes but Tor reckoned at this distance it would be no more frightening than a dirty old shirt caught on the branches of a tree. Both sides claimed Odin supported their cause.

There were at least two thousand warriors placed along the ridge line on either side of the central mud-coloured pavilion. Jarl Starki's force and a diverse, unruly collection of lesser jarls, thanes and *hersirs* were out on the extreme western flank — about four hundred men in all — and between them and the pavilion were about half of Jarl Sigurd Hring's own regional troops, some three hundred hard men from Sodermanland. Gathered round the big command tent itself were the king's picked bodyguards — two hundred of them, vicious brutes, in Tor's experience — as well as at least a hundred spearmen from all over the North belonging to the dozen or so mercenary heroes, and of course those strutting warriors of renown themselves.

This was the core of the Svear army, grouped around the Raven banner atop the mud-hued tent. The Danes, when they came, would probably aim straight for the centre of the line, for the king. Because with Sigurd Hring dead, the battle would be over – victory won for Harald Wartooth. That truth had occurred to Tor weeks ago.

To the east of the royal tent were the rest of the Sodermanland troops, another three hundred men, straddling the main road heading north. Then, looking east, a gap of almost half a mile before the first pickets of Jarl Ottar of Vastmanland's six hundred, and the two hundred Telemark archers under his command up on the cliffs.

'So is your famous Rekkr brother among them down there?' said Jarl Starki, gesturing southwards towards the Norrkoping plain and the distant Danish lines.

'Don't know,' said Tor, slapping the crumbs from her hands. Which was true. She had sent her private message to Bjarki with her friends but she had no idea if it had reached him. Valtyr, Garm and all the rest of them might have been drowned at sea on the way round the peninsula to Lodose. Bjarki might have refused to do as she had asked. He could be difficult sometimes. Maybe he was down there, maybe not. But it was her nervous jarl she was worried about. She had told him only the outline of her plan and his question had had a quavering uncertainty about it. She hoped he'd play his part in what she hoped to achieve. All he had to do was do what he was told.

Starki finished his meal, got up from the table and walked forwards a dozen jerky paces towards the lip of the escarpment. He looked to the south down the slope. Tor followed him and stood at his elbow, almost touching. He was quivering just a little.

Quietly, she said: 'Sigurd Hring has no respect for you, lord. But my brother Bjarki Bloodhand, King of Vastergotland, certainly does. And I, too, hold you in the highest esteem. My brother and I know you – and we know your quality. So if you will do as I ask, if you fulfil your role this day, you will get what you most desire. The prize will be yours; if you do what is required. Trust in me – and in my brother.'

A distant trumpet blew further along the ridge, a series of triple notes, brassy and urgent. It was a summons to the king's council as they both knew well.

'What if it goes wrong?' said Starki. 'What if the king discovers what we...'

'We will ford that river when we come to it, lord. And how could he know? Only you and I know what we have agreed. I've told no one of our plan. Have you?'

'No, no, I have not told any...'

'Then all will be well,' said Tor. 'Trust me. Now let us go to the council.'

—

Sigurd Hring was in full battle array, in a mail hauberk that fell to his knees, and which had been polished or scrubbed with sand until the links shone as if they were silver. He carried a fine, burnished helmet, with an eagle's feather atop the crown, snug in the crook of his arm, a fat seax was slung across his lean belly, and the fancy sword from Finnstorp, which Tor had indirectly given him, hung straight by his left-hand side. She glanced at Jarl Starki and saw that her lord was staring openly at the sword, a bitter expression marring his fine looks.

The king was surrounded by his bodyguards, twelve grim, hand-picked warriors, leaning on their spears like veterans, and giving everyone the hard eye. Tor had heard that they were the best fighters in Svealand. Each one a swaggering arsehole, too.

Not that she found them daunting. She was more nervous about the dozen so-called heroes who were also gathered in the command tent at that hour, waiting for the king's council. Hagnor the Fatbellied was swilling his ale from a huge ox horn by the central tent pole. He was dressed in a boiled leather chest-and-back corselet and two short-handled axes were stuck in his enormous belt. A long sword hung from his belt on one side, a seax on the other. He gave Tor a cheery, drunken leer when their gazes crossed. And she forced up a decent smile in return.

Erland the Snake was there too, standing with his arms folded across his chest at the back of the tent, near the rear flap, looking mock-solemn, as if he had just farted silently and was trying to pretend it were otherwise. Egil Skull-Cleaver stood like a true man-mountain a few yards away from the king, but still managing to tower over him. Egil held a long double-bladed Dane axe in his meaty right fist, making its five-foot length seem like a hatchet. And there were half a dozen other heroes and great jarls in the tent, including Jarl Ottar – who glared at Tor from across the crowded space, perhaps trying to intimidate her – and a dozen more thanes and *hersirs*.

'Jarl Ottar has the left flank, with the Telemark archers,' began Sigurd Hring briskly, 'Jarl Starki has the right flank with all the strongest *hersirs*, that is Bolgi, Fisk and Svartman and all their men. I will hold the centre here with the warriors of Sodermanland, and our new friends Egil, Hagnor, Erland and the rest of the heroes.'

The king had obviously decided to abandon any attempt at rousing rhetoric.

'This command tent is the heart of our line. This is the centre of the army,' said Sigurd Hring, and he stamped his foot on the earth floor to make his point. 'And these are your orders, people. They are simple: *not one step backwards*. We hold the enemy here. They must not break our lines. Do not move from your station unless I give the order, either to come in towards the centre, or to advance – which will mean an attack down the slope to drive the Danish dogs into the sea. You all understand?'

There was a general murmur of agreement.

'There are a great many enemies down there this morning, or so I'm told. But I swear to you, there will be a great deal fewer by the end of the day. Now, does everybody know the trumpet signals and the flag commands? Most important is the red banner, which means an advance, if that is hoisted above my tent, then we all...'

'Sire,' said Jarl Ottar. 'A messenger!'

The ranks of warriors opened and a frightened-looking young spearman took a few faltering steps towards the king. 'Sire,' he said, 'I have an urgent report for you.'

'Speak up, then, man,' said the king.

'The Danes are advancing, sire. Their whole battle line is coming towards us.'

—

The Danes were indeed advancing. Tor stood with Jarl Starki at the edge of the plateau, looking down the tree-stump-studded slope below them at the lines of tiny figures on the plain who were moving to a new position. They came on in two loose lines, walking over the pastures and fields, trampling green barley, until they were about a quarter of a mile from the bottom of the slope. Now Tor could make out individual warriors, the splash of a scarlet cloak, the colourful curving stripes on their shields, the gleam of sunlight on a polished helmet. She scanned the lines looking for the folk she knew, looking in truth for Bjarki. Her eye lingered on a tall blond man in the right of the first line but he was not her brother. Another grizzled fellow slightly resembled Kynwulf – but he was not the War Chief. Perhaps her message had got through; and perhaps Bjarki had decided to follow her instructions. Perhaps, if he did not get lost in the woods, he might be able to achieve the goal she had set for him.

She looked left along the Svear lines towards the Braviken inlet. It seemed that the whole edge of the plateau was lined with Svear warriors, all the way to the sheer cliffs above the sea. Then she looked right, fewer folk that way, and she could make out Jarl Starki's Silver Fish banner flapping in the distance, and beyond the dark mass of the endless trees – somewhere out there was the clearing where she had met the charcoal-burners. Beyond that, two days' march, was Finnstorp and the forge fires.

'When will he come?' Starki whispered in her ear. 'When will Bjarki be here?'

Before she could answer, she heard the squeal of a trumpet, and saw Sigurd Hring striding towards her, with Jarl Ottar and one of his oath-men stumbling along behind.

'They are asking for a parley,' said the king, pointing down the slope.

Tor looked and saw that the lines had coalesced at the foot of the slope, and a quartet of warriors had stepped forwards out of them, two dozen paces in advance of the shield wall, standing under a pair of green-leaf branches, the old sign of a parley.

'Go down within hailing distance, Starki, and see what they want,' said the King. 'Ottar will go with you. No need for too much talk. If they want to surrender now and kneel to me, I shall permit it. But it's full surrender or nothing, hear me?'

Jarl Starki mumbled something and, seizing Tor's arm, he began dragging her with him as he set off down the slope. Jarl Ottar was a few steps behind, with his senior oath-man. Tor broke Jarl Starki's hold, but then pulled her lord in close to her.

'Keep your nerve, my lord,' she whispered. 'Remain strong and say nothing, reveal nothing. We simply listen to them and report back to the king.'

The Danish line looked thin to Tor, the closer she got to it. A double rank of Danes, big, bearded, mostly armoured, standing behind a tightly linked wall of shields. Tor had the mad urge to walk forwards a dozen paces and kick the linked shields, to test their integrity. Thin. A weak line. She reckoned Bjarki or even one of the so-called heroes up on the escarpment could bullock through this line of men without too much difficulty. Was that because it was so long? She looked left, right and saw the *skjaldborg* stretched a quarter of a mile in each direction. That was a lot of warriors. But still it was an error of command. They should be in blocks – say five hundred warriors in each – three or four men deep. They would fight better then, each shield-man in a tight pack, supported, emboldened and watched over by his fellows. In a thick block of shields, it was harder to flee than to fight. Not that she thought of these men as cowards – but the shield wall had always been a place of terror.

She could hear Jarl Ottar and his man huffing down the last part of the slope behind her and focused on the four figures standing out in front of the Danish lines.

The big one in the middle was Harald Wartooth. She had never met the Danish king's *Armathr* before but the large, yellowish tooth that jutted out of his lower jaw could belong to no other man. He was staring at her as if he had never seen a shield-maiden. Frowning, as if he did not approve of women fighters on this manly field.

On his right was a lean oldster with a twisted spine that raised one shoulder above the other; she recognised him as a jarl called Lars, who had charge of the Dane-Work fortification in the south of Jutland. On his left was Widukind, Duke of Saxony, who favoured her with a smile. Tor, to her own irritation, found herself smiling back at her erstwhile lover. She immediately changed her expression to a fearsome scowl but a strange warmth glowed in her belly simply at the sight of him.

The fourth figure standing a little behind Widukind was Abbio the Crow. The man who had stolen Bjarki's glory in Rogaland, and who was betrothed to the lovely Edith of Saxony. Tor had no difficulty scowling at *him*. The raggedy *gothi* had painted his face pure white for the battle and his hair was clumped and spiked with honey to make it stand up in weird ways from his head. He was holding a nine-foot-long ash pole, the shaft clotted with black blood, in his right hand, and at the top of it was fixed a severed horse's head, painted in crazy red, yellow and white stripes. The animal's eyes had been replaced with pine cones, painted red, white and yellow, and they protruded horribly from the rotting animal's skull.

It was a *nithing* pole. A magical talisman designed to strike terror into the heart of a warrior, turn him into a coward, a *nithing*. The dark magic of the pole could make a man's bowels turn into writhing snakes, it was said, and make his own eyes smoulder in his head or burst into flame. It was powerful *seithr* and Tor found herself flinching at the sight of it.

Jarl Ottar said: 'You called us to parley!' He indicated the two leafy branches, planted in the turf on either side of the four Danes. 'What did you wish to say?'

241

'We come to you with an offer – and a promise,' said Harald Wartooth.

'Very well,' said Jarl Ottar. 'Let us hear them.'

'Yes, and be quick about it!' Jarl Starki chimed in. 'We don't have all day!'

Everyone looked at Jarl Starki in amazement. It was an absurd thing to say.

'You are in a very great haste to be slaughtered, I see,' said Harald Wartooth. 'Therefore I shall attempt to oblige you by being brief. The offer is simply this: if Sigurd Hring, Jarl of Sodermanland, will come down from his high perch and kneel before me – as King Siegfried's *Armathr* and representative on the field – and kiss my sword, swearing to do homage to Siegfried as his overlord and rightful King of the North before the month is up, he shall be acknowledged the King of Svealand. If he does this he may return to his own land and rule over it in peace.'

'The king rejects your offer,' said Jarl Ottar. 'He has no fear of you, nor your rabble of *nithings* – nor your grubby conjurer with his donkey's head on a stick!'

He gave a dismissive flick of his wrist towards Abbio. 'Sigurd Hring is King of the Svear by right – he owes fealty to no one, least of all a feeble grandsire of a Dane who sends his lackeys to do his fighting for him. Sigurd Hring will prove his claim to be King of the North on this field, on this day, with his courage and the prowess of his warriors and his oath-men, and by the obvious favour of Odin Shield-Splitter who always comes to the aid of the most valiant commander on the battlefield.'

'All he has to do is kneel and swear an oath,' said Widukind reasonably. 'Then we could cease all this nonsense and go home. There is no need for a pointless slaughter.'

The Wartooth turned on his Saxon ally and glared at him.

Tor, too, found herself despising the Saxon for his lack of spirit; still somehow wanting him, wanting his lean body, his hot mouth on hers, all at the same time.

Harald Wartooth spoke then as if Saxon had not. 'Very well,' he said, 'you have rejected our king's generous offer – with insults.

Now I shall make you a promise: when this battle is won, and Sigurd Hring's head is spiked on that *nithing* pole, I shall take my victorious men deep into Svealand and loose them on your women and children with fire and sword. There shall be no mercy, and the harrowing of your land shall be a lesson for a hundred years on the price of treason and the high risks of defying your rightful overlord. This is my promise to you. Svealand shall burn!'

'You now stand in Ostergotland,' said Jarl Ottar. 'Svealand begins at that line of barricades up there. Why don't you come up there now and try to enter our land!'

'And don't forget your flint and steel,' said Starki. 'And some dry kindling!'

Every member of the parley looked embarrassed at the jarl's remark.

'Hush now, lord,' said Tor firmly. 'Our discussions are concluded.'

Harald Wartooth stared at her, then looked at Jarl Starki, and finally Jarl Ottar.

'So be it!' he said.

As Tor and Jarl Starki plodded back up the slope again to the summit, Tor looked along the line of their fortifications. Some of the chopped-down trees had been split by carpenters and built into a kind of thick fence along the summit of the ridge. There were a few gaps, guarded by spearmen, to allow a sortie by the Svear warriors, but mostly it was an unbroken wall, centred on the king's muddy tent, and extending three or four hundred paces east and west on either side. A formidable obstacle.

Jarl Ottar and his man were slightly ahead of her and Starki, and as she strode through a narrow gap in the barricade, slightly to the left of the drab royal tent, her eye fell on a handsome warrior, a lean fellow with sandy hair, shaved at the sides to the bone. It was the victorious *Disablot* swordsman that Inge had loved. The young man who had sailed to Lodose to take her urgent message to her brother Bjarki.

It was Joralf.

Chapter Twenty-three

'I have hungered too long for this'

The branch under Bjarki's rump was a strong one, and it needed to be given his weight, but the bough still creaked alarmingly as he shifted to get a better look at the scene before his eyes. His lookout point was fifty feet up a spruce tree on the western end of the Kolmarden ridge, a mile east from the shores of Lake Glan, and about ten paces back into the thick forest that stretched seemingly for ever north into Svealand.

Beneath him were his followers from Lodose, lounging on the spruce needle carpet, munching their rations, and Garm the bear, who was looking up at Bjarki with a very human expression of disapproval in his yellow eyes. The bear had led them, unerringly, and without rest for two days and two nights, following the scent trail of urine that Tor had laid along the faintest of paths for seventy miles all the way from Finnstorp. And now, as a cruel reward for his endeavour, Bjarki had attached his leather collar and tied him securely to the trunk of a tree – the very tree atop which Bjarki was now perched.

Bjarki was too ashamed to hold Garm's accusing gaze and, instead, he looked south over the broad landscape in front of him. Down to his right was the shimmering blue expanse of Lake Glan, a lone fishing boat with a red sail visible on its calm waters. To his immediate left were the lines of the Svear warriors on the summit of the Kolmarden escarpment. He could clearly see Jarl Starki's position, half a mile away, marked by a long, limp pennant depicting his sigil of a silver fish on a blue field. A few hundred warriors were sitting on the ground around the blue flag, while some seemed to be milling about. A scant few dozen were standing to arms, in a line of shields on the lip of the escarpment, looking down at the flood plain below.

The great mass of the Svear army was also visible beyond Jarl Starki's small force, gathered around a huge mud-coloured pavilion, the flaps thrown open at the front, which had the Raven of Sigurd Hring flying from its pointed apex. That was the king's position. And Bjarki knew it would be the beating heart of the Svear line.

Bjarki could just make out beyond the tent, some miles off and a little further back from the royal centre, the sheer cliffs above the Braviken inlet, which were also manned by tiny stick-like warriors, many hundreds of them. There was a gap of at least a half mile between the mass of soldiery in the centre around the mud-coloured tent and the nearest defenders on the cliffs, and for a long moment Bjarki pondered if that gap might be a fruitful avenue of attack for the Danes.

There was a road leading up that way from the plain, a brown scar through the green countryside, along which men could advance. But their movements would be observed by the Svear centre and also by the cliff-defenders on the left flank, who would only need to shift their position half a mile westward to be able to block any attack through the gap; meanwhile, Sigurd Hring could simply wait for the Danes to scramble up the slope before swinging round and coming halfway down the slope to attack their vulnerable flanks as they advanced.

There was no way for the Danes to succeed on the far eastern side of the ridge.

There was another road from down on the plain that led up north-west towards Bjarki's own perch – and the position of Starki's men – but any attack on that side too would also be seen from the centre early on and could be blocked and easily flanked.

Sigurd Hring was in a commanding position on the lip of escarpment – he was not impregnable, but he had the advantage.

The Danes must be prepared to shed a lot of their warriors' blood if they sought to come up the steep hill and dislodge him.

The Danes.

Bjarki's people were lined up in one long shield wall, two men deep, along the base of the escarpment in the centre of the field. The line was alarmingly thin but it *was* extremely lengthy – perhaps as much as half a mile long. Bjarki reckoned it must contain a good three thousand warriors. Mostly Sjaellanders, he thought, Wartooth's own troops, and men from old King Siegfried's *hird*, as well as Danes from Jutland and all the various islands. His Vastergotland folk must be in there, too. Somewhere in that line was Mogils and Glamir Raeflisson and their five hundred brave warriors.

He puzzled for a while as to why Harald Wartooth should have ordered this odd, weakly extended formation – then abruptly arrived at his answer. For the nervous warriors looking down on the Danish shield wall from the Svear centre it would seem like an endless mass of enemies stretching almost as far as the eye could see in both directions. Harald Wartooth was not behaving as foolishly as it might seem. The old walrus was seeking to intimidate the foe with his numbers. A time-hallowed tactic.

Behind the long Danish shield wall, stretching all the way back several miles through the fields to the village of Norrkoping, were little knots of warriors sitting round fires, and small bands of men on the march, and some women, too, trudging back and forth between them. The women were probably water-carriers, assigned the duty of bringing water or ale to the fighting men in the wall, and dragging away the wounded to be given succour or perhaps, if the wound was severe, the merciful knife.

The knots of men around their fires were Danish reserves, probably levies, who had been summoned from the fields and sheep pastures to fight beside their lords. They would be used to fill the rear ranks of the shield wall when the battle line grew thin. Each would have a shield and spear, at the minimum, and if properly led, they could sometimes even be fearsome in the fray.

On the far west of the field, down by the shores of Lake Glan, due south of Bjarki's position, he could see horsemen, and horse lines. Not many – bringing a horse by ship to a distant battlefield was no easy task. But about three score animals were present on the field with riders, not that Bjarki thought they would be much use.

Now he could see movement, a few figures – four men he thought – were coming out of the shield wall, and holding up leafy branches. A parley! They took their position a couple of dozen paces in advance of the ranks of Danish warriors and waited. But not for long. There were figures coming down the tree-stump-studded slope from the Svear lines. Would Sigurd Hring confront Harald Wartooth in person? Or would he disdain to meet anyone other than a fellow king? It was too far for Bjarki to make out the faces of the people involved in the parley, but one of them on the Svear side, a small, slight figure, seemed very familiar to his eye. He caught a flash of bright red hair, recognised the proud bearing, and smiled happily to himself.

He looked down at Garm and called out, but quietly: 'You are going to see your mistress very soon, boy. We'll be with Tor within the hour. Won't that be fine, eh?'

The animal gave an affronted whine in response. Clearly Garm was still sulking.

Bjarki looked back at the centre of the field where the eight stick figures were now arguing about something. One of the men in the Svear side was gesticulating.

He knew well how these things went. The insults, the bravado, the threats. It was all a sham most of the time. A ritual with little meaning. Sure enough, now the Svear were turning around and plodding back up the slope to their lines. It was clear nothing had been resolved. They would fight. There could have been no other result.

Now – what was this? There was movement in the Danish ranks. Were they attacking? No, a grand reorganisation. Harald Wartooth was redeploying his warriors. Bjarki could see it now.

Not as smooth a manoeuvre as he might have liked, a little clumsy and disorganised, but there were three thousand men to muster down there, all seeming to move from their places at the same time. Some men were blundering into others; some men moving back and across. Others looped round the long line.

Slowly, very slowly, some kind of order began to emerge from the chaos. Three massive blocks of warriors – three divisions, a thousand shield men in each one – began to take shape. The reserves in the green fields behind the line were being marshalled, too. Bjarki could hear the call of distant trumpets, the rattle of drums. The knots of men previously sitting round their fires were up now and hurrying forwards, forming up in their own groups and lines, behind the three main blocks of warriors.

'He's going straight up the hill towards them,' said Bjarki aloud. 'Never mind subtlety, the mad old walrus is just going straight up against them – shield to shield.'

He shifted his numb arse and began slowly to climb back down from his perch.

His mind was spiralling – Tor was there! His sister would be in the midst of the shield wall that Harald Wartooth and three thousand charging warriors were about to assault. She would be in the path of the massive Danish attack. What was the matter with the *Armathr*? Could he not wait till Bjarki had a chance to enact Tor's plan?

He had clearly explained to Captain Mogils and to Glamir the law-speaker what Tor wanted him to do – and they had both sworn to pass the plan on to Harald Wartooth. Had the message not got through to the *Armathr*? Or was the Wartooth so monumentally pig-headed he did not care what Bjarki and his handful of brave folk were trying to achieve up here?

It didn't matter which. The attack was going in. And Tor was in grave danger.

Halfway down the tree, Bjarki paused and peered through the leafy branches. He could see young Joralf hurrying through the trees towards him – good! The youngster would bring fresh news.

And far below him on the plain, the first block of Wartooth's men, a thousand spears strong, was trotting towards the base of Kolmarden slope. The Danes were attacking. The great battle to decide who might have the right to call himself the King of the North had begun.

–

Bjarki faced Jarl Starki, surrounded by his ten Companions, with big Sambor barely restraining an eager Garm on his thick rope, and Joralf standing by watching. They were standing in the shade of an old elm tree on the western flank of the summit of the Kolmarden slope. The members of the jarl's *hird* were all around them, too, a thick crowd of more than two hundred warriors. Bjarki recognised one man, Gudrik, Tor's efficient lieutenant, the senior man who commanded the jarl's force when she was absent, and some other faces in the crowd, too.

'Where is my sister?' Bjarki said. He could sense the indecision in the jarl. And fear. Indeed, the young man looked as if he might shit his own trews at any moment.

'She is with the king,' said Jarl Starki. 'He dismissed *me* after we made our report on the parley – then he said he wanted to take counsel with her in his tent.'

'Does he suspect her?' Bjarki looked closely at the jarl. *Had he betrayed Tor?*

'I don't know,' quavered Starki. 'But the king may well be watching us.'

'It matters not,' said Bjarki. 'Now is the time. The Danes are, even as we speak, coming up the slope in force. And Sigurd Hring will soon be engaged to his front. Give the order to your *hird* and we'll hit him in the flank. The time to strike is now!'

'I don't know,' said Starki.

'I *do* know,' said Bjarki, feeling his frustration rise. 'Our wing of the battle line, this right flank, must unexpectedly turn on Sigurd Hring and attack and swiftly kill him. The battle will be over before it begins. This is Tor's plan. Did she not explain?'

'I don't know,' said Starki. 'Perhaps we should wait until Tor returns to me.'

'Tor is with the king,' grated Bjarki. 'She will be thrown into the battle in the centre with the king. We must attack now, kill Sigurd Hring and stop the battle.'

Jarl Starki opened his mouth, and Bjarki snapped: 'If you say "I don't know" one more time, jarl, I swear that I shall split your fat head open with my axe.'

Starki took a step backwards in alarm, the *hird* growled, hundreds of armed Norrland men now bristling at this threat from Bjarki. Garm, sensing the air, growled too. Sambor took a firmer grip on his leash. Bjarki could feel the familiar sensations seething in his veins. Mochta stirred deep in his heart; he felt her quicken and awake.

In the distance, he could already hear the wild war cries of the Danes as they approached the lip of the escarpment; the thump of spears beating against shield rims.

'Jarl Starki,' he said slowly and clearly, 'forgive my rudeness, but time is short. I must have your answer. Will you order your *hird* to attack Sigurd Hring from this flank, as you agreed? Will you seize your chance to become King of Svealand, as was promised by Tor, and supported by King Siegfried, the Wartooth and me? Will you make your move and bring this battle to an end? I must have an answer: yes or no?'

'I don't k…' began Jarl Starki.

Bjarki could feel the *gandr* swell inside his chest; he felt hot and also horribly breathless; madly itchy – he felt as if a horde of ants were crawling all over his skin.

'Stand aside, *nithing*,' growled Bjarki. 'Real warriors will undertake this task.'

Bjarki made a wide, sweeping gesture with his right hand, the hand holding his huge Dane-axe, and Jarl Starki stepped nimbly aside. With that one broad movement, a curtain of men opened in front of Bjarki and his twelve followers, leaving him with a clear line of sight from their position all the way to the big mud-coloured tent flying the Raven banner several hundred paces east along the long Kolmarden escarpment.

The *hird* and its over-timid jarl seemed to melt away to nothing. Bjarki looked around at his handful of loyal companions, at Kynwulf and Sambor, at Oddvin and Rask, at Joralf and Haugen Halfhand, and said: 'The king – the man who matters today is the Svear King. We kill Sigurd Hring now and the battle is won. Let's go.'

Bjarki could feel his vision blurring, the edges of his eyes tinged red; his heart was pounding, drumbeats vibrating in his veins. He felt light, stronger than ever, as if he could leap mountains in one bound, reach out a hand and touch the sky itself.

A voice inside him said: 'Yes, man-child, *yes*. I've hungered too long for this!'

Bjarki ran on light feet straight towards the royal tent, with Garm, now loosed of the thick rope, bounding effortlessly along beside him, and the *Felaki* behind him in a tight, silent pack. He had the long Dane-axe in his right hand and a large shield held high in his left. A sword hung from his left side and the Harva seax was slung across his lower belly. His body was clad in a mail hauberk that hung to his knees, and from his broad shoulders the tattered, streaked and yellow-brown-ish bearskin hung almost to his ankles; his head was shielded by a conical steel cap with a thick nasal guard and side flaps; his thick shins above his leather boots bore greaves of reinforced iron strips, just as his brawny forearms were warded by similarly made leather vambraces.

Two hundred paces ahead of him the horde of Danish warriors was crashing like a vast human wave against the timber barricades, the roaring noise of their battle shouts and the clash of iron against wood filling the air with the familiar din of battle.

Most of the Sodermanland warriors in this section of the Svear line were up against the barricades, hacking and screaming wildly at their Danish foemen over the chest-high wooden walls. Spears lancing out into the crush of humanity and coming back bloody, axes hammering down, crushing skulls, battering shields.

But there were several score men standing back from the timber wall, awaiting the order to go forwards and fill the gaps hewn by the surging Danish horde. And some of them turned, looked west, and gaped in horror. One nervous warrior shrieked and pointed at the charging bear, and the huge *berserkr*, his mouth creamy, beside it.

One of the Estonian mercenary heroes reacted better. He turned to face the oncoming threat, crouched low and braced his feet. But he alone stood against the dozen charging Lodose men, led by Bjarki and Garm, shield raised, his sword drawn.

Garm smashed straight into the Estonian, knocking the fellow flying backwards, his sword wheeling away, his shield clattering down. The bear ducked his head down low and bit once, his jaws crunched through the hero's head. The spell was broken.

The mud-coloured tent was now a mere hundred paces away. Despite the Danish attack clamouring at the barricade to their front, more and more Svear warriors were reacting to the unexpected flank assault of Bjarki and his men. Two Sodermanlanders locked shields and faced Bjarki, barring his path, two heads tucked behind their rims.

Bjarki screamed at them, a hideous bellow of wild, unnatural rage, which made them both immediately flinch back in terror. Then the Rekkr threw himself at the pair of them. His long Dane axe swung, a wide swooping blow, and one of the men's mailed shoulders was immediately sheared away, the other fellow dropped to his knees and cowered under his flimsy wooden disc. Bjarki smashed into him with his boot and kicked him sprawling away, then the Rekkr leapt over both terrified men, and pounded on, hardly breaking his stride. Only fifty paces to go to the royal tent.

All along the Kolmarden escarpment, many Svear warriors were now alert to the threat posed by Bjarki and his force. Men were shouting orders, some were levelling their spears, locking shields with their comrades – a handful stood in their way, in twos and threes, and Bjarki and Garm blew through them all like a mighty wind, the bear slashing with his heavy claws, Bjarki screaming, ripping and slicing with his Dane axe. They moved impossibly fast and left a trail of blood and broken men in their wake. The Companions raced after their king, just a scant dozen paces behind.

The battle at the line of the wooden barricade still seethed and surged, Svear and Dane tore at each other, men screaming in rage and pain; limbs sheared, flesh gouged, skulls shattered; blood flying as men scrabbled and stabbed each other and fell away moaning. But many of the men in the Svear line were casting fearful glances behind, unnerved by the whirlwind assault to their rear of *berserkr* and bear.

A thicker shield wall was forming just yards in front of the mud-coloured tent, and facing west. Towards Bjarki and the bear. A dozen men – no, more, a score of them now – trained warriors tightly packed in two ranks, a third rank forming up behind. And there – short, squat and ugly, Hagnor the Fatbellied, the famous outlaw hero, bellowing orders and pushing more of the Svear into his makeshift battle line.

Bjarki charged this new shield wall, his axe swinging, white froth flying, howls of battle joy erupting from his throat. He hacked at an uncovered Svear head, the sharp blade skittering off the bone and ripping away a clump of skin and hair; the man fell away backwards and the Rekkr barged with his full weight and momentum into the dense triple wall of Danish shields.

Which held.

Bjarki scrabbled for his footing in the mud, and heaved forwards again, his shoulders pressed hard against the wooden discs, a sword came looping out from over the top of the wall and smashed into his iron helm. Through his red battle haze, he glimpsed Hagnor's wide, red sweating face behind the hard blow. And the shine of his swinging blade coming again. And again. The hero's sword crunched down powerfully against the conical cap that protected the Rekkr's skull.

Bjarki's ears were now ringing from the blows, his senses swimming.

He screamed again and pounded in frustration at the implacable wall with his own shield, and the looping sword swooped again and crashed into his shoulder.

Yet now Garm's vast bulk was right beside him; he had a man's cross-gartered leg in his bloody jaws and was worrying it like a hound at a bone, biting through the woollen cloth, snarling, pulling, yanking the yelling man out of his place in the wall.

Bjarki bunched his massive thigh muscles and pushed hard one more time, an impossibly strong heave – and the whole shield wall caved in a fraction, the front rank shifting back just a few inches. Then the wall itself gave one huge convulsive heave and, like a bent branch springing back into place, it hurled Bjarki from its face.

The *berserkr* was thrown far back; he stumbled, dropped his shield and axe, tripped and fell, ploughing into the churned-up earth face first, falling to the ground in an ugly, undignified sprawl. The blows to his helm had made his vision blur; his sight came in, out, a blackness rising around him. He could feel greasy mud on his face, in his open mouth, between grasping fingers. The churned clay as cold as death.

Chapter Twenty-four

Fire in his belly

Tor watched them come up the stump-dotted slope with a good deal of detachment. Whether it was by design or not, the cut-off tree trunks made the Danish advance slower and less concentrated than it might have been. They could not link up into proper formations, since one man in the line would have to break ranks every so often to step over, or walk around, a thick, knee-high stump. So the Danes came on in twos and threes, piecemeal, occasionally forming a short man-chain of three or four, which soon dissolved. Leaving the stumps in place had been a master stroke, Tor realised. Erland the Snake, who was standing only three paces away, leaning a casual elbow on the barricade, had prepared this ground brilliantly.

She mentally saluted him.

As she watched the Danes laboriously stumble up the stump-obstructed slope – with one or two arcing arrows and javelins and the occasional hissing sling-stone claiming a Danish victim here and there – she lifted her own shield and spear and waited. Her mind went back to the conversation she had had in the king's tent right after the parley. And the reason why she was here now and not with Jarl Starki.

'Your jarl is weak,' said Sigurd Hring, his bearded face close to hers, so that no one else might hear. 'Do not say anything, woman, I don't have time to listen to your empty protestations of loyalty to young Starki. He is weak. You know it; I know it.'

Tor could smell mead on his breath, a sickly odour. Some warriors fought when drunk, she knew that, but it was not usually a sign of either great courage or strength.

'I cannot have weak jarls in my army – nor in my land. Nor in the North. I have spoken to him. I have told him that I shall be watching him closely during this fight, and he must prove his worth to me on this day of red battle – or I shall replace him.'

Tor could imagine how Jarl Starki would have taken that threat.

'I shall ensure he fights well,' said Tor. 'I'll put some fire in his belly.'

'No,' said the king. 'I do not want *you* to make him look brave. *He* must fight, and bravely. *He* must lead his warriors to victory – not you. I want you close to me.'

Tor stared at him.

'It is an honour,' Sigurd Hring said, half-smiling. 'You might recognise that. You've been chosen to fight in the centre, with me and my bodyguards and the hired heroes and all their men. We are the bravest. The best. If you fight well, and if Starki does not earn himself glory, I shall make you – my fiery Torfinna – jarl of Norrland.'

He knows, Tor thought. *Odin's arse! He knows of my plot to kill him. But how?*

'I am honour-bound to lead Jarl Starki's *hird* into battle today, sire,' she said.

'I am your king. You are honour-bound to obey me!' Sigurd Hring gave her another blast of half-digested mead. 'Starki will lead his *hird*. Lead them into battle.'

He doesn't know, Tor thought then. *He may suspect but he doesn't know for sure.*

'As you command, O my king,' Tor said, and bowed very low to him.

So she found herself standing at the barricade, grasping shield and spear, thirty yards in front of the royal tent, with a dozen heroes and their men all around her. She could almost feel the eyes of the king on her back. But there was nothing she could do. Instead, she watched, outwardly calm, as hundreds of Danes puffed up the slope in ones and twos towards her, the nearest only fifty yards away. She had no other choice.

To her immediate left was Connor the Black, the mad Hibernian viking, and beyond him Gummi and Gudfast – the two brothers from Estonia – and beyond them Krok of Frisia, who had not spoken to her since that night when he had implied she was a whore. Hagnor the Fatbellied was fussing about somewhere behind the lines with his retinue of twenty oath-men, near the open entrance to the royal tent, a reserve force for this small section of line. Sigurd Hring's greatest warriors were all here in the centre of his array, at the exact spot where the Danish hammer blow must fall.

She heard some disturbance behind her, shouts of alarm, the rapid movement of feet, the clash of steel, but she had no time to turn and look. For that moment, in a howling, thundering mass, the Danish attack hit the Svear barricades, and her world was filled with shouting warriors, huge and wild-eyed, their blades reaching for her.

Tor fought with a chilly precision, absorbing blows on her shield while her spear shot out like a lightning bolt, again and again, to steal the lives of the warriors in front of her. The sharp blade ripped into throats, punctured chests and sides, tore flaps from the ruddy cheeks of her foes. All around her the heroes and their men jostled and shoved, and fought like gods, their mighty blows striking down the Danes on the far side of the barricade with a joyful vigour. She dodged a wicked sword lunge, fended off a powerful chop from an axe – and felt rather than saw the axe-blade sink into the neck of the warrior next to her, a stranger, one of mad Connor's oath-men, who collapsed, sagging heavily against her, gargling noisily on his own up-welling gore.

The Danes boiled up against the timber wall like storm surf, wave after wave, more warriors surging forwards to fill the places of the men who had fallen, screaming their battle cries – Odin! Odin! – a swirling maelstrom of slicing steel, red, shouting faces and hot, spurting blood. Tor took a crunching blow that slipped off her shield rim and thumped into her leather-covered left shoulder, and stepped back, wincing at the blossom of pain in her upper arm. Raven-haired Connor pushed forwards eagerly into the space she had just vacated, his long sword already slick with Danish blood.

Tor found she was panting like a hunted beast, sucking air into her aching lungs; she was drenched in sweat, head to toe. And she watched in awe as Connor slew and hacked at the boiling horde in front of the barricade, killing, killing, and when no more Sword Danes stood against him he seemed – astonishingly – to be trying to climb over the barrier to get at the enemy.

'Get back down, lunatic!' Tor shouted. But Connor was far beyond her words. The Hibernian stood on the top of the timber wall, shaking his gory sword in the air. He let out one long, piss-curdling scream, then threw himself off the barricade into a seething mass of fresh Danes. His red sword rose once, and fell, cutting down an opponent, and as Tor moved forwards again to take his place on the correct side of the barrier, she saw Connor slash at a warrior, miss, lunge at another one and skewer him – then a bloody spear tip popped from the centre of his mailed back. A grievous wound, surely lethal, that would have dropped a lesser man. It just slowed Connor.

The dark-haired Hibernian staggered, the spear tip disappeared and, to Tor's amazement, the hero straightened and struck out with his bloody sword once more, hacking down a young Dane with a blond moustache who was just coming forwards. Connor cut him down, then another man, and plunged forwards into the crush of Danes down the slope. He jammed his sword tip into the eye of a screaming man. The sword was swallowed by the man's head. Trapped. An axe blow from the Hibernian's left-hand side swung in and carved the top of his own head clean away, and mad, brave Connor was no more.

The yelling scrum in front of the wall was thinned by now, whether by Connor's suicidal actions or the natural ebb of the fray. Tor leaned against the barricade, resting her weight. Her legs were trembling, her vision bright. The Danes were pulling back.

She realised that the noises of battle she could still hear were coming from *behind* her. She pushed off the barricade and turned to look and saw – to her absolute joy – a huge bear savaging the leg of a Svear warrior in a collapsing shield wall.

She shouted out: 'Garm! My sweet boy, you came.' But her words were lost in a burst of wild cheering all along the barricade at the ebbing of the Danish war-tide.

There was Bjarki, oaf-like, sprawled in the mud in front of the dissolving *skjald-borg*. A mob of *Felaki* there too – Kynwulf out in front – racing to protect their king.

Garm lumbered forwards into the loose ranks of the Svear, shoving warriors back and aside, his powerful forelimbs flicking out, ripping figures out of his bloody path. Joralf was beside him now, killing like a demon, his red sword flicking out like a serpent's tongue; and Sambor, too, wielding a huge axe with both hands, chopping down his opponents. Garm's giant form shouldered onwards, pushing right through the crumbling Svear formation, shrugging it away. Terrified men were jumping back, to get away from the unstoppable, blood-spattered bear and its lethal claws and teeth.

Kynwulf tucked in behind the bulk of the animal, with Rask on his right shoulder, and Oddvin on his left, all three men surging forwards towards the royal tent. The War Chief dropped a man with a lunge and twist of his sword – and at the same time Rask parried a sword blow from the right that would have killed his captain.

Tor snatched a glance back down the slope. The Danes had indeed pulled back a distance, fifty paces or so down the slope, but they were not running: she stared at a big warrior, a man she recognised. Hrolf? Hrafi? Something like that. A good fighter. The Danish captains were shouting, trying to drive the men back up the corpse-littered, stump-obstructed slope, urging them to assault the gory barricade once more.

An eviscerated man was lying screaming on the blood-splashed slope five yards in front of Tor. Had she wounded him? Was he one of Connor's victims? She had no idea. Tor ignored the dying man's screams and turned back towards the king's tent. And saw Hagnor the Fatbellied there swing his sword at Kynwulf, very fast, and the old *Felaki* catching the heavy blow on his shield, and returning the cut. Two of the Companions, Haugen and another man she didn't recognise, were helping a half-dazed Bjarki to his feet. The Svear warriors all along the escarpment barricade were pointing and staring – confused by the small but vicious fight taking place behind them. But now the Danes were coming again up the slope and the Svear captains all along the line were shouting at them to stand to, stand to, and stand fast.

The determined warriors of the Dane-Mark once again surged up against the barricade and Hralf or Hrolfi was now lunging at Tor with his spear, a snarl on his red lips, the point raking noisily across her iron helm. Tor battered the spear shaft aside with her shield and lanced her own spear forwards, forcing the man to stumble back.

He slipped and went down on one knee. Another Dane blundered into his place, and she gave him her spear tip right in the pit of his throat, then a sideways cut, the blade ripping open his neck in a welter of blood.

The space in front of her was empty again, and she turned to look at the scene before the tent thirty yards behind her.

She saw Bjarki, on his feet again, with a roar of rage, ripping off his battered helmet, hurling it at an enemy by the opening of the tent. He shook off all his Companions, too, who were helping him stand, and whipping his sword from its scabbard, he charged forwards once more and began hacking at two terrified Svear in the ruins of their shield wall.

One opponent swiftly fell to his slicing sword – the other ran, sprinting back inside the darkness of the mud-coloured tent. The bear was chewing on the arm of a wounded man. The wounded fellow strangely silent. Unconscious, perhaps. Or dead. Now Hagnor was the only man left standing from the former wall, wounded men, discarded weapons and corpses strewn all around him.

More Svear warriors were running towards the skirmish, coming from all sides. The alarm had gone out to all parts of the army. Suddenly, there was the king, bursting from inside his tent, in gleaming mail, shining helm, a drawn sword in hand.

Sigurd Hring surveyed the situation, raised his blade and bellowed: 'To me!'

Tor checked her front – the Danes were still holding back, hovering uncertainly, the nearest man twenty yards away. She looked round: behind her the bear was lumbering towards Hagnor the Fatbellied, the animal growling menacingly deep in his throat, his huge red mouth open, exposing two rows of wicked yellow teeth.

The fat man danced forwards, nimble as a deer on his feet, dodged left, jumped right and slashed quickly at the bear with his bloody sword. And struck the creature.

The sword blade bit deep into the bear's massive forearm. Tor screamed: 'Don't hurt my boy!' and abandoning her post at the barricade, she sprinted towards them.

Garm heard her voice. The huge beast turned and looked lovingly at Tor for a long moment, his yellow eyes glowing like candle flames. He gave a little mewl of pleasure and recognition. And Hagnor the Fatbellied jumped in again and plunged his sword right through the bear's meaty neck, the gory blade bursting out above the animal's black shaggy spine. Tor screamed – an agonised, wordless cry wrenched from deep within. She drew back her arm and hurled her spear at Hagnor.

The spear flew straight and true and plunged into the base of the hero's back, its tip punching through the iron rings and knocking the hero to the ground. Tor was on him an instant later, her sword raining mercilessly down at his shoulders and head.

She kept striking the fat man, hacking at him long after he was bloody and still.

Then Tor turned and threw herself on the wounded bear. Her arms encircling his thick neck. Mindless of the clash of metal all around her and the desperate shouts of men, she hugged the animal to her, and Garm whimpered and tried to lick her face.

The blood was welling thick and fast from the wound in his back, indeed his fur was already sodden, and Tor felt him shuddering. She released him and looked round.

Bjarki was at the centre of a knot of his own warriors, the Companions fighting with seax and sword with a desperate fury. There were Svear all around him but her brother had his hands down by his sides. His face was grey and his chin touching his chest as if he were an unstrung puppet from some mummer's fair attraction. As she watched, Kynwulf briskly slew two enemies, then simply shoved one out of his path with a stiff arm, and Rask, the woodsman, put an arrow through the belly of another.

The *Felaki* were embattled all around, some fighting individual duels with Svear warriors, and she saw that two of them were fallen and still, lying in the cold mud. Sambor, now weaponless, was crushing the life out of a Svear warrior with his hands.

The Danes were finally pulling back, for real this time, the tide of warriors retreating down the bloody slope, and all along the barricade the Svear warriors were once again cheering their victory, shouting praise at their survival to the skies.

There was no sign at all of the king. But blocking the entrance to the mud-coloured tent was a new triple-thick wall of well-locked shields, two score men or maybe even more – Tor recognised some of Sigurd Hring's elite bodyguards in there – and Egil Skull-Cleaver in the centre of the rear rank, towering over everyone and, now, looking accusingly straight at her. Many other Svear were also drifting back from the fight at the barricade to see what the commotion was around the royal tent.

And there, Tor saw, was a block of fresh troops coming forwards through the trees to the north – Wends, she thought, judging by their oblong shields, the king's reserve troops – a hundred foreign spearmen at least. It was no use – the surprise was gone. The king was gone – alerted to the danger. She could see some of the *Felaki* still fighting, exchanging blows with Svear guards, but the full heat and fury of battle had gone, and Bjarki was hunched over, silent, slathered in blood, blades dangling from his hands. Clearly he was utterly spent.

'Where the fuck is Jarl Starki?' she said, not meaning to say the words aloud. 'Where is the *hird*? Where are my men?' A panting Joralf was beside her. 'He would not fight,' he said. 'He could not decide if the time was right to attack the king.'

'That snivelling turd,' she said. Then: 'Fall back! Bjarki, we must fall back!'

Her brother turned to look at her, the wild Rekkr madness was visibly seeping out of him. He twisted his blood-spattered face into some kind of a crooked smile.

'Time to go, brother. We must fall back on Starki's *hird*.'

Bjarki nodded at her.

'Companions!' he called out, his voice weak and shaky. 'We shall retreat!'

The retreat was easier than Tor could possibly have hoped for. In the chaos of battle, no warrior was completely sure who was the foe and who was not. And many Svear were utterly done after the massive Danish assault. The eight surviving *Felaki*, Joralf and Sambor formed up in a tight pack around the exhausted Bjarki and the wounded bear and they trotted back along the line of the escarpment in a blade-bristling knot.

As they were leaving the vicinity of the royal tent, Tor heard Egil Skull-Cleaver shouting after them, calling them traitors and cowards, and urging all good, loyal men to come forward and cut them down like the treacherous dogs they were. But he did not choose to break up his tight-packed shield wall in front of the king's tent and pursue them himself, and no one seemed to heed him or to understand his orders. The Svear fighters along the barricades just watched in dazed, blood-spattered incomprehension as the tight, trotting group passed them by.

The king was still nowhere to be seen. And, in a few moments, Tor's friends were out of sight of the royal tent and heading briskly west along the long Svear line of battle towards the elm-tree position of Jarl Starki's *hird*.

No one raised a blade against them. No arrow was loosed. In a short while, they were under the elm. The Starki *hird*, when they saw Tor, opened their ranks.

'You have a choice to make now, lord,' she said a little later, looking into Jarl Starki's white, wide-eyed, appalled face. 'You can stay here and wait till Sigurd Hring wakes up to your treachery and marches west along the Kolmarden ridge to crush you. He has plenty of fresh men, you know. The Wendish reserves are coming up – I saw them. The king must now require your head after the attempt to kill him.'

Jarl Starki just goggled at her. 'What… what have you done to me, *Stallar*?'

'It is more what *you* did – or rather did *not* do. If you had done as my brother asked you, then Sigurd Hring would be dead, and you might be wearing his crown.'

'He said he was watching! The king knew what we planned. It was madness.'

'Nonetheless, you now have a choice. Stay here and let the king mount your indecisive head on a *nithing* pole. Or come down the hill with all of us and fight for the Danes. My brother will smooth your path. You might even redeem yourself.'

Jarl Starki stared at her, but only for a few moments longer. Then gave the order.

In the time it takes to boil an egg, almost the entire right wing of Sigurd Hring's army had deserted their posts. More than two hundred Svear streamed down the slope towards the shore of Lake Glan, with the angry shouts of their comrades in their ears.

Tor found Bjarki and the bear leaning against each other, in some sort of blood-soaked embrace. Yet her brother, bar a few cuts and bruises, seemed to be unharmed.

Her beloved Garm, on the other hand, was in very poor condition indeed.

Making good use of Sambor's strength, Tor and Bjarki had managed to get the bear down the wooden hillside, chivvying him to walk, and leaving great smears of bloody fur whenever the animal rested his body. Finally, when Garm eventually refused to move any more, Bjarki and Sambor were forced to lift the huge creature in their arms and carry him. Somehow they got Garm a mile or so from the enemy lines and down to a small tree-lined bay on the shore of the lake, where they let him rest.

The animal was whimpering and panting great, red-misted breaths by this point, in a world of pain. When Tor examined his two wounds, a deep cut across his right forearm, and a sword puncture in his neck, she felt a ball of rage forming in her belly.

'You'd better go and see Harald Wartooth yourself, oaf,' said Tor, 'or Starki and my *hird* will be cut to pieces by those cavalry over there. Sambor can help me here.'

Tor pointed to a couple of score of curious Danish riders, about half a mile to their south. These mounted troops seemed to be forming up in blocks of horse, ready to make a charge. The *hird*'s descent from the Kolmarden had not gone unnoticed.

Bjarki heaved himself to his feet. He staggered like a drunkard, clumsily missing his step on the uneven ground. He began to hack at some branches from the nearest ash tree with his Harva seax. But his blows were wild, feeble. Kynwulf came to help.

Tor frowned at her brother. 'Are you wounded?' she said.

'No, not truly... but I have no strength in my limbs,' said Bjarki. 'None.'

Tor squinted at him, absently stroking the bear's blood-matted right ear.

'Mochta has left you?' she said.

'She was singing inside me when we attacked the royal tent. I was so full of her rage and power. Brimming with her impossible Bear strength. Then, suddenly... When Garm was struck by Hagnor, it all went away. She's gone. She left me, weak and helpless, right in the middle of the fight. She's no longer there, Tor. She's gone, completely. I don't know where. But there is no Bear *gandr* inside me any more.'

Chapter Twenty-five

The grip of indecision

Bjarki got to the cavalry, with two green branches borne by two of the Companions waving over his head, just in time. Some sixty horsemen, Saxons from the north of their Frank-occupied country, Angrians, were on the very cusp of attacking the Svear infantry who had just tumbled higgledy-piggledy down to Kolmarden slope and onto the flat ground below. By good luck, their leader recognised Bjarki Bloodhand from his time in the Saxon wars.

'Where you going, Rekkr?' called out a captain named Vasti, reining in in front of him. Bjarki remembered the man from a big fight against the Christian Franks at Lubbecke. 'And who are those spearmen behind you? They look like Svear to me.'

'They are our allies,' said Bjarki. 'Jarl Starki's men – Svear who acknowledge Siegfried as the true King of the North. They are on our side – so leave them be, Captain Vasti. Where is Jarl Harald of Sjaelland now? I must take counsel with him.'

'They say you are a king yourself these days, Bjarki,' said Vasti. 'Is that so?'

'If they say so, it must be true,' grinned Bjarki. 'The Wartooth – where is he?'

Captain Vasti gave him a horse to ride and leaving his Companions jogging in the dust behind him, following after their king as fast as they could, Bjarki kicked the horse into a gallop and was soon a mile or two away in the thick of the Danish lines at the centre of the Kolmarden slope. He slowed his horse then, allowing the animal to pick its way through the groups of sitting or sprawling warriors. He saw that some men had already taken wounds. And, exhausted as he was, he could already see the signs of defeat written on their drawn, grimy, blood-speckled faces. The frontal attacks on the enemy up on the ridge had all failed. And many Danes had been killed.

Mochta, where are you? he said silently, speaking into his own empty heart.

There was no reply.

One older man with a stiff grey beard, seeing him approach, staggered to his feet and held out both his arms wide to halt Bjarki's progress. Bjarki reined in the horse and stared down at the fellow, who looked familiar, though Bjarki couldn't place him.

'You don't remember me,' the elderly warrior said.

'Should I remember you?' Bjarki replied. 'Are you a man of renown?'

'I am Malfinn – we met in Fröjet, in an ale-house there. Did you ever catch up with your kidnapped Saxon princess? Did you slaughter that maggot Hjorleif Illugi?'

Bjarki remembered him then. The old man who had given them precise sea-wise directions to the pirate's lair in distant Rogaland.

'I found her,' he said. 'And Hjorleif is dead. What is it to you?'

'You gave me silver for some information. I have more to share with you, if you have more silver to give me. I know you can easily spare it – King of Vastergotland.'

Bjarki looked closely at the man – measuring his quality. 'How come you to be here – in the battle?' he said. 'Why quit your warm comfortable ale-house in Fröjet?'

'The Wartooth stopped at the island of Gotland on his journey here – he was recruiting more spearmen. He offered me bright coin to fight, so here I am. Speaking of silver, will you buy what I offer? You will find it well worth the silver you spend.'

'What do you know?' said Bjarki.

'Silver first. It concerns your princess. And the man who ordered her abduction. Not Hjorleif but *his* master: the man who hired Hjorleif. What will you give for that?'

Bjarki stepped down from the saddle and walked up to the old man, looming over him, staring hard into his faded eyes. But the fellow's gaze was steady and clear. *It could be a trick*, Bjarki thought. *But what is there to lose? What value has coin on the day of bloody battle? The dead cannot spend it.*

He pulled a heavy purse from his belt and handed it over to Malfinn.

'Now talk. Tell me all you know of Hjorleif and Edith. And if I believe you have cheated me, or played me false in any way, I shall kill you. Speak only truth to me!'

Bjarki found Harald Wartooth in the middle of an angry conversation with Lars Crookback, Master of Hellingar and Jarl of South Jutland.

'No, my lord, I shall *not* withdraw my whole force to Norrkoping, I shall not hide in there like a coward and prepare defences against a coming Svear assault. The enemy is *there*, up there, on that very ridge.' Harald Wartooth stabbed his finger at the stump-dotted slope fifty yards in front of him. 'That is where Sigurd Hring now sits like an old mother hen on her comfortable nest! Teasing us. Mocking us. And that is where I shall go to fight that upstart lord on behalf of our good King Siegfried.'

Bjarki looked at the men surrounding the Wartooth. Lars Crookback was tugging worriedly at his beard. There was Widukind, also frowning and shaking his head unhappily, Abbio stood beside him, small, dark and filthy, staring at the ground.

Bjarki could not look at the *gothi* without thinking about Edith. And if he looked too long at the Crow-man fresh blood would almost certainly be spilled. He looked away, and saw Glamir, the Law-speaker of Lodose, who gave him a huge grin of genuine welcome, and Captain Mogils waving at him from the back of the crowd. And half a dozen other jarls and oath-men were there, many of whom nodded or smiled at him in a friendly fashion. And one half-glimpsed slender figure who, when he saw Bjarki's eye turn towards him, slipped quickly away back into the crowd.

'Jarl Harald,' said Lars, 'you have tried twice to take that accursèd ridge, and twice have you failed. And you have paid for that failure with the lives of my brave Jutlanders. It is madness to attempt another head-on assault. We must withdraw to the village, construct fortifications and invite Sigurd Hring to come down and attack us!'

'Who commands here, Crookback? Who represents our king before his army?'

'You do,' said Lars Crookback, looking mutinous. He opened his mouth to say something more, but Harald Wartooth interrupted him. 'That is an end to it. Prepare your men for another assault. I shall go forwards with you, with all our strength, and we shall chase that roosting fowl Sigurd Hring all the way back to his Uppsala coop!'

Harald Wartooth's eye fell on Bjarki. 'The King of Vastergotland! Here at last,' he said. 'I expected you to be present on the field of honour a little earlier, highness.'

'I told you I would be here on the first day of Heyannir. Today. And here I am.'

'It makes no matter. You are with us now. What tidings from your travels?'

'Jarl Starki and his *hird*, some two hundred Svealand warriors, have come over to our side. They are at present camped on the shores of Lake Glan, two miles west.'

'Starki, Starki, remind me – which one is he?'

'Starki is the Jarl of Norrland. My sister Tor has come down from their position on the Kolmarden with him. Were you not told of our plan? Jarl Starki held the Svear right flank secure. But my sister persuaded him to switch sides. Now he is with us.'

'I told him, highness,' said Glamir. 'I explained your plan in full to him twice.'

269

'There was some mention of tricks and traitors. It seemed a dishonourable ploy to me,' said Harald. 'Are you saying, Rekkr, the Svear right flank is *unguarded*?'

'I cannot say that. We left the position empty. We made an attempt on the life of Sigurd Hring; we hoped to catch him in his tent, but we failed. Then we came here.'

'I saw you,' said one of the Danish jarls. Bjarki did not know him. 'I saw you, Bloodhand, fighting with Hagnor the Fatbellied's men outside the upstart's tent. Your bodyguards with you. But your *sister* fought with the Svear. How can we trust *her*?'

'Tor enjoined Jarl Starki to change sides. And I vouch for her. She is with us.'

'Your sister killed some of my best men...' Bjarki noticed that this angry young jarl was lightly spotted with blood and there was a fresh cut along his jawline.

'If you seek redress, my lord, I am sure that either I or my sister Tor will be more than happy to oblige you – *after the battle*. If we survive it. But for now...'

'Be quiet all of you,' Harald Wartooth's voice boomed out. 'I have changed my mind. The King of Vastergotland's tidings change everything. The assault on Sigurd's centre will go in, commanded by Lars Crookback with his five hundred Jutland men.'

The hunchbacked jarl snarled: 'My lord, there is simply no chance of any...'

The Wartooth rolled right over him. 'But it will be a feint. A ruse. A distraction. The true attack, led by me, and two thousand of my Sjaellanders, supported by the brave warriors of Vastergotland, under their late-come king, will fall on the enemy's open right flank. We will strike Sigurd Hring there like a blow from Thor's hammer! There's not a moment to lose. King Bjarki, you are to come up with me. My men will go in first, you lag behind and reinforce us as you see fit. Yes? We must attack quickly before the Svear realise their weakness on the left flank. We must go now!'

Bjarki was distracted as Glamir the law-speaker and Captain Mogils marshalled his Vastergotland troops. As his five hundred shield-men formed up, in a single block a little behind the far more numerous Sjaellander warriors, Bjarki found himself staring in disbelief at the young man standing beside Harald Wartooth and holding up his Red Boar banner.

The king's ageing *Armathr* was now haranguing his people about the need for courage, strength and speed in their attack, and wagging one thick finger high in the air. But Bjarki was not watching the Wartooth's exhortations. His gaze was fixed on his *Merkismathr*, his banner man. He was almost certain that the young warrior carrying the Sjaellander's Boar flag was Rorik Hafnarsson – the man who had so cruelly poisoned his folk at Bearstead. He was looking at the murderer of poor Inge!

He was almost sure it was Rorik. Yet he could hardly credit his eyes.

The last word he had received from Tor about the murderer Rorik had said that the little weasel was in the service of Sigurd Hring, as Royal Huntsman, and yet here the fellow was, bold as brass, acting as an important functionary in the *Danish* host.

Bjarki's mind reeled. He fought through the dark fog of his exhaustion, trying to banish his own confusion – and failing. He wished more than anything to sleep. Even after an hour or two's slumber he might be able to fathom why this cunning worm was not up on the Kolmarden ridge with the Sveland foe but standing here under the Wartooth's banner. But that he could not do. There could be no sleep till they had assaulted the Svear lines and driven Sigurd Hring's men back into Sodermanland.

Yet in his mind was the wild urge to draw sword and sprint the hundred or so yards to Rorik, and immediately hack his stupid, murderous head from his shoulders.

He resisted the urge. With difficulty. He tucked it away in a part of his mind. He fought his tiredness too, and raised his chin.

He looked at the neat ranks of men now in front of him, many familiar, all five hundred now looking most expectantly at him.

'Men of Vastergotland,' he began, projecting his voice to reach the listeners in the rear ranks of the army. 'You know me – as I know all of you. I know your worth. I know your strength, your skill and your courage. And we shall need all of it today.'

He paused and surveyed the faces of the front rank. There was Baldur, who had won first prize for spear-throwing at the Feast of Idun, there was old Hedvig, from the Kullen hills, whose wife made fine mead. Brave warriors, good men – all of them.

'We're going up there,' Bjarki said, pointing to the slope, 'with Jarl Harald and his doughty Sjaellanders. And then we are going to show those Svear who we are. Follow my banner, hold tight, and we'll win a great victory before this day is done.'

Beside Bjarki, Glamir lifted his monarch's banner – a brown bear on a yellow field – high in the air. 'For Bjarki and Vastergotland!' the law-speaker bellowed.

And the assembled Vastergotland warriors echoed back his cry.

Kynwulf and the rest of the Companions gathered round Bjarki then. Kynwulf handed him his Dane axe, and Black Ivar handed him his shield. Rask carefully brushed some crumbs of dried mud from his tatty, yellowing bearskin cloak. Bjarki wished then that he had time enough to embrace Tor once more before the fight, but she was more than a mile away on the far side of the field, by Lake Glan with the wounded bear, her own people, and Jarl Starki's *hird*.

He could see the Sjaellanders were already moving off in a great pack – two thousand men – a great crowd of hurrying warriors streaming up the sunken road that headed roughly north-west from the bottom of the slope. This hidden road should take them almost to the summit of the Kolmarden without being seen from the top, and it would ultimately lead them to – with the gods' favour – the mostly empty western part of the line where the two hundred men of Starki's *hird* had once stood.

'Give us your blessing this day, Odin,' muttered Bjarki. Then, silently, *Mochta? Mochta – where are you? I need you with me now. I need you more than ever before.* He began to hum, deep in his chest, a four-note melody, ancient and powerful…

'Let's go up there – and show them all!' he shouted, and his Vastergotlanders cheered and moved off briskly, following in the dust of the far larger Sjaelland horde.

Bjarki continued to hum as he jogged forwards along the road, and as it began to climb the steep slope. His legs felt weak and watery; the weight of his shield dragged his arm. But he kept his head high and forced himself to take one step after another.

Mochta? he whispered a final time. There was no reply. Only an empty silence.

–

When the summit of the Kolmarden finally came into view at the top of the road, for one heart-lifting moment, Bjarki thought all would be well. The Sjaellanders ahead of him were cheering and shouting their battle cries. The ridge looked deserted.

Bjarki recognised the old elm tree that he had stood beneath to argue with Jarl Starki before his disastrous attempt on Sigurd Hring's life. There seemed to be no one there at all. The Svear right flank *was* completely unguarded. Perhaps they would all simply march up to the summit, and then turn right, eastwards, and then roll up the entire Svear force from this open flank. Over to his right, somewhere in the centre of the line, Bjarki could hear the long-suffering Jutlanders under poor Lars Crookback making a noisy assault on the barricades – the defensive line they had already come up against twice before. He hoped they would keep the foe amused just long enough for Harald Wartooth and his Sjaellanders to…

Then all of Bjarki's high hopes were dashed.

As if by some malignant *seithr*, a line of men had suddenly appeared at the top of the ridge. They seemed to pop up from nowhere. Perhaps two hundred warriors, fierce-looking wild men in rough hunting leathers and iron helms, in a tight double line, filling the crest. All with bows in their hands, and arrows already nocked.

They drew back their strings as one and, at a shouted order, loosed their shafts.

The Sjaellanders were seventy yards from the summit of the slope when the first wave of arrows sliced into them like a lethal storm. The air seemed thick with shafts. Bjarki could hear the meaty thud as arrows found their mark in flesh, and the *ting, ting* as steel arrowheads struck iron helm or shield boss. The front rank of Danes was wiped away by the first volley from the archers. Men were staggering everywhere on the slope, pricked with shafts, crying in pain, while the second rank of Sjaellanders just pushed them aside and ran, as fast as they could, upwards towards the enemy.

Telemark men, the famous bowmen, Bjarki thought. Fetched over from the Svear left flank, from above the cliffs overlooking the Braviken. A long way. That must have taken some time. Sigurd Hring had reacted swiftly to the betrayal by Jarl Starki. The knowledge hit Bjarki like a charging bullock: *This is going to be bad, very bad*.

'Shields high!' bellowed Bjarki. 'And *faster*, men of Vastergotland, *faster*. The quicker we get up there and at those archer bastards, the quicker this will all be over.'

The Telemark bowmen plucked fresh shafts, drew back their strings once more and loosed. Another hundred Danes were knocked back by the arrows' lethal sweep. Again and again, the bowmen sent waves of death into the ranks of running men.

Some shafts overflew the Sjaellanders and whistled into the mass of Bjarki's men. Two or three men cried out in pain. One old fellow fell to his knees, a shaft in his throat, spitting blood. But Harald Wartooth's rampaging warriors were now only twenty yards from the Kolmarden summit, howling with anger, ready to take a bloody revenge on the line of Telemark butchers. Another volley, another fresh slew of Danish dead and wounded, and strangely, almost miraculously, the cruel archers were moving back, back, drifting away, disappearing back from the lip of the ridge.

Just pausing to loose one final, parting shot before they vanished.

'They're running, the cowards!' Harald Wartooth's triumphant yell rang all around the hillside. 'Forwards for Siegfried; forwards for the glory of the Dane-Mark!'

It was true – the ridge line was once again empty. The archers were all gone.

Harald Wartooth, bounding ahead of his men like a fallow deer, was just below the line of the ridge. His drawn sword gleamed in the bright summer sunshine. He looked like a man of half his age, a true hero for the skalds to laud for ever and a day. And Rorik Hafnarsson, bearing the Red Boar banner, was only a few paces behind his lord. Harald stopped, turned back and hailed his scrambling troops, summoning them onwards, calling them to join him in his great victory at the summit of the hill. The Wartooth was waving both sword and shield high in the air to draw on his men.

But behind him, above him, the ridge line was once more filled with enemies.

A shield wall. A thick, well-knit enemy shield wall on the summit of the slope.

Again, Bjarki suspected some kind of magic. One moment the ridge was empty, and the next it was filled with men – many hundreds of men, many more than there had been archers. Squat, dark, shaggy men with linked shields, but oblong shields, not good round protectors such as the Norse carried. These alien shields were painted in black geometric lines and shapes, with lightning bolts, squares and diamonds. The warriors had iron helmets, and long ash spears, and they were packed just as tightly as any well-trained Dane-Mark or Svealand *skjald-borg*.

The appearance of the Wendish shield wall did not seem to daunt old Harald Wartooth in the slightest. He hurled himself up the last few yards of slope and straight at the nearest enemy. He slipped past his spear, and carved his sword down in the man's neck mid-way between the head and shoulder. Bright blood jetted upwards, but the man's horrible screams were drowned by the noise of an avalanche of battle-mad Danes rushing forwards the last few paces to join their heroic *Armathr* in the fray.

Bjarki halted his Vastergotlanders forty paces behind the battling Sjaellanders, telling his folk to catch their breath, keep shields high and wait for his order to attack.

He watched the raging fight, bouncing on the balls of his feet, exhaustion now forgotten, looking for an opening, a place where the weight of his five hundred men, piling in behind the Danes, could make the difference and break the wall of his foes.

The two sides seemed more or less matched – with perhaps a slight advantage to the Danes. And Bjarki knew that if he could only time the Vastergotland charge correctly, there was a chance they could turn this fight into a rout for the Wends.

The line of battle surged and swayed, back and forwards. Men yelling, slicing, shoving and cutting, bodies falling, blood spurting, spears flicking out from the shield line to rip away the lives of courageous men. Warriors hacked at their enemies' shields and tore at each other with their blades, punching their keen weapons forwards into the foemen's soft flesh. Occasionally, Bjarki could glimpse Harald Wartooth, fighting like a god of war, and always in the part of the battlefield where the fighting was fiercest; the old warrior slaying with a terrible fury; roaring for Odin to witness his deeds.

The Boar banner still flew behind the *Armathr*, although it wobbled and drooped alarmingly from time to time. Was that a breakthrough on the right? Bjarki craned his neck to see. The Wendish line seemed to be moving away, forced back by the Danes.

Bjarki could not be certain. He sensed Captain Mogils at his elbow.

'Not yet, captain,' he said. 'Not yet. We wait for exactly the right moment.'

'No, highness,' said Mogils. 'Look up over there!'

Bjarki looked left where Mogils was pointing; a hundred paces away, over beyond the edge of the heaving scrum of bloodied, writhing men. And saw the archers. The keen-eyed men of Telemark were back, but this time they were spilling down the slope on the extreme left of the battlefield and taking up positions in the few remaining trees on the slope on that side.

Now they were loosing, sending their wicked shafts in to the unguarded backs of the Sjaellanders who were surging obliviously against the Wendish lines. The black arrows flew, and thudded into the fighting Danes. One or two men saw the danger and shouted to their comrades; some of the rearmost men turned and raised shields.

Bjarki yelled: 'To me, Vastergotland! We shall sweep those bowmen away!'

He sprinted up the slope towards the massed archers of Telemark, his Dane axe raised, his shield high, with a howling mob of his subjects at his heels. The archers saw them coming, and immediately switched their aim, now targeting the attackers.

Bjarki felt the cool wind of a shaft ruffle his beard as he ran up the slope, feet pounding, lungs heaving, but he was among them in moments, the axe sweeping out to sink into the side of a man who was about to loose a shaft at him from a yard away.

The man screamed and folded himself around the axe blow and, as Bjarki paused to pull his weapon loose from the suck of the dying man's chest, he saw that Glamir and Mogils were already ahead of him, hacking and slicing into the more lightly armoured archers, slaying one man after another. The *Felaki*, too, were around him, and they went forwards together as a pack, killing as they advanced into the foe.

The Vastergotlanders surged forwards, too, a great moving mass of shouting men, and setting most of the archers quickly haring back up to the summit of the ridge where they disappeared once more. Those that were too late to run, or too proud, were cut down. Bjarki crushed the skull of a skinny bowman as he was turning to flee, then paused, panting hard. He could detect no feeling of Mochta in him *at all*.

The *gandr* was gone.

He looked over the field, scanning it for the next objective... and saw the approach of their doom. On the far right of the field, two hundred paces away, there were the shapes of men approaching, streaming down from the ridge, from far beyond this place of slaughter. Svealanders, Bjarki knew immediately, hundreds of fighters; he glimpsed a banner as well. Black raven on a white field: the sigil of Sigurd Hring.

In the Wendish centre, the battle still raged, but less fiercely. Bjarki saw Harald Wartooth standing tall and alone in the ring of bleeding, broken foes, a dozen yards in front of the still unshattered Wendish shield wall. The Sjaellanders had all pulled back a few yards from the wall, breathing hard, bloodied but still unbeaten. But some were yelling, and pointing over at the oncoming Svear. The *Armathr*, however, was laughing like a lunatic, his head thrown back, his mailed body slathered in gore, his long sword blade glistening red. There was Rorik Hafnarsson, standing a few paces behind his *Armathr*, the Boar standard lying at his feet, the ash shaft snapped in two.

And Rorik had a sword in his hands now, the blade silver-clean.

Harald Wartooth pointed to the right, towards the approaching mass of Svear warriors, jabbing hard with his index finger. He shouted: 'The usurper king has finally found the courage to face me! Come to me, O Jarl of Sodermanland; come here and I'll send you swiftly down to meet Queen Hel. Come to me, Sigurd Hr—'

And before Bjarki's astonished eyes, Rorik stepped forwards and shoved his clean sword blade deep into Harald Wartooth's back. It was a good, hard blow, which punched straight through the iron links of the Wartooth's byrnie and into his kidneys.

Harald Wartooth screamed out: 'Odinnnnnn!' and fell to his knees. He half lifted his own bloody sword in the air, brandished it, and Rorik stepped in once more and with one hack of his blade, he sliced the old warrior's head clean off at the neck.

The Sjaellanders howled and rushed towards Rorik in a pack. The Wends roared in triumph and their line surged forwards at the same time, and the two sides meshed together in a vast killing maelstrom, a heaving frenzy over the corpse of the *Armathr*. Rorik disappeared immediately into the gory, thrashing, hacking scrum, like a swift drowning man slipping down for ever beneath the raging waves of a winter tempest.

Bjarki looked up at the slope in front of him, and the ridge line. The Telemark archers were still up there, out of reach, a bare few visible now, but they were still loosing their lethal shafts. His men were milling about, looking to him for orders.

'Do we push on, sire?' said Glamir, beside him. 'Up on to the Kolmarden?'

Bjarki looked again at the struggling mass of Sjaellanders and Wends. One very young Dane towards the rear of the melee was shouting, 'The Wartooth is dead! Our *Armathr* is down! All is lost, my comrades!' and several of the men near him heard and were edging backwards. The terrified stripling then threw down his spear and shield, turned and ran like a hare down the hillside.

Beyond the still boiling heart of the battle, Bjarki could see the fresh Svear warriors – a good thousand of them – advancing under Sigurd Hring's Raven banner, beating spear shafts against shield in unison and shouting their hatred as they came.

Bjarki was suddenly gripped with a terrible indecision. If his Bear *gandr* had been with him he would have been forging ahead, eager for the slaughter, reckless, joyously killing, heedless of any tactic or stratagem. But Mochta was gone. He was alone. So Bjarki just stood there, the weight of his exhaustion immobilising him, unable to decide what to do next. He could not believe Rorik had slain the Wartooth.

The Danes decided the issue for him. More of them were streaming away down the slope. Indeed, the whole Danish line was crumbling. The Wends were pushing forwards, Sigurd Hring with his fresh troops was now fifty paces away on the right. An arrow pinged off Bjarki's helm. A sharp blow that shocked him from his torpor.

He remembered he was a king. He remembered that the lives of these folk were in his hands. 'Fall back!' he shouted. 'Vastergotland – we will fall back to the plain.'

Bjarki turned and began to stumble, loose-limbed, back down the bloody slope.

Chapter Twenty-six

The sweet stench of a disaster

Tor glanced west. The sun was about four handbreadths above the horizon. Two or three hours more of daylight, she reckoned. She turned back and looked along the length of the Kolmarden ridge that stretched right across the battlefield from Lake Glan to the distant inlets of the Braviken five miles away. She was standing on top of a huge boulder beside the lake, at least six feet above the water, which gave her a clear view of the long slope and the tiny stick-like figures that were stumbling down towards the plain, in ones and twos and little knots. Some had lost their shields, some all their weapons, most appeared to have some wound or were bloodied in some way. And so few of them were returning.

Such a different sight from an hour before when the proud horde of Sjaellander troops and Bjarki's five hundred Vastergotlanders had jogged eagerly up the sunken road, heading north-west towards the summit and victory. Tor had watched the thick column of warriors departing, the sunlight gleaming on the spear-points and the polished helmets, their painted shields catching the eye, and the banners flapping bravely in the wind. It had all seemed so festive, like a summer fair or some kind of celebration.

Not so festive now. On the wind, Tor caught the sweet stench of a disaster.

She jumped down from the rock, and called out to Gudrik, who was seated on the ground nearly, sharpening his sword.

'Fetch Starki to me,' she said. 'We need to move towards the centre.'

She explained to her lord that the *hird* must provide some sort of protection for the trickle of men coming down off the slopes – their defeat obvious in their postures.

But Jarl Starki seemed reluctant to move.

'That is Harald Wartooth's affair,' he said. 'It is not my concern.'

'We have just joined the Danish host,' said Tor. 'We must play our part for the good of the whole army. Or do you wish to make enemies of all the Danes, too?'

Mulishly, Jarl Starki looked at the ground. But he said nothing.

'Gudrik,' said Tor, 'get the *hird* ready to move. And send a runner to the Saxon cavalry yonder with this message. Tell their captain Vasti: We will be forming a defensive wall in the centre of the battlefield, half a mile back from the bottom of the slope. We will act as a secure rallying point for the Wartooth's retreating men, and for my brother's, too, when they come down from whatever catastrophe happened up there. And tell Captain Vasti that I shall be most obliged to him if he would form up his cavalry in two squadrons on either side to ward our flanks. Tell him it's urgent.'

By the time Tor had moved the *hird* the two miles to the centre of the battlefield and formed a decent battle line, with a screen of helpful Saxon cavalry on either flank, most of the Sjaellanders and Vastergotlanders had already come down from the slope. Now perhaps a thousand of the battered survivors of the battle on the ridge were sitting on the earth, sleeping or talking and drinking ale, making soup, and binding up their wounds behind her thin line of shields. Many had the blank look of men who have survived a disaster. The death of Harald Wartooth had hit the Danes hard.

A few of them were still trickling in, and most of the late-comers were wounded. And Tor reckoned the warriors who had not come down yet most likely never would.

'You think Sigurd Hring will attack us down here?' she asked Bjarki, who was swaying with tiredness but seemed, mercifully, largely unwounded. She knew her brother had marched two days and nights without rest, and fought two engagements.

'I don't know,' he mumbled. 'He *should* attack us now, if he has any sense.'

If Sigurd Hring came down from his ridge now and made an assault with all his strength, Tor knew, he could scatter the surviving Danes right across the field. But did *he* know that? And Sigurd's own warriors had taken a hard battering too that day.

'How's Garm?' asked Bjarki. 'Still asleep? You managed to stop the bleeding, I hope.' Her brother scrubbed his dirty face with his hand as if to rub away his fatigue.

'He is still holding on, my brave boy,' said Tor. 'I had some *hird* spearmen carry him to the village. He can recover his strength there in peace under a dry roof.'

'I must go see him – soon – but I am *so* tired. I think I will sleep here a little.'

'First, tell me again about Rorik and Harald Wartooth – I want to understand it.'

'Hmm. Rorik was acting as the Wartooth's *Merkismathr* – his banner man,' said Bjarki, yawning cavernously. 'Rorik went up to the Wendish wall with his *Armathr* – well, just behind him, then he stabbed Harald in the back. And chopped off his head.'

'We have some hot soup for you, highness,' said Oddvin, magically appearing.

Both Tor and Bjarki took the steaming bowls gratefully from the young *Felaki*, and sipped the fragrant liquid. It was leek and barley, with wild garlic in there, too.

'I still don't follow,' coughed Tor, after swallowing her mouthful too quickly.

'Rorik was playing both sides, I think,' said Bjarki. 'For the Wartooth he was his Danish spy in the camp of the enemy. But when things became too dangerous for him in Uppsala, thanks to you, he rejoined the Danes and the *Armathr* rewarded him with a role as his *Merkismathr*. Harald had spies in Svealand. Rorik was one of 'em.'

'He was half-Danish. His mother was a Dane,' said Tor. 'And Rorik kept on disappearing suddenly from Uppsala for long periods. Reporting back to his master – or to someone else who would relay his reports back to Harald Wartooth. Yes, that makes sense. But he murdered Harald Wartooth! Why would he do *that*, Bjarki?'

'Perhaps because his true loyalty was always to Sigurd Hring and to Svealand?'

'I see it,' said Tor. 'Sigurd Hring *knew* that Rorik was feeding information to Harald Wartooth – that is why he allowed him the freedom to come and go. But Sigurd truly owned him. Did the Danes get good information about the Svear army?'

'We all thought it was a lot weaker. We had no knowledge of the Wends at all.'

'There it is: Rorik was a spy with two masters. And secretly loyal to Svealand. He duped Harald Wartooth. So where do you think that murderous *nithing* is now?'

'Dead, almost certainly,' said Bjarki yawning again. 'The Sjael-landers will have torn him apart for what he did to the Wartooth. He was in the very heart of the battle.'

'Do you think Sigurd Hring will come down? Must we fight them again today?'

'Maybe. Wake me if he does – I must sleep now or I'll fall like a chopped tree.'

'You do that. I'm going to check on the *hird* lines and send out a few scouts.'

–

Bjarki lay down on the muddy turf and pulled his raggedy yellow bearskin cloak over his shoulders. Instantly, he was deeply asleep. He found himself in a thick pine forest, an endless gloomy twilight place of mossy trees and diffused greenish light. The close-growing boughs seemed to stretch out in all directions away from him, for ever, or so he believed. In front of him was a mature tree trunk, half-uprooted in some tremendous thunderstorm and snapped in two jagged pieces like a stick of some giant's kindling, the spiky points of the broken shafts as sharp as spears and angled up like a threat towards the enormous purple-grey sky.

A large black bear was sitting on its haunches in front of the nearest broken part of the tree and looking up at a cub, a sweet creature just a few months old, which was playing at one broken end of the thick bough, scampering and sliding, nearly tumbling off only to catch itself with its claws. Occasionally, the little animal let out coughing barks of distress. A sad, puny, deeply pathetic sound.

The adult bear slowly turned its huge head to look at Bjarki, who found himself standing a dozen yards away, naked as a baby, but in no discomfort from the lack of his clothing. The bear's eyes glowed red as coals, then she spoke in her deep voice.

'My cub is dying, man-child,' said Mochta, her voice throbbing with a mother's pain. 'Your cruel kind have pierced him with their sharp iron and his end is near.'

'I'm full of sorrow,' said Bjarki. 'I didn't mean for Garm to come to any harm in the fight. I did not. We love him, my sister and I, as much as we love any creature.'

'You made use of him in your quarrel. At your behest, he fought the bad men.'

'He is young and strong. Perhaps he will soon recover from his wounds.'

'He will not,' said the She-Bear. And, at that moment, the little cub fell off the broken tree stump and landed with a thump in the leaf litter. Mochta ambled over and sniffed the cub, which began to whine pitifully. The Mother of Bears gave the little creature a loving lick with her long red tongue, and the quieted animal closed its eyes.

'That is not Garm,' said Bjarki. 'Our Garm is near as big as you now, Mochta.'

'This is not the animal you call Garm,' said the She-Bear. 'This is the *gandr* of my cub. Like the living bear-flesh my child inhabits, a *gandr* must grow into itself.'

The little bear gave a mewl of distress, and his mother nuzzled him with her snout. 'If the bear-flesh that supports my child dies,' she said, 'if it perishes before this half-formed *gandr* grows into its strength, my cub will be no more in this realm or any other. You're to blame, man-child. You let the Sword-Svear destroy my child.'

'My regret is a knife in my belly. Is *that* why you left me in the midst of battle?'

The She-Bear said nothing but gave a great, wet, slobbery sniff. The cub was lying on its back now, perfectly still, its little paws in the air. Its eyes were still closed.

'What mother can feast when her child is dying?' said Mochta quietly.

'Is there nothing that can be done for Garm?' said Bjarki. 'Nothing at all?'

The bear swung around again and pointed her snout at him. Her eyes glowed red once more with her anger. But Bjarki saw the wet tracks of tears on her black muzzle.

'The cage of flesh that contains my sweet cub is mortifying, it is fading to mere meat,' the *gandr* said. 'When his heart ceases its beating, my child will be no more, the spirit of my cub will be dispersed on the winds of time, gone for ever. Unless...'

'Unless what?' said Bjarki.

'Unless you wake up right *now*, oaf,' said the bear, but in Tor's most strident tone, 'I shall pour this boiling-hot water all over your fat head and scald you awake!'

Bjarki sat up. It was nearly dusk. He had slept deeply for perhaps three hours. Tor was standing over him with a large bowl of steaming water.

'I thought you might like a wash,' she said, seeing that her brother was finally conscious. 'From the stink of you, it's been a good long while since your last one.'

Bjarki grunted something rude and gingerly accepted the hot water-filled bowl. 'I wash myself almost every week,' he muttered, 'whether I need a wash or not.'

Tor squatted by him as he made his ablutions, and spoke quietly, so that no one else could hear. 'I fear, oaf, that Sigurd Hring will come down in the night and fall on us while we sleep.

My scouts say they have seen his men moving about on the slope. We should withdraw back to the village. In Norrkoping, we can build fortifications between the houses and give a better account of ourselves when he does come down.'

Bjarki splashed his face and neck with the delightfully hot water, and scrubbed his filthy hands and forearms. The water in the bowl turned dark from dried blood.

He wiped his face with his shirt, then he looked directly at Tor – and nodded.

'That is sensible, sis,' he said. 'We cannot hope to beat them fighting here.'

Tor reached out and gripped his big shoulder. Then she stood and walked away.

Bjarki got slowly to his feet and looked around him. The day was dying and the dozens of warriors gathered around him threw long shadows across the fields. Bjarki turned slowly again and looked due north, and he too could clearly see enemy warriors now moving about on the lower, stump-dotted slopes of the Kolmarden only half a mile away. Svear scouts, he reckoned, but in force. At least two *lith* of spearmen, or perhaps even some of the fearsome Telemark archers. They were not formed for an attack but they *were* definitely a threat. They should not waste any more time before pulling back to a more easily defensible position.

'Get all our Vastergotland folk up and ready to move,' he said to Kynwulf, who was hovering nearby with a clean towel. 'And fetch Glamir and Mogils to me as soon as you can. Who commands the Danes? Is it Lars Crookback now the Wartooth's dead?'

They gathered up a few more leaderless Danish warriors like a broom gathering crumbs, as the Vastergotlanders and the Sjael-lander survivors of the fight on the ridge and Jarl Starki's intact *hird* made their way south across the fields and pastures.

The Saxon cavalry on their flanks had disappeared. Bjarki did not know when – or where they had gone to. There was no sign of any other Saxons, either. As they all trudged south across the darkling ground, heading towards the small huts, fishing bothies and barns of Norrkoping, Bjarki kept glancing nervously eastwards towards the Braviken inlet. He did not like what he saw. Not at all. Ships, dozens of ships, loosing their moorings, spreading their sails and gliding towards the distant sea.

The Danes had been badly beaten on the slopes of the Kolmarden; their leader Harald Wartooth was dead. Many had had enough, and were quitting the battlefield.

Chapter Twenty-seven

'We stand here and fight'

It was full dark by the time Tor made it to Norrkoping. There was, mercifully, no sign of the victorious Svear sweeping down the Kolmarden slope and flooding across the plain behind them. Bjarki's man Glamir, with help from a dozen other men, was organising a field kitchen and cooking up several cauldrons of hot fish stew made from looted dried and salted cod to feed the Vastergotland troops. And Gudrik was passing out cupfuls of barley grain to the folk of the *hird* so they could make their own pottage. Tor herself had no appetite and went to find Garm, who had been placed in a small fisherman's hut on the eastern edge of the village. She spent a little time with the sleeping animal, talking to him and singing one of the lullabies she had heard Inge sing in the longhouse in Bearstead once. The bear did not move. But, when she checked, he was still breathing. When she was certain that her boy was comfortable, with a blanket draped over his huge silent form in the corner of the hut, she went out into the darkness to find her brother and discuss their plans.

'We could make a run for it,' she said, when she finally found Bjarki and Lars Crookback and another Danish jarl, sharing a leather bag of ale beside a watch fire, just outside the northern edge of the village. 'There are still ships in the Braviken.'

'I heard that Widukind of Saxony has already left,' said the jarl, a middle-aged man called Lofarr, from the north of Jutland. 'He and the weird creature of his that looks like a bedraggled blackbird were seen getting into a ship at dusk and heading out to sea. The horsemen went with them. They left their mounts loose on the bank and boarded ships. The battle is lost. I do not see why *we* should not save our skins.'

'The battle is *not* lost,' said Lars. 'And we are *not* running away. I will not go back home to my king and tell him that he must submit to the upstart Sigurd Hring.'

'What is the point of throwing our lives away?' said Tor. 'Who cares who is King of the North? It's not a real title. We haven't had one for many a year.'

'I gave my oath to King Siegfried that I would support his cause with all my strength; that I would offer my life in the service of his honour,' said Lars, his eyes glittering. 'The King of Vastergotland – your brother – also made this same oath. I am no oath-breaker. I do not serve whomever it suits my taste on any particular day!'

Tor bristled: 'Are you saying that I do? Are you calling me a filthy traitor?'

'I only ask: where were you standing this morning, shield-maiden?'

Tor felt as if she had been punched in the belly. She took a loud, gasping breath.

'I should cut you down, jarl, for that remark,' she said, holding on tight to her rage. 'But I will forbear and say only this. I made my oath to *my* lord, Jarl Starki – I have not broken it. I made no promise *at all* to Sigurd Hring. I have betrayed no one.'

'And where exactly is your famous Jarl Starki this fine evening?' asked Lars Crookback. 'Perhaps we should listen to his wise counsel, instead of his servant's.'

'I am here,' said Starki, stepping out of the shadows. 'And my counsel is this: we must fight. We must stand here and fight the usurper. With my *hird* and the men of Vastergotland, and the Danish survivors of the assaults on the Kolmarden, who are yet coming into Norrkoping in ones and twos, even now – if you did not know it – we still number more than fifteen hundred fighting men. A not-inconsiderable army – and Sigurd Hring must also have suffered from the Wartooth's attacks on his lines. I would say we are almost evenly matched with the Svear force and, with caution and no more reckless assaults, with the help of the gods, we may yet prevail.'

'A sly-minded man might say, jarl,' Lars Crookback said, 'that *you* have no alternative but to fight on. You cannot return to your lands unless Sigurd is defeated.'

'I have just heard *you* say almost the same thing, Crookback,' said Jarl Starki. 'That you would not go home to your king in Jutland unless Sigurd Hring is beaten.'

'It is agreed, then,' said Bjarki. 'We do not run – we stand here and fight.'

-

They made their dispositions: with Bjarki and more than four hundred men of Vastergotland in the centre, with Starki's two-hundred strong *hird*, combined with Lars and the remnants of his Jutlanders on the right, and Lofarr on the left of the line, in the position of honour, with the surviving Sjaelland warriors who used to follow the Wartooth. Then Tor met her brother in the darkness a little north of the battle lines. They sat together on the ground, sharing a jug of mead, and looking across the plain at the bar of the Kolmarden and the line of twinkling campfires along the ridge.

'He's in no hurry to come down, is he?' said Tor, after a little while.

'Why would he be?' said her brother. 'Sigurd Hring is hoping we will decide to make another suicidal charge up that hill to all die conveniently on his barricades.'

'He'll have to come down and fight us either tonight or tomorrow,' Tor said. 'It's either that or he packs up and goes home. Sigurd Hring would never do that.'

'Mm-hmm,' said Bjarki. 'Likely he will come down to us in the morning.'

'What would Harald Wartooth do if he was alive? If Rorik had not killed him?' asked Tor. 'I mean after that bloody fight on the ridge. What would he do now?'

'He would be forcing us to make another assault up that slope. The mad fool.'

They sat for a while. Then Tor said: 'It's a good thing that the Wartooth is dead, then. But it irks me Rorik is no more. I wanted so much to kill him myself. I dreamed of boiling him alive and listening to the music of his screams. Inge will never have her revenge now. I would wish him still alive, in truth, oaf, only so I could end him.'

'Talking of dreams,' said Bjarki, 'Mochta spoke to me in one. She blames me for the wounds Garm took. That's why she left me in the fight before the tent. She said: "What mother can feast when her child is dying?" I do not think I can summon her bear-strength in the battle tomorrow. I may never be able to use her power again.'

Tor said nothing for a while. She was thinking of her Garm, silent and still in his hut, barely alive. And of Inge, cold and dead in her grave. As beautiful as the frost.

'Try not to get yourself killed tomorrow, oaf. Keep the *Felaki* close by you.'

'You too. But no man lives for ever. What was the saying Kynwulf always liked to repeat? Fear not death – for the hour of your doom is set and none may escape it.'

'Kynwulf is a miserable old goat. His doom may be set. We might escape ours.'

Sigurd Hring came down from the Kolmarden ridge in the morning and his army slowly spread across the plain north of Norrkoping like spilled honey on a tabletop.

The warriors of Siegfried's army came out a little way from the village to meet them and formed up in three great battalions in a long, curving bow shape. By mid-morning the two sides were facing each other, no more than a bowshot apart – two lines of shaggy men in leather and ring-mail, spears, helms and axes glinting.

Tor, Bjarki, Jarl Starki and Jarl Lars pushed out of the throng and came to stand two dozen yards in front of the Svear army. There was a ripple of movement in the enemy lines and out came the man who claimed to be King of the North, Sigurd Hring, followed by Jarl Ottar of Vastmanland, Erland the Snake, and Egil Skull-Cleaver, who towered over the others by at least a head. They walked forwards a couple of dozen paces until all eight leaders were only a short spear-toss apart.

Tor studied the four foes and her eyes caught those of Erland the Snake. He winked at her and grinned like a naughty child. She returned him her fiercest scowl.

'If you have come to beg for mercy,' began Sigurd Hring, 'I shall listen to your petition with an open mind – but…' he pointed his unsheathed sword in turn at Jarl Starki and then at Tor '…but that man there and that woman's lives must be forfeit. They are both traitors to their rightful king, snivelling cowards, ungrateful worms who deserve…'

Bjarki held up a palm. 'Could we forgo all the usual nonsense, the threats, the insults, the old grudges, the disobliging references to people's mothers, and simply each say what we have to say. We are going to fight today – we all know this is true.'

'You in a hurry to die, Fire Born?' growled Egil Skull-Cleaver, his voice was as deep and gravelly as Mochta's but somehow less full of life.

'Not at all. I plan to live. Are *you* frightened to face death, Egil?' said Bjarki.

Egil spat copiously on the turf. 'I am certainly not frightened of you, Rekkr.'

'Then, by all the gods, let us try to limit the amount of blood shed this day,' said Bjarki. 'We have already spilled plenty on this field. Enough men have died. Both sides have fought with great courage and honour. I therefore propose this: the battle's final outcome shall be decided by a contest of champions. Just two warriors. Me against the Skull-Cleaver here. If I win, you all go back to Svealand in peace, and Sigurd Hring bends the knee to King Siegfried and renounces his absurd claim to be King of the North. If I lose, our people shall cease hostilities and depart this land, and Sigurd Hring may call himself whatever he likes in Svealand. What say you, king?'

'No,' said Sigurd Hring flatly. 'I shall take the lives of Jarl Starki and Torfinna Hildarsdottir before this day is out. And I would very much like to see your foolish brains spilled out on the earth, too, Bjarki Bloodhand, simply for refusing the honour of serving me. However... I do agree to a contest of champions. Three champions: the Fire Born against the Skull-Cleaver, Jarl Starki against Jarl Ottar and...'

Before he could finish, Erland the Snake stepped forwards.

'I beg the honour of fighting the shield-maiden,' he said. 'If Tor Hildarsdottir is minded to accept my challenge.'

Bjarki looked at Tor with a raised eyebrow, who merely shrugged in reply.

'So be it,' said Bjarki. 'Three single combats to decide the fate of the North.'

'Hold a moment,' said Jarl Starki. 'Tor is my champion. By rights she should fight Jarl Ottar in my place. That is what a jarl's champions are for, are they not? To do the actual fighting. After all, a man does not keep a dog and bark himself.'

'You think I'm your dog?' said Tor, incredulously. 'More importantly, you want me to fight and defeat both Erland the Snake *and* Jarl Ottar? One after the other?'

'You could do it, *Stallar*. I know you have the skills to beat them both. Easily.'

'No,' said Sigurd Hring. 'Jarl Starki must fight or there are no contests at all.'

'Are you a coward, Starki?' said Jarl Ottar. 'Are you a shit-breeches *nithing*?'

The two jarls glared at each other.

'I will gladly slice open *your* overstuffed guts, old man,' Jarl Starki said.

–

Tor faced Erland the Snake at a distance of two sword lengths, each one armed with a sword and shield, and a seax in their belts. Behind her she could hear the cheers and shouts of the Danes urging her on to victory, and beyond her opponent, the Svear were shaking their spears in the air to encourage their champion. With many hundred, even thousands watching, it seemed less like a battlefield than a market-day sword-match, with a couple of travelling warriors demonstrating their skills for the local yokels.

But this was no game. No entertainment. Sigurd Hring, who was standing twenty feet away, behind and to the left of Erland, lifted an arm and said, 'Ready?'

Lars Crookback, standing opposite Sigurd and behind her, said, 'Ready, Tor?'

She gave a brisk nod, never taking her eyes off Erland, who was still grinning insolently at her, gently swishing his long sword in front of him like a hazel switch.

'Fight,' said Sigurd Hring.

'Let's see what you've got, little one,' said Erland. 'Come on girl, do your best!'

Tor controlled her anger. She edged a little closer, watching the swordsman's eyes. They were green and brown like a snake's, narrow and mean, despite the lazy smile on his face. She took a step to her left, closer but circling, and when Erland made the corresponding step to his left, she changed direction and leapt towards him. Her first cut arced towards his head – and he blocked with his shield and lunged, and Tor heard the blade scratching across her shield's boss as she pushed the strike wide.

Then they were battering at each other like maniacs, sword meeting shield, steel cracking against wood, strike and parry, hack and block. Blow and counterblow.

Tor felt the wind of Erland's sword across the top of her head, in a move she had not even seen. By the gods, he was fast. Faster than any opponent she had ever had. Their shields thumped together and she shoved against him with all her strength, but he did not budge. They were locked in place, and Tor sensed the downward sword blow aimed at her left foot, and moved her limb out of its path just in time and, now off balance, Erland shoved her shield hard and she tumbled backwards. She landed on her back; immediately rolled as Erland's sword thudded into the earth beside her ear.

'You're a nimble little thing, aren't you?' said Erland, as Tor bounced back to her feet and set her fighting stance once more. She glared at him over her shield.

Tor attacked again, a feint at his head to make him raise his shield, the blow turning into a low slash at his knees. But Erland, divining her ruse, had not raised his shield, he saw through the feint and her sword snicked against his lowered shield rim and cut a groove in the turf. Erland's weasel-fast counterstrike skidded over the face of her shield and clanged against her helmet, and she only managed to avoid a second cut taking off her head at the neck by dropping suddenly, humiliatingly, to her knees.

Erland backed off and graciously allowed her to rise. Still smiling irritatingly.

'You are doing much better than I expected,' he said. 'You're really quite good.'

'Don't toy with her, Erland, finish the silly bitch off,' shouted Sigurd Hring.

Tor felt shaky and weak. He was the better fighter, there was no question about it. And much stronger, too. But now she was angry. She circled him once again. Went in for a probing hack to his grinning head, and jumped back to avoid his counterstroke.

The roar of the crowd had stilled to a few scattered shouts. She heard Bjarki's bellowing voice. 'You've got him, Tor! Tear the guts out of that lump of pig-dung.'

Tor gritted her teeth. She came in again, strike, shield block, strike. Erland lunged at her face and she took the point hard on her own shield. Then he was coming at her with a speed that was scarcely believable: his sword point was everywhere, jabbing, slicing, hacking high and swooping in low at her ankles. She parried with her sword, swung her shield desperately across her body to keep his liquid, dancing blade away from her flesh. But he was nowhere and everywhere, forcing her back. And back. She stumbled and tripped again, falling flat on the ground, swiped away a lunge at her eyes with a flick of her blade, rolled desperately to avoid a massive killing chop aimed right at her head. Half got to her feet, just able to block a swing at her shoulder, surged upwards, only just keeping his blade at bay. He swung at her, aiming for the gap between her shield and her sword – and slipped in loose dirt, falling to his knee with a loud curse. And Tor, smelling victory, charged forwards, her sword lifted.

And a shaved heartbeat before she struck, she stopped. Recalling, in a blinding flash of memory, the trick that Erland had demonstrated in the sword square in Uppsala all those weeks ago. She stopped just short of committing to her own blow, and as she remembered it, Erland the Snake lunged forwards with his sword, his whole long body fully extended, the wicked steel lancing out towards her unguarded belly.

Had she not stopped, the sword would have met her backbone. But she had held back just enough, and now, quick as thought, she changed the angle of her own strike, powered the blade down and hacked instead at Erland's outstretched right hand – the hand holding the sword that would surely have gutted her.

And sliced the hand clean off at the wrist.

Erland screamed – a terrible peal of pain and horror. And an instant later the severed arm was pumping out gore, spattering the very blade that made his wound.

The great swordsman sagged back, hugging his mutilated arm with his shield hand, and Tor took two steps back, raising her own sword high in the air.

'Does anyone dispute my victory?' she bellowed, shaking the blood-painted sword so hard that red droplets fell like a warm rain all about her.

The Danes were all chanting: 'Tor! – Tor! – Tor!' The Svear were making a low growling noise, like a thousand angry dogs restrained by a thousand leather leashes.

Sigurd Hring came forwards and looked down at Erland the Snake, who had now slumped and passed out from the pain of his wound in a puddle of his own fluids.

'Take him away,' Sigurd Hring said, beckoning over two of his warriors. Then he looked straight at Tor, a cold implacable fury burning like ice-fire in his pale eyes.

'Next contest!' he said.

Chapter Twenty-eight

The sacrificial bull

When Bjarki had congratulated Tor, and wrapped her up in his own warm bearskin cloak, he went back to the front of the shield wall to find a place to watch the next bout.

Jarl Starki looked terrified, standing there shaking slightly with sword and shield in drooping hands, as Jarl Ottar performed some ostentatious, even comical stretching exercises about twenty yards away to the cheers and jests of his Vastmanland men.

Bjarki pushed forwards to stand by Starki's side. The young man seemed even smaller and frailer than ever. He placed one big padded hand on the jarl's shoulder and said: 'He's old and he's fat and he hasn't fought a duel for many, many years.'

Starki turned to look at him. His eyes were massive. 'Neither have I,' he said.

'But you can take him, lord, I know it,' said Bjarki. 'He will tire before you, so make him run, don't stand toe to toe with him, swapping blows. He is strong. But he is *not* fast. Make him chase you. Then jump in when he is tired out and go for his hands or his feet. Forget about his chest or his head. He'll be looking to protect them. If you wound him in the foot, or the hand, just like Tor did, he will be at your mercy. I know you of old, Jarl Starki: you will be the victor of this match. Just make him run.'

Bjarki watched as the two men squared up to each other, again both armed alike with sword and shield. The two jarls circled each other for a brief moment, then Starki gave a wild shout and rushed straight at Ottar, and began raining sword blows at his opponent's helmeted head. The Jarl of Vastmanland was a little taken aback by the ferocity of the assault, but he kept his shield high and absorbed the battering.

Bjarki yelled: 'Back off, lord, and make him come to you. Make him run!'

Jarl Starki ignored his advice. Instead, his hammering at Ottar's defences took on a whole new manic energy. Starki slashed and hewed and hacked at Ottar with his sword but with no real skill beyond his youthful strength and agility. He used his long blade like a whip to lash his enemy. But while Jarl Ottar might have been fat, he was also an experienced warrior, and he weathered the storm, warding off ever-wilder blows with his own sword and shield, and occasionally ducking under a wide slash or swing. And when Jarl Starki stepped back panting, already spent, Ottar moved in towards him, feinted low at his legs to make Starki drop his shield, then switched the angle of the strike, aimed higher, and stabbed him through the throat with a thrust of his steel.

And Jarl Starki was down, on his knees, bleeding heavily and coughing his life blood on the grass. The assembled mass of thousands of men went quiet. Starki toppled onto his side, coughed out a great gout of blood, the final one, then lay still.

Then the cheering and jeering began from the ranks for the Svear.

Bjarki went forwards and scooped up Starki's gory body in his arms and carried it back to the Danish lines, handing the mortally wounded jarl to Gudrik and some other members of his *hird*. He found nothing good to say to the jarl's man except: 'He did not die a coward.' And Gudrik nodded in mute agreement before bearing him away.

'Next contest!' shouted Sigurd Hring. He was rubbing his hands with joy, and the smile on his face could have split his head in two. Bjarki gave him such a ferocious glare that the would-be King of the North went quite pale, and quickly looked away.

Tor came up to Bjarki and handed him his Dane axe, his helm and a thick oak-plank shield – a heavy object, heavier than the usual lime-wood, but reassuringly solid. The long Harva seax blade was already slung over his loins in its usual place.

'Is your *gandr* with you?' she asked, tying the leather thongs of the bearskin cloak she had borrowed around his neck. 'Will Mochta help you? Is she here now?'

'I don't need her,' Bjarki replied, shaking his arms to get some blood into them. 'Egil Skull-Cleaver is no more than a big, dull, lumbering bull ripe for the sacrifice.'

'Call on Odin. Tell the All-Father you will kill this giant as an offering to him.'

Bjarki put the helmet on his head, a plain steel cap with a thick nasal guard, and fastened the ties under his chin. Then he hefted the axe and shield, and looked into Tor's eyes. 'Oh, old Spear-Shaker is watching our deeds, you can be sure of that.'

'Go and slay the sacrificial bull, then,' she said, briefly gripping his forearm.

Bjarki nodded, turned and strode out into the space between the two armies.

For all his bold talk, Bjarki could not prevent a chill of fear running down his spine when he saw Egil Skull-Cleaver emerge from the ranks of the Svear. The hero was enormous, at least half a head taller than Bjarki, thick and muscular in body and limb. A bull was right – Bjarki knew he could not encompass that neck with both hands.

Mochta, are you there? said Bjarki into his heart. *Heed me now and come to my aid, I beg you.* He despised himself for making this plea. But when he looked at this gigantic fellow, this human-bull, he knew he could not defeat him.

Odin, lend me strength.

Egil began by rolling his head from side to side, to loosen his muscles. He was holding a double-headed axe, with a long shaft like a Dane axe but with two curved brightly polished blades on either side of the five-foot-long ash pole. It was a stupid, showy weapon, to Bjarki's eye. Impractical. And the shield he carried was equally ridiculous. It was a plain, white lime-wood

301

disc inexpertly painted with a black skull that was dribbling blood from the crown. For an ordinary man it would have been a decent protection, but in Egil's huge hands it was absurdly small, like a wooden plate.

Egil had also painted his own bald skull crimson with madder dye and his face was marked with three thick black lines across his huge nose and cheeks. He wore a leather cuirass, reinforced with small plates of iron stitched onto the hide. He grinned at Bjarki then, revealing teeth that had been filed into little points – some kind of *seithr*, perhaps. Or a way to make himself seem more fearsome. If that was the case, he did not need it: he already seemed like a monster from some terrible nightmare.

The Svear crowd was chanting Egil's name, rhythmically, over and over.

The Danish side took up the challenge: 'Bjarki! – Bjarki! – Bjarki the Rekkr!'

'Are you both ready?' asked Sigurd Hring. He'd recovered his little smirk.

Bjarki ignored the Svear king, carefully observing Egil, trying to see a weakness in his opponent. Egil lifted both the shield and the double axe in the air, exposing his muscle-slabbed naked arms and matted hairy armpits, and let out a vast, animal roar.

The Svear warriors behind him echoed his cry, screaming and shouting out his name, urging him to kill the enemy, to split open his feeble skull. Bjarki took a firmer grip on his Dane axe and shield and waited, weight balanced on the balls of his feet.

'This last bout will decide the battle!' said Sigurd Hring. 'Now – fight!'

Egil Skull-Cleaver began to stomp over the turf towards Bjarki. He moved well, easily, if a little heavily. He walked right up to Bjarki and swiftly launched a massive axe-swing at his head, a colossal swooping blow that would certainly have chopped his skull wide open if it had landed. But Bjarki ducked under the hissing blow, took a quick step in and surged forwards, using all his own not inconsiderable strength to hurl his body, shield-first, against Egil's chest. An ordinary man would surely have been knocked flying, perhaps with several ribs cracked and a vital organ mashed to pulp by the impact. But Bjarki's heavy body merely bounced off Egil's torso – it felt as if he had charged into an oak tree – and as Bjarki staggered away, the giant loosed another massive swing with his double-axe, that might easily have severed Bjarki's left arm had it not been protected by his shield. The wood gave an almighty crack at the blow, which Bjarki felt all the way up to his shoulder, but the inch-thick oak did not break.

Before Bjarki could recover, the giant was above him, swinging again, a great downward chop, and the Rekkr only just managed to avoid the shining steel blade which thumped past him into the ground, and buried itself in the turf six inches deep. Bjarki swung his own axe, a wild blow, which Egil caught easily on his silly shield and shrugged away like a child's slap. Bjarki scrambled to his feet, backing away.

The roars of the crowd were deafening. But Bjarki thought he could hear Tor's voice among them urging him to slaughter the sacrificial bull, slay this evil beast.

Mochta, I thought we had an agreement – where are you?

No reply.

Bjarki stood tall. The *gandr* was gone. No help was coming. He must face this monster on his own. *Am I a weakling?* he asked himself. *Am I a coward? I'm neither.* He moved in with purpose, dodged a mighty axe swing from the giant and hacked.

His axe clipped the side of Egil's shield and thumped into Egil's iron-reinforced leather corselet. Egil gave a loud grunt of pain. But Bjarki's axe had not penetrated.

Bjarki danced back out of range, but Egil was lumbering towards him, swinging the huge axe with just one hand, and making complicated patterns in the air. Bjarki backed away, away, keeping his shield high. Egil shouted: 'For mighty Thor!' and launched a ferocious blow at Bjarki's left shoulder, which landed on the thick shield, chopped straight through the seasoned oak and clanged hard against Bjarki's helmet.

Momentarily disorientated, Bjarki stumbled to the right and, by sheer luck, Egil's second massive swipe missed him only by a hair. His vision cleared and he saw that his shield was half gone, a semi-disc extending below his left forearm. He hurriedly shook the wood-wreckage off and took a grip on the shaft of the Dane axe with both hands. Egil struck again and Bjarki was forced to block the strike with the shaft of his own axe, the two ash poles cracking together, the sharp double-blade stopping an inch from his nose. He shoved the axe away from him and went on the attack, swinging at Egil's ankles. The giant simply hopped out of the path of his axe.

Bjarki struck again, the Dane axe powering towards Egil's ribs on the left. The Dane axe stuck in the lime-wood of the tiny shield, punching through the thin boards but without hitting Egil's forearm. As Bjarki wrestled with the weapon, trying to tug it free from the grip of the lime-wood, Egil slashed at Bjarki's right hand on the ash shaft of the axe, missed and cut straight through the pole, leaving Bjarki with a two-foot stick in his left hand. He darted down to retrieve the blade of the severed axe which was now in the mud by Egil's feet, and as his fingers reached for it, Egil kicked him full in the face, flipping his body away and backwards.

Bjarki landed on his back, turned himself over and scuttled away on all fours, his head ringing from the kick, his eyes blurring with the pain.

He got to his feet, swaying, and quickly drew the seax from its sheath. Shield gone, Dane axe gone – the long Harva blade in his right hand now his only weapon.

Egil advanced on him slowly; he seemed to be chuckling at some joke.

The Svear crowd, now just a few yards from his right shoulder, were chanting: 'Kill... kill... kill the Dane! Kill... kill... the Dane. Kill... kill...'

But Bjarki heard one high, familiar female voice shout out: 'Stop playing the fool, oaf – stop wasting time. Just slaughter the big dumb ox and be done with it!'

Bjarki crouched down, weight forwards, knees bent, seax in his right hand, left hand clenched in a fist. Egil approached slowly

– not out of caution, Bjarki realised, but to savour his inevitable victory. The giant stopped three yards away from Bjarki and violently shook his left arm. The partly damaged little shield rattled on his forearm, the gaps between the boards clearly visible. Egil leaned his head in behind the shield, undid a buckle or strap with his teeth, still keeping his eyes fixed on Bjarki, and shook off and hurled away the small damaged elm-wood shield.

'Makes it more equal,' he rumbled. 'Besides, I do not think I shall be needing that encumbrance for much longer. Are you ready to meet Odin, Bjarki Bloodhand?'

'Always ready, Skull-Cleaver. Are you not? Do you wish to live for ever?'

Egil was already in motion. He leapt forwards, moving faster than Bjarki had thought possible for such a man, and he swung the huge double-headed axe in a long, low, vicious arc aimed straight at Bjarki's left-hand side. The Rekkr had no way of blocking this powerful lateral blow, no way of preventing the sharp steel blade from plunging through his ribs and tearing through his internal organs, ripping his frail life from this Middle-Earth in a matter of a few agonising, gory moments.

But Bjarki did not wait to receive the blow. He took his own fast step forwards, at almost exactly the same time as Egil, and he dived, helmeted head first, straight towards the giant's belly, thrusting forwards with all the strength in his extremely powerful thighs. As the shining double axe was slicing through the empty air where the Rekkr's body had been only an instant before, Bjarki's iron-clad head, propelled with all his remaining strength, was smashing into Egil's open midriff like a battering ram. The full weight of Bjarki's not inconsiderable frame crashed into Egil's body, a fleshly thunderbolt, the point of impact being just below the giant's sternum.

All the air was forced from Egil's lungs in one vast, paralysing whoosh.

The giant was hurled to the ground, the axe spilling from his grasp, with Bjarki's weight on top of him – and a moment later the foot-long Harva seax was questing for his flesh, Bjarki's point flickering out and sliding into his left side, pushing deep into his belly and bursting right out his other side. Bjarki roared out his rage, and punched the seax home again, striking higher this time, the blade sinking into his chest just below the nipple. He hauled out the wet blade and struck again, slicing into Egil's right armpit and ripping through muscle, sinew and bone. Bjarki struck a final time: the fine blade seeking out the giant's throat and slicing through flesh, artery and windpipe.

Then Bjarki pushed himself off the huge, convulsing, gore-spraying body, and stood tall on his own feet above the wreckage of his foe. He lifted both his bloody fists and his dripping blade above his gore-spattered head and turned to the Danes' lines, letting out a long, inchoate howl of victory. His people cheered him: the cry of 'Bloodhand... Bloodhand... Bloodhand!' rang out across the plain of Norrkoping.

After a little while, Bjarki dropped his hands. And the cheering died away. He wiped the gory seax clean on his breeches, sheathed it once more at his waist and turned and walked over to Sigurd Hring – who was still staring with astonished horror at the ruined body of his champion Egil Skull-Cleaver lying on the bloody turf.

'Sigurd Hring,' said Bjarki, 'King of Svealand and Jarl of Sodermanland, the contest of champions is complete. Torfinna Hildarsdottir defeated Erland the Snake; Jarl Ottar defeated Jarl Starki; and I have now slain Egil Skull-Cleaver. The Danes of King Siegfried are the victors of this combat by two matches to one and by the rules agreed before, the victory belongs to our side. Let there be no more blood spilled this day – nor for many years afterwards. The issue is decided. You will go to the Dane-Mark within the week, kneel and do homage to King Siegfried for your kingdom, for ever renouncing your claim to be the King of the North. We, for our part, will take to our ships and return to our homes to mourn our many war dead in a fitting fashion.'

'What are you babbling about, fool?' said Sigurd Hring. 'Are you mad?'

'The agreement,' said Bjarki. 'We won the contest of champions. You lost.'

Sigurd Hring ignored Bjarki he turned to face the bristling Svear battle line.

He took a breath, pointed at Bjarki and yelled: 'Somebody kill this idiot Dane!'

Bjarki said, reasonably: 'Highness, the agreement we reached means that...'

Sigurd Hring was still shouting at his army: 'What are you waiting for? Death to all Danes! Kill them! Kill them all now! Forwards the Svear nation! Forwards!'

The whole Svear line, more than a thousand warriors, surged forwards into battle.

Chapter Twenty-nine

A feast for the ravens

Tor, standing watching with the members of the Starki *hird*, had always suspected that Sigurd Hring was not to be trusted, but even she was shocked by the abrupt turn of events after Bjarki had dispatched Egil Skull-Cleaver. One moment, Bjarki was being chased round the field by Egil, looking as if at any moment he would be chopped down, the next he had turned the tables, Egil was dead and, after an exchange with Sigurd, it seemed the whole Svear nation was howling towards them.

She yelled: '*Skjald-borg!*' in her loudest battle voice and felt all the well-trained Starki *hird*-men around her instinctively begin to move into their positions.

As she hefted her shield, she called out to Bjarki: 'Get back here, oaf!' and just as the words were out of her mouth, a spear sailed out of the Svear lines and cracked into the back of Bjarki's iron helmet and her brother fell like a dropped sack of oats.

She felt someone jostle her shoulder roughly and push past, then more men pushing through, and saw the *Felaki* – the eight surviving Companions – hurtling forwards towards their fallen leader. She had half a mind to follow and rescue Bjarki's body from the charging Svear, but common sense prevailed. If eight of the finest warriors in the North could not retrieve the unconscious King of Vastergotland from the midst of a full-pitched battle, then nine could not do it either.

Yet the warriors of Vastergotland seemed to have a different view – even while the Starki *hird* was forming its impeccable shield wall around her, hundreds of other warriors were rushing recklessly forwards to engage the Svear, screaming their battle cries – 'Bjarki the King!' and 'Save our lord!' – and hurtling into the chaos of battle.

The *Felaki* were all crouched around their king by now, facing outwards, shields up, spears out, in a tight defensive ring, and old Kynwulf had Bjarki's limp body slung over his shoulder. Now, stumbling under his unconscious weight, the War Chief was moving back towards the Danish lines, with the steel-edged ring of Companions around them, spearing any man who came within range of their points.

'Here, Kynwulf, bring him here,' Tor called out. Men were fighting all along the lines, hacking at each other, clashing steel and screaming either in pain or rage.

Yet the War Chief heard and responded.

'Open ranks!' Tor shouted, and her wall parted just enough to admit the *Felaki* and their senseless lord, before snapping shut, the double line of shields linked tightly once more. And, just in time, a dozen running Svear warriors crashed up against the shield wall. Screaming their hatred, lunging with spears and hacking with their swords. The *hird* bore the weight of their frenzied assault, then threw the enemy off their shields, their own spears jabbing out to end the lives of the Svear attackers.

'Hold them here,' Tor shouted to Gudrik, over the clashing tumult of battle. The *Merkismathr* was three men along from her in the front rank of the wall. He nodded his assent. Javelins and arrows were hissing over her head but Tor ignored them.

'We need to be the rock in the stormy sea,' she shouted to Gudrik, 'a rock any drowning Dane can cling to. Thicken your ranks with any of ours who join you and try to extend your flanks. Don't attack. We need to survive this. Where's Jarl Lars?'

'Over yonder, Tor,' said Gudrik, jerking his head east. 'The Crookback has his Danes in order. They are trying to push on and advance against the Svear left flank.'

'Advance?' yelled Tor. 'He's got the right spirit. But don't *you* get any similar thoughts. Stay here. Be like the rock. Hold them off. I'll be back with you very soon.'

Tor took one quick look at the battlefield beyond the steady line of her *hird*'s shield wall and saw a swirling storm of chaos. The Vastergotlander folk were fighting with a rare fury, driven mad at the sight of their fallen king, battering at the scrum of Svear who had been unleashed by Sigurd Hring's treacherous order. An arrow flashed past her ear and, as she flinched back, her eye alighted on the hero brothers Gummi and Gudfast, who were fighting together, back pressed against back, amid a jostle of Bjarki's Vastergotlanders, killing with a swift, terrible, dance-like elegance.

A hundred yards to her front she could just glimpse the Raven banner of Sigurd Hring, flying over a company of Svear warriors who were not yet engaged in the fray.

She ran back to the group of Companions who were standing beside the body of Bjarki, all facing outward, a few yards behind the rearmost rank of the *hird* wall.

Bjarki lay, unmoving, his eyes closed.

Tor seized Kynwulf's shoulder. 'How is he?'

Kynwulf gave her a crooked grin. 'That spear knocked him senseless but he will live. The king is strong.' He pointed to an inch-deep dent in Bjarki's iron helmet.

'Well, he is no good to anyone here,' said Tor. 'Take him back into the village and put him in the hut with Garm. It's the one next to the ale-house beside the...'

'I know where it is,' said Kynwulf. 'But I will stay here to fight off these Svear dogs. I'll send young Oddvin, he is strong enough to carry the king safely back to the bear's hut, and to stand guard over him there until he awakens.

'Good. Will you fight beside me this day of battle, War Chief? I have a plan.'

'Gladly. Together you and I will make a feast for the ravens. What is the plan?'

'The same as before. To kill Sigurd Hring.' Tor pointed to the Raven banner streaming out in the Svear lines a hundred paces away beyond the chaotic melee.

'I'm with you. The *Felaki* are with you, honoured sister of our king.'

–

They gathered up more than two score Danes who had become separated from their own companies, and a few dozen Vaster-gotlanders. Those that had not already been killed by their own reckless fury. And Tor sent a runner to Lars Crookback on the left wing and another to try to find Jarl Loffar whom she thought must be somewhere on the right. The battle in front of the *hird*'s shield wall had abated somewhat, the Svear had pulled back to reform their battle line, but the ground they abandoned was strewn with the bodies of the wounded and the fallen. One man, she could not tell if he was Svear, Dane or Vastergotlander, had been wounded in the face and blinded and was staggering between the two sides, moaning and calling piteously for a friend named Olaf. She could hear the Svear leaders exhorting their men to show courage.

Tor was not one for speeches but she knew she ought to say something.

'Warriors of the Starki *hird*,' she yelled. 'Your jarl has been slain. Your friends and comrades have been slaughtered. Shall we now go forth to avenge them all?'

And the men of the *hird* responded with a rousing wave of cheering and shouts of vengeance. Tor, with Kynwulf at her side, pushed forwards to the front and centre of the shield wall, the rest of the *Felaki* pushing in right behind them.

Tor bellowed: 'Boar's Snout!' and immediately felt the jostle and shove of the *hird*-men behind her flowing into the new trian-gular formation, the long hours of practice in the fields outside Uppsala bearing sweet fruit. She and Kynwulf locked their shields together and formed the face of the snout and the other *Felaki* slotted in behind them in three ranks, then four and so on until the whole wedge was in place.

Tor hefted her spear, resting it on the rim of her shield, and shouted: 'Forwards! Forwards for Bjarki Bloodhand! Forwards for Odin's favour – and victory!' and they stepped off, lurching en masse towards the Svear line a hundred yards away.

The formation was tight but they stumbled as they stepped on the bodies of the fallen. Tor heard a wounded man scream under her boot but she ignored it, heading straight for the Raven banner of Sigurd Hring. Once they were twenty yards from the enemy lines, close enough to see the faces of her foes awaiting them, they charged.

The Boar's Snout, with Tor and Kynwulf at its tip, and more than three hundred men behind them, punched into the Svear battle line like an axe striking a mound of wet clay. The Boar's Snout plunged into the mass of the enemy, with Tor and Kynwulf lancing out their spears at the faces of their foes. And there it stuck fast.

The forward motion stopped. Tor was aware of a blow striking her helm, and a battering of swords against her shield. She shouted: 'Push! Push forwards, you milksops!' And felt the power of Boar's Snout surge behind her, forcing her further into the mass of the enemy. They were now in the centre of a surging scrum of shouting warriors. Tor's spear flew out and back, plunging into screaming, red-mouthed faces. She struck again, and again, men falling like stalks before a scythe.

The Boar's Snout ground forwards. The pressure on Tor's back was immense. But they *were* moving, slowly pushing their way through the thick Svear battle line.

An axe looped out of nowhere and she ducked in behind her shield and felt the blow land on the man at her left shoulder – Harknut, her nearest comrade on that side, howled in pain and she felt the pressure of his shield against her spine cease, a vacant space where a good man had once been. A Svear warrior barged into the void to her left, hacking down at her with the sword, but she caught the blow, by luck, mostly, on the edge of her shield, and then Haugen Halfhand was there beside her, filling poor Harknut's place, his long spear streaking out by her ear to claim her enemy's life.

They forged onwards, shoving ever deeper into the heart of the enemy. A sword blow chopped the shaft of her spear in two and, without missing a step, she pulled out her seax and pushed on, shoving with her shield against the crush, stabbing low with the wicked blade. She was half-aware that a sword blow had struck Kynwulf – he half-dropped but came up bellowing back to his feet, his face now wet and bloody. They surged onwards together, the grizzled Goth warrior and the nimble shield-maiden, and felt the enemy line dissolve before them. Suddenly there was space where there had been a crush of shouting men and glancing steel, the foe scattered, reluctant to attack.

'Forwards,' yelled Tor. 'Forwards for Bjarki and victory!'

The Boar's Snout had become looser, raggedy where so many men had fallen. But it was now in clear ground beyond the broken enemy and Tor could see the banner of Sigurd Hring only a dozen paces in front of her, and a tight ring of grey mailed warriors all around it. And there was the grizzled usurper – red-faced in his rage – gesticulating, shouting, pointing at her, ordering his oathmen to attack her.

And, by all the gods, there beside Sigurd was a face she knew – and hated with all her being. A man she had believed to be dead on the Kolmarden slope. Rorik Hafnarsson, murderer of Inge, Ulli and the Honeyman, the poisoner of the Bearstead women and children, scowling like a whipped child under a helm too big for him.

'Forwards!' she yelled, shoving aside one sword-waving Svear with her shield, barging into another and wielding her seax, stabbing, till the blade came back bloody.

She heard shouts to her left of 'Crookback! Crookback!' and saw that a mass of more than hundred Danes were bounding forwards on that eastern side, with Jarl Lars, grasping a red sword to the fore, leading his men to close in and slaughter the foe.

She looked again for Sigurd Hring and saw he was edging backwards, through the bristling ring of his bodyguards. There was no sign of Rorik. Now a huge figure was coming forwards towards her, brandishing sword and shield – Krok of Frisia.

Krok shouted: 'Come to me, you whore! We have a matter to resolve!'

But Tor was still looking beyond him. Sigurd Hring was nowhere to be seen, and neither was Rorik – and the king's banner was retreating, now a good forty yards away, moving slowly back across the fields towards the shadow of the Kolmarden.

Tor shouted: 'No! Come back, you coward – come and fight me, Sigurd Hring!'

Yet Krok the hero was before her, directly in her path, his long, shining sword already slicing down towards her head. Her own shield was too far down and she had no time to raise it. She saw the falling sword blade above her, she saw her doom... And Haugen Halfhand shoved roughly forwards and lofted his own shield and caught the massive hero's blow full on the boss with a mighty clang.

Tor spat at the Frisian, jumped forwards, mashed her shield against his, and as they were locked together for an instant, she reached behind his body to jab at his kidneys with her long seax. But the tall hero's fine mail deflected her seax blow and Krok shoved her away with his shield and was swinging at her again with his sword.

She heard a grunt of effort from Kynwulf behind her, felt a whistle of wind by her cheek, and a black spear flew past her ear and plunged into Krok's mailed side.

The Frisian staggered back and Tor leapt up at him and jammed the seax blade into the side of his neck and they both fell in a heap to the earth. Tor pulled back and stabbed him again, the blade punching into the back of his skull below his helm rim. Krok convulsed like a madman for a dozen heartbeats, spitting, cursing, then lay still.

Tor rolled off his body and stood up.

The Svear were running. The mass of men below the Svear king's Raven banner was now seventy yards away, and retreating fast. Ahead of her and to the right, Lars Crookback's men were cheering their victory. Punching their bloody spears into the sky. A few Svear stood their ground, warding their king's retreat, but when the Danes approached them, they threw away their shields, turned tail, and fled across the fields.

The whole Svear battle line was now in full retreat. Tor bent over and leaned her hands on her knees, heaving in great, deep breaths like a runner after a ten-mile race.

She looked over her whole aching body and saw that she had a small puncture wound on the side of her left thigh, an arrow or small knife, perhaps. She hadn't noticed it in the heat of the battle. Kynwulf came to stand by her, also breathing hard.

All along the Danish lines the warriors were cheering. And the Svear were now half a mile away and still running north, back towards the slopes of the Kolmarden.

Some Danes who had followed after them, looking for the easy slaughter of beaten men, were turning back and returning to their captains and their comrades.

Kynwulf said: 'We beat them. I didn't think we could do it, but we beat them.'

'We failed,' said Tor. 'I failed again. Sigurd Hring escaped. They're *not* beaten. We pushed them back. There are still a thousand Svear warriors on the field.'

'We beat them,' said Kynwulf. 'By the time you're as old as I am, Tor, you'll know to savour every victory that comes your way. There are few enough in this life.'

–

They pulled back into the village of Norrkoping, leaving their many hundreds of Svear and Danish dead on the field for future burning or burial – when they had the time and the strength. For now they looked to their wounded and pulled back into the meagre shelter of the village buildings and Tor, with the help of Gudrik, who was unscathed, and the five surviving *Felaki*, set about organising soup for every warrior.

It looked set to rain and menacing black clouds were looming in the south.

Lars Crookback was badly wounded, a deep spear thrust to his guts, and looked likely to die but he was surprisingly controlled, even calm, when Tor went to see him.

'We gave them a rare thrashing,' he said. 'My Jutlanders were just magnificent! What a battle! I've never seen the like. If the All-Father was watching – and I'm sure he was, he wouldn't miss a battle like *that* – he can't be less than impressed with us.'

'You set your mind on healing up, jarl,' said Tor. 'Don't excite yourself.'

'Healing up? I took a bastard Svear's blade to the guts – right in there. I'm done for, woman. No good pretending otherwise. But, after the slaughter we inflicted, after the courage we showed, I believe I'll be feasting in the Hall of the Slain before long.'

Jarl Lofarr was dead too, killed in the initial Svear attack. Harknut and two of the newly joined *Felaki* were no more, as were scores of the Starki *hird* – men who had performed so bravely in the Boar's Snout. Tor felt numb with sorrow. Her hurt leg was painful, too. So she went to look in on Bjarki, bringing him hot soup and ale.

He was lying beside the curled form of Garm, the poor animal still breathing faintly. Tor knelt beside her brother's unconscious body, and set the food beside him.

'You need to wake up, oaf,' she said softly, pulling a blanket over him. 'We are going to need you.' She looked up at Oddvin, who was standing by the door of the shed. 'Has he opened his eyes, at all?' she asked. The young *Felaki* shook his head.

When she had eaten, and bound up her leg wound, she sought out Kynwulf, Glamir Raeflisson and Captain Mogils, who were standing by a hay barn on the northern edge of the village, looking out at the battlefield. There were stooped figures flitting from body to body, bending and robbing the fallen – both the wounded and the dead. These were the villagers of Norrkoping, she guessed, who had fled before the battle and were creeping back to their fields to gain what they could from the carnage.

'Kynwulf,' she said, 'will you take a dozen of my unwounded *hird* spearmen and clear those human-ravens off the field. Kill them if you have to. Those wounded Svear fought with honour today – they do not deserve to be knifed for an arm ring or some other trinket. When we have time, we will tend to them, and burn all the dead.'

'As you command,' said Kynwulf – and he trotted away, calling out for men.

'Do you think they will come at us again?' asked Mogils. He had a bad cut on his brow that had formed a scab but was still dribbling watery blood down his cheek.

'I don't know. We must assume so – and must be ready for them if they do,' she replied. 'Will you take charge of the living Danes and ward the left flank?'

'There must be someone alive more important than me,' said the young warrior.

'I don't think so but, if there is, ask him to help you. The left flank, yes?'

Captain Mogils nodded tiredly. Her own exhaustion was a shadow on her mind. It was not much later than noon but she felt she had been awake for several weeks.

'How is the king?' said Glamir the law-speaker. 'Bjarki still lives, I hope.'

'He is sleeping like a milk-fed baby. I think he will recover but he is taking his own sweet time about it. How many of your Vastergotlanders are still on their feet?'

'A hundred, maybe a hundred and twenty,' replied Glamir. 'There are many new widows now in Lodose – although they do not know it yet. Can we go home soon?'

'Form them up on the right – between us and the ships. I want to give Bjarki a little more time to return to his senses. The decision should be his. If we leave the battlefield now, Sigurd Hring will claim victory and it will all have been for naught. If we can hold here today, maybe, if we wait for Sigurd Hring to retreat, we can…'

'Torfinna Hildarsdottir,' said a new voice. And Tor turned to see a very young Danish spearman, a skinny boy no more than twelve or thirteen years of age, looking earnestly at her. 'I was sent to find you – or the King of Vastergotland – is he with you? Or Jarl Lars Crookback, or… or any high personage who is among the living.'

'What is the matter?'

'I've been guarding the baggage in the rear – I missed the whole battle. But my friend Olli saw a plume of dust to the south, a lot of people, warriors, we think, coming towards us. An army – we saw many glints of sun on metal. They are coming here.'

Tor limped to the southern side of the village, followed by the Danish boy. He helped her to clamber on top of a small house with a thatched roof, where she shaded her eyes and looked south over the plains of Ostergotland. There it was: a fresh force, two or three miles away, hundreds strong, coming straight towards them. She thought she could make out banners, blowing in the strengthening breeze. And wolf pelts.

Ostergotlanders, she thought. *The Wulfings. The Wolf twins Fidor and Fodor.*

And they were all heading directly for Norrkoping.

Chapter Thirty

Know when to walk away

Bjarki found himself lying on a black, rocky shore, beside a lapping black lake, with a vast lead-grey sky arcing overhead devoid of sun, moon or stars. He sat up. His head was aching, throbbing, and he gingerly felt the back of his skull and discovered a large swelling that was tender to the touch. He recalled the fight with Egil Skull-Cleaver, he recalled winning the bout and killing Egil. But had the giant somehow felled him before he himself died? No, he had spoken to Sigurd Hring, who had broken the agreement and ordered all the Svear to attack.

So was he now dead?

He looked around him and saw several large boulders, even blacker than the shore, and a thick-trunked tree growing out over the water of the lake, but nothing moving, absolutely nothing living as far as the eye could see. No birds, no animals.

'Mochta!' he shouted. And his own echoing voice made his head ache harder than ever. 'Mochta, where are you? I know this is one of your worlds. Come out.'

One of the small boulders uncurled and revealed itself as a bear cub, the size of a large puppy. It lifted its snout towards Bjarki and sniffed. Then it began to whine.

Bjarki walked over and picked up the cub, which was surprisingly heavy. He gently stroked its fur. 'Garm,' he said. 'Is that you, boy? Is this your *gandr* form?'

The bear cub nuzzled into the crook of his arm, and he continued stroking its fur, feeling to see if it had any injuries. But the animal was whole, if clearly unwell.

'I am sorry for what happened to you, Garm,' Bjarki said. 'I should have protected you from Hagnor the Fatbellied. I should have fought beside you and warded you. I failed you, boy. Does it help you to know that Tor killed Hagnor?'

'What is one meat-bag to a *gandr*?' said Mochta, and Bjarki watched as another huge boulder uncurled and became the Mother of Bears. 'Do you, man-child, care deeply for the sheep that is slaughtered to make your nightly mutton?'

'Hagnor injured Garm – and Tor took her revenge on him for that insult. This kind of thing matters much to we folk, if not to you *gandir*. It is a question of honour.'

'What care I for honour when my child is dying?' Mochta said, with a snarl.

'Tor and I will do anything we can – when the battle is over – to save poor Garm. There are several fine healers with the army, and some wise *gothi*, too...'

'That bag of flesh that contained my child is already dead, fool. It is beginning to rot and will be food for the worms by the time you wake. And my *child* – the creature you hold in your arms – will be dead, too, in the merest blink of an eye.'

As if obeying a command, the little cub began to whine and cough weakly.

'What can I do?'

'You know what to do, man-child.'

'I do not.'

'My own mangy bear-carcass is long gone. You slew me in the snowy forest long ago. Cut off my bear head. Have you forgotten? Yet I still live. I live *inside you*.'

'What are you saying?'

'I am saying, you empty-headed fool of a man-child, that the price of my strength is the survival of my cub. He will give you his power, too. Summon him!'

–

Bjarki sat up blinking, his head splitting, his mouth as dry as dust. He looked around and saw a cup of ale and a bowl of cold, congealed leek soup beside him. Beyond that on the earth floor was his Harva seax and scabbard. Someone – a *Felaki*, he guessed – had retrieved it, cleaned the blood from it and laid it out beside him ready for use.

He drank the ale down in one draught but could not face the soup. Then he looked a little further into the dim shed in which he found himself. And saw the mounded shape of Garm, lying in the corner. He shuffled over, every step a blinding skewer through his temple, and knelt down next to the young bear. He felt his snout, and his nose. Cold. He lifted one of the creature's eyelids and saw a milky film over the eye. He knelt down and put his ear right next to the bear's nostrils. No breath. And feeling through the blood-sticky fur around the neck he tried, fruitlessly, to find any pulse.

He sat back on his heels, and looked at the corpse of his animal companion.

'Goodbye, my boy,' he said, the tears already running down his bearded cheeks. 'Goodbye, my loyal friend. Sleep well, Garm, in whatever world you find yourself.'

He pulled the blanket over Garm's head, and gave the bear one last loving pat, before standing up and, when his head had stopped reeling, he strapped on the belt and seax, donned his tattered cloak, and pushed his way out of the door of the shed.

The world outside the fishing shed was painfully bright, and filled with running and shouting folk. He reached out a hand and grabbed a passing Danish spearman.

'What is happening?'

'They are coming!' the man was panicking, struggling to free himself from Bjarki's grip. 'They are coming to kill us. Thousands of them. Wolf-men. Wulfings!'

The young spearman tugged himself away and ran off, going eastwards.

Bjarki knew not what to make of that. He saw Sambor lumbering towards him, the big man moving surprisingly swiftly.

He stopped in front of Bjarki, panting hard. 'Your sister. Sent me. To fetch. You. Carry you. If I must. We go. Now. To the ships.'

Bjarki jogged beside Sambor, running with the rest of the crowd of warriors, east, through the village of Norrkoping and out the other side towards the Braviken, towards the southern inlet of the sea where the remaining Danish ships were moored.

He found Tor near the mouth of a narrow neck of dry land, fifty paces across, that jutted out into the waters of the Braviken with two wide channels of sea on either side. Beyond his sister, Bjarki could see three or four moored ships, and men already moving about on board. The *Felaki* were also on the neck of land. Jorulf was standing beside Tor, with Captain Mogils and Glamir the law-speaker close by, and several Vastergotland men milling about, along with many faces that he did not know at all.

'What's amiss?' he asked Tor, looking into her drawn face. 'We won the duels but Sigurd Hring played us false. Did we fight? What happened when I was out?'

'Too much to tell now,' said Tor. 'We beat Sigurd in a straight-up shield-fight, pushed him back towards the Kolmarden, but we were badly mauled, too. Then, when we thought it was all over, the Ostergotlanders appeared suddenly; they came up from the south – you remember Fidor and Fodor? – well, they are with Helgi the Wulfing now. And when the Wulfing army appeared, Sigurd Hring came back down from the Kolmarden, advancing with at least a thousand men. So now we have Svear coming at us from the north, and Wulfings coming up from the south. And we have only a few hundred warriors left who are unhurt. I made the decision to make a run for it. There seemed no point dying here for nothing. We've lost the battle. A warrior must know when to walk away. It's time to go, and go swiftly.'

'Garm is dead,' said Bjarki. 'I left his body in the fishing shed. I'm so sorry.'

Tor closed her eyes, and gave a sniff. 'I felt it – I felt something an hour ago, an overwhelming darkness. Like a black cloud covering the sun. My lovely boy!'

Bjarki opened his arms and they embraced each other, squeezing tightly.

'Highness,' said Kynwulf from Bjarki's elbow. 'I've something to show you.'

'Give me a moment, War Chief,' Bjarki said. He took Tor by both shoulders. 'We'll mourn our boy later – I have something to tell you – but first what's the plan?'

Tor sniffed again and wiped her nose with the back of her hand.

'This is a decent position,' she said. 'Water on both sides. They can't get round our flanks. The plan is simple: we hold them here for as long as we can while we get our wounded and the rest of our people get on board the remaining ships. Then, at the last moment, we all make a run for it. And may the All-Father give wings to our feet.'

'Highness,' said Kynwulf again, 'I have something here that may please you.'

'Yes, yes, what is it?' said Bjarki crossly. His head was pulsing like a drumbeat.

'You will like it,' said Tor. 'It may be one good thing to come out of this mess.'

Kynwulf led Bjarki through the crush of warriors, on to the narrow strip of sandy land between the two sea channels, and pointed to a huddled figure of a young man on the ground, roped, gagged and bound up like a market-day goose, with Rask standing over the sad, hunched figure, beaming with pride and leaning on his spear.

It was Rorik Hafnarsson.

'How? How did you catch him?' Bjarki was astonished.

'I found him on the battlefield. Leg injured by a spear thrust. He was trying to crawl back towards the Kolmarden. Kynwulf and I, and some of the Starki *hird*-men, went out to scare away the corpse-looters – and we found him. The one who poisoned little Inge and our folk in Bearstead. We found you, Rorik, didn't we? We found you, you nasty, murdering bastard,' said Rask. He kicked Rorik hard in the face.

The diminutive *Felaki* warrior said: 'We have strict instructions not to kill the slimy wretch yet. Tor's orders. She says she's saving him for something special.'

Bjarki shivered when he heard those words. But all he said was: 'Be sure you keep him safe, Rask. Don't let him escape. You've done fine work here.'

They made their battle line across the fifty-yard-wide entrance to the sandy peninsula, and somehow got all their folk, including the wounded, behind them on the spit of land. While many were engaged in the slow and painful business of getting the injured warriors on board the ships, Bjarki took Glamir Raeflisson, who had been loading the hurt Vastergotlanders, off to one side, away from the bustle and noise.

'If I live to see another dawn,' Bjarki said, 'there is something I have to do, a deed that will mean that I will not be able to return to Vastergotland for some time. I'll be gone for months – or perhaps years. It may be that I never return to Lodose.'

'But, highness, whatever you feel you must do, we will all support you in your task,' said Glamir. 'Come home when you've done the deed, for without a king...'

Bjarki held up his hand. 'Time is short, my friend. Believe me, if I live out this day I shall do something that will make me the enemy of many powerful men. They will seek my destruction. I will be hunted like a wolf right across the Middle-Realm. I would not bring that fate down upon Lodose. I would not have my people destroyed for what I must do for my own personal satisfaction. You do not need a king. No, do not argue, Glamir. You did not have a king in Vastergotland for many a year before I was sent to you, yet you thrived under your father Raefli's rule. What I ask you, Glamir, is that you take up your father's burden and rule Vastergotland in my stead, as my *Armathr*, standing in my hall, speaking with my voice, undertaking all the duties of a king but without his crown. Can you do that for me, law-speaker;

can you do that for me, Glamir Raeflisson, my friend and most courageous comrade?'

Glamir's pale face seemed even whiter. 'Only till you return to us, highness.'

'Till I return,' agreed Bjarki. 'For however long a time that might prove to be.'

Glamir knelt, took Bjarki's hand and kissed it: 'As you command, my king.'

Bjarki heard shouts from the line of shields across the mouth of the neck of land, people calling out his name. He clapped Glamir on the shoulder and turned to go.

By the time he got to the thin defensive line of shields, it was clear what had caused the alarm. There were scores of lean, grey-clad figures flitting between the buildings of Norrkoping, running in ones and twos, but all heading towards them. The Wulfings had arrived in the village. Joralf touched his arm and pointed to the north-west, where Bjarki could see three columns of marching men on the plain under the black Raven banners of Sigurd Hring. A thousand Svealand warriors there at least.

He knew then that Tor had been correct. They could not hope to match these combined enemies. He bellowed: 'Make haste, people, we leave within the hour!'

His height allowed him to see over the heads of the Danish shield wall across the entrance to the neck and he saw that now one or two wolfskin-clad warriors were emerging from the house and barns of Norrkoping. They approached the Danish *skjald-borg* cautiously, like hungry scavengers approaching a tempting carcass, but mindful of the dangers it represented, and stopped a long spear-throw away to stare.

Then more Wulfings emerged. Perhaps a hundred men were gathered now in front of their walls, still at a respectful distance, and Bjarki thought he recognised Fidor among the thickening crowd, and there beside him Fodor – the Wolf twins looking even more savage than usual, their faces painted with black and white stripes, their bodies clad in furs in place of armour. Bjarki pushed through the ranks until he found Tor in the front rank, glaring at the enemy with Captain Mogils beside her.

'There will be the usual challenges,' Bjarki said quietly. 'The usual threats and boasts. But I want *you*, Tor, to do all the boasting and threatening for our side. You and Captain Mogils, if he wants to help, you two parley to them. Keep them talking for as long as you can. Ask for a long truce. An hour if you can get it. If they want a duel, a contest of champions, fine. Agree. Or say you need time to think. You'll know what to do. Give me just a little time to prepare myself. And when the time is right – well, you will know when – clear a wide path and simply let me come through.'

'What are you going to do?' asked Tor.

'You will see!' Bjarki grinned at her. 'When it happens, ignore the danger to me. Maybe my doom *is* set for today. Who can say? Get everyone to the ships. Don't wait for me. Go with them. If you love me, Tor, do exactly as I say – I beg you.'

He pushed back through the Danish shield wall to the rear section, a patch of open ground behind the last rank of spearmen. He glanced along the peninsula, the hundred-yard strip of land between the two inlets, observing the loading of the last few remaining ships with the Danish warriors' goods and possessions; the delicate urgency of frightened men carrying their wounded friends on board. As he looked on, one large vessel, a round *knarr*, packed with pale bearded faces, dropped its red and white sail, loosed her moorings and nosed gently out into the waters of the Braviken.

Bjarki went over to a stack of spare weapons, those which had not yet been loaded onto the ships. He selected a Dane axe with a good solid shaft and a sharp enough blade, and an iron helmet of the right size. He found a pair of worn leather vambraces for his forearms, and a pair of greaves for his shins, and strapped them on. He settled the yellowing bearskin around his mailed shoulders, getting it right, loosened the Harva seax in its sheath across his loins, put on the helm and tied it securely. Then he sat cross-legged on the grass, and laid the axe across his knees.

He could hear the shouts from the wall of warriors behind him; and Tor's voice calm and confident, and something that sounded like the howling of wild wolves.

He breathed out and composed his mind – and realised his head no longer ached.

Then he began to hum.

It was a simple four-note tune, repetitive, rhythmical, ancient and terrible, which vibrated deep within his heart. He felt his chest expanding with the hum, his blood pumping harder and hotter, and a weird sense of collapsing in on his own body. His mind was filled with the colour red, then a growing black. And then gold. A golden void appeared at the centre of his being. An empty core of impossible light and heat.

Mochta, are you there? he asked himself silently. *Garm, are you there as well?*

'I am here,' said the She-Bear. 'And I sense you have summoned my cub.'

Garm – are you there? Are you truly inside my heart?

'I greet you with joy, Bear-brother,' said Garm, a soft, warm, light-timbre, golden voice, very different to Mocha's dark, menacing growl. 'You are a creature I have known all my days in the Middle-Realm,' said Garm. 'But I have known you in all the other worlds as well. I see you. You are the cheese-giver and playmate. But you are also my protector, provider and friend. I am glad we are together at last in this realm, Bear-brother. We will achieve much now we're joined together in spirit.'

Will you lend me your strength on this day of battle?

'Gladly,' said the younger *gandr*. 'You and I are one – your heart is my home.'

'You shall have my power, too,' growled Mochta. 'And my gratitude. But we are hungry, man-child. Near starved to death. It is past time for us to gorge on the blood of your foes. Unleash our joint strength – and let carnage be our just reward.'

Bjarki rose to his feet. He drew the seax from its scabbard and raised the Dane axe high in the air. He was suddenly swamped with a great, golden, shimmering rage, pulsing with raw sun-like power, brimming with a barely contained and appalling violence. He felt more alive than he had ever felt before – stronger and fleeter than in any of his wildest *berserkr* furies. He knew he could uproot a mountain range and crush the snowy peaks to dust in his bare hands; he knew he could fly faster than a hunting eagle; slay a giant with one punch; swim the widest ocean like a mighty salmon; or even leap into the sky and pull down the fiery sun from its dutiful course.

He could feel both Mochta and Garm pumping their power into his head, chest, belly and limbs. He could barely contain his expanding golden heart within his body.

He threw back his head and screamed: a long, bubbling torrent of joy and rage.

Then he charged.

Chapter Thirty-one

'Ignore the danger to me'

Tor watched the crowd of Wulfings thicken into an army in front of the Danish shield wall. Over to the north-west, the three marching columns of Sigurd Hring were a mile away, but they would be here within half a handspan of the sun – if she could see the sun. The world had turned grey – dark clouds were streaming in from the south and the wind was gusting. They were in for a drenching, but was that an advantage or not?

A tall figure was pushing himself out from the ranks. His rich, green, hooded cloak was trimmed with wolf fur, and he had a thin circlet of gold around his head, holding back his grey locks, and a fine sword, and a seax too, belted around his waist. Tor recognised him from the Great Hall at Uppsala some months ago – it was Helgi the Wulfing, the man who dared not name himself as King of Ostergotland but the same man, too, who refused to kneel before Sigurd Hring and make an oath to him.

Tor reckoned both those matters had changed since that encounter in Uppsala.

The man spoke and proved one of Tor's suspicions correct: 'I am King Helgi, lord of Ostergotland, and I desire to speak with my fellow king, Bjarki of Vastergotland.'

'He's a little busy now, hound-master,' said Tor. And the tight-packed and nervous Danish shield wall behind her erupted in guffaws and titters at her insult.

Helgi frowned, and a dozen fur-clad warriors came forwards to stand on either side in support of their king. Tor recognised two of them, Fidor on the left and Fodor on the right, among the other fierce-looking Wulfings. She nodded in greeting at the two Fire Born. The Wolf twins stared as if they'd never seen her before in their lives.

'Summon the so-called King of Vastergotland to me now,' growled Helgi, he sounded like a man with scant patience. 'I would speak only with him on this day.'

'He's occupied. I'm his sister. Say to me whatever you would say to Bjarki.'

Fidor came forwards and whispered something in Helgi's ear. The king scowled.

'Very well, Torfinna Hildarsdottir, you may repeat to your brother this message. Are you listening? For too long the people of Ostergotland and Vastergotland have been divided, set against each other by our enemies. We are folk of one blood, one spirit – we are all Goths whether we live on the east or the west side of Lake Vattern – and we should stand together as one people. United. I sent my two envoys to Lodose some weeks ago to propose this very union. I humbled myself. I made many accommodations to your Rekkr brother. I said that Bjarki Bloodhand, as the heir of Angantyr, might rule as king over *all* of us. I said I would bend the knee to him and take the loyal oath, for the sake of uniting our one Goth nation under one true king.'

Helgi paused and took a deep breath. Tor could see he was agitated. Very angry.

'I offered Bjarki the hand of my eldest daughter Ynghildr, to bind this new arrangement, to make it endure, solemn and dynastic. I was prepared to sacrifice my precious girl, the shining full moon of my life, for the sake of the union of our folk.

'This was the message I conveyed to Bjarki Bloodhand through my envoys Fidor and Fodor. And his reply? He flatly refused me. He bluntly said no. He said he preferred to serve the Danish king – a feeble old foreigner – instead of ruling justly over his own people and mine. He chose the path of a thrall, not that of a king. His ancestor Angantyr would never have behaved in such a slavish, cowardly fashion.'

Tor said: 'You might regret calling Bjarki a coward – and a slave. You will only make him upset. And I don't think you would like to meet him when he's upset.'

'I know he is Fire Born. That does not frighten me. I also have wild Rekkar who kill at my command.' At this, Fidor and Fodor each gave Tor a stiff bow. 'But allow me to complete my message, Torfinna Hildarsdottir. I shall not trouble you much longer.'

'Bark as much as you like, Helgi the Houndling. I'm in no great hurry today.'

Tor could not help betraying herself as a liar, and spoiling a fine insult, too, by snatching a look north-east. The three Svear columns were a quarter of a mile away now – and closing in fast. *Where was Bjarki?* She could not stall Helgi much longer.

'So I pondered Bjarki's refusal,' said Helgi. 'And thought about my own refusal to bend the knee to Sigurd Hring. I decided that both refusals were errors. Yet I also knew that I was correct: that Gotland – east and west – must have its own king. So I went to see Sigurd Hring in secret, and I *did* bend the knee to him. I kissed his fancy new sword and acknowledged him as the one, true King of the North, my overlord.

'Sigurd Hring, for his part, has raised me up and recognised me as the first King of Gotland since great Angantyr, who was my ancestor too, went to the Hall of the Slain. But there can be only one King of Goths – Sigurd and I both understood this – which is why your brother Bjarki, and all who stand him, must be sent into the void.'

Tor heard a huge sound behind her, a long scream of battle-rage, louder than any noise she had ever heard, coming from behind the Danish shield wall. She muttered something to Mogils, who stood beside her, then she stepped forwards from the ranks.

'This all seems far too complicated for a plain Svear girl like me to grasp,' she said. 'Too many kings for my silly brain to get a grip on. King of Vastergotland, King of Ostergotland, King of Goths, King of the North – it's all so very confusing. I think it might be best if you explained everything again – to my brother Bjarki Bloodhand.'

At her words, the tight-knit ranks of the Danish shield wall parted like a curtain, and something enormous and golden and deadly, something moving very fast indeed, and scream-laughing as it came, hurtled through the lane made in the Danish ranks, and hurled itself at the self-proclaimed King of the Goths and all his warriors.

—

The Rekkr erupted like a ball of golden fire into the Wulfings, his axe and seax a whirling sphere of sharp, swinging steel and fury, the yellow-ish cloak streaming out behind him like a train. He moved almost too swiftly for the human eye to track – so much faster than Tor had ever imagined a warrior could move; he danced and hewed, he spun and slaughtered. So fast, she had only the tracings of his movements in her eyes, and the fleeting impression of a shining brilliance. The Fire Born warrior slew Helgi first, hacking the King of the Goths down before the Wulfing could even draw his sword, slicing right through his left shoulder to expose his purple chest cavity.

Tor had never seen Bjarki like this before: she had seen him in his *berserkr* fury a dozen times, but never like this. He had the power of a thousand suns; a dazzlingly bright, exploding core of molten fury. Her brother was so swift, and so unstoppably powerful, that he seemed to glow with some uncanny inner power. He destroyed Helgi in a split instant and exploded into the deep ranks of the Wulfings, slaying left and right. All Tor could make out was a rolling flash of golden violence; a whirlwind of light and heat, spraying blood, arcing blades. She watched open mouthed, frozen, as Bjarki sliced down the Ostergotlanders, surging through them, leaving a reeking path behind him.

But Tor was not the only warrior who was shamefully slow to react.

The Wolf-twins were still standing over the ruined body of their king, howling and grunting and mashing their gums, summoning their Wolf *gandr* to them.

Of the two, Fodor was the first to react to the stunning assault. He threw himself after the Rekkr, charging into the mass of his own comrades, snarling, gnashing his teeth, filled with rage by his awakened *gandr.* Bjarki, froth-lipped and bloody, stood in the centre of a circle of terrified Ostergotlander spearmen. He saw Fodor coming for him and snarled in recognition, as one creature salutes another alike.

They threw themselves at each other like long-separated lovers, axe and seax flashing, clashing, sparks exploding. Bjarki flailed at Fodor with his bloody Dane axe, a scything, decapitating blow, but Fodor, creamy froth ringing his jaws, too, smashed it away with his shield. His brother Fidor, then, also entered the fray – he crunched his sword into Bjarki's mailed and bearskin-covered back a moment later, and the Rekkr felt the blow bite. He turned his shaggy head and spat blood at Fidor.

Then Bjarki hurled himself, his blades swinging, at the both of them.

The three Rekkar hacked and swiped at each other, blows landing, screams and growls and howls, and swift, swirling action. Faster than a dog-fight; bloodier, too.

The rest of the Ostergotlander warriors, bizarrely, were hanging back, hesitant. Observing the battle. The shock of the death of their king, and the slaughter of so many of their comrades by this terrifying apparition, combined with the lightning-fast battle between the Wolf twins and Bjarki, had made them unsure of what to do.

The melee of the three Fire Born warriors was a tumbling mass of flashing steel, golden light, billowing dust and blood-spraying chaos. The Wulfings eyed the three combatants as if it was a contest of champions. But their captains bellowed at them and they began to surround the whirling trio, to hem them, encircle them with shields.

Tor's first instinct was to rush to Bjarki's defence. To break up the forming circle. But 'ignore the danger to me' was one of the last things Bjarki had said.

'No,' said Tor aloud. 'I will not. I need you alive, oaf. You're no good to anyone dead.' Then: 'Companions, to me! *Felaki* to my side. Time to protect your king!'

'Captain Mogils!' she shouted. And the young man, who was right beside her, flinched at the volume of her cry. 'Your task is to get all of the rest of them aboard quickly,' said Tor more quietly. 'Every one of our warriors on a ship, *now* – don't wait. Go now!' She slapped him on the shoulder and shoved him away from her.

She cupped her hands around her mouth and bellowed: '*Felaki*! With me!'

There were four eager faces, including Kynwulf, at her elbow. 'The king said to leave him to fight,' the War Chief said. 'He said he might slay *us* in his madness!'

'Fuck that,' repeated Tor. 'We must get him out of it! I need him. As do you.'

Sambor was beside her, too, A horrible spiked club grasped in his meaty hands.

'Not you. Get on a ship, any ship, get on board, you stupid ogre,' shouted Tor.

'I fight,' said the big Polans. 'For Inge. For Bjarki. Maybe for you, too.'

Joralf, too, was by her side: 'They're going to kill Bjarki if we don't go now!'

It was true. Several Wulfings had made up their minds to join the fray with Bjarki and the two Wolf twins. One was immediately killed by a backward swinging axe blow from Bjarki that crushed his skull. But another man leapt in and jabbed a spear into Bjarki's broad back, up near his shoulder blade, making the Rekkr scream.

'We go in, pull Bjarki out of there – then we run!' said Tor. 'Yes? Let's go.'

Had she looked behind her as she ran, Tor would have seen Captain Mogils shoving and pushing, and cursing the Danes, urging them to break up the shield wall and run back towards the ships while they still could. Sigurd Hring, too, was upon them. The first arrows of his Telemark archers pattering down onto the fleeing Danes. The first running man died, gargling his own blood from a shaft in his neck.

But a few Danes, and a dozen Vastergotlander warriors, ignored Mogils's orders and rushed forwards with Tor and the *Felaki* to rescue their beleaguered king.

This tiny handful piled into the circle of shields around Bjarki and the twins.

And the rest of the Wulfing army rushed forwards as one to meet them.

The battle heaved and raged and spun around Tor. Sambor was a wonder of destructive fury, smiting Ostergotlanders with his huge spiked club like a giant swatting away a swarm of dwarves. Young Joralf, at her left side, killed with a fine, chilly precision, piercing belly and throat, dropping man after man. Kynwulf, Haugen Halfhand, Oddvin, and a new fellow called Black Ivar tore into the Wulfings' shield-circle around the battling trio. Their combined attack swept the Wulfings back and away, to expose the sight of her tiring brother's unequal combat. She saw one of the Wolf twins lunge at her brother – and miss – and snag Bjarki's yellow-brown bear cloak and rip a section of the thick fur clean away. And the other twin, who had worked his way behind him, lifted his sword and chopped at the back of Bjarki's head. His sword clanged against his iron helm and Bjarki roared with rage, spun, swung and sank his axe deep into the Wolf Rekkr's left side, a lethal blow.

No man could survive that.

It was Fodor, Tor believed, though she could not be certain. He gave a noise like a whine, a big *whooff* of breath, and slumped to the turf.

'Bjarki, we must go!' she yelled and, astonishingly, her brother turned, looked directly at her – and even heard her. He stared at her, his face blood-slathered and froth-speckled, but he was *there*, he recognised her. At that same moment, Fidor threw himself screaming his rage at the Rekkr's other side. The two Fire Born men went down in a tangle of limbs, Bjarki lost both his Harva

seax and Dane axe, and Tor saw him pounding his clenched fist
into Fidor's face as they rolled over and over. There was a gigantic
crack and the grey skies were split with white lightning. The
heavens opened wide and the battlefield was suddenly drowned
in falling water.

Fidor punched his sword pommel hard into Bjarki's face.

Tor yelled: 'Sambor!' and 'Kynwulf!' and charged forwards,
her own sword sweeping out to strike at Fidor's head. The blow
skidded off the top of Fidor's iron helmet, and the Wolf warrior
rolled away, snarling and spitting. He tried to stand but slipped
on the sodden grass. Sambor and Kynwulf rushed forwards now
and each seized one of Bjarki's huge arms and, with Tor guarding
them, her sword out, ready to strike, the two men began hauling
the fallen Fire Born towards the peninsula.

'Back!' shouted Tor, 'Everybody back!' as the hard rain fell like
a waterfall.

She looked north and could see Sigurd Hring himself with a
wall of warriors behind him, so close, his sword drawn, extended,
and pointing directly at her.

The drumming of the rain made his shouted words inaudible.
Tor turned and ran, back up the narrow peninsula, towards the
last remaining ships.

The thunder rumbled and white light smashed the sky. The
downpour was so heavy it was almost impossible to breathe. Tor,
gasping, spitting rain water, took one glance back at the Wulfing
army, and at Fidor down on his knees and cradling the body of
his brother. And the last of the Danes and Vastergotlanders hard
on her heels.

She put her own head down and ran.

She slipped and slid, her wounded leg flaring like fire, pain
right down to the thigh bone, and ignoring the agony and peering
through the murk and wet, saw that only one ship was still moored
on the bank, a lean vessel with a blue sail, already hoisted. She
could see the faces of her friends already on board, Rask and
his cheery imp's grin, Mogils, looking anxious, and there was

Sambor, and Kynwulf, the War Chief, standing at the steering oar, both making beckoning motions with their hands.

There was no sign of Bjarki. She slowed her pace and looked behind her. A couple of Danes and Oddvin and that was all. No one else was chasing her. The Wulfings – their king dead – were leaderless, milling about, disinclined to pursue them with any kind of eagerness. A lone spear launched out from the loose mass of their foes and fell short. A few arrows, too, mingled with the hissing rain.

Tor ran on. As she neared the ship, she tried to slow and skidded in the mud and crashed belly-first into the wooden side of the ship. She saw Oddvin vault effortlessly over the side ahead of her. But she could not move, all the breath having been knocked from her body. She gasped like a fish. And Sambor, suddenly there, leaned forwards, grabbed her with both massive hands and hauled her on board, lifting her high and dumping her on one of the rowing chests in the belly of the vessel.

Kynwulf was shouting: 'Loose that rope – no, not that one, you fool, the mooring rope.' And strong backs were pushing the ship away from the side of the bank with the rowing oars, and out into the waters of the Braviken. And Kynwulf was shouting something again about raising the rain-drenched sail. A final enemy arrow fell on them and thwacked into the hull, just two inches away from her right boot.

Tor was entranced by it. An elegant, deadly object. When she looked up next, there was Bjarki, soaking, dripping watery blood, his bear-cloak a sodden ruin, but he was grinning lopsidedly at her, more or less whole, and on his feet, though swaying badly, and saying something kind she couldn't make out over the dull roar of the rain.

Epilogue

A swift and difficult decision
Ten days later

Bjarki watched the guard from his position of concealment in the shadowed corner where a large grain store abutted a small forge about halfway down the hill in Viby, a bowshot away from the royal hall. The guard was a young man, with a spear, iron helmet and a long blue cloak. He was likely a Saxon, judging by his corn-coloured hair and red cheeks, and he seemed bored. The door he was guarding led into a small hall a dozen paces long, one of the royal guest houses, and so indicated by the elaborate curling dragon carved above the lintel.

The guard yawned. Bjarki found he was yawning, too.

'Come on, come on,' he muttered under his breath. His chief fear was that the occupant of the house would be summoned to the great feast he knew was being prepared in the royal hall. Not that there would be much joyful celebration at the feast – the whole of Viby was muted and sullen as a result of the failure of Harald Wartooth to achieve victory for the Danes at Norrkoping. If the Jarl of Sjaelland had survived the battle, he would have been disgraced, perhaps even punished by his king. His memory was already cursed by many of the common folk of the Dane-Mark – how many households had lost a husband, brother or son to his pride and folly? And in a week or two, King Siegfried himself would be forced to undertake the sea journey to Uppsala – an arduous voyage for an elderly man – and once there he must humble himself before Sigurd Hring, kneel before the victorious monarch, swear fealty, and confirm him, and all his heirs, as the rightful King of the North.

Bjarki was glad he would not be there to witness the old king's humiliation.

King Siegfried and his court, the people of Viby and all the good folk of the Dane-Mark, had been diminished by defeat. Yet Bjarki had more urgent things on his mind this night. His most pressing concern was this: would King Siegfried send a full squad of Danish spearmen, say a dozen men, to accompany the honoured guest who now resided in the guest hall to the high wedding feast he was giving that night? If so, it would completely spoil everything that Bjarki had so carefully planned.

Bjarki heard the sound of voices and the slosh of boots on the muddy street, and he felt his whole body tense. Two figures came around the corner from the direction of the royal hall, clearly warriors, a man and a woman. The man was a tall, young blond fellow – a Goth by blood but one who could easily be mistaken for a Saxon. The woman was a short, lithe, wiry, red-headed shield-maiden, a little scarred by war.

They appeared to be very drunk and called out cheerfully to the bored Saxon guard at the door of the guest hall. 'An ale-house, we must find another ale-house!'

The pair stopped in front of the guard, grinning like idiots. 'Hey, friend,' said the woman, 'is there a place you can suggest, one with sweet ale and good music?'

'And women, lots of pretty girls!' said the man. 'Tell us the right way, friend.'

'Olaf, you horny pig-fucker. Am I not woman enough for you?'

The guard, chuckling, stepped forwards into the street to point down the road and give them directions to the port, and Bjarki emerged from the shadows like a *draugr*.

In three long strides he was behind the Saxon guard, a seax in his hand. He struck. Using the bone hilt of the fighting knife, he delivered a short hard blow to the guard's temple. And the young man folded at the knees and slumped into the mud.

'Quick! Help me, Tor,' whispered Bjarki. 'We must get him off the street before someone comes!' They stripped the blue cloak off the unconscious man, and took his spear and helm, too, and Oddvin, the 'horny pig-fucker', stood in his place at the hall door, fastening the distinctive cloak around his shoulders while Bjarki and his sister bound the guard's hands, gagged him and carried him quickly inside the guest house.

Once inside, Bjarki left Tor with the prisoner and walked forwards towards the fireplace where a lone slender figure was sitting, working with a needle and thread on a piece of elaborate embroidery. Bjarki coughed, a little artificially, but just loud enough, and the figure by the fire turned, saw him and gave a little involuntary cry.

'Don't be alarmed, Edith,' said Bjarki. 'It's only me. I need to speak to you.'

'Bjarki,' she said and she threw aside her embroidery and rushed forwards and enfolded him in a warm embrace. They held each other for a long while, breathing each other in, and then Bjarki, very gently, pushed her body away from his.

'I must speak with you, Edith,' he repeated. 'It is important. And time is short.'

'Speak then,' sniffed Edith. For some reason, tears were welling up in her eyes.

'I know that tonight is your wedding feast. I know that tonight the king will honour you and Abbio in his hall, and that tomorrow the senior *gothi* will perform the ceremony in the sacred grove. But before all that happens I must tell you one thing.'

Bjarki paused, looking for a long, long time into her lovely face.

'Say it,' said Edith, with a touch of impatience. 'Just say the words to me.'

'I love you,' said Bjarki. 'I love you with all my heart. And I cannot let you be married to that… vile-smelling, raggedy *nithing*, without first admitting that I love you and I would love you and live with you for the rest of my life; but also without telling you

341

this: Abbio is not the man you think he is. He is evil. He is the man who paid Hjorleif to kidnap you and take you away to Rogaland. We were all deceived.'

'How do you know this?' Edith seized one of Bjarki's big hands in both of hers.

'I met a man on the battlefield – just by chance. He was a man called Malfinn whom I thought had originally helped me to find you in Ymirsfjord. He gave me directions to the viking fortress. But when I met him again at Norrkoping, and gave him some more money, he told me I had been deceived by Abbio the Crow. He said Abbio had arranged the kidnap – that the Crow had long had dealings with both Hjorleif and his master Einar the Cruel, that they had been spies of sorts, gatherers of important information for Abbio and your brother. *Abbio paid them to kidnap you!*'

Tor said: 'You need to hurry this along, oaf. Siegfried's men could be here at any moment to take Edith to the feast. Put your proposal to her, and let us be gone.'

'I will tell you more another time but, briefly, Abbio wanted me to go to Rogaland to kill them all and rescue you – he fed me information to make this happen. He aimed all along to take the credit. He hoped, at least Malfinn thinks this, that you would be so grateful to Abbio that you would fall in love with him for saving your life. And since I, this dim-witted Rekkr, had killed the Ymirsfjord vikings...'

'Bjarki,' said Tor from the doorway. 'We need to go! Ask her – ask her now.'

'Ask me what?' said Edith.

'I ask you to come with me. I ask you to make a swift and difficult decision. I have a ship in the harbour, and my people are there, ready to depart. We will go to Ymirsfjord, to the fortress there. We will be safe for a time, I think. So I ask you, I beg you – come with me right now. Let us go from this place. We will be reviled...'

'Yes,' said Edith.

'You are sure? We will be outlaws, we will be hunted by Danes, Saxons, your brother, everyone. They'll say I stole you, they'll say that you're a dirty...'

'I said yes!' Edith grabbed Bjarki's big head in her two hands and kissed him on the mouth. A long kiss. Only ended by Tor's call of 'Enough, you two, we must go!'

'I love you, Bjarki,' said Edith. 'I think I have always loved you. Your strength, your kindness. Now I know that Abbio is a deceitful coward, I feel no obligation to him – or to my brother, or any of them. Let's go, let us run, let us be free of them all!'

-

The log-built temple in the compound at Ymirsfjord was lit with a score of candles, their soft light illuminating the stern wooden face of the All-Father, who watched events with a brooding silence. The door to the victim-cage was open, its former occupant bound to the wooden pillar in the centre of the stuffy chamber. He had been stripped and gagged, and his skinny body shivered from both cold and fear.

Bjarki, Tor and Kynwulf stood by the far wall observing him, their arms folded across their chests. Impassive. Stern. Implacable. The prisoner rolled his eyes in his terror, trying to communicate something with them, trying to make some connection with these three that might save his life. But there would be no mercy that night.

Tor stepped forwards: 'Heed me, Odin; heed me Spear-Shaker. Heed me All-Father, the Wanderer. Heed my dark deed this night and the justice of my revenge.'

The prisoner gave a wriggle of terror, constrained by the ropes that secured him to the pillar. His eyes were huge, and as Tor reached forwards to seize his beardless jaw and look into his face, Rorik released his bladder and urine splattered the floor.

'You must know why I am doing this, Rorik, son of Hafnar,' said Tor, looking into his eyes. 'It is important to me that you know why this shall be your doom. And why there are some friends of mine in the afterlife who are eager to meet you again. Ulli Thorsson was the steward of Bearstead and my friend and comrade. You or your men hanged him by the neck – for no good reason at all.

'To my lasting shame I did not swiftly punish you for that. Then you returned to Bearstead, looking to kill me – and using the coward's weapon, poison, you slew my daughter Inge as well as the wives and children of my *Felaki* friends, and the Honey Hunter, too – eight innocent lives you stole with your poison on that accursèd day.

'I did not punish you for that, either, Rorik Hafnarsson. Not swiftly enough. Lastly, you murdered Harald Wartooth, the *Armathr* of the King of the Danes, playing him false with your lies and treacherously slaying him to gain favour with your true lord Sigurd Hring. All of these folk will be waiting for you in the afterlife. You shall serve as their slave. You shall be their wretched thrall till the end of time.'

Bjarki heard the sound of drums and women chanting from outside the temple.

'Your doom fast approaches,' said Tor. 'Do you have any words to say before you cross over to the other side?'

Tor pulled the gag from Rorik's mouth, and a torrent of words spilled out.

'Mercy, I beg you, have mercy on me. I killed Ulli, yes, but he was old and useless – and you had fled, and I was angry with you for humiliating me. And the honey – yes, I left the honey, but I was only trying to kill you – my enemy – as you tried to kill me in the forest in the hunt. I had to kill you – or you would kill me. We were at war. It was an act of war against you. The others were not intended to die.'

'Yet you cared not who ate the honey cakes. And Harald Wartooth?'

'He wanted to die. The Wartooth asked me to kill him. Indeed, he ordered me to do it. He said that when he had killed enough of his foes, when he had gained enough glory to be granted a place in the Hall of the Slain, I was to cut his head off, kill him instantly. He asked for a good death! I swear it. He died in battle, a sword in his hand; it was what the *Armathr* wanted. I cannot be blamed for it. I obeyed his command.'

'Liar!' said Tor.

'Tor, the Wartooth said something of the like to me in Lodose,' said Bjarki.

'Hmm,' said Tor.

The wooden door of the temple opened and the Lady Edith came into the dark low space. She was dressed in a pure white gown. Her fine oval face, fixed and stern, was painted unnaturally white with some paste, perhaps chalk. Her lips were coloured a dark purplish, bruise-like shade, and her eyes were rimmed with lines of the same hue, as well as black and crimson. Her long hair was arranged into tight plaits, oiled, stiffened with glue and dyed white, red and purple, and looked like a nest of snakes as she moved into the chamber. She looked solemn, frightening, but utterly beautiful. She was singing, a wild, eldritch song that stood all the short hairs on Bjarki's neck erect.

Behind her filed in the few women of Ymirsfjord. Their high singing and swift drumming complemented Edith's voice, increasing in volume as they had all entered.

Bjarki saw that in Edith's hand she carried a stone knife, as broad as a chestnut leaf, its ridges seeming to ripple in the yellow light from the temple's many candles.

Rorik saw her and let out a moan of fear. Tor stepped in very close to him then.

'You will greet Harald Wartooth in the next world – and maybe he will plead for you. But for Inge and Ulli, and the others, you shall die this night. You die to honour Odin, and his son Vidarr, and to feed the *Disir* – and for my own personal pleasure.'

She pulled the cloth gag up again over Rorik's mouth, silencing him for ever.

The eldritch singing reached a loud crescendo, then suddenly ceased, and Edith stepped forwards. 'Odin! Hear us, All-Father, draw near and accept this *blot* sacrifice. *Disir* of Rogaland, gather now, come spirits of Ymirsfjord, take your seats at the table of the gods! Here is your meat and drink, *Disir* – sisters, here is your lawful portion!'

She stepped forwards briskly and sliced once, a hard and smooth strike, across Rorik's bare neck. The stone knife cut deeply into his flesh and a jet of bright blood immediately fountained into the air, splashing on the earthen ground, then dribbling down the naked victim's body, and against the ancient oak-wood of the Odin pillar.

Rorik jerked and twitched for a time. His feet drumming against the pillar. Then he stopped, went still, and his blood-washed body slumped loose against the ropes.

Historical Note

> The intolerable clash of arms filled the air with an incredible thunder. The steam of the wounds suddenly hung a mist over the sky; the daylight was hidden under the hail of spears...

So wrote Saxo Grammaticus, the twelfth-century chronicler of Danish history in Part 1, Book 8 of *Gesta Danorum*. The medieval scribe was writing in Latin of the horrors of the legendary Battle of Brávellir, which probably took place sometime in the late eighth century on the plain below the wooded Kolmarden ridge between the territories of Svealand and Ostergotland. He was re-imagining the battle using descriptions from the Norse sagas and writing more than four hundred years after the event – if, indeed, this battle ever happened at all – and so his work must be taken with a large pinch of salt. Nevertheless, this was the battle I used as a rough model for the great slaughter at the end of *King of the North*.

I first came across this extraordinary conflict not in Saxo's writing, nor in the sagas, but in a brilliant historical novel called *A Sacred Storm*, the second volume of the superb Wanderer Chronicles, written by a friend of mine, Theodore Brun. If you enjoyed this book, I urge you to read his novel – which, I am relieved to say, has a completely different take on the semi-mythical battle. I have since done a fair bit of research on the battle myself, but I cannot deny that Theo's fine novel gave me the original idea for *King of the North*, and he has very kindly said he doesn't mind at all.

As I say, I have done the battle quite differently to Theo – and, indeed, I have departed also from the legend to a large degree to make the story fit in with my own Fire Born 'universe' and the various Scandinavian kings and jarls established in my previous novels. However, the original story of the Battle of Brávellir goes something like this: the King of the Danes, Harald Wartooth, was growing old and losing his sight, and he wanted to have one last good fight before the end to ensure himself a place among the valiant in Odin's Hall of the Slain. He wanted a 'good' death in battle and so sent a message to Sigurd Hring, the King of Svealand, inviting him to join him in a great glorious bloodletting at a suitable place near the Braviken fjord between Sigurd's territory and the land of the East Geats.

The Svear king agreed and they allowed seven years to plan for this epic encounter, with each side recruiting many famous warriors from across the North. The heroes flocked to both their banners from as far afield as Ireland and Lithuania, Frisia and the Slavic lands – two hundred thousand warriors took part in the battle, we are told, although this is surely a huge exaggeration – and these warriors also came equipped with the most wonderfully descriptive Viking names, the flavour of which I have tried to give to my own fictional combatants.

Harald Wartooth – who may or may not have gored his enemies on his weirdly protruding tooth – was joined by the heroes Are the One-eyed, Dag the Fat and Hoth-brodd the Indomitable. Sigurd Hring recruited Egil the Bald, Einar the Fatbellied and Erling the Snake. Into the mix of these 'historical' heroes, I added my own Bjarki Bloodhand and Tor the Shield-Maiden – apparently there were another three hundred shield-maidens fighting at Brávellir, as well as the famous archers of Telemark.

The events of the battle in my novel differ greatly to the legend – with the many unwise Danish attacks up the stump-dotted slope of the Kolmarden being somewhat unlikely. In Saxo's telling of it, Harald Wartooth uses a chariot on the plain below the ridge with scythes on the wheels, à la Boudicca, to mow down his foes. But the most extraordinary event in the battle occurred when Harald was killed by his own steward who, riding with him in the lethal chariot, decided Harald had won enough glory and crushed his skull with a club at the height of the fray. The steward may, in fact, have been Odin in disguise, rather than the Wartooth's faithful old retainer, but what a plot twist! I knew I had to include that surprising death in my version of the story.

In the legend, Sigurd Hring won the day, and it is claimed (unconvincingly) that forty thousand people died in the terrible slaughter. In my book, I have reduced the numbers of participants to a far more credible ten thousand, and switched the allies of the opposing armies around a little simply because I wanted Bjarki to be King of Vastergotland and he and Tor to be initially on opposing sides in the great showdown. In the sagas, the Vastergotlanders fought alongside the Svears and the Ostergotlanders were allied to the men of the Dane-Mark. The Slavic Wends also fought on the Danish side.

The title of King of the North is my own invention, although the royal houses of Svealand and the Dane-Mark, from the little we know of them in this period, appear to have been interconnected by blood and marriage, as well as sharing a common Norse culture. The first historically recognised King of the Danes is Gorm the Old, and he ruled in the early to mid tenth century – a hundred and fifty years after my Siegfried. Before this era all Danish kings are semi-legendary and most rule only in the realm of myth.

The old sacrifice

There is little doubt, given the archeological evidence, that the people of the North practised human sacrifice from time to time and that the old temple at Uppsala was an important cult centre of their pagan religion. What we don't know is exactly *how* the rituals were performed. Probably in different ways according to region and the era they were performed in. We only know about them from Christian chroniclers, to whom they were an abomination. Saxo writes in *Gesta Danorum*: 'Also Frey, the regent of the gods, took his abode not far from Uppsala, where he … paid to the gods abominable offerings, by beginning to slaughter human victims.'

The scene at the beginning of the book, in which Einar the Cruel was sacrificed in the *Disablot* ceremony, was inspired by a photograph I saw going round on Twitter last year that records the final moments of a German general called Anton Dostler, a war criminal. The picture shows him as he is being tied to the stake before execution by an American firing squad. The look in Dostler's eyes as he stares directly into the camera still haunts me. He knew he was going to die, he knew his captors would have no mercy – he had ordered the execution of fifteen US prisoners of war in cold blood – yet he is trying with all his might to preserve his courage right up until the end.

He was ritually slain by the victors of the war. And I like to think that people don't change very much over time. So, while I have no sympathy for Nazi war criminals, you might well argue that General Dostler was, in fact, a latter-day human sacrifice made to the gods of victory.

Acknowledgements

No novel is the creation of just one person and, while my name goes on the cover as the author, there are several important people who have also helped substantially in the making of *King of the North*. I would like to thank Craig Lye, my superb editor at Canelo and a tireless champion of the Fire Born series, and Miranda Ward, for her restrained yet meticulous copy-editing. My agent Ian Drury of Sheil Land Associates deserves a very special thank-you for his long-term support of my novel writing career and for connecting me with the brilliant Canelo publishing crew in the first place. And, lastly, I must thank my generous brother John Brodie Donald for providing the elegant map of the North at the front of this book.

Angus Donald
Tonbridge, May 2023